BLACKBIRD RISING

KERI ARTHUR

ISBN: 978-0-6484973-4-9

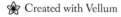 Created with Vellum

With thanks to:

The Lulus
Indigo Chick Designs
Hot Tree Editing
Debbie from DP+
Robyn E.
Quymie G.
The lovely ladies from Central Vic Writers
J Caleb Designs for the brilliant cover

ONE

The old suspension bridge creaked under my weight. The sound echoed across the stillness, as sharp as a demon's cackle. A thick fog hid the world from sight—not even the navigation lights were visible at the far end of King's Island, and that was bad news for any ships or yachts navigating toward the main port. The island might be small, but she'd been the cause of many shipwrecks over the centuries, before the lights had been installed.

The silence was as thick as the fog. There was no birdsong, no sound of traffic, and absolutely no indication that a major town lay behind me. I could have been alone in this place. *Should* have been alone, given King's Island was a place few ventured near these days.

But I wasn't.

Someone was out there, watching from afar. While there was no immediate sense of danger, unease still crawled across my skin. Not only had there been reports of strange flashes of light in this area of late, but also of demonic activity. Then there were the disappearances ...

only three so far, which wasn't much for a city the size of Ainslyn and might be nothing more than coincidence.

Still ...

I scanned the swirling blanket of gray, my sense of responsibility warring with the need to play it safe. My grandmother wouldn't, in any way, begrudge caution, but she was also a stickler when it came to duty. Though few these days remembered the Witch King's true name or the reason his sword had been buried hilt-deep into stone on the island's highest peak, the De Montfort line had long borne the task of looking after the memorial. For countless centuries, De Montfort women had made this same journey across the bridge on the first day of the new year. Mo—who hated being referred to as Gran—had been doing it for nigh on eighty years, but she'd recently taken a tumble down the stairs of our bookstore and fractured her leg, so the duty had fallen to me. She could have flown over, of course, but I rather suspected she'd taken one look at the weather this morning and decided I was more than capable of doing the blessing by myself this year. Which I was, of course, but it still felt odd not to have her by my side. Her absence, however, had nothing to do with the growing tide of uneasiness.

I flexed my fingers and did my best to ignore it. I was neither defenseless nor without means to quickly flee. Like Mo and those hundreds of other De Montfort women before us, I was a blackbird. The freedom and safety of the skies was mine to claim with little more than the flick of an internal switch. Of course, that same switch was somewhat faulty in my particular case; I might have inherited the gene that allowed us to shift shape, but I'd somehow totally skipped the aptitude for healing magic that should have come with it. The lack was made even more annoying by

2

the fact that my twin brother, Max, had inherited Mom's ability to manipulate the weather and had undergone full training at the Okoro Academy.

The old arch that signified the end of the footbridge loomed out of the fog. It was an ornate and beautiful structure despite the fact both time and the weather were taking a toll on the decorative metalwork that adorned the two stone pillars. At the very top of the arch, untouched by the rust tarnishing the rest of it, was a shield bearing a red cross and a white rose. It was said to be the Witch King's, but I personally doubted it. It was far too small to be of any real use to a man who'd supposedly been seven feet tall.

I walked under the arch and headed up the long hill that led to the monument, glad to be on ground that didn't bounce under every step. Trees loomed, their windswept forms ghostly and surreal in the fog. Despite the fact the island was a haven for wildlife, there was little movement in the undergrowth and no birdsong filling the predawn darkness. The pulse of unease grew stronger, and I warily scanned the area ahead. The fog clung to the branches of the old elms and oaks that dominated this part of the island, forming a ghostly veil that covered the entire path. There was absolutely no sign that anyone or anything had moved through here recently, so why did my innate inner sense of wrongness suggest that the fog lied? That someone had not only taken this path but was now waiting up ahead?

I didn't know, but it was way past time I did something about it. I swung the backpack off, then opened it up and pulled out my daggers. While it was illegal for non-adepts to carry blessed blades, I'd gotten around the ruling on a technicality. I might not be able perform magic but I *was* immune to it—a rather weird anomaly considering the ability to shift shape was in itself a form of magic. It was the immunity rather than the shape shifting that allowed me to carry.

According to Mo, the two daggers—Vita and Nex, which meant, quite literally, life and death—had been handed to the firstborn female of each generation at puberty since medieval times. De Montforts might traditionally be healers, but we'd once also been warriors who could both give *and* take life. These daggers were the conduits through which that power had been channeled.

I might not have inherited all the De Montfort magic, but these blades at least gave me some access to the power that should have been my birthright. After generations of being the focus point for countless De Montfort warriors, the blades had gained a life and energy of their own. Demons were certainly wary of them—I knew that from experience.

I strapped on the sheaths, then swung the pack over my shoulders and quickly continued up the path. The veil parted before me, a wave of gray that did absolutely nothing to calm my nerves—especially given the crunch of stones under my feet seemed abnormally loud in the silence. Whoever—whatever—waited ahead had ample enough warning of my presence.

Though I suspected they didn't really need it.

I finally came out onto open ground, and my gaze automatically moved to the right. On a good day you could see the entire city from this vantage point, but not even the aviation lights topping the office high-rises in the western sector beyond the old town's walls were visible this morning. Which more than likely meant the airport was closed—a fact that wouldn't please Max, given he was supposed to be headed to Paris for a week's vacation today.

The monument was situated on what had become

known as "the king's knob"—a sharp projection of rock that jutted out at an angle on the highest point of the island. A wide field of flat gray stone ringed this outcrop and, despite the wildflowers that grew in abundance all over the peak in spring, it always remained empty of life. Not even weeds survived there. No one really knew why for sure, but Mo's theory was that when the Witch King had thrust the blade into the stone, the last vestiges of the sword's power had bled into the ground and forever sterilized it.

In the distance, something stirred—a shadow that looked man-shaped but could have been anything, including the stump of a tree briefly visible through the fog. I gripped Nex's hilt, finding comfort in the soft pulse of the blade's power.

More movement, and then light flashed. Blue light, sharp and intense against the curtain of gray. Energy shivered through the air, its force so strong the hairs at the back of my neck stood on end.

It wasn't magic; it was something else. Something that spoke of violent storms and the ferocity of lightning.

Another pulse, brighter than before. Vita and Nex responded, emitting a light that bled past their scabbards and gave the fog a cobalt glow.

Unease sharpened into fear. In all the time the daggers had been mine, they'd never responded in such a manner to an exterior force, be it magic or something more elemental in nature. I had no idea what it meant; no idea if the force that lay up ahead was good or bad. It certainly didn't feel foul, but that was no indicator of truth. Some of the most dangerous spells ever created were the ones that hid behind the screen of harmlessness.

The light ahead abruptly disappeared, and the still-dawning day seemed colder for it. I hurried forward, even though part of me wanted to do nothing more than turn and run in the opposite direction. But I'd yet to make the blessing that would protect the sword for another year and until I did, there could be no retreat. Mo certainly wouldn't have.

I hit the stone platform that surrounded the monument, and the curtain of gray melted away, revealing the evenly spaced monoliths that ran around the perimeter. In the center of this circle stood the knob and the hump of stone that held the Witch King's sword. There was no immediate evidence it had been tampered with, and nothing to indicate a spell had been cast. If the activity I'd glimpsed had involved demons, their acidic stench would still stain the air. The only things I could actually smell were vague hints of cardamom, fresh bergamot, and lavender—all of which had a synthetic undertone that suggested it was cologne-based rather than natural. That basically confirmed my instincts. Someone *had* been here.

But doing what?

And what on earth had caused those blue pulses?

I warily approached the outcrop of rock. The cologne's scent grew stronger, suggesting whatever had been going on involved the monument. I skirted the knob but once again couldn't see or feel anything that suggested magic—no lingering wisps of power, no discarded spell strings.

I frowned and returned to the rear of the rock. The hump that held the sword loomed above me, though the hilt wasn't visible from where I stood. Again, there was nothing here to suggest anything untoward had been going on.

And yet my fear continued to build.

I shivered and shoved a hand into the hollow smoothed by countless others doing the exact same thing, and stepped up onto the rock. The teasing scents got stronger and I hesitated, once again scanning the stone that held the sword. There wasn't even the usual scrawl of graffiti that often happened as the blessing wore off and the kids moved in.

I scrambled upward, and the visible portion of the Witch King's sword came into view, gleaming in the soft light of the dawning day. It was a rather ornate sword for a weapon that had been used in war—intricate runes ran the visible length of the silver blade, and the cross guard and hilt were heavily etched and decorated with silver and gold. The pommel had been shaped into a rose whose petals were made with gold.

It was all that gold that made the blessing a necessity.

I swung the backpack off, but as I bent to open it, I noticed something odd—far more of the blade was visible than usual.

Had someone moved it? Or had the sword become loose and somehow worked its way up?

I reached out and tentatively wrapped my fingers around the grip. Blue light pulsed, and energy caressed my hand, a sharp but electric force that made my fingers burn and my heart race. A gasp escaped and I instinctively let go and stepped back, teetering briefly on the edge of the knob before I caught my balance.

The damn sword was the source of light and magic I'd felt earlier.

I stared at it, more than a little unwilling to believe it was possible, despite the evidence of my own eyes. In all the years I'd been coming up here with Mo, the sword had been utterly inert. As far as I knew, that had been the case ever since the Witch King had declared, with his dying breath, that only the next true king would draw the sword from the stone.

Ainslyn's royal line had since merged with human

monarchs, who ruled from their palace in London, and the world in general had all but forgotten the Witch King's existence. Even history books had relegated his presence, his victories—which included saving human and witch alike from the dark elf sorcerer who sought to claim this realm as his own—and his sword to the ranks of myth and legend.

But Uhtric Aquitaine was no myth and neither was the power of his sword.

Which begged the question, why had it come to life now?

And why had it reacted to my touch, however faintly? The De Montforts had no links to the Aquitaine kings as far as I was aware, and there were few enough true descendants left these days anyway. My gaze dropped to the stone that held the sword; the inscription was as unreadable now as it always had been. Why I expected anything else I couldn't say, but I had a bad feeling the sooner we uncovered what it said, the better.

I hesitated, then stepped forward and gripped the hilt a second time. Once again, that otherworldly force rose, pulsing through my body, a wave that rushed through limb, muscle, and bone, as if it were seeking something.

Or accessing something.

I frowned at the thought and tightened my grip, trying to pull the sword from the stone. It didn't budge, which was no real surprise given the fact I was female and also lacked the prerequisite Aquitaine blood. It did mean, however, that someone from that line had been here, testing his link to the sword. It wouldn't be the first time and certainly wouldn't be the last.

But it was, as far as I knew, the first time the sword had actually responded.

I scanned the emptiness around me. The awareness of

being watched remained, but there was something else moving through the distant fog now. Something that spoke of darkness.

I released the sword and quickly emptied the backpack of its contents. After carefully placing the short white candles in a circle around the hump of stone, I lit them one by one. Then I grabbed the twin bottles of sanctified water, took a deep breath that did little to calm my nerves, and waited for the sun to crest the horizon.

It seemed to take an eternity for the first rays of the new day to spear the sky. I waited, tension running through me, as the light grew stronger and the sky was painted orange and gold. Then the sun crested the horizon, the sword began to glow, and the golden rose on the pommel gently unfurled.

Now, an inner voice whispered.

I raised the vials of sanctified water and slowly moved around the sword's base, calling on the power of the sun and the moon to protect the blade through the upcoming year, to keep it safe from darkness and all else who might wish it harm. As the words ran across the silence, a force sharper and more ethereal than any mere spell rose. The sanctified water hit the base of the sword's stony sheath, and the air shimmered in response; the power of the blessing took hold, becoming a visible force that crept upward toward the blade. When the rays of the sun combined with the blessing's shimmer, a shaft of golden light shot from the unfurled center of the rose. As that light dissipated, the blessing's shimmer melded into the rock and the sword stopped glowing. I closed my eyes and sighed in relief. The sword was safe for another year.

I knelt to place the now empty vials back into the pack. A soft noise ran across the stillness, one that sounded an awful lot like the scratch of a claw against stone. I froze, goose bumps racing across my skin and my heart seeming to lodge somewhere in the vicinity of my throat.

For several seconds, there was only silence. Then that one scratch became two, and two became three ...

I swallowed heavily and clamped down on the thick wave of fear. This wasn't the first time I'd come across demons. I might do nothing more than help run a book and healing store, but I was still a De Montfort. Juvenile demons seeking to boost their standing amongst their brethren routinely went after the low- or no-powered members of the various witch clans.

I tied the vials safely into the pack, my skin twitching with awareness. Then I took a deep breath in a vague attempt to calm my nerves, drew Nex and Vita, and rose. White light flickered down the edges of the blades, and a hiss rose from the demons gathering below the knob.

May the gods help me ...

This wasn't a couple of juveniles out to test their prowess. This was something far more serious.

There were over a dozen demons standing within the stone circle, and at least eight of them were winged. While instinct might be clamoring for me to change shape and flee, that was probably the worst thing I could do. Blackbirds weren't equipped to fight demons on wing—neither our beaks nor our claws were designed to tear through leathery hides. I had more hope of survival in human form, but against so many ...

I tightened my grip on the daggers. I was a De Montfort, however underpowered, and I'd been well trained by Mo. I could and would survive this.

The biggest of the gathered demons stepped forward. He was an ugly son of a bitch, with mismatched yellow daggers for teeth and eyes that were as orange as the skies. His red wings fanned lightly, making him appear even bigger, and his thick, sharp claws flexed in and out of their sheaths.

"Leave this place." His voice was a guttural smear of sound, harsh and ugly against the glory of the golden sunrise. "Leave, and never return."

I shifted my stance and braced for attack. "If you seek to destroy the sword, you've arrived too late. The blessing has already been made."

They hissed again, the collective sound discordant and grating.

"Leave," the leader replied. "Or die."

Demons weren't exactly known for their generosity, and I seriously doubted they were actually intending to let me go. So why were they even bothering to offer the possibility of escape? Was it merely a game? Or was something stranger happening here?

"Sorry." I raised my daggers in readiness. "No can do."

He made a motion with one clawed hand, and the demons attacked en masse. I cut, slashed, and thrust at claws, teeth, and bodies, Nex and Vita blurred beacons of brightness in the shadows and death that all but swamped me. Seconds of survival turned into minutes. Two lay dead at the foot of the knob, but there were so many more ... a writhing, stinking wall of them that wanted nothing more than to rend me into tiny, unrecognizable bits of flesh.

An unholy scream to my left ... I flinched and slashed Nex sideways, felt the stinging spurt of blood across my cheek. Movement to the right ... I shifted. Too late. Claws raked my left arm, shredding my coat and sending me stumbling sideways. I went down, smashing one knee against the stone but somehow remaining upright, and thrust up with

Vita. Her blade pierced the palm of a demon attempting to cleave me in two and, with a quick circular flick, I severed his hand. His howl briefly overran the screeching of the others and stirred them into an even greater frenzy. Talons tore at me, shredding clothes and skin, drawing blood and staining the air with my fear. I pressed back against the outcrop of stone that held the sword and fought on, slashing the face of one leering imp to the bone and then cutting the neck of another. As his blood spurted across my face, something silver flashed across the far corner of my vision and the demons momentarily gave way.

Then a hand grabbed the collar of my jacket and unceremoniously hauled me upright.

"Back to back," a deep, velvety voice said.

I didn't question his sudden appearance. I just obeyed and continued fighting the demonic wave that seemed to have no end, all the while aware of the play of the stranger's muscles against my spine and the fierce howl of his sword.

A shadow loomed high, and the air screamed. I glanced up, saw three demons diving down, their claws extended and gleaming with bloody fire in the sunrise. I raised Nex and Vita and smacked their blades together to form a cross; a force that was far wilder than mere magic sparked to life, and lightning shot from the tips of each blade, cutting upward. Two demons were hit, but the third dropped through their cinders, a scream on his lips and death in his eyes.

"Drop low," the stranger ordered.

I did, and his sword swung over my head, cleaving the demon's limbs, then sheathing itself deep in his torso.

As two halves of the demon's body fell to either side of the knob and his blood sprayed all around us, another scream rent the air. I twisted around and saw the lead demon take flight. But he wasn't attacking, he was leaving, his wings gleaming like dripping blood in the brightness of the dawn.

No other demons had survived.

I briefly closed my eyes and took a deep, shuddering breath. With the help of the stranger and a whole lot of good fortune, I'd survived.

"I need to thank you ..." The words trailed off.

The stranger, like the red demon, had disappeared.

TWO

I spun and quickly scanned the area, but there was absolutely no sign of him. The color-stained sky was also clear. The only indication that I hadn't been alone up here was the sheer number of broken and bloody bodies littering the knob's base—and even those were now disintegrating as the sun's rays shone more fully on them.

Why had he left without saying anything? While I appreciated the rescue, I'd also have appreciated knowing to whom I owed my life. I didn't think he was a witch—he hadn't felt like one and he certainly hadn't used magic against the demons—only a sword that had screamed in delight every time it tasted the blood of its enemies. Besides, few witches used swords these days to channel power through, simply because they were considered too cumbersome for everyday use. Most resorted to daggers similar in style to mine, or long hairpins that were both intricate in design and very deadly.

After one more look around, I stripped off what was left of my jacket and used it to wipe Nex and Vita clean. I'd still have to wash them with sanctified water once I got home, as demon blood did horrible things to metal. Of course, it also did horrible things to clothing—everything I was currently wearing would have to be burned, as there was no way to get the stench out.

I sheathed the blades and used the coat to wipe off the rest of my clothes as best I could. Then I carefully peeled away the remnants of my shirt to examine the various wounds. The worst of them was my left arm—three deep slashes that ran from shoulder to elbow and already showed signs of festering. Thankfully, I hadn't been hit hard enough for bone to show, but unless I tended to it now, the arm would be nigh on unusable within twenty minutes. All sorts of nasty germs and diseases clung to a demon's claws—it was one of the reasons so many died even if they survived the initial attack.

I grabbed my pack and pulled out the medical kit. Inside was a vial of sanctified water and another containing an antiseptic sealer that was one of Mo's specialties. After uncorking the water, I carefully poured it over the various wounds and gritted my teeth against the scream that sprang to my lips. The water bubbled and hissed for several very painful minutes, but by the end of it all the wounds looked far cleaner. Once the reaction had ceased, I wiped my arm down with a clean cloth and then applied Mo's concoction. The thick green goop filled the three cuts and then hardened, forming a waterproof seal that would allow the wound to heal from the inside out while protecting it from infection.

I put my shirt back on, tossed the medical kit into the pack, and then grabbed the bloody remnants of my coat and headed back to the bridge. The wildlife that had been so absent earlier was now back in full force; squirrels scurried across the path and the air was alive with birdsong. At least

I now knew that silence from the local wildlife was not only a good indicator of predators being in the area but also demons.

My old Mini sat alone in the parking area, its red-and-white paintwork vivid against the surrounding greenery. I threw the pack onto the passenger seat, then dug out a couple of largish plastic bags from the trunk, using one to cover my seat and the other to dump my coat into. While I'd never be using it again, I wasn't about to leave it behind. Not when the shredded sleeve probably had remnants of skin and blood on it. I might be immune to outside magic, but dark-path witches had long used skin, blood, or even hair as a "spoor" for demons to hunt.

Someone—or something—had wanted me to walk away from the sword. That same someone or something might now decide they'd be better off if I was dead. I had no idea why that might be so, but I certainly wasn't about to risk having another encounter with that red demon or more of his crew.

I jumped into the driver's seat and started the Mini. The engine rumbled sweetly, and I couldn't help grinning. Max could keep his shiny electric sports car; for me, there was nothing better than the sound of an old petrol engine—even if they were damn expensive to run these days.

I shifted gear and left, winding my way out of the peninsula park and onto the main highway that ran around Ainslyn's more modern city center and on to the old walled town. By the time I arrived, my left arm was aching, thanks to constant gear changes.

I carefully drove through the Petergate Gatehouse and wound my way through the tiny streets until I reached Foss-gate Road, where our book and healing store—Healing Words—was located. Long-term parking wasn't allowed along the street, but Mo had purchased the remnants of the smithy opposite, simply because it came with enough land to park three cars. Not that many people used vehicles to get around the old town—there were so many car-unfriendly lanes it was generally easier to walk. And for those who didn't want to—or actually couldn't—walk, tourist buses ran around the perimeter of the entire city, and there were also electric two- and three-wheel bikes for tourists to hire.

I reversed into the parking area, noting that while Mo's Nissan Leaf was here, Max's Jag wasn't. It was rather unusual for him to be out of bed at this hour, but maybe he'd already left for the airport.

I grabbed all my gear and climbed out of the Mini. This area was mainly retail, so the cobblestone street was empty and quiet and—given it was the first day of the new year and most of the retail stores and museums were closed—would remain that way until tomorrow.

Healing Words was situated in a three-story, single-fronted building squeezed in between two larger terraces. Its red brick was darkened by years of grime, but the heritage green-and-gold woodwork surrounding the front window and inset, half-glass door had been repainted last year, and subsequently stood out against the classic black-and-white detailing of the shops on either side. The front window display was jam-packed with books, healing potions and charms, and pretty soaps. The latter three were aimed at all the tourists who wandered along this street on their way to the nearby Shambles—an area that contained some of the oldest timber-framed buildings remaining in England. The various snickelways that led off the Shambles had once contained the retail bases of five of the witch houses, but none of us remained there now.

The Valeriun, Okoro, and Chens had moved their business headquarters across to the relocated city center over a century ago in order to be closer to the new port. The Lancasters still retained a major retail presence in the old city, but they, like us, had basically been forced out of the Shambles after the other three witch houses had gifted the area to the heritage council. They still owned much of the surrounding area, however, and made a good living from rents. Mo, Max, and I weren't exactly poor either—we owned quite a number of residential and retail buildings within the old city—but we were the only De Montforts living here now, and there were maybe a dozen left across the entire UK. The only three I actually knew were my cousins in London, but they didn't venture down to Ainslyn much these days. In fact, the last time I'd seen Ada, Gareth, or Henry, I'd been three years old and both my parents and theirs had still been alive.

I unlocked the front door, and the small bell above it chimed, the sound echoing cheerfully through the stillness.

"That you, Gwen?"

The voice was rich and melodious and brought a smile to my lips. "Yep. I'll be up in a minute."

"Good. You can cook me breakfast." Mo paused. "I'm getting a faint whiff of demon—did you strike some trouble?"

"You could say that. Hang on while I go dump some clothes in the burner."

"I'll put the kettle on while you do, then." A soft thumping followed the comment as she hobbled across to the small kitchen. Guilt stirred, although in truth there was little I could do about the length of time it would take her leg to heal. I was a healer-free zone, Max had inherited Mom's storm-control powers rather than De Montfort healing ability and, for some weird reason no one had ever been able to explain, healers weren't able to heal themselves.

I walked through the shelves containing books and other oddities, heading for the sectioned-off rear of the store. There were a number of smaller rooms here—an office, a storeroom, and, in a separate, magically shielded rear room, an old boiler and laundry. It had once provided the hot water for the building, but these days we basically just used it to get rid of the occasional spell paraphernalia that couldn't be thrown out with regular rubbish.

I stripped off and chucked everything—including my bagged coat and my shoes—into the boiler, then lit it. Once I'd cleansed my daggers, I grabbed a towel from the nearby stack, wrapped it around me, and padded barefoot upstairs.

The first floor had been split into two areas—Mo's bedroom was at the rear of the building, and an open kitchen-living area lay to the front. Richly colored tapestries hung on roughly plastered walls, and rugs far older than my grandmother covered the wooden floorboards. The furniture was a mismatch of centuries—new sofas and a big-screen TV juxtaposed against a midcentury teak table and a Regency sideboard. The kitchen was filled with a colorful array of art-deco cabinetry, and the upright stove came straight out of the sixties. It was a mix that shouldn't have worked but somehow did.

Mo glanced around as I appeared. She was a tall, thin woman with plaited gray hair that hung down to her ass and merry blue eyes whose irises were ringed with gold—a feature of all De Montforts and something else I hadn't inherited. Her clothing style could only be described as bohemian—this morning she'd donned patchwork harem trousers and a loose-fitting embroidered top. She didn't look much older than fifty, and I could only hope I looked that good when I hit that age—a mere twenty years from now—let alone when I reached her actual age, which was ninety-five.

She sniffed loudly and then grimaced. "Move right on up to the shower, my girl, because you—" She stopped, her expression concerned. "What the fuck have you done to your arm?"

"Got swiped by a demon. I sterilized it and put your goop on, though."

"It's still looking a little too red around the edges for my liking. Go get clean—and make sure you use the nullifying soap, because I'm not healing anything when you stink worse than a demon left too long in the sun."

A saying that made no sense, given demons left in the sun didn't actually *get* the chance to stink, but I nodded and continued on up the stairs. There were a total of three rooms on the second floor; my bedroom lay at the front over-looking the street while Max's was at the rear with a side window that looked into next door's small rear courtyard. A bathroom divided the two and, though little bigger than a water closet, it somehow fit a full-sized shower and a vanity basin as well as the toilet. Mo, who preferred a bath, had installed a small en suite in her bedroom downstairs. Which was just as well, given how long Max tended to spend in the bathroom getting ready for work every morning.

Not that he spent all that much time here lately.

Once I'd deposited my daggers safely in my room, I grabbed the nullifying soap—which was basically a mix of lavender, lemon, and cinnamon oils mixed with a sprinkle of Mo's healing magic—then switched on the shower taps and waited for the water to get hot.

It took a good ten minutes to scrub the smell from my

skin, and by that time the heat of the water had washed the green goop away and my arm had begun to throb again. I threw on a pair of sweatpants and a tank top and then headed downstairs.

Mo tsked. "Made a right mess of that, didn't you? Sit down and tell me what happened while I patch you up."

I obeyed. My immunity to magic had never curtailed Mo's ability to heal the various cuts and scrapes I'd gotten over the years. Apparently, this was due to the fact that, although I didn't have access to the healing magic, it nevertheless resided somewhere in my DNA.

As explanations went, it didn't really make a lot of sense, but I'd learned long ago straight answers were not something Mo was keen on.

Her power rose, a heated golden force that stirred both around and through my skin, rising and falling in strength as her interest was snagged by a story detail. Eventually, though, she made a satisfied grunt and withdrew her power. I flexed my fingers and then moved my arm around. The wound had completely healed; only three faint pink scars remained, and I knew from experience those would fade.

"Thanks, Mo."

She nodded. "I do feel the need to point out that if you'd used Nex and Vita sooner, you mightn't have been injured at all."

"I'm a power-deficient De Montfort, remember, and the potency of the daggers is not unlimited." Something else I knew from experience.

She made a clucking sound that spoke of disagreement, and I raised an eyebrow. "And what is that supposed to mean?"

"Nothing for now. Tell me more about the knight who rescued you."

"Only if you tell me why the daggers reacted to the pulse coming from the Witch King's sword."

"Probably because they came from the same forge and were made of the same steel."

I blinked. "Why would we have daggers made in the king's forge? We were never connected to the Aquitaines—were we?"

She pursed her lips. "Yes and no. There are plenty of tales of De Montforts being the trusted right hand of many a king."

"And yet there are no De Montforts mentioned in any of the old history books I've read on the Aquitaines."

"That's because there was a fatal falling out between the two lines. Kings can be such touchy creatures." She paused. "Or so I've heard. Now, the screaming sword."

"There's nothing to tell. I didn't actually see it—I just heard it."

"I'm gathering the same can be said of the man who wielded it?"

"We were back to back, and he disappeared the moment the last of the demons fled."

She grunted. "That's not good."

I frowned. "Why?"

She waved a hand. "I can't get into nitty-gritties on an empty stomach. I'll make the toast while you fry up the bacon."

I rolled my eyes but nevertheless got up and grabbed the bacon from the fridge. Once breakfast had been made and the tea was steeping in the cozy-covered pot, she said, "There's only one group of witches who used such a weapon, and I've not heard from them for a very long time. I thought perhaps the line had died out."

"Obviously not." I made myself a bacon butty and took

a bite. "And the only witch line that's currently near extinction is ours."

"Ours and, to some extent, the Aquitaine, although the latter doesn't really count because it's prophesized to rise again when darkness does."

It would be hard to rise if the bloodline no longer existed, but I didn't bother pointing that out. She'd only get sidetracked telling me why the impossible was possible and, right now, I needed to know more about who or what my rescuer was.

"There are only six witch lines in all if we include the Aquitaines, and nothing I've read about the Chens, Valeriuns, or Okoros suggest they've ever used swords that screamed."

And given the sheer force those three houses often channeled through their blades—the elements of earth, water, and air respectively—if ever weapons were going to scream, it would surely be theirs. Of course, controlling those elements for the benefit of mankind—or not, depending on who might have hired them—was also the reason those three had garnered great wealth. More so than the Lancasters—whose magic was of the personal kind and therefore dependent on the strength of the mage—and the De Montforts ever had, at any rate. Mankind continued to be fascinated with magic, but it had never been a path to great wealth for the Lancasters. And the huge leaps in the study, development, and practice of medicine over the last few hundred years had lessened humanity's need for our help.

Mo grabbed the teapot and poured us both a cup—hers in fine china, mine in an old Disney mug. "If you search far enough back into history, you'll see mention of the seventh line, but they've long been absent from the witch council *and* witch records."

"And they're the ones who used the screaming swords?"

She nodded. "They were known as spirit blades, and they contained the souls of those witches whose penance on death was to destroy the dark forces whose power they'd coveted in life."

"Nasty." I spooned some sugar into my mug and then took a sip. "What house controlled them, and why did you think they'd died out?"

"Their surname was Durant, but most knew them simply as the Blackbirds."

I blinked. "I thought we were the only shape-shifting witches?"

"We are."

"Then why were they handed that nickname and not us?" Especially given it wasn't unusual for De Montfort males—just like our avian counterparts—to have a much darker skin tone than females, who were usually brown. Hell, that was the very reason why few realized Max and I were twins—he was a true De Montfort in looks while I'd inherited Mom's Eurasian coloring—white skin, blonde hair, and black eyes. Even in bird form, I was pale.

"It wasn't a nickname, as such. The Blackbirds were an order of warriors who could manipulate both darkness and light, and they were longtime protectors of king and crown."

Meaning my stranger hadn't actually disappeared—he'd simply orchestrated the sunrise to make it *appear* that he had. "When did they disappear?"

"Not long after Uhtric sheathed the sword in stone."

"So the guy today could just be someone who had the good fortune to find one of their blades?"

"Only Blackbirds can control the blades—if he had one, then he is of that line."

"Huh." I leaned back in the chair and finished the last bit of my butty. "Why would he come to my rescue?"

"Anyone with any drop of decency would have done the same."

"I wouldn't be so certain of that." Not in this day and age.

"So young, and yet so cynical."

I smiled. "With some reason."

"Perhaps." She took a sip of her tea, her expression thoughtful. "I think we need to talk to our Blackbird and uncover why they've suddenly become active."

"And how are we going to do that when the man can manipulate light and disappear at will?"

"I dare say he'll find us. In the meantime, we should head over to the King's Tower after breakfast."

The King's Tower was the only intact remnant of Uhtric's castle and, these days, was little more than a tourist attraction and museum.

"Aside from the fact it's closed—"

"Since when has a damn padlock ever stopped me getting into a place?"

"Well, never, but there's also the cameras and alarms to deal with."

She waved a hand. "Only on the upper levels. The vaults aren't monitored."

"Which doesn't help when you get to said vaults via the alarmed ground floor."

"Actually, no, you don't. Like any wise king, Uhtric had escape tunnels."

"If you know about them, the heritage council surely does."

"If there were any witches on it, they might. But that's never been the case, and for this very reason."

I raised an eyebrow. "You're saying some ancient Chen witch figured out we'd need access into the place so we could trace a warrior long thought dead, and set about disguising the tunnel?"

She tsked and slapped my right arm. "No, idiot. And it wasn't the Chens who hid the tunnel—it was the Lancasters."

Meaning the protections were based on personal rather than earth magic. "Then how are you getting through them? Or are you going to call in Barney to help?"

Barney Lancaster was the latest in a long line of lovers and, at fifty-five, was probably one of her oldest. I really wished I had half her luck when it came to attracting the opposite sex.

"I don't need the help of any damn man, young lady, and you well know that."

It was snootily said and made me grin. "Yes, but if it's Lancaster magic—"

"It won't make a jot of difference. I've been getting in and out of the place for years undetected."

"How, when personal magic is supposedly not our thing?"

She waved the point away. "Ask no questions, be told no lies."

I rolled my eyes and picked up my tea to wash down the last bit of toast. "So, why do we need to go to the vaults?"

"Because they're one of five repositories of witch history. The disguised tunnel allows us to come and go at will."

"I take it, then, that the repository portion of the vaults

isn't accessible to the heritage council or those who run the museum?"

"Of course not. They use it as a storeroom and regularly swap out pieces. Uhtric's throne is currently on display in the old hall, so we will have to go back when the museum is open to check that out."

I made myself another butty. "And why would we need to do that? I've seen the throne—there's really nothing remarkable about it."

In fact, Uhtric's throne was the total opposite of his sword—basic and plain, except for the slight embellishment of gold adorning the roses lining the throne's crest rail.

"Be that as it may," Mo said. "I think it might still be useful."

I didn't bother asking why, because she wouldn't damn well tell me. She had that "don't bother me with inane questions" look in her eyes—which generally meant she was running on a gut feeling rather than any logical reasoning.

"Where's the entrance to the tunnel?"

"At St. Mary's Abbey."

Which was just outside the old wall, between the river and the Hanging Gate precinct. "They're ruins."

"Well, they are now, but they weren't back then. The tunnel entrance is hidden within one of the remaining wall sections."

And had no doubt been protected magically, which was probably why it still stood after the vast majority of the structure had been destroyed during Henry VIII's dissolution of the monasteries.

I glanced at my watch; it was just past eight o'clock. "What time do you want to head over?"

"I'll finish my tea and then we'll go. Given the early

hour and the fact it's New Year's Day, there aren't going to be many out on the street as yet."

And those that were probably weren't going to be paying attention to what was happening at the ruins of an old abbey. I drained my cup and rose. "We driving or flying?"

She hesitated. "Flying would probably be quicker."

I nodded and headed upstairs to get ready. After doing my teeth, I changed into warmer clothing, grabbed a small flashlight, and then walked into Max's room to open his window. For someone who was generally a neat freak, his room was a goddamn mess. Drawers were open and clothes were everywhere. It almost looked as if someone had searched it—but that was impossible given the protections placed around this building. Besides, why on earth would anyone want to search my brother's room?

Mo fluttered in, her brown plumage streaked with gold in the light filtering in through the open window. She squawked loudly—no doubt a demand I immediately follow —and then flew out.

I smiled and reached for the inner magic that allowed me to shift. It flared immediately, a thick wave of heat that rolled through muscle, sinew, and bone, altering and miniaturizing all that I was in human form and shifting it across to my bird persona. Thankfully, the magic that allowed us to shift also took care of whatever we were wearing, though it couldn't alter silver-based jewelry or weapons such as my daggers. I could carry them, even though they were a damn heavy burden for a blackbird, but I didn't really think I'd need them today.

And crossed mental fingers that I hadn't just tempted fate.

The rush of power reached its peak and there was a

moment of nothingness—a moment where I was neither human nor blackbird, but held in unfeeling suspension somewhere between the two—and then I was winged, and the freedom and the glory of the skies was mine.

I flew out of the window and soared upward, following the brown speck that was Mo. It didn't take us long to get to the Museum Gardens, where the abbey's ruins were. Though some fog still blanketed the area, it was nowhere near as thick as it had been on the island, and even from up high, visibility was reasonable. There were a few people on Dame's Walk—the promenade that followed the banks of the Ainslyn River from the old port to the new—but the only thing to be seen in the gardens was the rubbish people had left behind after last night's celebrations.

I circled down, calling to my human shape when I was close to the ground, and then flexed my shoulders to rid my muscles of the last vestiges of the changing magic.

St. Mary's Abbey had once been amongst the richest in England, but there was little enough left of it now—just a long sidewall and a solitary corner edge that was disconnected from the rest.

Mo stood in front of the latter, and it dwarfed her. She wasn't short by any means, but the crumbling ruins towered above her by a good twenty feet. I jogged over, each breath stirring the thin veil of gray that still clung stubbornly to the stones.

"The entrance should be right about here somewhere ..." She ran her fingers across the thick curve of a column, golden sparks following her touch like a comet's tail.

I frowned. "Is that fireshow part of the protection? Or is it something you're doing?"

"Bit of both." Her reply was absent, her gaze narrowed.

"But De Montforts—"

"Are many things, most of them unexpected. It's your certainty of what *can't* be done that's hampering what can, my girl."

I raised my eyebrows. "Care to explain that?"

"Of course not." There was a soft click, followed by a distant rumble. Then the air shimmered, revealing a slowly opening and very narrow stone door.

"You've raised me and Max since we were three years old and, in all that time, I've never seen you perform personal magic."

She glanced at me, clearly amused. "What do you think the stuff I put in the soaps is?"

"Healing magic, not personal."

She waved her free hand. "Same, same. And I do have a speck of Lancaster blood in me—my grandfather was one of them. Ready?"

My gaze went from her to the doorway. The stone stairs that descended down into deeper darkness were wet and somewhat slimy-looking. "Are you going to be able to handle the stairs and the tunnel?"

"I've got my moonboot on—I'll be fine."

I glanced down. "That boot is bigger than the damn stair treads. Why don't you shift shape? I've got a flashlight—"

"Stop fussing and just get a move on before someone notices us and comes to investigate."

"There's no one currently here in the park *to* investigate," I retorted, but nevertheless flicked on the flashlight and then squeezed sideways through the door and into the tunnel.

The walls were every bit as damp and wet as the steps, and the air drifting up from the deeper bowels of the place was rank and musty. "For something that's supposedly the repository of all witch knowledge, this place doesn't appear to have been used much."

"That's because youngsters today think they know it all." She poked me in the side with a stiffened finger. "Get a move on—we haven't all day."

Actually, we *did*, because the store was closed and neither of us had anything else on today. This evening was a different matter entirely. It was the first night of the year, and that was the traditional party time for witches—a time where we could let off steam in witch-only venues, freeing us from the worry of upsetting human sensibilities. I was meeting my two best friends—Ginny, who was also a cousin, and Mia—this evening at The Marquis, one of the many old pubs owned by Mia's parents and one of two traditional party venues for Ainslyn witches. Drinking, dancing, and, if we were lucky, sex were all on the cards. Although if past pub exploits were anything to go by, we'd probably end up just plotting our next holiday abroad. The men overseas seemed to appreciate us more.

With a smile twitching my lips, I started down the steps, taking it slow and keeping half an eye on Mo to make sure she was okay and didn't slip. Thankfully, we both made it to the base of the stairs without a problem. The minute Mo stepped off the last step, the door above us shut and darkness closed in. My tiny flashlight wasn't doing a whole lot to lift it.

I moved forward cautiously. The moisture trickling down the walls collected in a central gutter that ushered it into the deeper shadows ahead. The smell of disuse and age grew stronger the further we moved into the tunnel, but underneath ran three vague but very familiar scents—

cardamom, bergamot, and lavender. The same scents I'd smelled over on the island this morning.

Tension rippled through me, and I couldn't help but wonder if fate was about to teach me a lesson. "We may have a problem."

It was softly said but echoed as loudly as any shout. Up ahead, something stirred in response. Something that felt unnaturally dark and powerful.

Magic.

"It would appear so," Mo murmured. "I'm not recognizing the tells, though."

All magic, personal or otherwise, had tells—magical indicators that were unique to every witch. I could pick the tells of all those I'd grown up with as well as most of Mo's friends. I could also track the tells of strangers—something Mo had insisted I learn, though I had no idea why. She certainly hadn't forced Max to learn the skill, although that might have been due to the fact the Okoros had undertaken his schooling from a very early age.

"Suggesting it's an outsider?"

"Possibly." Her energy slithered through the shadows, testing and tasting what lay ahead. "It's some sort of concealing spell. Whoever it is doesn't want anyone to see them."

"Wonder why?"

"I'm thinking there could be no good reason behind it. Get a move on, my girl, before whoever it is completes whatever mischief he or she is up to."

I increased my pace, and the sound of our steps echoed ever more loudly, a drumbeat even the dead couldn't miss. The cologne-based scent grew no stronger, making me wonder if this was the only tunnel in and out of the old vaults. A canny king would probably have had more than one escape route.

Then, from up ahead, came a soft glimmer, one that spread a flickering, pale yellow glow across the old stone wall that curved to the right up ahead.

I frowned, unease stirring, as that yellow glow became brighter, fiercer, and a wave of heat rolled over us.

My gut clenched.

That glow wasn't magic.

It was fire.

There was a goddamn fire in the heart of the vaults.

THREE

"**G**wen, fly!"

I obeyed without thought, shifting shape between one step and another, then rocketing toward the fire rather than away. Mo was only a few wing sweeps behind me but her anger was a sharp wave that all but smothered my senses.

Though I wondered why, it was impossible to ask in this form. While there were some who could communicate telepathically when in either human or bird form, our particular branch of the De Montfort tree was not amongst their number.

I swept around the corner and was confronted by a wall of stone. I shifted the angle of my wings to slow down and then realized the light of the flames shone *through* the stone. The wall was an illusion.

Mo swept past me and arrowed into it. I swore—which came out a harsh squawk—and quickly followed. The illusion's magic briefly caressed my feathers and then I was on the other side, surrounded by heat, thick smoke, and the sharp crackle of the fire.

Why on earth weren't the alarms going off?

Surely if this area was used to store artifacts, both alarms and sprinklers would have been installed. Unless, of course, the person behind the fire had disabled them.

My gaze went to the flames that billowed past a secondary wall illusion and threatened the nearby furniture items. The fire was fierce, but I had no sense of magic being used to enhance it. Whatever fuel fed these flames was natural.

Mo shifted shape and then raised her hands. "Grab the extinguisher, Gwen."

Magic poured from her fingertips, a force as strong as a wave. I had no idea what she was attempting or even what type of magic it was. It certainly wasn't personal—it was far more elemental in feel.

I spotted the fire extinguisher near an exit sign and flew across. Once I'd shifted to human form, I tugged the extinguisher free from its holder and then pulled the pin to break the tamper seal.

By the time I'd run back, the false wall was down and the fuel source revealed. The flames raged through the first section of a vast shelving unit filled with ancient-looking books. Mo's magic flowed either side of this unit, shielding and protecting its sister shelves.

"Aim at the base of the fire and gradually sweep upward."

Mo's voice was distant, her expression one of intense concentration. The energy pouring from her fingertips was so fierce it made the small hairs on my arms and neck rise.

I squeezed the extinguisher's trigger handles together, and foam sprayed out. It didn't immediately smother the flames, but I swept the nozzle back and forth, covering the base of the unit before working upward. White smoke billowed, catching in my throat and making me cough, but the foam eventually did its job.

When the last flicker of fire was erased, I released the handles and put the extinguisher down. Only the books on the top shelf of this first section of shelving had escaped major damage; the rest were a charred and stinking mess.

Mo lowered her hands, but her magic lingered in the air, tiny wisps of power that hung like fireflies in the darkness. She took a deep, somewhat shuddering breath and then walked past me to inspect the shelf.

"It's the goddamn history section that's been hit."

I grabbed the flashlight, but the yellowish beam just made the damage seem all that much worse.

"Why would someone want to burn history books? It's not like there aren't plenty of libraries containing the oral and written history of the witch houses."

"Yes, but this is the only place that holds, amongst other things, the full birth records of all seven houses, dating back since before the time of the Witch King. And there are books missing."

My gaze shot to the charred remnants. "How can you tell?"

She motioned toward the top shelf. "Whoever set the fire wasn't counting on anyone getting here so fast. Books four, six, and eight are gone."

I pointed the flashlight up. The top shelf contained the birth records of the Aquitaines. My heart began to beat a little faster. "Someone's looking for Uhtric's heirs."

"Well, I don't think it's a coincidence that you were attacked on the day of blessing—the one day of the year the sword is vulnerable."

"Except the sword wasn't attacked—someone had been

trying to draw it. And the demons didn't hit until after the blessing was completed."

"Which could have been a matter of mistiming on their part. Demons aren't the brightest creatures sometimes."

Could have been, but wasn't, her tone seemed to imply. "Do you think demons are also responsible for this fire?"

Mo shook her head. "Demons ain't got the smarts to get past the protections around the tower. Whoever did this was a witch of some standing."

"A Lancaster?"

"Maybe, although as I said earlier, it wasn't anyone from around here."

"Could it have been the man who raised the sword this morning? I know the Aquitaines generally aren't capable of personal magic, but given the line isn't pure anymore—"

"There are a few direct descendants left, even if they no longer live in these parts." Mo frowned. "I think I'd better contact Jackie up north and see if she can track down the two up there."

Jackie was one of Mo's old school friends, if I remembered right. I'd never actually met her, but they talked regularly on the phone. "If someone intends to go after the competition, why now? That sword has been stuck in stone for hundreds of years and even we—the last of its guardians here in Ainslyn—don't know what Uhtric ultimately intended beyond saving it for the next true king."

Which in itself was rather odd given that Uhtric, at the time of his death, had one son and two daughters. Surely either his son or his grandsons, however young they'd been at the time, would have fit that description.

"The sword is a weapon against darkness and exists because evil exists," Mo said. "But such power can be dangerous in the wrong hands, so the sword is always sheathed until the time comes again for its use."

I blinked. "That sounds as if Uhtric wasn't the first to draw the sword."

"He wasn't—there were two others before him. The sword is not a part of Aquitaine rule, even if only one who wears the crown can draw it."

Which was news to me and made me wonder just how much more there was to the story of the sword and the crown than I'd been taught. "But the crown—and the rule—of the Aquitaine kings no longer exists."

"Their rule might be long over, but the crown remains."

I frowned. "Isn't it a replica on display in the Tower of London? Wasn't the real one destroyed in the cleansing of artifacts that happened after Layton married Elizabeth?"

Layton had been the very last king to sit on the Aquitaine throne. Not only had his marriage to Elizabeth of York combined human and witch royalty and signaled the end of true witch rule in England, it had also handed his descendants a means of curtailing any magical attacks on human monarchs—one that was still in force today.

"Yes, it is," Mo said. "But the real crown wasn't destroyed in the cleansing—it disappeared weeks before the marriage."

"But he was wearing it the night of the ceremony."

"That was a hastily created copy—the very one that now sits in the Tower. No one knows for sure who took the true crown, but some suspect the Blackbirds were involved."

My confusion deepened. "Why would anyone think that, given their duty was to protect the king?"

"Their duty was to crown more than king, and Layton in his madness was in the process of destroying everything they'd sworn—on their lives—to protect. It was obviously enough to draw them out of what I can only presume was a self-imposed exile."

"Layton wasn't mad—"

"You didn't know him."

"Neither did you. You're old, Gran, but you're not *that* old."

She swatted my arm. "Call me that again, and I'll curse your sex life for the next month."

"Go for it. It's not like it'll affect me in the slightest."

In fact, I'd been in a serious rut ever since Tris had left to chase work in London ten months ago. He'd been my first boyfriend, and while we were no longer romantically involved, we remained in the "friends with benefits" category.

Mo shook her head, her sad expression countered by the twinkle in her eyes. "It's sometimes hard to believe we came from the same gene pool. Must be the Okoro blood in you."

"I doubt *that* has anything to do with it." Max never had any trouble getting partners, and he'd obviously inherited far more Okoro genes than me.

"Then perhaps I should—"

"No."

"Just a tiny little—"

"No. Definitely not. I'd rather remain celibate for the rest of my life than have you magic someone into it."

"Oh, I wouldn't do anything too permanent. Just a week or two, to ease some of the tension."

"My tension levels are just fine, and I'm perfectly capable of taking care of my own needs if necessary."

"No granddaughter of mine should be reduced to self-service—seriously, what is wrong with the young men in this town?"

I shrugged. It was Mia's theory that we were all simply

"too much woman" for them to handle. I rather suspected it more a case of "familiarity breeds contempt." We'd grown up with most of our male peers, and they all had one thing in common—a very high opinion of their prowess, be it magical or sexual. Thankfully, Tris had never really fit into that category. Maybe I needed to head up to London for a week or two ... although I never liked going anywhere uninvited, and Tris had all but fallen off the map these past few months. He didn't even text me anymore, despite the fact we used to talk on the phone every other day.

"I'm not having this conversation with you yet again, Mo, so if you'll excuse me, I'll go check why the damn alarms aren't working."

Her chuckle followed me. I ignored it and walked around the basement's perimeter, scanning the ceiling for smoke alarms and sprinklers. There were a dozen of the latter and six of the former, and a telltale shimmer surrounded each of them. I stopped under the one near the exit door.

"Found something?" Mo said.

I glanced across at her. She had her phone in hand but had obviously told whoever was on the other end to hold. "The smoke detectors are shielded by magic."

"And the source?"

I returned my gaze to the alarm. "I'm not sure ... it's almost elemental but darker in feel."

"Define darker."

I narrowed my gaze and looked past the shimmer to examine the twisting strings of energy of the spell. It was unlike anything I'd ever seen before and reeked of evil. "If I had to guess, I'd say it was demonic in nature, which make no sense given demons aren't capable of magic."

"There's more living in Darkside than just demons, Gwen, and many of them are capable of magic."

Darkside was basically a reflection of our world that existed in the same space but on a different plane. Through means no one really understood, gateways had formed between our plane and theirs. The major gateway—Hell's Gill—was the one Uhtric had sealed. Minor gateways still existed, but for the most part they were located in regional cities rather than major. Generally, the only demons that came through were either minor or juvenile, with the occasional appearance of the winged warrior class. There'd been no full-blown, coordinated attacks since Uhtric's time.

I looked across at Mo again. "Uhtric's war destroyed the dark elves."

"No, Uhtric merely re-caged them, and the effort basically killed him. You cannot destroy all those who live in shadows—not without killing all those who live in light. One is a reflection of the other."

"Oh, that's just—" I paused and cocked my head. After a moment, I heard it again—a very faint *tick, tick*. It was coming from the other side of the exit door, and moving away rather than toward us. Someone—or something—else was in the building. "Mo, is this door alarmed?"

"As far as I'm aware, only the upstairs exit doors and the exhibits are. Why?"

"There's someone moving around on the floor above us."

"Could be security running a check, but take Einar with you, just in case." She whipped the long knife from under her coat. "And be careful. We have no idea what else the bastard who lit the fire might have been up to."

I walked across. Einar was far older than even my daggers, and had been carved out of a solid piece of stone that was as black as ink. I had a similar stone knife but mine was plain, unadorned, and held absolutely no power. The glyphs that ran down Einar's blade glowed briefly at my touch, as if in recognition, and then faded back into darkness. As the hilt warmed in my grip, a soft but steady pulse rose from the stony heart of the blade. Mo had once told me that it was nothing more than the lingering echo of the power that had once flowed through it, but I'd always suspected there was far more to this blade than that.

Which was a pretty common suspicion when it came to my grandmother. I loved her to bits, but her often enigmatic replies to my questions were more than a little frustrating.

I turned and walked back to the door. The handle was cool against my fingertips, despite the lingering heat in the air. Tension pulsed through me, and my grip tightened on Einar's hilt. The blade's inner beat grew stronger and made me wonder if it was somehow echoing my fears.

I cautiously opened the door and peered out. An unadorned stone corridor led to ancient stairs that spiraled upward. I stepped out, then froze as the ticking stopped and a thick wave of awareness rolled through the air.

Not mine.

The intruder's.

My pulse rate leapt, and my breath caught in my throat. The silence stretched on, eating at my nerves.

After what seemed like an eternity, the ticking resumed, but more cautiously than before. Recognition stirred.

Claws.

The ticking was the sound of claws against stone. There was a demon in the tower.

But how was that even possible, given the time? Demons couldn't move around in daylight, and there'd been no hint of their stench in the tunnel we'd used.

So why was it here? Did it have its own agenda or was it working with whoever had lit the fire? While it was extremely rare to find a witch willing to deal with demons—those who did cross that line were swiftly and brutally dealt with—it was also unlikely that the demon's presence here was a coincidence. Somehow, the fire, the attack on the island, and this demon were all connected.

It was the *how* we needed to uncover.

I padded forward silently, my gaze on the stairs but every other sense focused on the sound coming from the floor above.

The ticking stopped again. I paused, one hand on the wall as I looked up. The curving nature of the staircase made it impossible to see anything, but even so, the imminent sense of danger jumped tenfold.

I rolled my shoulders and then cautiously continued on. Once I'd neared the top of the stairs, I stopped again. The simple rope barrier stretched across the exit arch swayed lightly, though the air itself was still. I couldn't see a great deal of the main hall from where I stood, but I knew the layout well enough. The old tower was quadrilobate in shape, rather than the usual circular design, with each "lobe" holding different functions. The one to my immediate left contained toilet facilities—updated for modern sensibilities, of course—while the two opposite were now the souvenir shop and the display room, which currently held the throne, amongst other things. The floor above—the most intact and original portion of the tower—contained the bedchambers.

The intruder was in the display room.

I took a deep breath, then ascended the remaining steps and carefully peered around the edge of the archway. The main hall was empty, but the motes of dust dancing in the light streaming through the window slits spoke of recent movement.

My gaze went to the doorway of the opposite lobe. I couldn't see any sign of movement but the ticking had now given way to a steady thump, thump. The intruder was hitting something.

I stepped over the rope barrier and walked on, my sneakers making little sound on the old stone floor. Even so, I was barely halfway across the great hall when the thumping stopped and that wave of awareness rolled over me again.

I paused, my grip tightening on Einar's hilt. Nothing moved. Nothing rushed out at me.

But just as I was about to walk on, energy surged, a force that was both fierce and foul. Its source wasn't one of the witch houses remaining today. Wasn't a creation of light.

It was born of darkness. Of ill intent.

Smoky strings of magic slithered through the doorway and slunk toward me. Goose bumps fled across my skin, but I somehow held still against the instinctive need to run. While the design of the spell as a whole was unfamiliar, some of the outer strings held similarities to a probing spell. That being the case, running might just set off whatever retaliatory action had been woven through the rest of it.

Einar began to glow fiercely, and the blade's power pulsed outward in waves. I had no idea what it intended or whether it would, in any way, be a match for the dark spell, and had no immediate desire to find out. Especially given that, in my hands, Einar was little more than a razor-sharp blade with a thirst for demon blood.

And it certainly wasn't a demon standing in the throne room.

I hastily shoved the knife under my shirt, against my skin, and vaguely hoped my natural immunity to magic would somehow shield the pulsing. Several strings broke away from the main part of the dark spell and slithered toward me. It took every ounce of willpower to remain still, to not react as the smoky snakes wound up my legs. They might be insubstantial wisps, but they were heavy with a sense of depravation. I shuddered, and the strings paused, their ends rising sharply and snapping back and forth, as if ready to strike.

Magic surged.

Its source wasn't the snakes or even the unseen intruder. It was Mo, casting a sunsphere spell and, I suspected, deliberately drawing the probe away from me. She would have sensed its creation, and the fact she hadn't come flying up the stairs to confront the intruder meant she thought me more than capable of dealing with the spell's creator.

Which should have gone a ways to calming my inner tension, but didn't.

The snakes unwound themselves from my legs and chased after the main spell, slithering into the stairwell. I sucked in a deep breath and then pulled Einar free and continued on.

The thumping resumed.

I padded across to the open doorway and pressed back against the wall. After another of those useless deep breaths, I edged forward and peered around the doorframe.

The throne had been pulled away from its position against the far wall and the shards of both physical and magical alarms lay in pieces around its base.

Standing side-on to it, with an axe in his hands, was a man. He was tall and thin, with pale gray skin and long white hair that was held back in a ponytail by an elaborate metal barrette. His face was long and gaunt, and his ears pointed, their ends tipped with black metal that matched the color of his armor. My gut began to churn.

A dark elf.

Here, in the last remaining remnant of the Witch King's castle.

Fuck.

He looked up at that moment and our gazes met. His eyes were red—all red, no white—and his pupils narrow and oval in shape, rather like a snake's.

A long, slow grin stretched thin blue lips and, in a casual manner, he rested the axe against the splintered and broken back of the throne and then reached for his sword. Anticipation gleamed in his eyes, and for one weird moment, I got the impression he knew who I was.

But that was impossible ... wasn't it?

"Fortune favors the dark realm, it would seem," he said. "You will not escape us a second time, little witch."

I'd been expecting the guttural harshness of the demons, but the dark elf's voice was deep and as sweet as honey. It only made me fear him more.

But his comment basically confirmed my fears; the attack on the island had not been aimed at the sword but rather me. *Why* was the question that now needed an answer—though it was one I was unlikely to get from this elf.

I stepped fully into the doorway. He could certainly stick me like a pig, given the length of his sword, but at least the stone frame offered some protection against a full swing.

I raised Einar; the long knife looked totally inadequate against the dark elf's blade, even if blue-white flames now caressed its sharp edges and the glyphs pulsed with power.

Or perhaps it was hunger. There was certainly a deep eagerness in the inner beat now.

The dark elf stepped clear of the partially destroyed throne and strode toward me, his bony feet bare, metal-clad claws scraping the flagstones with every step. I shifted my feet, lightly adjusting weight and balance. He might have the advantage of reach, but hopefully I was lighter and faster.

But I'd never fought a dark elf before and had no idea if they could move with the grace and speed of their literary cousins.

"Perhaps," a deep but familiar voice said, "you would allow me the pleasure of taking care of this one."

I jumped, and only a deep sense of self-preservation prevented me from instinctively swinging around and attacking. I had no doubt the minute I looked away, the dark elf would charge.

I stepped to one side and waved the mysterious stranger through. "Be my guest."

Air caressed my face as he strode past, but he was wrapped in light and basically invisible. My gaze went to the dark elf. He'd stopped and was regarding the doorway with a quizzical expression. He'd obviously heard our conversation but as yet hadn't seen the Blackbird.

Then his nostrils flared, his gaze narrowed, and he spun, his sword flashing up to meet another. The sound of metal against metal rang out, and the fight that followed was swift and brutal but rather weird to watch, given only one of the two combatants was visible.

The stranger's sword, I noted, was silent. Perhaps it only hungered for demon blood.

The fight ended with the dark elf partially going down, blood spurting from a wound that ran the length of his thigh

47

and took a chunk out of his knee. A heartbeat later, his head was on the floor and rolling toward me. His expression was one of shock, and black blood and god knows what else spurted from what remained of his neck.

My stomach rose abruptly, and I bolted for the ladies', where I lost every bit of food I'd eaten that morning and perhaps a bit more.

After a final few dry heaves, a hand appeared to the left of my face, plucked Einar from my grasp, and then gave me a plastic cup of bluish-looking water.

"Rinse your mouth with this—it'll take away the aftertaste."

Mo, not the stranger.

"Thanks." I accepted it gratefully and quickly swished. It tasted vaguely of mint and lemon, so why it was blue I had no idea. "I take it our stranger has yet again disappeared?"

"Indeed, I have not," that deep voice said.

I straightened abruptly and looked around. He leaned against the bathroom doorframe, his arms crossed and his pose casual. The sword that had so swiftly dispatched the dark elf was nowhere to be seen, though the slightest shimmer near his left shoulder suggested it was now sheathed across his back—a position historians had spent centuries saying was illogical, as it was all but impossible to draw a long sword held in such a position. Unless, of course, you had gorilla arms, and the stranger certainly didn't.

They were, however, very well muscled, a point emphasized by the somewhat bloody material of his shirt being stretched to breaking point around the bicep area.

The rest of him wasn't exactly shabby, either.

He was tall and, rather surprisingly, considering those arms and the width of his shoulders, built more like an athlete than a weight lifter. His short hair was as black as sin, his eyes the most startling shade of jade, and his face ... gorgeous didn't even begin to do it justice. The man looked like an angel ... albeit an angel with a sword that screamed like a banshee.

Mo cleared her throat, amused speculation evident in the quick glance she cast my way, and then said, "To what do we owe the honor of your presence, my dear Blackbird?"

One dark eyebrow winged upward. "You know what I am."

It was a statement rather than a question, and Mo's amusement grew. "Of course I know. There're not many in this world who control soul blades."

"There're not many in this world who would even recognize one."

"Ah, but I'm far older than I look. What do you want, Blackbird, and why are you here?"

Just for an instant, amusement flirted with his lips, and my heart did a weird sort of flutter. I rather suspected a full-blown smile would have it stopping entirely.

"The fact that I've saved the life of your granddaughter twice now is not enough?"

Meaning he knew exactly who we were. That should have had trepidation rising, but the fact was, if he'd intended me harm he could have done so at any time, either this morning or now.

"Said granddaughter is more than capable of saving herself," Mo said. "And Blackbirds were not known for acting against either demons or dark elves unless they threatened the crown or king. Gwen is clearly neither."

He nodded, his gaze flickering to mine. I felt the weight of it all the way down to my toes. "No. It is her brother I seek."

It was on the tip of my tongue to say, "all the good-looking ones usually are," but I somehow managed to restrain it. "Why?"

He lifted one shoulder, a small motion that was somehow elegant in the extreme. "I'm merely a foot soldier doing as I'm told."

Mo snorted. "For such a pretty man, you can't lie for shit. You got a name or do we just keep calling you Blackbird?"

Once again a smile ghosted his lips. Once again my heart did its weird little dance.

"Lucas Durant, at your service, ma'am." He didn't exactly do a full bow, but he did incline his head. Maybe courtly manners were a prerequisite for Blackbirds.

"I'm too young to be handed the 'ma'am' moniker, so you'd best keep it to yourself and call me Moscelyne."

"It is indeed an honor to use the great mage's first—"

"Stop talking shit, Lucas," Mo cut in. "Why are you here? Tell us, or leave. We've too much yet to do to be playing word games with you."

"Fair enough." He pushed away from the frame, all amusement falling from his countenance. "There have been a number of dark elf incursions of late, most of them centered around the few remaining artifacts from Uhtric's era. Five of us have been dispatched to guard said artifacts—Ainslyn is my patch."

Which at least partly explained his appearance on the island and here at the keep—they were the only two places in Ainslyn that still held original pieces from Uhtric's reign. "And my brother? Where does he fit into all this?"

His gaze met mine, and this time the shiver that ran through me had nothing to do with desire or attraction. Those jade depths were now a sea of cold distance.

But why?

Max had certainly walked the edge of civilized behavior more than once, but he'd never crossed that line and stepped into the shadow realms. I was his damn sister—his twin. I would have sensed it if he'd strayed so far from the light.

"I simply want to speak to him. Nothing more, nothing less." He paused. "At least at this point."

"You don't think my grandson is responsible for these events, do you?" Mo's tone was extremely polite—a sure warning of trouble brewing to anyone who knew her. "Because I have to warn you, such an accusation will not be well met unless you can produce proof."

Lucas's gaze flicked to hers, but its absence from mine in no way eased the inner chill. "As far as I'm aware, no, we do not."

She crossed her arms and studied our Blackbird for several seconds. Judging him, judging his words. Believing them, up to a point. "Then what do you wish to speak to him about?"

Lucas hesitated. "There was a break-in at the British Museum a few nights ago. Someone fitting his description was seen leaving the area."

"Was anything actually taken?"

"The sovereign ring."

Mo's eyebrows rose. "The one on display is fake, isn't it?"

"Yes—the thief obviously wasn't aware of that fact."

"I take it the real one remains safe?"

A smile touched his lips. "It's been safe for centuries."

Meaning the Blackbirds had it, not the nation.

"Good." Mo paused. "I take it there's video evidence of this thief?"

"No. Whoever broke in used a light shield."

"Given the only witch group capable of such a feat are the Durants," she commented, "I presume you're searching amongst your own ranks for the culprit?"

"No, because it was a spell rather than a manipulation of light. We were called in as soon as the alarms sounded and found the fading traces of it."

I raised my eyebrows. "Given the world in general thinks the Blackbirds are as dead as Uhtric's line, who called you in?"

"The one person who knows we are not," he replied. "Queen Eleanor."

"You still serve the royal family?" I couldn't contain my surprise. "Why? It's not like the royal line—past or present —is magic capable."

Layton might have given humans the means of ruling over us all, but his marriage to Elizabeth had never produced an heir capable of witchcraft. Even though subsequent kings and queens had periodically taken witch partners, the result had never altered. It appeared there was something in human biology that nullified whatever gene enabled us to either create magic or control the elements.

"While that's true," Lucas said, "what relics remain from Uhtric's rule are part of the royal treasures, and it is to those pieces our duty lies."

"Does that include the crown?" I asked. "The real crown, not the fake one on show in the Tower of London?"

Surprise flickered in his eyes. "What makes you think the crown is fake? It *is* the one that Layton wore on the day of his marriage."

Mo's phone beeped, cutting off my reply. She pulled the phone out of her pocket and glanced at it. "Barney just arrived downstairs. Why don't you two go see what that damn dark elf was up to in the throne room, then come downstairs and help us clean up the mess?"

"I have other—"

"No doubt," Mo cut in crisply. "But if you want my help finding my grandson, you'll be doing as I say."

His dark eyebrow winged upward again, but he didn't argue. He simply stepped to one side and motioned her through. Then he glanced back at me. The remoteness remained. "Would you prefer to wait here?"

"No, I damn well would not." I dumped the cup in the nearby waste bin. "I wasn't expecting a decapitation, that's all."

Wasn't expecting so much blood and gore and fluid stuff to come spraying out of a severed head.

My stomach rolled at the thought, but I ignored it and strode past him. His scent teased my nostrils, a warm mix of musk, sandalwood, and cinnamon. It was rich and sexy and made my insides quiver and my body ache with the need to just—

I cut the rest of that thought off, suddenly glad he was behind me and unable to see the heat creeping across my cheeks. I'd been in the presence of sexy men before—hell, Tris wasn't exactly a slouch when it came to the hot guy stakes—but this was the first time I'd had a reaction at such a base, almost primeval, level.

I cleared my throat and tried to corral my unruly hormones. "The crown in the Tower might be the one he wore at his marriage, but it's not the Witch King's Crown. It disappeared several weeks before the ceremony."

"Says who?"

There was amusement in his tone, but I didn't look back. Too much heat remained in my cheeks. "Says Mo."

"And she is the keeper of all knowledge regarding Uhtric in Ainslyn?"

"She's a De Montfort, one who has spent most of her life protecting the king's sword and studying what information remains about Uhtric and his line. So yeah, I guess she is." I risked a glance his way. "You never did answer the question as to why you're here at the King's Tower."

"I've been staying here," he said. "The beds upstairs are old but comfortable, and it kept me close to the throne."

I guess it wouldn't have been hard for someone who could manipulate light to make it appear a room was empty when it was not. How he'd gotten around the security measures after hours was a different matter.

I stepped around the dark elf's head and tried to ignore the liquid it still leaked. His body wasn't much better, but at least there were no eyes staring up at me.

"If you're staying here, why didn't you stop whoever started the damn fire? Surely you must have felt him breaking the illusion and spelling the alarms?"

"Yes, but then the dark elf entered, and I thought it better to discover what he was up to."

Suggesting he might not know what the vaults contained—or didn't care. I stepped over the broken barriers and stopped in front of the throne. The arms were shattered and part of the back splintered and broken, but overall it remained in pretty good shape considering it had been hacked at with a great big axe.

"Why would they want to destroy the throne? It's not required in a crowning ceremony, is it?"

"Officially no; generally the crown is placed on the head of a kneeling monarch. Perhaps they're merely being cautious."

"Then why not simply take it rather than make such an inept attempt to destroy it?"

"Dark elves do not think as we do."

I shifted position and spotted deep indentations across the back of the throne, just under the still intact portion of the crest rail—something I'd never seen before, thanks to the way the throne was generally displayed.

I brushed my fingers across the old wood. The indentations were more than deep scratches from past misuse. There almost seemed to be a pattern to them. I frowned and pulled out my flashlight. The dull light didn't really reveal all that much more.

Lucas bent to study them; it placed his face entirely too close to mine and had his scent once again filling my nostrils. I bit my bottom lip, using the pain to override sensory input. It helped. A little.

"Those scratches appear to be glyphs of some kind. Give me the flashlight."

I did so, careful not to let our fingers brush. "Why can't you just make the light in the room brighter?"

"Light manipulation is more about concealment." His reply was absent as he brushed his fingers across the wood. "There're several lines of words, but I'm not recognizing the style. It's very old—perhaps even older than the throne."

I frowned. "Didn't Uhtric have this one made after the original was destroyed in a fire?"

"They salvaged fragments, apparently."

"Huh." My gaze returned to the glyphs. "Do you think it's some sort of prophecy? Or warning?"

He shrugged, his shoulders brushing mine and igniting the inner fires yet again. Damn, this was *strange*.

"It could be either, but I think the more pertinent question is, how did that dark elf know about them when we did not?"

"We" being the Blackbirds, obviously. "Whatever it says, they certainly didn't want us to see it. What's the plan?"

"We hide and protect the throne, obviously."

"I'm sure the heritage council will just love that."

"They won't even know."

"Seriously? You think they're not going to miss one of their main attractions?"

He gave me a look—one that was a weird mix of amusement and cool distance. "Obviously, a replacement will be brought in."

I raised my eyebrows. "Meaning your lot has fake thrones just handily hanging about?"

The amusement got stronger, and my pulse rate did a happy little skip. "Illusion and a stand-in will do the trick short-term. We'll have a proper replica created if it's deemed necessary."

"Huh." I took out my phone and took a couple of photos. I had no idea whether Mo would be able to understand the glyphs—or if they'd even be visible in the photos—but a couple of the symbols did echo the ones on Einar. "So what do we do with it now?"

"I'll run some protections around it, then ring headquarters and apprise them of the situation. I'll meet you downstairs in a few minutes."

I hesitated, then nodded and headed out of the room. Breathing suddenly became a whole lot easier. I shook my head and made a mental note to get over my reluctance to go where I possibly wasn't wanted and ring Tris. The need for sex was obviously a whole lot more dire than I'd presumed.

I clattered down the stairs and found Mo and Barney studying the wall to the left of the storage area, directly opposite the tunnel we'd used. The sunsphere Mo had created to distract the snakes hovered near the burned remnants, but it was still bright enough to light the entire area.

"What's up?"

"Another tunnel entrance," Barney said. He was a well-built man with silver-gray hair, craggy but handsome features, and kind brown eyes.

"Well, there obviously had to be, given our arsonist didn't come through the abbey one." I stopped beside them and studied the wall in question. Vague strings of energy drifted across the stone surface but there was nothing to suggest a major spell at work. I brushed my fingers across the stone. "It feels solid rather than an illusion."

"Well, there'd be little point in having an illusion that any Tom, Dick, and Harriett could fall through." Mo's tone was amused. "But in this case, it *is* an actual wall. The tunnel is to the left, just below that white stone."

The white stone was actually a pebble, and it was situated a mere two feet above the floor. "That suggests it's not a very big tunnel."

"It's not, which is why we've never used it, and why you and our Blackbird can have the honor of exploring it. Barney and I are far too old to be clambering about on hands and knees."

I snorted. "Only in certain situations."

Barney's brown eyes twinkled. "Have you been listening at the door again?"

"Don't need to. The pair of you aren't exactly quiet."

Mo patted Barney's arm. "Just ignore her. The poor

child is suffering a distinct lack of sexual satisfaction at the moment."

"Seriously, can we save such comments for a more appropriate time and place?" I motioned toward the concealed tunnel. "Where does it come out?"

"According to our records, the old docks," Barney said. "But the exact location is a little fuzzy. We also have no idea what condition it's in."

"Our arsonist obviously used it, so it can't be in too bad a state."

"True."

Mo glanced past me. "Where's our Blackbird?"

"Upstairs ringing his people. He's taking the throne into custody."

Barney raised silvering eyebrows. "Why?"

"The dark elf was attempting to destroy it—maybe because there're glyphs on the crest rail."

Mo held out her hand. "You obviously took photos."

I handed her my phone. She enlarged the photos and studied them intently for several minutes. "The glyphs certainly hold some similarity to the ones on Einar, but it's hard to make out what they're saying."

"Send them to me," Barney said. "I've a nephew who could probably enhance them for us."

She nodded and immediately forwarded them. As his phone beeped, Lucas stepped into the vault. The sheer force of his presence had me sucking in air ... and I couldn't help but wonder if it was something to do with his witch power—a natural magnetism that came with the ability to manipulate light, perhaps.

His gaze swept the three of us and then came to rest on the destruction. "Do we know if anything was taken?"

"Aquitaine lineage records." Barney held out his hand. "Barnaby Lancaster, head of Ainslyn's witch council."

Lucas introduced himself and briefly clasped Barney's hand. "Book numbers?"

"Four, six, and eight," Mo said.

"Those being the lineage records of Uhtric's son and two daughters."

"And you know that instantly how?" I asked, unable to keep the skepticism out of my voice.

"Because I'm a Blackbird, and it is our duty to know such things." Amusement touched his tone again but failed to register in his expression. "It does surprise me that the books were taken *after* the attempt to draw the sword this morning rather than before."

"An oddity that also occurred to me," Mo said. "I've asked Jacqueline Lancaster to check on the two known descendants working up her way."

Lucas nodded, an indication that he knew exactly who Jackie was. "Owain—another member of our order—has been sent up there, so no doubt their paths will cross."

"Excellent," Mo said crisply. "In the meantime, I suggest you get that gorgeous butt of yours into the tunnel and see if our arsonist has left any clues behind. My grand-daughter will accomp—"

"That is unnecessary—"

"I beg to differ," Mo cut in. "This is my town, Blackbird, and you had best never forgot that."

Barney cleared his throat. "Our town, you mean."

"Of course, dear boy." Mo patted his arm. Barney's expression was one of tolerant amusement. She made a "come here" motion with her fingers, and the sunsphere skittered across the room. "Use this to light the way—the batteries in that flashlight look ready to fail."

Lucas studied her for a second and then followed the sunsphere into the tunnel. I couldn't help but note that the man's jeans hugged him in all the right ways.

"You can thank me later," Mo said, clearly knowing exactly where my thoughts—and eyes—were. "In the meantime, in you go."

She didn't offer Einar, which meant she didn't expect us to hit any trouble. I dropped and, on hands and knees, pushed through the illusion into the tunnel. The air was dank and filled with rot and age. Moisture dripped off the walls, fat drops that landed on my head and neck and made me shiver. Riverlets ran past my fingertips, and in the distance, lit by the golden light of the sphere just ahead of Lucas, strings of moss swayed lightly. Either someone had only recently traversed this tunnel or the exit was open.

What was absent were the teasing scents I'd now smelled twice. But I guessed that was to be expected if the exit was open. The fresh air could have dispersed them by now, even if it weren't doing such a great job with the rest of the smells in this place.

I shuffled forward, trying my best to keep my gaze on the ground rather than the well-formed butt ahead of me. It was a task that became increasingly easier as the tunnel's walls closed in and the sharp edges of rock threatened to shred my shoulders if I wasn't careful. Whoever created this tunnel certainly hadn't bothered with niceties like smooth walls.

"Given the trouble we're having moving through this tunnel, I have to wonder how our arsonist got three books through here." I inched past an outcrop of rock that had a hooked edge not dissimilar to a crocheting needle. "There's not enough height for a backpack and there's no evidence of anything having been slid along the floor."

Lucas pushed sideways past an even larger outcrop. Sharp edges scraped across his chest, tearing open his shirt and slicing into skin. "He could have used some sort of hover spell."

I reached the outcrop and shuffled past sideways. Unfortunately, my breasts didn't fare a whole lot better than his shirt, and I swore.

He immediately glanced back at me. "You okay?"

I nodded, despite the stinging. "I'm not seeing any left-over spell strings though."

"If he'd created the spell in the vaults, you likely wouldn't. Not given how fast the leftover echoes of such a minor spell fade."

Which was true enough and somewhat frustrating. We continued on. The tunnel got no smaller, but it did get wetter and colder, the latter thanks in part to what looked to be an old brick stormwater drain joining it. Thankfully, this also meant we could stand rather than crawl, but it didn't ease the chill settling into my bones.

After another ten minutes or so, daylight began to invade the tunnel and the cry of gulls filled the air. Lucas stepped over the remnants of a metal grate, then stopped. I did the same, wiping the moisture from my face with the sleeve of my sweater as I looked around. While I didn't immediately recognize the area, the stormwater outlet sloped down to the sea, and just above that was a set of stairs that curved away to my right.

But to my left ...

I instinctively backed away, my heart lodged some-where in my throat and my mind not wanting to believe what my eyes were seeing.

The gateway was six feet high and made of a stone that shone a deep, dangerous blue-black in the light of day. Like the gateway bridge that provided an entry point onto the island, it was arched, but the carvings here were grotesque abominations that depicted demons both cavorting with and destroying human figures. I could almost hear the screaming of all those being fucked, tortured, and hacked, often all at the same time ...

I gulped and tore my gaze away.

The archway had no door and to anyone not witch-born, would appear to be totally blocked by stone.

But that was an illusion.

And this was something I'd never thought I'd see. Not here in the heart of old Ainslyn, at any rate.

An open gateway into Darkside.

FOUR

"Well, that at least explains how the dark elf got into the tower." Lucas's voice was grim.

I eyed the entrance uneasily and fought the urge to run deep into sunlight. "How could a new gateway appear without anyone knowing?"

Especially here, in Ainslyn?

"It didn't. It's an old one that's been reopened."

"Deliberately? Or did the locks placed on the gate fail naturally?"

"The locks on all the minor gates have been gradually failing over the last half century, but in this case, they were deliberately smashed."

"How can you tell?"

"There were light locks here—" He pointed to an area on the right side of the gate—just above what looked to be a demonic orgy—then swept his hand around the arch. "As well as here, and here. If you look closely enough, you can see the stretched and torn remnants of them."

I crossed my arms and studied the gateway. After a moment, I spotted them; they spoke of thunder and lightning as much as magic, and reminded me a little of the power that had pulsed from the sword. Entwined within those remnants were several tiny strings that had a vaguely familiar feel. I frowned, trying to pinpoint why, but there simply wasn't enough magic left.

"Whoever broke the seal was a witch rather than a dark elf—"

"Not just a witch," Lucas cut in. "But one with Aquitaine blood. Only an heir could smash the lock open like this."

"Why would an heir—especially one intent on claiming the crown—want to do that? No one wins if Darkside is unleashed."

He glanced at me, expression shuttered. "Power. It's always about the power."

"Uhtric's heir has access to more power than most witches could ever imagine."

"Once he draws the sword, yes. But what if he's not so well endowed, magically? What if he seeks help to claim what should not be his?"

"But from demons? Or dark elves? That makes no sense at all."

Lucas shrugged. "To you and I, perhaps. To someone who would go to any lengths to attain power? Perhaps not."

"But—" I stopped and shook my head. Until we knew more about the person behind all this, there was little point in guessing at motives. "If you're aware the locks are fading, why isn't something being done to strengthen them?"

"The magic's source was Uhtric's. None of us can alter or even reinforce the spell."

"But you could've placed backup light spells around them."

His smile held little warmth. "We did, and yes, they're

regularly reinforced. Having too many open gateways is not something any of us want—not when Uhtric's crown remains unclaimed."

"It's unclaimed because your lot have it hidden."

"So the rumors would have you believe."

My gaze narrowed. "Your people *don't* have the crown?"

He raised an eyebrow, his expression giving little away. "There's no doubting you're of Moscelyne's bloodline, is there?"

"Meaning what?"

"Nothing."

"I've heard that enough times from Mo to know the opposite is generally true." Annoyance ran through my voice, despite my best effort to keep it in. "What of the Hell's Gill gate then? Is that magic still holding strong?"

"Yes. But if it *is* an heir behind all this and they *have* teamed with Darkside, then we'll be in real trouble."

"Why, if the magic locking Hell's Gill is holding strong?"

"Because the sword is the key to the gate. What it locked in, it can also unlock."

"Well, fuck, isn't that great news."

"I'm surprised you didn't know."

"You wouldn't be if you knew Mo better. She has a tendency to dish information only as needed."

He grunted. "Why don't you walk on and see if there's any sign of our arsonist. I need to shore up this gate to prevent further incursions."

"Said arsonist will be well gone by now. If you want me to leave, Lucas, just say it."

"Luc."

I frowned. "What?"

"Call me Luc. And yes, I need you to leave. There's a chance either the demons or the dark elves will sense the new restrictions being placed over the doorway and attack. While demons might be incinerated by sunlight, dark elves are a touch more resilient."

"Then consider me gone." I hesitated. "Are you coming back to our place once you've finished?"

"Yes. Moscelyne has yet to answer my question about your brother."

"I wish you luck on getting that sort of information without giving out some of your own first."

I spun on a heel and walked away. His gaze was an uneasy heat that burned into my spine and sent shivers dancing across my skin. There was no doubting I was fiercely attracted to the man, but there was also something about him that made the more sensible bits of me wary. He was, after all, hunting my brother, and I had a bad feeling he would do anything—use anyone—to get to him.

It was the "why" that bothered me. There was more to the story than what he'd already told us.

I jumped over a wave that lapped the edge of the water-course, then bounded up the steps leading up to the narrow but long sea wall that curved around the bay, providing a safe harbor for what had once been a major fishing hub. These days, the only vessels using it were small pleasure craft, and even then, they were few and far between. The new port, which was close not only to the city and the relo-cated fish markets, but also a vibrant café scene and nightlife, was where most boats moored these days.

At least the fog had finally burned off; though it remained chilly, the skies were clear and blue. I drew in a deep breath to wash the smell of rot and darkness from my lungs and glanced around. As suspected, there was no sign of our arsonist—but then, he was hardly going to hang about the scene of his crime or leave an easy clue or two for someone like me to follow.

I scanned the pretty pastel houses that lined Beach Road, but couldn't see anything that tweaked my instincts. Aside from the cafés that belonged to the two small hotels situated at either end of the old harbor, there was nothing open.

I hesitated, then strode back along the sea wall and onto Dame's Walk. After pausing on the edge of the cobblestone street for a couple of push bikes to go past, I jogged back to the first hotel and scanned the entrance to see if there was any indication that a witch might have stepped inside. It was, at best, a vague hope, as only the strongest of witches left "presence trails," as I liked to call them. There might be no indication that our arsonist belonged to the upper eche-lon, but there was also no indication that he *didn't*.

Unfortunately, there was no vague glimmer, no fading wisps of energy or power. Oh well ...

I shoved my cold hands into the front pockets of my torn and grubby sweater, then headed back along the street, all senses alert but finding nothing untoward. Once I'd checked the other hotel, I swung into a small lane and wound my way through the multitude of streets until I was home.

After grabbing a hot shower to warm the chill from my bones, I tended to the scrapes on my breasts—which were thankfully minor—then made a pot of tea and plonked down on the sofa. It was well after eleven, so if the fog had cleared the airport as quickly as it had here, Max should be in Paris by now.

I grabbed my phone, hit his number, and waited for the call to go through. The phone rang ... and rang. Either he was screening calls or he had his phone switched off, and the latter wasn't likely.

Just as the automated message service was about to kick in, there was a soft click and then he said, voice dry, "Well, if it isn't my dear sister. What's up this time?"

"Plenty." I quickly filled him in. "The Blackbird also wants to talk to you about a break-in at the British Museum a few days ago."

He snorted, the sound one of contempt. "Of course he does."

The back of my neck prickled. "You were there at that time?"

"Of course I was—I had to do a presentation at the Okoro Foundation, remember?"

No, I did not. "But why would he think you're involved in the break-in? Was the meeting near the museum?"

"Close to. But I dare say the cause was more the altercation I had with one of his compatriots a day or so later."

"*What?* Why?"

"He tried to question me. I was late for a date. Let's just say things got a little heated."

"Is that why you suddenly decided you needed time off in Paris? And why there's such a mess in your bedroom?"

"Could be." Amusement ran through his voice. "Although the latter is also due to the fact I couldn't immediately find something I needed and then not having the time to clean up."

"Damn it, Max, why didn't you tell us any of this?"

I could almost see his shrug. "I thought the situation would blow over and didn't want to worry Mo."

"Didn't want to get dressed-down by her, more likely."

"That might also be true." The amusement was deeper. "Listen, I need you to cover for me—"

"No."

"Sis—"

"Don't 'sis' me. You assaulted someone. I'm not covering that sort of shit up, Max. Not anymore."

"Fine." His voice was curt. "Give him my number, then. But I'm not coming home until my damn holiday is up."

"Fine." I paused. "Did you have any trouble flying out this morning?"

"No—why would I?"

"The fog, dummy."

"It was gone by the time we got to the airport."

"We?" My eyebrows rose. "I thought you and Liam had broken up?"

"We did—ages ago."

"So is this a new lover? Or a new business opportunity?" Max didn't really have that many friends. Not of late, anyway.

"Both, but until the formalities are over and the deal delivered, it's all hush-hush. But it's going to change our lives, Gwen."

The excitement in his voice had my eyebrows rising again. "I actually don't want my life changed—I'm quite happy as I am." Well, aside from the whole lack of sex thing, anyway.

"And that's why I was sent to the Okoro Academy and you were not."

I snorted. "The fact you have the Okoro ability to control storms might have had something to do with it, too."

"As I've said before, I can feel the power in you, Gwen. You're just too damn scared to step outside your safe little box and reach for it."

That was the second time today I'd been told something

like that, and it did not make me happy. "Thanks, bro. Love you too."

He laughed. "Back at you, sis. See you next weekend."

"You want me to pick you up?"

He hesitated. "No. I'm not sure yet what time my flight is, so I'll catch a cab—"

"That'll cost a fortune."

"And neither of us are poor." He hesitated, and then added more seriously, "Be wary of the Blackbird. They possess a magnetism that can be hard to resist, but it's nothing more than a part of their game. A means to an end. Their end goal is always the protection of the crown and nothing—and no one—else matters."

His verbalization of my own doubts had unease deepening. "Thanks for the warning, but I do have to ask ... how come you know so much about them?"

"Mo isn't the only Uhtric scholar in town, no matter what she claims. The Okoro and Aquitaine bloodlines have been intermingled for centuries and their library is vast."

Something else I didn't know. "Does it have lineage records? Because it might be a good place for us to search for—"

"Leave it to the Blackbirds," he cut in. "That is, after all, what they live for."

"Max, I was attacked. First by demons, and then by a dark elf." And more worryingly, the dark elf had actually stated I would not escape "them" again. He might now be dead, but the "them" were not. "I'm not going to sit idly by and let those bastards have a third go at me. I want to know what the hell is going on."

Max grunted. It was not a happy sound. "Then at least wait until I get—"

"No."

"Gwen, be sensible—"

"Not when my life is on the line, brother."

He swore. "Just be careful then. Keep in the light and remember, these bastards don't give up once they've got their mind set on a kill."

"I'm always careful."

He grunted. "See you in a week, then."

"You will."

I hung up and shoved my phone onto the coffee table. After drinking my tea, I headed downstairs to tidy up the store and get a few things ready for tomorrow's opening. As night closed in, Mo sent me a text saying they were still covering up the mess and that we'd talk more tomorrow.

With Luc obviously also not coming, I headed upstairs to get ready for my night out.

"Hey, babe." Ginny brushed a kiss on my cheek, then perched on the stool beside me. "This place is rocking tonight."

"That's hardly surprising—there're only two pubs open tonight."

And only The Marquis had The Seagulls playing—a three-piece rock group that had become a firm favorite with the pub's patrons. The result was a packed bar and the doors being closed early thanks to safety concerns. Ginny, who was—as usual—late, had undoubtedly only gotten in because Mia had left word with the door staff.

"True, but it leaves little enough room for dancing. Where's Mia?"

"Getting hot and heavy with Jonny."

"Seriously?" Her head whipped around, sending the

long length of her plaited black hair flying and forcing me to lean back to avoid getting smacked in the face. "She must be desperate, poor woman."

I laughed and motioned at the bartender. He nodded, and three seconds later, Ginny had her favorite drink—a whiskey on the rocks—sitting in front of her. It paid to be best friends with the owner's daughter.

She took a sip and sighed in appreciation. "There's nothing finer than Chivas Regal." She paused. "Except maybe a hot man serving me Chivas Regal, and they're few and far between in this town."

"A truer word has never been spoken. What's been happening?"

She wrinkled her nose. "Mom's been making 'it's about time' noises again."

I snorted. I adored my aunt, but she was a total homebody who'd married at seventeen and had her first child at eighteen. She really couldn't understand why Ginny wasn't following in her footsteps. "And what did you say this time?"

"That if she was so intent on seeing me married and pregnant, there's a rather nice but totally human sergeant in my division that I quite fancy."

I laughed. "Oh, to have been a fly on the wall."

Ginny's grin was decidedly devilish. "Yeah. I might even go out with said sergeant, just to give her conniptions. So, who or what has upset your equilibrium?"

I drank some bubbly. "What makes you think something has?"

"Aside from the fact you just avoided answering the question, you mean?" She made a circular motion toward my torso. "It's all those tension vibes you're radiating."

While Ginny hadn't inherited the family's ability to

control storms, she was sensitive to any and all fluctuations in the air, and could track people, animals, or even vehicles via the lingering swirls of color and currents that followed their movement. Which was why she worked at the major crimes unit as a specialist detective.

I grimaced. "It's been a rough day."

She leaned forward, her dark eyes sparkling with interest. "Really? Feel free to unleash on your cousin—she has the shoulders to handle it."

I smiled. Ginny was all of five feet one and petite in build ... but woe betide anyone who mistook either for weakness.

I gave her the bare bones basics and she blinked several times before saying, "Well, shit."

"Yeah." I gulped down my bubbly and then motioned for another.

"What's Mo planning to do?"

I shrugged. "Find the heirs, for a start. Then I suppose we'll need to figure out which one of them is trying to erase records of the others."

Ginny wrinkled her nose. "And why you've suddenly become a target. I mean, really, that makes no sense."

"No." I smiled my thanks at the bartender as he delivered my drink. "Although Max did make an interesting observation—that the Okoros and the Aquitaine bloodlines have been intermingled for centuries."

"Which still doesn't explain why they're after you. I mean, you're female."

"Huh, who'd have guessed *that*? It's not like I have any giveaway bits."

My voice was dry, and she grinned. "All of which are kinda hard to miss in that dress you're almost wearing. The blue really suits you, by the way."

"Thanks." I raised my glass and clicked it against hers. "It could simply be a matter of me currently being the last of the De Montforts who's tending the sword—and the weakest. They're not likely to go after Mo—even demons have better sense than that."

"True." She sipped her whiskey. "It's also true that the mixing of our line with the Aquitaines hasn't done a goddamn thing for his human heirs."

"Yes, but it still leaves the possibility that an Okoro *could* be one of the heirs."

"You've met my brothers—do any of them seem likely to hold royal blood to you?"

I laughed. "Well, no. I'm thinking more a different branch of the Okoro tree."

Especially given that if one of Ainslyn's Okoros did have royal blood, however small a fraction, Mo would have mentioned it. She might not have had a reason to do so in the past, but today had changed all that.

"Possibly." Ginny's expression was thoughtful. "I could look in the family bible—that's where all the births and deaths have been recorded over the centuries. I might find something there."

"That would be great." Mo might have already asked, but it didn't hurt to double up.

"And now," Ginny said. "Let's move on to a more important subject—the gorgeous Blackbird."

I raised an eyebrow. "I never said he was gorgeous."

"You didn't have to. Your vibes got all hot and bothered just mentioning him."

I grinned. "Okay, so he *is* gorgeous, but like me he does not."

"Then you're not expecting to see him again?"

"Oh, I will, probably tomorrow, given he's chasing after Max."

"Huh." The devilish light entered her eyes again. "I might just pop around ... I'm in need of some new soaps."

"Which will do you absolutely no good. According to Max, Blackbirds aren't interested in anyone or anything except achieving their aims."

"Yes, but they must have sex sometimes—otherwise the line would have died out by now."

"Also true." I grinned. "It'll be interesting to see if he has the same magnetic effect on you as he does me."

"Magnetic effect?" another voice cut in. "Who?"

"No male in this room, that's for sure," I replied.

Mia squished between the two of us and vaguely waved a hand. Her drink of choice—a Brewdog Beer—was swiftly delivered, an action that was met by heated grumbling from those standing nearby. Mia flashed them an unrepentant grin and raised her beer, adding, "It's just one of the many benefits of your folks owning the bar."

"And can I just add," Ginny said, "there's nothing magnetic about you right now, dear Mia. You're all red and sweaty."

"Dancing does that to a girl. You should try it sometime —it might get the happy juices flowing."

"If they're flowing for someone like Jonny, count me out."

"I'll have you know he's damn good—"

"No, stop right there," Ginny cut in. "I do not need those images invading my brain."

Mia grinned. At five-ten, she was two inches taller than me, with blue-gray eyes, short brown hair, and a slender build. "Ladies, this is the one night a year we can truly let our hair down—so to speak—so get out onto the dance floor and damn well relax."

With that, she drained her beer, grabbed Ginny's hand, and dragged her off the barstool. Ginny yelped and reached for me, and the two of us were pulled only a little unwillingly onto the dance floor. Where, it had to be said, much fun was had over the next few hours.

Midnight had come and gone when a muscular pair of arms slid around my waist and then pulled me back against a body that was hard and firm. As uninvited lips brushed my neck, I thrust back hard with my elbow.

There was a deep "oomph" and the arms fell away. I swung around, ready to unleash verbally, and then blinked in surprise.

"Tris?"

"Yeah." He straightened and rubbed his solar plexus. "Some welcome home there, Gwenny."

I laughed and bounded into his arms. He caught me with another "oomph," a sound that was lost as our lips met and I kissed him with all the hunger and frustration that had built up over the last few months.

"My, my," he said eventually, his golden eyes sparkling with heat and desire. "I think someone missed me."

"You have no idea." I kissed him again, this time quickly, then released him and tugged my dress back down my thighs. "What brings you back home?"

"Work."

"And are you staying at your parents' place?"

"Not when I have every intention of having loud and vigorous sex with my ex." He glanced past me. "Hey, ladies, nice to see you again. Mind if I steal your girl away for a few hours?"

Ginny's eyes twinkled wickedly. "If it's only for a few hours, she's going to be mighty disappointed."

Tris laughed and wrapped an arm around my waist. "Shall we catch up for lunch tomorrow? My treat?"

Mia frowned and placed the back of her hand against his forehead. "He *is* running a bit of a temperature ..."

Tris laughed again and swatted her hand away. "It's not *that* rare."

"Oh, it is," Ginny replied. "Work must be good."

"I landed a big contract a few weeks ago," he said. "I can afford it now."

"You're a Chen," Mia said dryly. "You could afford the moon if you wanted it."

"My parents' money is *not* mine." There was an odd edge in his tone that had me frowning. "Anyway, does The Bean Fairy at one o'clock suit everyone?"

"We should be over the worst of our hangovers by then," Ginny said. "Have fun, kiddies."

He nodded and swept me away. After paying my bill and grabbing my coat, I tucked my arm through his and said, "Is there yet another problem with your parents?"

He grimaced. "It's nothing more than the usual."

"Surely they can't be disappointed now that you've landed a good job?"

"They're Chens. I could marry into the royal family and they'd still think Leon would have done better." He shrugged. "But let's not spoil the mood. I've missed you."

"Really? Because you've got a funny way of showing it."

"I've been busy—"

"Not a worthy excuse."

"It is when you're doing nothing more than working or sleeping."

I raised my eyebrows, a grin twitching my lips. "No time for sex?"

"None at all." His expression was sorrowful but somewhat countered by the glimmer in his eyes.

No time for sex, my ass. "So that whole hard and fast comment—"

"Was no exaggeration."

"Huh." I studied the street for a moment. "Where are you staying?"

"At The Cherry Tree."

Which happened to be nice and close. "I suggest we hurry along then."

"I do like your thinking."

It only took a few minutes to get to his room, but we didn't make it to the bed. Hell, we barely made it past the door. He slammed it shut, then pushed me against it, his mouth claiming mine, his kiss as demanding as his touch, setting me aflame and making me ache with desire in a matter of seconds. I moaned, a sound that drew a deep growl from the back of his throat, and a heartbeat later, my dress and underclothing were on the floor. I tore off his shirt, undid his trousers, my fingers shaking with the force of my need. With another growl, he lifted me up. I wrapped my legs around his waist and drove him inside, but there was no pause to enjoy the utter perfection of that moment. He was moving, thrusting, and it was all heat and urgent desperation. Desire built, and built, until my body was so tightly wound it felt ready to shatter. Then my orgasm hit, and I was shaking, groaning, and shuddering. A heartbeat later, he came.

When I was capable of speaking again, I rested my forehead against his and chuckled softly. "I think it's safe to say we both needed that."

"Yes." He hesitated. "You're still protected, aren't you?"

I pulled back a little to look at him. "It's a little late to be asking that."

"Yeah." He didn't in the least look repentant. "Sorry."

"As it happens, I am. Little Chens running around my feet isn't something I want right now." Or ever, if I was at all honest. I loved him as a friend, and I certainly enjoyed his company sexually, but that was it. That indefinable something—a connection that was far more than mere physical attraction, even if that was initially part of it—was missing.

Said connection hadn't been missing when it came to Luc ...

I shoved the thought away and dropped a kiss on the tip of Tris's nose. "Shall we take this to the bed?"

"Sounds like a plan."

He carried me over, placed me down, and then leapt onto the bed beside me, almost bouncing me off in the process. He laughed and pulled me close again. "Prepare to be further ravished, my dear friend."

There was little talking for the rest of the night. And while I thoroughly enjoyed every moment, part of me—a tiny, probably overcritical part—couldn't help but notice the differences in him. He was more physical—his love-making more dominant and even a little rougher—than usual, and I had to wonder why. Was it simply a matter of the time we'd spent apart deepening the already obvious differences between us? Or was there something else behind the change? I didn't know, but it did disconcert me.

I finally fell asleep just on dawn, and woke to the soft rumble of traffic some hours later. I opened a bleary eye and looked around the room. It was a typical hotel room—a window overlooking the street to the right, a bathroom to the left, a little desk and chair on one side of the door, and a small wooden wardrobe on the other.

"Tris?" I said softly.

No answer came. I frowned and squished down the pillows to look at the clock. It was nearly eleven. I should have been at the bookstore an hour ago. I groaned, then flung the covers off and padded naked and shivering into the bathroom. There, stuck to one edge of the mirror, was a note.

Got an emergency call from work earlier, it said. *Won't make lunch, will ring you later.*

I tugged the note free then tossed it into the bin. I wasn't entirely surprised he'd backed out of lunch. Tris was many things, but he'd never been overly generous when it came to money. He had good reason, of course. His parents adored his elder brother and doted on his youngest—who, at ten, was twenty-one years younger—but Tris had inherited his mother's ability for personal magic rather than the more prestigious Chen control of earth. Nothing he did had ever been good enough—which, perhaps, explained the anger I'd sensed in him last night.

Perhaps.

I took a quick shower then got dressed, collected my shoes, and walked home barefoot. My feet were frozen by the time I arrived, but better that than having blisters all over them. The shoes were divine, but they were not designed to walk any sort of distance.

I pushed through the front door. Mo was replenishing the soap near the cash register and said, without looking around, "Go warm those feet, then make us both a sandwich and a cup of tea."

I nodded. "How did things go at the tower?"

"Updates later. Your feet are a strange blue-white—go warm them before you get a chill or something."

I'd long gotten over wondering how she knew such things without actually looking around. "I'm hardier than that."

"You'll need to be."

"Another of those statements you won't explain. You are so annoying sometimes."

"I'm your grandmother. It's part of the job description." She finally looked around, her smile wide. "And hey, at least I'm not nagging you to get married and produce wee bairns."

I snorted. "No, but I daresay only because you're too busy bemoaning my lack of sex."

"A problem that has apparently been rectified, if the satisfaction practically oozing from your pores is anything to go by. Go."

I rolled my eyes and bounded up the stairs. Once I'd sent Ginny and Mia a text telling them lunch was off, I pulled on a thick pair of woolly socks, shoved my feet into my slippers, and then set about making the tea and sandwiches.

"There's enough there to feed an army," Mo commented, her eyes twinkling. "You really did have a good night, didn't you?"

"And no breakfast." I placed the tray on the small table near the counter, then grabbed a beef and onion relish sandwich and sat down. "How did the cleanup at the vault go?"

She reached for a ham and cheese sandwich. "We reinstated the fake wall and called in Erika to sweep out the stench of fire, but it's going to take some time to sort through the remains of the books and see if anything can be salvaged."

Erika was Ginny's mom and my aunt. "And the throne? Did you manage to get upstairs to take a look at it?"

"Before it was snatched away by the Blackbirds, you mean?"

"Yes, and don't start."

She raised her eyebrows, devilment in her eyes. "I have no idea as to what you're referring."

"Of course you don't."

She chuckled softly. "The glyphs are definitely from Einar's era, which means that particular piece of wood is older than the throne itself. Couldn't make it all out, but there's mention of the Blackbirds, the sword, and light being reborn."

"Helpful."

"Once Barney's nephew enhances that photo you took, I should be able to work out the rest of it."

"And hopefully why the dark elf didn't want us reading it." I finished the rest of my sandwich and reached for another. "Did you call Jackie?"

Mo's amusement fled. "Yes, a couple of times, but she hasn't answered. It's rather worrying."

"Maybe she's just been busy."

"Maybe." Mo picked up the teapot and poured us both a cup. "She's never usually this slow in responding, though."

"Do you want to fly up there today and check? It won't hurt to close the store early."

There certainly hadn't been many people walking past in the time I'd been sitting here, and the few that had hadn't even glanced into our window. But then, it was winter and, despite the blue sky, damn cold. Sensible tourists would no doubt be inside a café or a pub by now, having a meal and a drink.

She hesitated and then nodded. "I've a gut feeling something is wrong, and it never pays to ignore that sort of stuff."

Especially when it was Mo's gut. "I don't suppose Ginny came in this morning, did she?"

"Yes, she did, on the pretense of buying soap, but hanging around an extraordinarily long time. I gather you told her about Lucas?"

"Indeed I did." I hesitated. "Are we expecting him to come in today?"

"Tomorrow at eleven."

"Ah."

Amusement creased the corners of Mo's eyes. "Is that an, 'Ah, I'm looking forward to it' or more an 'Ah, my attraction to the man scares me and I just might hide'."

I whacked her lightly on the arm—which only served to increase her amusement. "I don't run from anyone."

"Which does not address the rest of my question."

"Deliberately so. You're amused enough." I picked up my Disney mug. "When I was talking to Max last night, he said that part of a Blackbird's power was an intense sexual magnetism—is that true?"

"I wouldn't have said that was the province of Blackbirds—it was generally something attributed to the Aquitaine line, thanks to their ability to draw on the power of all four elements." She shrugged. "It's part of the reason why the Aquitaines and the De Montforts were—for a few brief centuries—all but interchangeable."

Only Mo would ever describe centuries as being "brief." "And *that* is yet another snippet of information you've not imparted before now."

"I haven't?" she said, feigning innocence. "How remiss of me."

I rolled my eyes. "What about the Blackbirds? Given

they were responsible for the safety of the royal house, did that lead to a liaison or two?"

"Sexual shenanigans undoubtedly happened with Aquitaine queens but the Blackbirds were only ever male."

"That doesn't mean a liaison or two couldn't have happened with a king. Homosexuality was around back then, you know."

"Of course it was, but the Blackbirds were, as a general rule, highly ethical, and having a relationship with the man you were supposed to be protecting would have betrayed said ethics."

I reached for another sandwich. "But having a relationship with his Queen didn't?"

"Apparently not." Her eyes sparkled wickedly. "I'm sure you could break down his barriers if you wish. You are, after all, my granddaughter."

"Thanks, but I'm not *that* interested in the man." I ignored her sharp laugh of disbelief. "If there was such a crossover between De Montforts and the Aquitaines way back in the dark ages, is it at all possible that Max could be one of the heirs?"

Mo hesitated, indecision briefly flaring through her expression. Before I could ask why, she said, "It is, although the link between the two houses was severed long before Uhtric was crowned."

Which did not preclude the possibility that Max could be a very distant heir. "What about the Okoros?"

"Also possible—especially given Queen Eleanor's grandmother was an Okoro. Not from the Ainslyn branch, though."

"Are any of these distant heirs up Jackie's way?"

"One Okoro, plus a couple of brothers who are descendants of Uhtric's older sister."

"Why is Jackie looking after them rather than the Blackbirds?"

Mo shrugged. "She's an Aquitaine scholar and history professor. She likes knowing these sorts of things."

There was more to it than that, of that I was sure. I drained the last bit of my tea and then rose. "I'll close things up and do the till if you want to head upstairs and get ready."

She nodded, picked up another sandwich, and then hobbled toward the stairs. I walked across to the door to flip the Open sign over and then lock the door. It didn't take long to do the day's takings—although sales had been a little better than I'd presumed. Once I'd locked it in the safe, I headed upstairs to get ready for the flight.

Mo was already waiting in Max's room. "Bit of a mess, isn't it? I've a right mind to text him and tell him off. If he wants to live in a brothel, he can get his own place."

I smiled and tossed my daggers onto the bed. I'd tied the sheaths together and created a small loop at the top to make carrying them a little easier. "I've already done that. He said he couldn't find something he needed and then didn't have time to restore order afterward."

Mo harrumphed. "Poor excuse. You ready?"

I nodded and motioned her to proceed. Once she'd shifted shape and flown out of the window, I did the same, sweeping up the daggers on my way through.

Jackie lived in Amble, a small seaside town in Northumberland. It was far quicker to fly there than it would have been to drive, but the effort of carrying my daggers had weariness beating through me by the time we arrived. Mo was luckier—Einar was stone, so at least the shifting magic was able to incorporate the blade in the same manner as it did her clothes.

We swept over the small town, heading toward the coast and the North Sea, then circled down toward an old graveyard and shifted shape behind a weird, A-shaped stone gateway that led precisely nowhere.

I strapped on my daggers, then glanced around. As areas went, it wasn't particularly inviting. But then, we *were* standing in a cemetery. "Where's Jackie's house?"

"Across the road."

Meaning the small pebbledash bungalow that was all but dwarfed by its newer-looking two-story neighbors. The grass in the front yard was longish, the bare rosebushes lining the timber fence in need of a prune, and there was smoke drifting from a small chimney. "She may be a scholar, but she's not much of a gardener, is she?"

"No." Mo's voice was uneasy. "I'm not liking the feel of this, Gwen."

My gaze shot back to the house. I couldn't feel anything untoward, but then, I likely wouldn't, given the lack of magical ability. "How do you want to play this?"

Mo hesitated, her gaze sweeping the surrounding area for a second. Other than a woman on a motor scooter driving toward us on the footpath, there was little movement and few sounds beyond the crashing of waves on the shoreline behind us.

"You jump the fence and go in through the back. I'll distract them from the front."

"Them?" One hand automatically found a knife hilt.

"Yeah. There's someone else in there."

"Then you be careful."

A smile touched her lips. "You too, darling girl. Meet you in the middle."

I jogged across the road, then waited a second or two for the old woman on the motor scooter to drive past before I jumped the front fence and clambered over the taller, secondary fence. The back yard was neater than the front, and featured a small clothesline, a paved dining area, and more roses sitting against the fence that divided the bungalow from its taller neighbors. Magic floated in the air, but the glittering strings were little more than the remnants of a protection spell that had been smashed open.

I ducked under the open single window and walked to the back door. It wasn't locked, and the door opened into a small galley kitchen.

I drew Nex, then took a deep breath and stepped inside.

The first scent I noticed was thick and metallic.

Blood. And not just a little bit.

The second was more acidic, and so strong my skin crawled.

Mo was wrong.

There *wasn't* someone else here.

There was some*thing*.

A goddamn demon.

FIVE

I drew Vita and, gripping both daggers tightly, padded quietly through the kitchen, keeping out of the light filtering in through the window above the kitchen sink to avoid creating an unwanted shadow. The scent of blood and demon grew stronger near the sliding door that led into the next room, and I paused, waiting for Mo to create her distraction. The smack of flesh against flesh filled the air, and the desire to run in and stop the bastard surged. But I had no idea how many demons were in that room, no idea if they'd set all this up as a trap, and no desire to find out the hard way.

A heartbeat later, knuckles rapped sharply on glass; the sound echoed through the small bungalow. It was swiftly followed by the scrabble of claws on floorboards.

The demon, on the run.

I darted out of the kitchen, caught a quick glimpse of bloody, broken flesh before spotting the demon's tail disappearing into the room opposite—the same room that had the open window.

I swore and bolted after it. Flames flickered down Nex

and Vita's sharp blades, as if in anticipation, and the stench of the demon grew stronger, catching in my throat and making me gag. I slid around the door and saw it half in, half out of the window. Why it thought that was a good idea given sunlight would kill it, I had no idea—and no intention of discovering whether it was carrying some form of light protection.

I raised Nex and Vita and slapped their blades together. Lightning shot out, twin forks that turned brown scaly flesh into ash in a matter of seconds. As the soot of his remains drifted to the carpet, I sheathed both daggers and half turned to walk out, and then caught sight of something gleaming against the wall under the window. I frowned and walked over.

It was a ring. A shiny, blue-stone ring.

I bent to pick it up, but evil prickled across my skin, and I sharply withdrew my fingers. Instead, I slid Nex's tip through its center then lifted it up. Flames ran down the blade and surrounded the ring, flaring brighter for several seconds. Once they'd died down, the stone looked dull. Whatever evil had lain within it had obviously been rendered inert.

I slipped it into my palm then resheathed Nex and closed the window. By the time I walked back into the living room, Mo was kneeling down next to the bloody figure lying on the living room floor.

"How is she?"

Mo glanced up, her face drawn but her expression furious. "Unconscious, but alive. Her leg was shattered, and it had punctured the artery. I've healed them both, but I've still her arm and smashed cheek to go."

If she did both of those, she'd end up in hospital too—and wouldn't care, I knew. "No internal injuries?"

"No, thank god. The severed artery was dangerous enough."

"You want me to call the police and an ambulance?"

"Already have. What happened to the demon?"

"Ashed him."

"Good, although I would have liked to know what he damn well wanted."

"He obviously wasn't sent here to kill her. Not straight away, at least." I offered her the ring. "He left this behind."

She plucked it from my fingers and sucked in a breath. "I haven't seen one of these for decades."

"What is it?"

"It's an oath ring—one that usually binds one or more demons to a dark practitioner."

"That makes sense, because that demon certainly wasn't responsible for breaking the spells around this place."

"No. And yet I didn't see or sense the presence of another witch." She rolled the ring across her fingertips. "What color was the demon?"

"Brown."

"It's unusual for such a demon to be bound by an oath ring. They're basically little more than for-hire thugs and their services can be bought by as little as a few gold pieces."

A smile touched my lips. "There're not many witches around these days who have easy access to a stash of gold coins."

Her gaze flashed to mine. "You know what I mean."

I nodded. "Why would a witch—even one with a darker bent—risk throwing their lot in with demons?"

She shrugged. "If your intent is thuggery, then it's one way of getting it done without personal blowback."

I snorted. "Unless, of course, another witch catches the whiff of demon on you."

"There are ways and means of neutralizing such scents, as you well know." She shoved the ring into her pocket. "Can you check the rest of the house before the cops get here? It'd be good to know if the place was searched before Jackie was beaten up."

I skirted the two of them and moved across to the door that led into a small hallway. The layout of the house was pretty basic—there was a bedroom, a bathroom, and this living room to the right of the front door, while two more bedrooms and the kitchen lay on the left. I walked into the smaller of the two rooms in this section of the house. There was a double bed against one wall and a wardrobe to the right of the door. The small window opposite looked out to a wooden fence and let little light in, thanks to the proximity of the terrace house next door. I walked over to the wardrobe and opened it. Inside was an assortment of clothes, coats, and shoes. I opened a couple of the boxes sitting at the base of the robe but found nothing except knickknacks. I closed the doors and scanned the room again, but nothing here even remotely tugged at my instincts.

I spun and walked up the hall to the next room. I'd been expecting a master bedroom, but it was in fact a study. A long, antique-looking desk sat under the window, and the other three walls were lined with bookcases stacked to the brim with books.

I went across to the desk and shuffled through the papers. One of them was a half-finished Okoro genealogical tree, with a list of names to one side. Some of them had been crossed out and placed in the tree, while others had yet to be moved. Max's name was at the bottom, with Gareth, Henry, and someone named Jules listed above him.

Ginny's brothers, I noted, were *not* on the side list,

which was rather odd considering her mom and mine were sisters.

I briefly scanned the rest of the names, but none of them were familiar.

Why was Jackie bothering to trace the Okoro line? Even if there *was* a distant connection, surely if she was looking for the true heir—and given her connection to Mo, that was indeed likely—it would have made more sense to study either the Aquitaine or Valeriun bloodlines? All of the direct heirs would have to be killed before the names listed here would be in any danger.

But why were Gareth and Henry on the list? As far as I knew, neither their mom nor grandmother had any Okoro connection. I skimmed the tree and saw that their great-grandmother's parents were Valeriun and Okoro.

Given they'd both been placed above Max and the unknown Jules, that surely meant that link back to the Aquitaines was stronger than Mom's.

I tucked the papers into my pocket and then went through the rest of them. Most were end-of-term history papers on English royalty in need of grading. There were, I noted in amusement, going to be some failures amongst them.

The drawers on the left side of the desk held various bits of stationery, and the ones on the right were locked. I half thought about forcing them open, but given the age of the desk, didn't think it would be appreciated. Especially when Mo could magic it open within a second.

I walked over to the nearest bookshelf and then scanned it to see if there was anything a demon might have wanted. They were mostly the generic type of history books you'd find in college libraries, although the bookcase on the back wall held a number of more ancient-looking tomes. One of them snagged at my instincts. I carefully reached up and slid it out. I couldn't read the title thanks to the fact it was Latin, but there was what I presumed was a handwritten translation just inside the cover that said "The Fables of Kings from the Time of Swords." I carefully flicked through. It was exquisitely and lavishly decorated, the vellum pages inked with gold and bright, beautiful illustrations.

There were a couple of names I recognized, including Uhtric himself. Interestingly, the sword he carried in the illustration was not the one currently buried in the stone, as it was far plainer. An everyday sword, perhaps. Uhtric was also the last entry in the book, although there were blank pages following his section, so maybe it was simply never finished.

I closed the book and continued my inspection, but nothing else caught my eye. As the distant wail of sirens began to intrude on the silence, I headed back to the living area.

"The ambulance is almost here. How is she now?"

"Still unconscious but breathing easier." Mo's gaze met mine. Lines of tiredness now edged her eyes and cratered her cheeks. "Did you find anything?"

I showed her the family tree. "Do you think we should warn Gareth and Henry?"

She hesitated. "I'll give them a call once Jackie is in hospital and tell them to take extra precautions. And the book?"

"It's fables, and I'm not sure why it tugged at my instincts, but—"

"Your instincts are almost as reliable as my gut, so I daresay something will be found on closer inspection. You want to take them home and look after them until I get back?"

I raised my eyebrows. "You don't want me to accompany you to the hospital?"

A smile touched her lips. "We both know how uncomfortable you'd be there."

That was something of an understatement. I might have only been three when Mom had fought for her life after the accident that had killed Dad, but the years had not erased the horror of watching her slowly die, no matter what anyone did or tried.

I swallowed heavily and pushed the memories back into their box. "Yes, but given what's happened—"

"This attack is the very reason I don't want you with us. Whoever is behind this is hunting for something. I wouldn't be surprised if our shop is the next on their list."

"Demons won't get through your protections—"

"They got through Jackie's easily enough, and hers were every bit as strong as mine."

Given the brief glimpse I'd gotten of the various spell strings, that wasn't exactly true. "Keep me updated then." I glanced around as the siren stopped. "You want me to get the door?"

She shook her head and climbed to her feet. "You'd best leave, especially given you're carrying Nex and Vita."

I frowned. "I'm legally allowed—"

"Yes, but country coppers don't always agree with such rules, and I know Jackie was pulled up the few times she wore her hair-blades."

I grunted and, at the sound of slamming doors, headed back through the kitchen and out the back door. I tucked the papers inside the book and then carefully slid it inside my jacket. Once secure, I undid my daggers, looped them together again, and then checked no one in the nearby houses was looking my way. With the coast clear, I shifted to my blackbird shape and flew home.

By the time I was back in Max's room, weariness pulsed through me. I changed to human form, stumbled forward before catching my balance, and then stood there, one hand gripping the doorframe as I sucked in desperate breaths. I wasn't unfit—I flew a couple of times a week to keep in flying trim—but this time I'd been carrying more than double my blackbird body weight. No matter how much I might have built up my muscles, that would always take its toll.

Once my limbs had stopped trembling and my breathing had calmed to a more normal rate, I unzipped my coat and pulled out the book. Where did I put the thing to keep it safe? I looked toward my bedroom, but if someone were to break in, that would probably be the first place they'd look, especially if they were still hunting me.

I frowned at the mess surrounding me, but instinct whispered against storing it in Max's room. Why, I had no idea, but I wasn't about to gainsay it.

I picked up my daggers and then clattered down to the living room. After studying the entire area for a few moments, I decided hiding it in plain sight was the best option. I walked over to the coffee table and its multiple number of books, and shoved the fables into the middle of a stack. Once it was covered with the other books, I stood back. The disguise was perfect, thanks to the fact that many of Mo's books were not only yellowed but also reeked of age. The nearby scented candle only barely covered it up.

I dumped the daggers on the sofa, made myself a pot of tea, then sat down and flicked on the TV. After surfing through the channels, I settled on a wildlife documentary and turned the sound down to a murmur. Within minutes, I was fast asleep.

I wasn't sure what woke me.

I must have slipped sideways sometime during the afternoon, because Nex's hilt was digging into my side. The room was dark, and rain beat heavily on the windowpane to my right, a normally soothing sound that somehow scratched at my nerves. The TV had switched to standby mode, and the bright red light gave the immediate area an eerie glow.

Then, from downstairs, came the soft creak of a floorboard.

Someone was walking around the shop.

I slipped a hand underneath my body and pulled the daggers free. The footsteps moved toward the stairs.

I pushed upright, slipped off my shoes, and then rose, a knife in each hand. No flames ran down their sharp sides, suggesting the intruder was human rather than demon. Which perhaps also explained why the spells hadn't reacted —they were tuned more to preventing dark intrusions rather than stopping ordinary folk. Even so, anyone intent on mischief—human or not—should have had some trouble getting through the spells, which probably meant the intruder had at least some magical knowledge.

The stairs creaked as someone climbed. The air fairly crackled with tension, and I had no idea whether it was his or mine.

I moved around the sofa, carefully avoiding the loose boards as I crossed the room and pressed my back against the wall near the end of the stairs. From this position, I'd see the intruder long before he ever saw me.

The intruder paused near the top of the stairs. My

breath caught in my throat, and my grip tightened on the hilt of my daggers.

After several minutes, the footsteps continued, and a shadow appeared on the landing. He wore dark clothes and a hood pulled over his head and smelled of wind and rain rather than demon. That didn't ease my tension any.

He paused again. I held still, not daring to even breathe. After several tense seconds, he moved.

So did I.

In one fluid motion, I grabbed a fistful of hair with one hand and with the other pressed the point of one knife against the base of his neck where it met the spine. "Move, and I'll push this goddamn blade right through your fucking neck."

The figure froze. Then an all too familiar voice said, "What the fuck, Gwen?"

"Tris?" I didn't lower my knife. Not immediately. "What the hell do you think you're up to?"

"What do you think I'm up to? I came here to see you. Put the knife away before you stab me or something."

"Not until you explain why you snuck in rather than simply knock. Or hell, even call first? And how did you get in? I didn't feel you unlock any of Gran's spells."

While Tris could perform general magic, his true gift was the ability to unpick any sort of lock, be it physical or magical. It had gotten us into—and out of—a whole lot of trouble in the so-called "wilder days" of our youth. Not that any of us had been truly wild—not in comparison to Max, at any rate.

But he certainly knew better than to use that here.

"I didn't need to—you gave me a key, remember?"

"You gave that key back to me."

He cleared his throat. "I may or may not have had a copy made."

"Why?"

"Just in case we ever got back together. Officially, I mean, rather than just for sex."

"Sex and friendship is all I want from you. Give me the damn key. Slowly."

He reached into his pocket and then held up the dead-lock's key. I plucked it from his fingers and pocketed it. "Now answer the question—why didn't you ring or knock?"

"Because I wanted to surprise you. Won't be fucking doing that again, let me assure you."

"Good." I finally lowered the knife then stepped back and switched on the lights and heating. Maybe it was just the aftereffects of being woken so abruptly, but it felt like a damn freezer in here.

Tris turned; his face was pale, but fury burned in his eyes. He didn't like being so completely caught out.

Too fucking bad.

"Would you like a coffee or would you rather something stronger?"

"Whiskey, straight, if you've got it."

"I do." I turned and walked back to the sofa, sheathing my daggers and then depositing them both on the kitchen counter, out of his way. Why I felt the need to do that I had no idea; maybe it was just the anger still radiating from him.

Or maybe it was a rekindling of the feeling that *this* Tris wasn't the man who'd left me with a kiss and a happy laugh ten months ago. A feeling that said he'd changed in ways I couldn't yet imagine.

I grabbed the Jameson bottle and a couple of glasses out of the booze cupboard and then moved back to the sofa. He sat beside me somewhat warily.

Once I'd slid a glass across to him, he picked it up and contemplated it for a second. "So what has made you so jumpy?"

I raised an eyebrow. "I was woken from a dead-to-the-world sleep by floorboards creaking. What did you expect me to do?"

"What about asking who the hell it was before you shoved a knife into the base of their neck?" His voice rumbled with the anger he was barely repressing. "Don't you know how easy it is to kill someone like that?"

"Yes, and you will note that I barely even pricked your skin."

He snorted. "If I'd retaliated—"

"You would have come off second best. Your magic washes over me, remember?"

He grunted, an unhappy sound that matched his expression. "So why not flee like a normal female?"

I sipped the whiskey. The happy burn did little to erase the doubts and questions still crowding my mind. "Because I'm not a normal female. Besides, Mo would have had serious words with me if I'd flown rather than defended our home."

"She's as goddamn crazy as you are." He looked around. "Where is she?"

"Up north, visiting a sick friend."

A gleam entered his eyes. One I was all too familiar with, but which lacked its usual power over me tonight.

"Then we're all alone here this evening?" he mused. "How fortunate."

I raised my eyebrows. "And how do you know Max won't be back?"

"He won't."

I frowned. "Well, no, but why are—"

"Let's order in some dinner," he cut in, "then finish that fine bottle of whiskey and go test out the springs on that old bed of yours ... or did you finally update the thing?"

Despite my misgivings, I couldn't help but smile. "Don't be mocking the bed. A lot of good times were had there."

"So that would be a no, you haven't replaced it."

"I might have if I'd been heartbroken about you leaving, but I wasn't, so—" I shrugged.

"Ouch." He slapped a hand against his chest. "Wounded to the core."

"Yeah, right." I rolled the amber liquid around in my glass for several seconds. "I'm not up to it tonight, Tris. I have to run the shop myself tomorrow, and I need to sleep."

"We can do the sleep thing—"

"No."

"Huh." He contemplated me for a second, and then knocked back his drink. "Then I guess I'll go and leave you to it. Dinner tomorrow night instead?"

"Sure." I hesitated. "Do you mind if I invite Ginny and Mia? You do owe them a meal, remember."

Something flickered through his eyes. Annoyance at being called on his offer, perhaps. "Sure, but it'll have to be a pub meal. Those two can eat, and the new job isn't paying that well."

"What *is* your job? You've never really said."

"I work for a specialist locksmith company." He shrugged. "It's nothing fancy but it suits my skills, the pay is good, and if I play my cards right, I'll be helping to run things within the year."

"How long are you in Ainslyn?"

"Uncertain at this point. It depends on how the current job plays out." He pushed to his feet. "I'll let myself out."

"I'll come down with you, just to make sure the door is locked."

His eyebrows rose. "You don't trust me?"

"It's not that." Though it was. Partially. "There've been some odd things happening—"

"What sort of things?" he cut in, frowning.

"A couple of demon attacks." I shrugged. "Nothing I can't handle."

"Gwen, if demons have the scent of your blood in their nostrils, they won't stop until you're dead. It might be better if you weren't here alone."

I hesitated, half tempted. I'd already been caught literally napping once; I really didn't need it to happen again. And yet ... I just couldn't shake the vague sense of unease. I shook my head. "I'll be fine. Really."

"I get you need to sleep alone, but I could stay in Max's room, if you'd like."

I touched his arm lightly. "Thank you. Really. But this place is ringed with protections, and no mere demon will get past them."

A dark elf, however, might be another matter entirely.

His frown deepened. "Are you sure?"

"Yes." I squeezed his arm. "But thank you for the offer. I appreciate it."

"No problems. But once I leave, I suggest you close and lock Max's window."

I blinked. "How—"

"There's a stream of cold air sweeping down the stairs, Gwen." His voice was dry. "And Max's room sits almost directly opposite them. It doesn't take a genius to put two and two together."

A logical, practical answer. So why wasn't I believing it?

What was wrong with me that I was suddenly distrusting a man I'd known all my life?

"Thanks for the reminder."

He swung around and headed for the stairs. "Do you want me to pick you up tomorrow night, or shall we meet somewhere?"

I hesitated again. "Probably best to meet, given I'm not entirely sure yet what's happening with Mo."

"What about the Red Gryphon? They do decent meals, and at least Mia isn't stuck with her parents staring at her all night."

"They stopped worrying about her ages ago," I said, smiling. "But the Gryphon would be good. Shall we say seven?"

He nodded. "I'll book a table when I get home."

I followed him across to the front door but found my gaze sweeping the shadows, looking for who knows what. I caught the edge of the door to stop it crashing back, but the wind howled in, chilling me to the core. I shivered. "It's pretty nasty out there—did you drive or walk?"

"Walk. My timing, as usual, leaves a lot to be desired."

I half smiled. "Do you want to borrow an umbrella? Or a coat?"

He shook his head. "I might head to the pub down the road and wait out the storm. Or grab an Uber from there."

"Don't get too wet. Wouldn't want you catching a cold before tomorrow night."

A smile teased his lips. "I'm not going to back out of our date a second time. Even I'm not that much of a bastard."

I snorted and pushed him out the door. "Go, because that wind is fucking cold and I need to shut the door."

He swooped in for a quick kiss, then flashed me a cheeky grin, doffed an imaginary hat, and headed out into the storm. Just like old times, I thought, and wondered again if it was simply the events of the last twenty-four hours making me jumpy.

I closed and locked the door but didn't immediately head upstairs. Instead, I walked through the store, trying to figure out why my instincts were itching. There was nothing out of place, nothing that had been touched or moved. And yet ... what? It was damnably annoying that instinct wasn't giving even the slightest clue.

I swore and swung around ... only to see a pale figure looming in the doorway. Recognition hit a second *after* the squeak of fright escaped.

Lucas.

It was *Lucas*.

I took a deep, somewhat shuddery breath, and said, "You're quite a few hours early, Blackbird."

"Yes, but I have to talk to you."

I wasn't entirely sure talking was something I'd be capable of in his presence—not in the close confines of our store, anyway.

"About what?"

"Are you seriously going to make me stand out here in the wind and the rain, and talk to you through the *door*?"

It would be better for my hormones if you did ... I walked over, unlocked the door, and then motioned him inside. Though he was wearing a coat, it obviously wasn't water-proof, because the bits of shirt visible around the collar and chest were sodden. Water dripped steadily from the ends of his dark hair, and his nose practically glowed red.

Sadly, it in no way detracted from his gorgeousness.

"Don't they provide you lot with wet weather gear?"

"Yes, but I forgot how swiftly the weather can change and was caught out."

"We live in England. Quick weather changes aren't exactly unknown."

"Perhaps, but I was stationed overseas for the last few years and simply forgot." He stripped off his coat and then looked around. The wet white shirt, I couldn't help but notice, clung to his skin, highlighting a muscular chest and washboard abs. And the wet jeans ... I mentally smacked myself, plucked the jacket from his fingers, and then walked across to the coat hook. "What were you doing overseas?"

"Protecting assets."

I risked a look over my shoulder. He still looked like wet perfection. "What sort of assets?"

A smile touched his lips, and my pulse did its crazy little dance again. Mo might have stated the Blackbirds weren't sexually magnetic, but this man was making a total liar out of her.

"I can't say—and for their safety as much as anything else."

Meaning the asset was a person. Which made sense, given they were in the business of protecting kings.

"Would you like to come upstairs? It's warmer, and you look cold."

"I am." He motioned me to precede him, the movement elegant. "Lead the way."

I walked across to the stairs. A breeze teased my hair as I neared the top, and I remembered I hadn't yet closed Max's window.

I glanced over my shoulder. Luc's eyes gleamed in the shadows, the jade depths filled with a heat that burned all the way down to my toes. But it was gone in an instant, making me wonder if I'd imagined it.

"Do you want to get out of those wet clothes? I doubt

we've any that'll fit you, but I can grab you a dressing gown to wear while we toss your clothes in the dryer."

He hesitated and then shook his head. "A towel would be useful, though, if it's not too much trouble."

"It's really not." I motioned toward the living area. "Help yourself to either whiskey or coffee. Clean cups are in the cupboard above the microwave. I've just got to duck upstairs to close a window."

He nodded and walked away, leaving behind a little puddle of water at the top of the stairs.

I spun on a heel and bounded up the next set of stairs. The wind was stronger on the second floor, which was odd. I hadn't left the window open that far—I stopped abruptly.

The air wasn't just cold; it was filled with the scent of demon.

SIX

I didn't worry about how or why it had gotten past Mo's spells. I simply reacted.

Three quick steps had me in Max's room. At the very last moment, the demon sensed my approach and swung around, but by that time I was already in the air, arrowing feetfirst towards him.

He screamed and raised his talons, but the blow missed and he got no further. I hit him hard and, with a squeal that was more surprise than pain, he was flung backward, out the window and down to the ground. There was a soft but sickening crack, followed by silence.

I hit the carpet, rolled to my feet, and ran to the window. The demon lay below me, dark liquid leaking across the concrete under his head. He'd hit hard enough to be killed, and I couldn't be sad about that.

A hand came down on my shoulder, and I did another of those damn squeaks even as I swung around and buried my fist into a stomach that felt like steel. There was another oomph, and then my hand was caught and held tight.

I looked up into jade eyes that glittered with the barest hint of pain. "Oh. Sorry."

"My fault entirely." He didn't quite wheeze, but his voice was nowhere near as deep and seductive as it normally was. "Where's the demon?"

"I kicked it out the window. It's dead on the concrete below."

He pressed past me and looked out. "A brown—how the hell did a brown get past all the protections layered around this place?"

"The same way his mate at Jackie's did—with help."

He frowned. "Has there been any word on how Jackie is?"

"Not yet." I paused. "I'm gathering you've talked to Mo recently?"

"She rang me a few hours ago. It's part of the reason I'm here."

"The other reason being my brother?"

"Yes." He slammed the window shut. "I'll go around and get rid of the body. It might be worth putting in a call to your grandmother to see if Jackie has regained consciousness. We need to know what the demons are after, both there and here."

I nodded and followed him downstairs. "You're coming back?"

"Yes. I'll knock on the door."

Once he'd left and the door was locked again, I pulled my phone out of my back pocket. Thankfully, my drop onto the carpet hadn't done it any damage.

I hit Mo's number then walked back up to Max's room and peered out the window. Luc knelt next to the demon's body, examining it while he talked on his phone. I leaned against the window frame and admired the play of muscles so evident under the wet shirt.

Mo finally answered. "I haven't anything to tell you yet, which is why I haven't called."

I frowned. "She hasn't regained consciousness?"

"No. They've done some blood tests, and it appears she was drugged."

"Why the hell would a demon drug her? Especially if he was intent on torturing the information out of her?"

"Don't know, but I have some theories."

"You always do."

She chuckled softly. "I think whoever is responsible for breaking her protection spells is also behind the drug."

"And when it didn't work quickly enough, they resorted to torture."

"Yes." She paused. "Any problems there?"

I told her about the demon. "I have no idea what he was after, but he was definitely looking for something."

Mo grunted. "The mess in that room might be the sole reason he didn't succeed."

"I guess so." Luc walked over to one of the rubbish bins lining the back of the small courtyard and pulled out a large, black plastic bag. After emptying its contents, he moved back and shoved the demon's body into it. "Why did you send Luc here?"

"Because I thought you'd like the company."

"I'm being serious."

"Oh, so am I."

"Mo, seriously, quit it."

She chuckled again. "Okay, so it's not just about giving you pretty company. It's rather obvious someone is after you, and I'm a little worried they might be trying to get to Max through you."

I frowned. "Why would you think that? What has Max done that I don't know about?"

"I don't actually know, and that's the problem. But he's been rather evasive of late, and that worries me."

"He's been evasive for years; I don't think it's altered much in the last few months."

"Maybe." She didn't sound convinced. "Anyway, I know you're well able to take care of yourself under most circumstances, but I'm thinking it's better to be safe than sorry. Especially since I can't be there."

"But why Luc? You don't even know him."

"I don't have to. He's a Blackbird."

"The order might have changed a little in the centuries since the last Witch King."

"Some things in this world are eternal, and some things never change. The Blackbirds are the latter."

"Evil being the former, I take it?"

"Amongst other things, yes."

Which had me wondering what other things she might have been talking about, but I knew from long experience it was pointless asking. If and when she wanted me to know, she'd tell me.

"I know Max has always been a bit wild, but he's only ever dabbled in the shadows. There has to be a mistake; it can't have been him at the museum—for a start, creating a light shield isn't in his skill set."

"No, but such a spell can be purchased easily enough. But until he gets home, we won't know the truth."

Meaning she intended to grill him—and she was damn good at getting to the truth of the matter when she wanted. We'd both learned that very early on in our lives.

"I'll give him another call tonight and see if he has any

idea what the demon was after." I paused. "Do you think it could be the book I took?"

"How would they know we have it? Besides, if they'd been after that particular book, they would have had enough time to grab it before we got there."

Especially since whoever had shattered Jackie's protection spells was long gone by the time we arrived.

"After you call your brother," Mo continued, "Search his room. You might get lucky."

"Doubtful, given I have no idea what I'm looking for."

"Trust your instincts; as I've said, they're usually pretty good."

"Except when there's a pretty man in the room, apparently."

She chuckled again. "Happy birthday, my dear."

I snorted. "Aside from the fact it's weeks away, I'd rather something more practical."

"Seriously? Whose loins did you come out of again?"

"Not yours, thankfully. And Mother was far more reserved—"

"Don't believe the cock and bull stories your aunt tells you. Those two were the very definition of wild—at least until your mom met your dad."

"So how come you've never mentioned this before now?"

"Because your brother was wild enough for the two of you. I was an old woman even then and couldn't possibly have coped with both of you testing the limits."

I smiled. "Mo, if there's one thing you've never been, it's old." Not when it came to physical or mental strength, anyway.

"Ha! Tell that to the birth certificate."

"I've seen that certificate, and the year is mysteriously fudged out."

"Well, we can't have every Tom, Dick, or Barney knowing a girl's true age, now can we?"

"I suppose not." Though I doubted Barney would actually care, given he was totally smitten. "Make sure you ring once you've talked to Jackie."

"You make sure to enjoy the local scenery."

She hung up before I could reply. I shook my head and hit Max's number, but this time it went to voicemail.

"Brother, I need you to ring me the minute you get this —no matter what the time. It's urgent."

As I shoved my phone back into my pocket, a man-shaped shadow flowed over the fence below and shook Luc's hand, I pushed back from the window and began my search, starting with the drawers the demon had been standing near. There was nothing that tweaked my instincts, so I moved on. I was barely halfway through the mess when someone rapped loudly on the door downstairs.

I took a quick look out the window; all evidence that a demon had died on the concrete below had disappeared, and neither Luc nor his shadowed partner were visible.

I rattled down the stairs, then opened the door. "Who was the man helping you with the demon? Another Blackbird?"

"Why do you always insist on asking questions while I'm standing in the wind and the rain?"

"Maybe I just like the soaked-to-the-skin look on you." Which was a little closer to the truth than I should ever have admitted. I stood to one side and waved him in. "Unless you're only staying for a second, you really need to get out of those wet clothes and let me dry them for you."

"That perhaps would be for the best, especially since I intend to stay the night."

"What? No. I don't care what Mo said, I don't need a babysitter." Especially one capable of getting my hormones in such a twist.

He glanced over his shoulder, his expression serious. "That demon—a simple brown demon—somehow got through all the spells that surround this place. He unlikely did so alone, and I doubt whoever is behind the intrusion will abandon whatever ill they were attempting."

"Yes, but I'm fully capable of looking after myself."

"Yes, but the next time they might send more than just a brown." He shrugged. "Besides, until I catch up with your brother, I am, I'm afraid, your shadow."

"To repeat my previous statement, no. Besides, I'm going out for dinner tomorrow night, and I do not need nor want a scowling shadow."

"The dinner being with the man who left here a few minutes before I arrived?"

He couldn't quite disguise his contempt, and my gaze narrowed. "Yes—why?"

He hesitated. "No reason."

"Mo's right—you can't lie for shit, Blackbird. Give."

His mouth ticked upward ever so slightly, though the amusement didn't quite touch his eyes. "Tristan Chen has something of a reputation in London."

I locked the front door. "What type of reputation?"

"There have been rumors of him accepting commissions for work that's less than legal. We've never been able to prove anything, however."

I frowned. "And why would the Blackbirds even be keeping an eye on him? The Chens have never been related —in any way—to the royal line, as far as I'm aware."

"True, but we always keep an eye on those who socialize with heirs."

"And he is?"

"He was dating the sister of one for a few months, yes."

So much for Tris's claim of having no love life—not that I'd actually believed him. "And this is why you don't like him?"

Surprise flickered briefly through his eyes. "I never said that."

"You didn't have to." I motioned toward the stairs. "Why don't we continue this conversation once you've had a shower and warmed up?"

Again he hesitated. I couldn't help but wonder if he'd sensed my attraction and didn't want to be placed in a situation that could be misconstrued.

"That would be good," he said eventually.

I nodded and once again went upstairs. After grabbing a towel and one of Gran's woolen bath robes—which was a man's, simply because she preferred their length and sturdiness over the typical woman's robe—I told him to strip off in the bathroom and toss his clothes out to me.

Once I'd shoved them all into the dryer, I sent Mia and Ginny a text, telling them they were to join Tris and me for dinner tomorrow night. Then I pulled a pizza out of the freezer, added extra cheese and bacon, and put it in the oven.

Luc came down fifteen minutes later. He was wearing Mo's gown, but his feet were bare and his sword was visible and slung over one shoulder.

My gaze slid down his long length and came to an abrupt halt at his feet. "Hobbit toes."

Confusion crossed his face. "What?"

"You have hobbit toes."

He frowned down at his feet. "They are an appropriate length for my size."

No doubt other bits of him were, too ... I cleared my throat and pushed the resulting images away. "Yes, but they're extraordinarily hairy." Which his chest—or the bit not covered by the dressing gown—was not.

"That, sadly, is genetic, and has long been the bane of my mother. She has them waxed regularly."

"She'd have no other choice if she wanted to wear pretty shoes."

"Only a woman would think that way."

"Only a man would make such a chauvinistic comment. Would you like a drink?"

"A coffee, please."

I turned on the kettle, then crossed my arms and leaned back against the counter while he placed his sword on the top of the couch and then sat down. He stretched his long legs under the coffee table and crossed them at the ankles. Everything the man did was goddamn elegant.

"Why don't you like Tris?" I asked eventually.

"I don't know what you gleaned from my expression, but you're mistaken. I neither like nor dislike him. I simply don't trust him."

"Why?"

Again his mouth twitched. "As I've already noted, you are very much of your grandmother's bloodline."

I frowned. "Meaning what?"

"Meaning she also has a reputation for never leaving a question unasked."

"And Blackbirds have a reputation for avoiding them. But if you want our help, you need to be a little more forthcoming."

He sighed; it was a sound edged with frustration. "We

suspect Tristan Chen dated Monika Aquitaine in order to glean information from her. A large amount of money appeared in his account a few days after they'd split."

"Could have been a coincidence."

"Unlikely, given this is not the first time in the last eight months it has happened."

"The other incidents also involved heirs?"

"No." He paused. "We also don't think it's a coincidence he turned up here after a ten-month absence to reignite a relationship with the sister of someone we're interested in."

Neither did I, when it was put like that—especially after his break-in effort. "Have you any idea who paid him?"

Luc shook his head. "We've been trying to trace them back, but we're not having much luck so far."

"But you must have some idea which of the heirs is making a play for the crown. I mean, how many of them are there?"

"Thirteen direct descendants, seven indirect. Three who were murdered."

"Recently?"

"Within the last month, yes."

"I take it the remaining heirs are now all being watched?"

"Those we can find are."

"And is Max one them?"

He hesitated. "Only very indirectly."

"What about my cousins?"

"Gareth and Henry? Slightly closer than Max, but still so far down the tree they're not likely to be hit."

I hoped he was right, because I had few enough De Montfort relatives as it was. "And is Max the real reason you came to Ainslyn? You're on protection detail?"

This time, the smile was full-blown and my stomach flip-flopped. The man really was too good looking for my own good.

"As I said, I was sent here to guard the remaining artifacts. The fact that a distant heir lives here on a part-time basis was not a consideration, given it's very unlikely his hand will ever lift the sword. I do, however, need to talk to him about that break-in at the museum."

"I did ask him about it. He denies any involvement."

"Does he also deny attacking the Blackbird sent to question him?"

"No. And be warned, he'll probably do it again to anyone who gets in his way when he's late for an appointment." As the kettle began to boil, I reached up to grab a cup out of the cupboard. "How do you like your coffee?"

"Strong, black, and no sugar."

I shuddered. "Good god, how do you drink it like that?"

His smile grew. "My palate has always preferred sharp things over sweet."

Something in the way he said that had my gaze stabbing toward him. There was nothing in his expression to suggest he'd been referring to anything other than the coffee, and yet I couldn't escape the notion that he had.

I made his drink and passed it over, doing my best to ignore the tremor that ran across my skin when our fingers brushed. Thankfully, the timer on the oven went off, so I grabbed a tea towel, pulled out the pizza and, once it was sliced, put it on the coffee table with a couple of plates.

"Help yourself."

He did so. With gusto.

Once it was gone, I poured myself another whiskey, then tucked one leg under and sat down so that I was facing him. It put my shoulder a little too close to the tip of his sword; even though it was sheathed, it pulsed with an almost otherworldly power. Which, no doubt, was due to the fact it had a spirit locked within its steel.

I sipped my drink and then said, "You know, I might just do a little careful probing when I'm out with Tris tomorrow."

"This is no game—"

"I'm well aware of that." A hint of annoyance crept into my voice. "But if Tris is in any way involved in something shady with one of the heirs, I want to know how and why. Especially when my brother's life might well be on the line."

"As I said, it's doubtful he's in danger."

"Which does not totally erase the possibility. My brother's life is not something I'm willing to risk." I took another drink and tried not to think about the task I'd just set myself. If Tris wasn't involved, then my actions might well destroy a friendship I still valued. And if he was ... I shoved the thought aside. I'd deal with that if and when it eventuated. "Now, as to the matter of you staying here—"

"That's not open to negotiation, I'm afraid, if only because there'd be hell to pay with your grandmother if I allowed anything to happen to you while she was away."

"My grandmother is well aware just how well I can protect—"

"Perhaps, but she told me to stay here and guard you, and that's exactly what I intend to do. She's not a fool. Nor, I believe, is her granddaughter."

"Flattery is not going to win me over."

"I'd be disappointed if it did." He patted the sword lying on top of the sofa. "Hecate and I will ensure there are no further incursions."

I blinked. "You named your sword after a mythological goddess of the underworld?"

"No. That was her name before she transgressed."

"Can you and she communicate?"

"After a fashion. She is one of the older spirits, and her language is sometimes difficult to understand."

"If she's that old, why hasn't her language evolved? She's had the time to learn, hasn't she?"

"Yes, but not the desire. She destroys demons because she must, but helpfulness in other ways isn't always guaranteed."

"I had no idea souls retained their personalities after death."

"Only the very strong ones do."

Which Hecate obviously was. "Has she always been constrained to this sword?"

"Yes. If a spirit blade is broken, the soul is destroyed. That is part of their penance for dealing with darkness. It's also the reason so many of these swords survive—they have no desire to meet their ultimate end and will do all in their power to protect their casing."

"Huh." I downed my drink and then rose. "The sofa pulls out to a bed, and there's pillows and blankets in the laundry cupboard downstairs. You're welcome to help yourself to coffee and whatever food there is in the fridge."

He nodded. "Sleep well."

"Thank you." I stepped over his legs and then went up to my room. And despite the fact I was inordinately aware of him moving around downstairs, I quickly fell asleep.

When I clattered back down the following morning, he was fully dressed and on the phone. I flicked on the kettle, then tossed a couple of slices of bread into the toaster, all the while pretending not to listen to his conversation even though my ears were flapping so hard it's a wonder I didn't take flight. Unfortunately, he hung up before I got much more than the fact there was another break-in at the King's Tower, and a "meet you there in ten."

"You're off, I take it," I said.

He nodded and rose. "There's been more demon activity at the King's Tower. I'll be back tonight."

"I've got a date, remember. I may not be back at all."

He contemplated this for a second, his expression giving nothing away. "To reiterate, be careful. We have no idea what game Tristan Chen plays."

"But at least I now know he is playing a game. That gives me an advantage."

"Perhaps." He picked Hecate up and slung her over his shoulder. The air shimmered briefly as she disappeared.

"How does that actually work?" I asked.

"How does what work?"

I waved a hand in the general direction of his shoulder. "The light covering your sword? I didn't see or feel a spell— it just happened."

He nodded. "I've been doing that sort of concealment for so long, it's basically automatic."

"But when you disappeared on King's Island, there was no rush of magic either."

"No, because what we do isn't a spell, as such. It's a manipulation of either light or darkness."

"So why are you called Blackbirds when it's light you seem to manipulate more?"

"That wasn't always the case, and we weren't always *just* the king's guards." He shrugged. "And the rest of your questions can wait. I really must be gone."

Once he'd left, I ate my breakfast and then opened the shop. The rest of the day passed relatively quickly—while I wasn't rushed off my feet, there was a steady trickle of customers, most of them purchasing Mo's soaps, perfumes, and the occasional magical trinket. I closed at five, did the till, and then replenished everything for tomorrow's trade.

Mo rang just on six.

"Has she woken yet?" I asked.

"Yes, but I'm up here for another night. They want to keep her in for another two days, so I'm waiting for her family to arrive and take over watch duty before I leave."

"You think it's possible she's still a target?"

"Yes, as they didn't get what they wanted."

"Which was?"

"The Valeriun family bible."

"Why in the hell are they after *that*?"

"Because Uhtric's older sister—Rodella—married Marcus Valeriun and produced a son. She was widowed soon after, and subsequently married her second cousin—Phillip Aquitaine. Marcus's family raised his boy, as Phillip refused to have the seed of another under his roof."

"Doesn't he sound like a charmer?"

"It was pretty commonplace in those days."

Maybe, but that didn't make it right or fair. "If they're after the Valeriun family bible, it suggests Marcus's son produced heirs that could hold a claim to the throne. I take it she hasn't actually got the bible?"

"No, and neither do the Valeriuns."

"So where is it? She must have some idea if she's been researching them."

"She said it was taken into safekeeping some years ago by a witch or witches unknown. She suspects it might be in one of the repositories."

The back of my neck prickled. "There was another break-in at the King's Tower this morning."

"They were probably looking for the bible, but they wouldn't have had any success. It's not there."

I frowned. "How can you be so sure? There were thousands of books in that damn place—you can't know them all."

"No, but a centuries-old family bible is pretty damn special, and not something I'd have missed."

"Do we have one?" If we did, I'd certainly never seen it.

"No. It was destroyed long ago."

"How?"

"Fire, I'm afraid." I could almost see her shrug. "It happened just before the First World War and, by then, there were bigger things to worry about than replacing a family bible."

"Shame."

"Or, perhaps, fortunate, given everything else that's happening at the moment. We don't need demons, dark elves, and whoever else might be behind all this to be coming after another item."

I frowned. "What I don't get is, why would the dark elves even be colluding with anyone? I mean, they're powerful sorcerers in their own right—"

"Yes, but they're restricted by their ability to only move in darkness. You'll find human help behind all their past incursions."

"Even the one that Uhtric stopped?"

"Indeed. In that case, it was one of his most valued advisors who betrayed him."

"How come none of this stuff is ever mentioned in the history books?"

"Because history is invariably written by men who are more concerned about promoting the greatness of the victor." She paused, and someone murmured in the background, though it was too soft for me to make out. "Jackie says it's also possible that the bible is being kept in one of the Blackbird libraries. They've a long habit of collecting artifacts relevant to the throne."

"And misplacing them, if a comment Luc made about the crown is anything to go by."

"Well, if the Blackbirds don't know where the real crown is, then it's likely no others will—and right now, that's a good thing."

"Do they require the real crown to proceed with the coronation? Or will the replica do? It was the crown placed on Layton's head, after all."

She hesitated. "In all honesty, I don't know, although there is far more to a coronation than just a crown."

"Did you ask Jackie why she was tracing Okoros?"

"There was some theory that Marcus's son married into the Okoro line."

My gut clenched. "If that's true, then Max, Gareth, and Henry just moved from indirect to direct heirs."

"Except she didn't get far enough into her research to uncover whether the theory held any truth."

"Which just might be a good thing—if she's uncertain about the link, maybe others will be too."

"A fine theory if it wasn't for the fact indirect heirs are being taken out. Someone obviously thinks they're a danger."

"A statement that does nothing to ease my fears." I paused. "I gather Luc told you about the indirect heirs when you talked to him earlier?"

"Yes. And your brother is slipperier than a wet rat down a drainpipe." Amusement edged her voice. "They won't find him an easy target."

That was certainly true enough. "Did you ring Gareth and Henry?"

"Yes, but I'm not sure they were convinced by my statement they needed to increase their personal protections for the next few weeks."

"You didn't tell them about heirs being killed?"

"I did. Not sure they believed that, either."

Which pretty much summed the two of them up. If you couldn't provide concrete evidence to back your claims, they remained skeptical.

"Given the bible seems to be the key here, I'll mention it to Luc when I see him. He can contact his people and see if they're holding it."

"Are you staying overnight at Tris's again?"

"How do you even know I'm going out with him tonight?"

She chuckled. "Because I'm an old woman who sees all."

I snorted. "Right. And I don't know." I quickly told her what Luc had said. "I'm planning a little careful digging first, and I'll get Ginny to read the current of his reactions for me."

"If you're interested in tracking his movements without him knowing, there's a locator charm and receiver sitting in my knickers drawer."

"Because where else would you keep such a thing." My voice was dry, and she chuckled again.

"Given there're few who'd want to go through an old lady's knickers, there is no safer spot to keep valuables."

Meaning there was probably a whole lot more tucked in that drawer than a simple locating charm. "How do I activate it, given I can't do magic?"

"It is that sort of attitude that prevents you, you know."

"Mo, you were the one who told me magic was not my forte."

"And I dare say I had good reason at the time. Can't remember it though."

"Believing that." *Not.* "How about you just answer the question?"

"Activation is simple—just pull the charm free of the casing and place it somewhere inconspicuous. The receiver has a range of a couple of kilometers."

"How long will the signal last?"

"A couple of days, if we're lucky. And it's probably better to stick it in his car rather than on his person. I know that opens the possibility of losing him, but he might just sense its presence if it's placed too close."

And he probably would, given how familiar he was with Mo's magic after all these years. "I might ask Ginny or Mia if they can look after the store for us tomorrow. That way, I can still tail him if you're not back in time."

"Okay, but don't drive that car of yours when doing so. It's far too noticeable."

"I don't need a car to follow someone."

"No, but if he *is* involved in this damn mess, then he may well be on the lookout for blackbirds. Of course," she added, "You can always ask Luc—"

"No, and stop it."

She laughed. "Fine. But don't be moaning to me about the lack of eligible men in Ainslyn any more. Even when a tasty morsel is shoved your way, you won't bite."

"Said morsel has shown absolutely no interest." Which wasn't exactly true, if the flash of heat I'd briefly glimpsed was anything to go by. "And now, I must be going. Talk later."

I hung up on another laugh. I shook my head and then

got ready for my date, settling on jeans, sensible shoes, and a fluffy mohair sweater. After grabbing the charm, my purse and a thick, warm coat, I called a cab and headed across to the Red Gryphon.

Ginny and Mia were already inside and waiting. I kissed them both on the cheek and then stripped off my coat and sat down opposite.

"So, what's all this actually about?" Ginny interlaced her fingers and then leaned her chin on them. "Because we all know Tris would not have volunteered to pay for tonight's meal."

I hesitated as a waiter came over and took our drinks order. "I want an opinion."

"On Tris?" Mia said. "Why?"

"He's changed and I just—" I hesitated and then shrugged.

"You think he's up to something," Ginny said. It was a statement rather than a question.

"Yes, but I'm not sure what. I could be overreacting, but still—"

"Your vibes are telling me that statement is not something you believe," Ginny said. "If that's the case, why not just walk away? It's not like you have an emotional connection. It's just a sex thing."

I smiled. "The sex thing is very good."

"Obviously, given you've still got that 'well sated' glow happening." Mia's voice was dry. "Good sex is never worth losing good sense over, however."

"Says the woman who spent five nights with Gerard Barker simply because her parents said he was an inept loser." My tone echoed hers. "Which he was, by the way."

"Yes, and this is why I can speak with such authority. Been there, done that, and it's totally not worth the trouble."

"This is a rather different situation."

"Perhaps." Ginny's gaze flicked past me. "He's here."

"Color me surprised," Mia muttered. "I felt sure he'd bunk out at the last moment again."

"The meal hasn't been eaten and paid for yet," Ginny replied, and then flashed a bright smile. "Tris. Nice to see you again."

"Ladies." He dropped a kiss on my cheek, then pulled out the chair beside me. "Thanks for coming out on such a horrendous evening. You really shouldn't have."

Mia grinned. "Oh come on, it's not often that Tristan Chen bankrolls a meal—"

"And it's something you'd best not get used to," he cut in equably. "The budget, by the way, does not stretch to lobster."

"Which is out of season and not likely to be on the menu." Ginny flashed a smile as the waiter returned with our drinks. Once Tris had ordered a beer, she added, "So what's been happening since you left us?"

He shrugged. "Nothing much. Working for a specialist locksmith company and enjoying big city life."

"And big city girls?" Mia asked, amused.

"Maybe one or two."

"Oh yeah?" My voice held a teasing note. "I thought you said you were all alone and lonely?"

A smile twitched his lips. "I may have exaggerated."

"So you *are* seeing someone," Ginny said.

"We recently split, so no, I'm not."

I shifted to look at him more fully. "Why did you split?"

He shrugged again. "Her parents didn't approve."

"Since when has that ever worried you?" I asked.

"It didn't." He studied me for a second, his expression ...

odd. "But I'm not the only one telling white lies when it comes to relationships."

"Meaning what?"

"That I wasn't the only man you saw last night."

I blinked. "You were watching the shop?"

"No. I just happened to glance around as he entered."

My gaze flickered to Ginny's. She shook her head slightly. A lie. "That was a friend of Mo's, not mine, and he damn well slept on the sofa."

Tris held up his hands. "It doesn't matter to me where he slept."

Like hell it didn't. But why? I doubted his reaction was in any way territorial; Tris had never been one to get jealous, even when we'd been an item. So maybe it was confirmation that Luc was right—Tris *was* using me as a means to gather information on my brother, and anyone else I might be seeing was simply a possible problem.

What we really needed to know was who was pulling Tris's strings, and what did they want with my brother? Rather frustratingly, they were the two questions I *couldn't* ask right now.

The conversation moved on, and in many ways, it felt like old times. But I couldn't help noticing that, when it came to any real information about his life or his job, he remained vague. Which only increased my uneasiness.

His phone rang just as we finished our coffee; after glancing at the screen, he grimaced and said, "Sorry, I have to take this."

As he went outside, I looked at Ginny. "What do you think?"

"There's definitely a darker edge to his output now," she said. "And there's certainly a whole lot more anger. I can't pin either to a specific cause, though."

"They could be a result of him just breaking up with someone he liked," Mia said.

"Maybe." Ginny wrinkled her nose. "If feels deeper than that. More disturbed than that. It's ... strange."

"Yes, it is." I crossed my arms and leaned on the table. "Which is why I'm going to follow him—"

"Not alone, you're not," Mia said instantly.

I glanced at her. "I've already had Mo and Luc telling me to be careful—I don't need you getting overly protective as well."

"Luc?" Mia's gaze snapped between the two of us. "Who is this Luc you speak of? Or is he the man making Tris all unfriendly?"

"The latter," Ginny said, before I could, "And apparently he's as hot as all get out."

"Then I obviously need an immediate introduction."

I raised my eyebrows. "So all thoughts of a protection detail have now been abandoned?"

"Hell, no." Mia's grin flashed. "It just means I'll be over there in the morning to check him out."

"I take it," Ginny said, "that the plan to follow Tris means you're sleeping with him tonight?"

I shook my head. "There's a theory he's using me to get to Max. Until I know whether that's true or not, he and I will not be hitting the sheets."

Mia frowned. "Won't that make him suspicious, given you literally bounced into his arms the other night?"

"It probably would if he was sticking around for the rest of this evening," I said. "But I'm betting that call means he won't."

"If he *is* up to something," Ginny said, "he's going to notice a car tailing him, whether or not he knows it. People up to no good tend to be aware of such things."

"Which is why I'll be using one of Mo's tracking charms. Once I attach it to his car, we can follow from a safe distance."

"Your gran never ceases to amaze me," Mia said. "She always seems to have an answer or a spell, no matter what the problem or situation."

"According to her, it's because she's lived so long."

"Trouble with that answer is, as a De Montfort, she's not supposed to be able do half the things she does."

Ginny's voice was dry, and I grinned. "Apparently, no one ever advised her of this fact."

"Tris is coming back," Mia warned softly, "and, judging by the look on his face, the evening is indeed about to end."

"Sorry, ladies." Tris stopped behind his chair. "That was work with an urgent job. Gwen, do you want a ride home?"

I hesitated and glanced at Ginny and Mia.

"Go," Mia said. "We'll catch up later."

I rose and grabbed my coat off the chair. Tris got his wallet out and dumped some cash on the table. "Just in case you think I'm trying to run out on you ladies without paying the bill again."

"I would never think that about you, Tris. Honestly."

He gave Mia a wry look. "Say that with a little more sincerity, and I might just believe you."

She chuckled softly. "Don't work too hard."

"Never do." He helped me into my coat, and then motioned me to precede him. I slung my handbag over my shoulder, shivering as the night air hit. At least it had stopped raining.

"Where are you parked?"

"Just down the road."

Once we got to his car, he opened the door and helped me in. As he moved around to the driver side, I popped the charm out of the casing and quickly slipped it under the seat. It clipped onto something, suggesting it was magnetic.

He pulled out of the parking spot and made his way quickly through the streets. The bookstore was dark, but I had no idea if that meant Luc wasn't there. If he could manipulate darkness, he could probably see very easily in it.

"Your guest not staying tonight?" Tris asked, in a voice that tried to be casual but didn't quite succeed.

"Damned if I know—he's not my guest." I leaned across the center console and dropped a kiss on his cheek. "Keep warm tonight."

His smile certainly held little enough of it. "I'll ring soon."

"No problem." I climbed out, shivering as a blast of cold air caught the ends of my coat and tugged them wide. I'd barely closed the car door when Tris zoomed off. Obviously, his job was an urgent one. I opened the front door, and stepped inside.

"Luc, you here?"

There was no response, so I sent a message to Ginny, telling her I was home. Then I grabbed the tracking receiver, which happened to be a very old iPhone. Usually spells and technology did not play well together, but Mo had a knack for doing things others thought impossible. I switched on the phone; after several runs of magical static, the screen came to life. It showed a basic street map with a green dot moving steadily away.

Lights swept across the dark street outside. I waited until Mia's small white Fiesta stopped, then exited the shop, slammed the door shut, and jumped into the back seat.

"Where to?" Mia said.

"Straight ahead."

Ginny twisted around in her seat. "The tracker uses an

iPhone? Your gran could make a mint selling that sort of thing to the partners of cheats the world over."

I smiled. "Because she really needs the money. Left at the next street."

"Hey, a good cash flow never goes astray. And maybe if Tris had one, he wouldn't be up to no good."

Something within me doubted it would have made any difference—at least not now. He was too set in his ways, too used to scrimping and saving and sometimes even stealing to get what he wanted. His parents had never been truly harsh or ungiving, but they certainly hadn't pandered to his desires as they had his brothers.

We continued to follow the soft green blip, eventually leaving Ainslyn behind and heading out on the M62.

"You think we're heading toward Manchester?" Mia said, after a while.

"At this stage, who knows?"

"I think the more important question is, what are we going to do once he does get to his destination?" Ginny said. "We're too far behind him to have any chance of finding him if he goes inside somewhere."

"What we need is something personal of his," Mia said. "Like hair. I could use it to pin his whereabouts."

Mia's magic was of the general kind, which meant she used actual spells and drew on personal strength to bring them to life. Like many Lancasters, she'd learned her craft under the tutelage of her parents, rather than going to any sort of witch university. It was also why her parents now ran pubs rather than relying on their spellcraft for income. Personal magic always took a toll on its creator, and it was rare to find anyone over fifty offering spell services.

"The only way I'm likely to get something personal is to

go back to the hotel with him—and I'm not keen on doing that right now."

"Understandably," Ginny said. "But you do have a Blackbird in your midst, and he could certainly get in and out of the hotel room without detection."

"True." I glanced down at the iPhone as it beeped. Tris had stopped. "Take the next exit."

"Ordsell? What the hell is in Ordsell?" Mia asked.

"That," Ginny said, ever practical, "is hopefully what we're about to find out."

After a few more turns, we found his car in the crowded parking lot behind McDonald's.

"He can't be hungry—not after everything he ate tonight."

"The man *has* got a really good appetite, and not just for food," I said blandly, and ducked away from Ginny's slap with a laugh.

"I did not need to know that," she said. "What do we do now? We can't go in—he'll see us."

"Yes." I twisted around. Tris had parked in a back bay underneath one of the light poles. He obviously wasn't afraid of anyone spotting him. "I might shift shape and go over. He's not going to notice a blackbird hanging onto the guttering and peering in through the top of the windows."

"Probably not, but keep away from the really well-lit areas."

I nodded and climbed out of the car, shivering once again as the cold air hit. After quickly shifting, I flew across and settled on the roof. No one appeared to take any interest in me, so I strutted forward, gripped the edge of the gutter with my claws, and then peered over the edge, spreading my wings and flapping lightly to maintain balance.

The place was packed with late-night patrons, and I couldn't immediately see him.

I flew across to the roadside edge and repeated the process. Still nothing. Maybe he'd simply dumped his car here and walked to his destination.

Hoping that wasn't the case, I tried the KFC side of the building, and finally spotted him. He was talking to a slender, black-haired man who had his back to me. I shuffled along a little, trying to get a glimpse of the stranger's face, but the angle was wrong. He was, however, right on trend clothes-wise, wearing brown-black commando boots that had probably never seen any terrain other than the sidewalk, black jeans, and a brown leather bomber jacket that had a darker brown patch on the right elbow.

My pulse rate stalled, and then zoomed up several notches.

My brother had bought exactly the same jacket only a few weeks ago.

SEVEN

I t couldn't possibly be Max.

He was in Paris, not Ordsell.

Besides, there were probably tons of people who owned the same jacket, given how reverently Max followed fashion trends.

But the only way to be sure was to get closer ... and to do so without being spotted by either man. I looked over my shoulder. Now that I knew their position, I might be able see them through the windows on the other side of the restaurant. It was worth a try, even though the place was crowded.

I padded across the rooftop and peered down over the gutter again. Unfortunately, there were several tall men sitting at the table directly in front of Tris's, and I couldn't see anything more than the stranger's dark hair and his somewhat blurry forehead. I swore and edged sideways, but the result was the same. Tris had positioned himself very carefully indeed. There was nothing I could do now but hope they weren't settling in for a long discussion—especially since—in my experience, anyway—feathers didn't provide all that much protection against the bitterness of the wind.

Mo would definitely have called me soft.

The minutes slipped by. I shifted from one foot to the other, huddling closer to the D in the McDonald's sign in an effort to keep a little warmer. After a while, the doors below opened and then Tris said, "I'll go pick her up now and update you tomorrow."

I didn't hear the reply because it was too damn soft. Frustrated, I took to the sky and flew high enough to see them both without being obvious. The stranger strode toward a silver Volkswagen Golf, which at least eased my fears. Max wouldn't be caught dead in such an ordinary little car.

I swung around in an attempt to get a better look at his face, but it remained blurred. He had to be using some sort of magic to conceal his features, even if I couldn't immediately see any spell strings. But maybe I wouldn't—there were plenty of short-term charms capable of achieving a blurry effect without having to resort to bigger magic.

I circled around, undecided what I should do next. The stranger was obviously involved in whatever was going on and had to be a target, but I couldn't let Tris go either ...

I swore again and flew across to Mia's Fiesta. Once Tris had driven out of the parking lot, I shifted shape and opened the car door.

"Was he meeting anyone?" Ginny immediately said.

"Yes, but there was some kind of magic being employed to blur his face." I reached in, grabbed my handbag, and then handed her the tracker. "I'm going to follow the stranger—can you two keep tailing Tris and see what he's up to?"

"Sure." Ginny activated the screen and waited for the

green dot to appear. "If anything drastic happens, I'll message."

"Just be careful," I said.

"That's my middle name," Mia said cheerfully.

I snorted. "Meet me back at the store later."

"No matter what the time? Because it could be late, depending on what he's doing."

I hesitated. "If it's after midnight, just drop the tracker back at the shop. I'll need it tomorrow—which reminds me, if Mo doesn't get home in time to open up tomorrow morning, would one of you be able to hold the fort until she does?"

"Happy to," Mia said. "Especially if the gorgeous man will be hanging about."

"That is an unknown."

"Better than absolutely not." Her smile faded. "Be careful, Gwen."

I nodded, then slammed the door shut and stepped back as they left. Across the road, the Volkswagen's lights came on. I shifted shape and flew high, circling lazily as the stranger left the parking lot and drove toward Manchester. Eventually, he swung onto the motorway and then onto the M6, where his speed increased. I managed to keep him in sight for almost two hours—mostly by flying in a straight line rather than following the motorway's twists and turns. In the end, I had to quit. Few birds could fly at full speed for more than one hundred kilometers; I might be stronger than the average blackbird thanks to the fact some human strength did carry over in the change, but I also had to keep enough in reserve to fly home. I dipped low enough to catch the number plate, then turned and headed home at a far slower pace. I was barely halfway there when a storm swept in. It made flying bloody horrid.

It was well after midnight by the time I reached Ainslyn. I shifted shape and dropped down the last foot or so to the pavement, but my legs gave way and I stumbled forward, grabbing at the edge of the window frame to save myself but ending up on my knees anyway. For several minutes, I didn't have the strength to move. The rain soaked through my clothes and chilled my skin, and my breath wheezed in and out of burning lungs. Every inch of me shook, and my arms were all but numb. Overhead, lightning flashed; a heartbeat later, the sky rumbled ominously. The night was about to get a whole lot worse. I needed to get up; needed to get inside and warm up. A dram or two of whiskey wouldn't go astray either ...

The front door opened and then Luc said, "What the hell ...?"

I sucked in more air and glanced up. "How the fuck did you get in?"

"Your grandmother told me where the spare key was."

"Which was on the roof of a three-story building and you can't fly."

"You're seriously going to have this conversation in the middle of a damn storm? You really are certifiable, aren't you?"

"No, I'm just—"

The rest of that sentence gave way to a yelp as he stepped forward and somehow lifted me into his arms from my kneeling position.

I didn't struggle. I didn't have the energy. And yet I felt obliged to offer a token protest. "I can walk—"

"Looked like it."

"Seriously, just put me down—"

"When we're upstairs."

"Luc—"

"Shut up, woman, and just relax."

I shut up, but I didn't relax. He felt too damn good—too damn warm and strong—for *my* own good. Relaxing into him would be like putting cake in front of me and then telling me not to eat it. It was simply impossible.

After kicking the door shut, he headed up the stairs, his footsteps echoing in the shadowed silence and his breath remaining even. I was no lightweight, so it spoke volumes about his strength. He deposited me in the bathroom, his fingers warm and steady on my aching arms while I found some strength and locked my knees into position.

"Shower and warm up," he said. "I'll go put on the kettle."

"I think something stronger will be needed. Lace a hot chocolate with a good dash of whiskey."

He shuddered. "Seriously? There should be a law against combinations like that."

"You, dear Blackbird, obviously haven't lived."

"If living is partying on such a waste of good whiskey, then no, I haven't. Got your land legs now?"

I nodded, waited until the door was shut, then leaned wearily against it and closed my eyes. I really, *really*, wanted nothing more than to crawl into bed and sleep, but Luc needed to know about tonight's events.

I swung my purse off my shoulder and pulled out my phone. There was a text from Ginny that detailed what Tris had done after I'd left them—which, apparently, was pick up a woman and take her to a small brick factory that had no signage or anything else to indicate what was inside. He left without her twenty minutes later via the front door of the pub next door and then headed back to his hotel, where he picked up a different woman. She sent me the factory's address, apologized for not leaving the tracker, and said Mia would be at the shop by eight thirty.

I sent them both a quick thank-you, then placed my phone onto the vanity and hit the shower. Running the hot water out didn't do a whole lot to ease the ache in my limbs.

After pulling on pants and a warm sweater, I shoved my feet into slippers and headed downstairs. Luc was standing in front of the stove, stirring the contents of a small pot. Hecate was visible and resting against the nearby fridge. He looked up as I appeared and then did something of a double take.

"What are those?" He made a vague motion toward my feet, and I grinned.

"Zombie slippers—aren't they awesome?"

"That's certainly one description—not one I'd use, mind you." He motioned toward the sofa. "Sit. The abomination you requested is almost ready."

I tucked one leg under and plonked down. "How bad was the break-in?"

"No major destruction this time, although some of the books in the library appear to have been thrown."

"They were frustrated because they didn't find what they were looking for."

"It would seem so." He poured the hot chocolate into my mug—my favorite Disney one, I noted with amusement, which meant he already knew me better than Tris ever had —and then topped it up with a generous amount of whiskey. After adding more into a separate glass, he picked up both and walked over. "The air was tainted by a metallic-ash scent, so at least one of them was a dark elf."

I accepted the enhanced chocolate with a nod of thanks. "I'm surprised they got through all the reinforcements Mo and Barney placed around the tunnels and that chamber."

He shrugged and sat down at the opposite end of the sofa. Out of touching distance, I couldn't help but think. "All magic can be broken—you just have to be familiar with the type of spell being used."

"Problem is, Mo's well known for using the unfamiliar."

"Which is why I called Barney; he said it would have taken a lock mage of some power to break the combination of their spells."

I sipped my chocolate and watched him over the rim. His face was expressionless but we both knew what he was implying.

"As far as I'm aware, Tris doesn't know about the tunnels. If he used another means of entry, it would have been caught on tape."

"It wasn't, because he didn't. The dark elves are obviously using the tunnel near their gateway, so if he's working with them—"

"That's the one thing I can't believe he'd do."

"Can't? Or won't?"

"Both." I grimaced. "He's a friend who was once a whole lot more. I really don't want to think he could have fallen that far."

He studied me for a moment. "I gather—given the condition in which you arrived—that you did track him after your dinner?"

I nodded and updated him on everything we'd discovered. Which wasn't a whole lot, if I was at all honest. He pulled out his phone and made a note of the number plate. "I see if I can pull some strings and get it traced."

"Good." I took another drink and felt the happy burn all the way down to my toes. "Jackie's finally awake, by the way. The demons were after the Valeriun family bible."

Understanding flickered through his beautiful eyes. "They're trying to track down Luis's line."

"Luis being Rodella and Marcus's son, I take it?"

He nodded. "Did they take the bible or is it still in safe-keeping somewhere?"

"Jackie didn't have it—she was looking for it."

"She must have gotten close, otherwise they wouldn't have attacked her."

"I'd have thought it'd make more sense to wait until *after* she had it."

"But you're sensible." He glanced down at the slippers. "Mostly."

I smiled and took another drink. The man did make damn fine whiskey-laced hot chocolate. "The bible was supposedly taken into safekeeping quite a while back by a person or persons unknown. Mo said it's likely to be in either another repository or in Blackbird safekeeping somewhere."

"The latter is certainly possible, although I've not heard of its existence at headquarters."

"And just where is that?" I asked curiously. "Do you live in modern premises? Or are you all monks who live in one big old monastery-like building?"

Amusement creased the corners of his mouth, but my pulse rate barely even fluttered. Apparently, even *it* was too damn weary to do anything more. "Whatever gave you the idea that we were monks?"

I smiled. "Hey, you *are* a secretive organization. It leads to rumors and speculation."

"Well, we're not, and we certainly don't live in a monastery. In fact, our current headquarters in Covent Gardens was once a rather notorious tavern in the seven-teenth century."

"Do any of you live there?"

"Only if a full meeting has been called and there's no accommodation elsewhere. I own a manor house in Somerset and, for the most part, that's where I live."

"With your family?"

He smiled, though his eyes remained wary. "No. Nor am I married or otherwise entailed, if that's your next question."

"'Entailed' is a very odd way of describing a relationship."

"Many would say I'm a very odd man."

He wasn't going to get an argument about *that* from me. "I thought I'd head over in the morning to check the warehouse out. If you've nothing pressing to do, would you be able to break into Tris's room and steal some hair from his comb?"

Luc's eyebrows rose. "Why?"

"Mo's charm is stuck in his car, which only gets us so far. Mia needs his DNA to create something more refined."

"Then we'll do both—I doubt it's wise for you to go into that warehouse alone given the attacks—"

"Splitting forces would be quicker—"

"But not safer," he cut in. "Your grandmother would agree with me."

Yes, she would, but not for the reasons he was presuming. Still, after what that dark elf had said, it was better to err on the side of caution. "Then we'll take your car—"

"Motorcycle."

Oh dear ... "Really?"

His eyebrows rose. "You don't like motorcycles?"

"Love them." Probably a little *too* much—which was fine when riding with someone I was also sleeping with, but Luc had shown nothing but wariness.

"Then what's the problem?"

"There isn't one. I was just surprised."

I did my best to ignore the glint in his eyes—a glint suggesting he knew well enough what my problem was. Only time would tell whether he'd be similarly ... perturbed ... by sharing the close quarters of a motorcycle. I suspected he wouldn't be; the attraction seemed very one-sided at the moment. Either that, or he had a will of iron when it came to that sort of stuff.

"I guess," I added, "that it does make an odd sort of sense, given it *is* the modern-day equivalent of a war horse."

"You're not the first to note that." He studied me for a second. "Have you heard from your brother as yet?"

"No." And tried to ignore the insidious whisper that said maybe *that* was because he was still in the silver car driving god knew where.

"And you're sure he *is* in Paris?"

No. "He wouldn't lie to me. He never has in the past, no matter what he was up to."

Luc's expression was less than convinced. "Perhaps Mo could run a tracer spell on him."

I hesitated and then nodded. If nothing else, it would tell me once and for all whether my fears about the man in the silver car were correct. I drained the rest of my drink and placed the mug on the coffee table. "I'd better get some sleep. Are you staying or going?"

Another smile touched his lips. "Despite you wishing otherwise, I'm staying. I'd rather not risk your grandmother's wrath."

"I somehow think fear and you are not often companions."

"And in that, you'd be wrong." He raised his glass. "Sleep well."

I flashed him a smile, saw a brief spark in his eyes that might have been desire but was more than likely my imagination and wishful thinking, and once again headed upstairs alone.

———

The smell of bacon woke me the next morning. I pushed the blankets away from my face and glanced blearily at my phone. Eight o'clock. *Fuck.*

I threw myself out of bed and shivered into jeans and a thick woolen sweater. After doing my teeth and twisting my hair into a topknot to tame it, I grabbed my phone and trundled down the stairs. Mo was in the kitchen. Luc was nowhere to be seen.

I ignored the sliver of disappointment and walked over to the breadbox. "How's Jackie?"

"Good, considering. I convinced her it would be better for everyone's sake if she disappeared for a few days. Once she's released, she'll take up the offer of a friend and head over to Portugal."

I dropped four slices of bread into the toaster. "Is she okay to get on a plane?"

Mo nodded. "Just the bruising remains, and as bad as it looks, it isn't dangerous."

"That's at least something." I leaned back against the counter and crossed my arms. "Was she able to give you a description of the man who was with the demon?"

"No, but she said he was a witch of some power, because he unpicked her spells with ease and was in the house before she could really react."

I rubbed my arms and tried not to think about Tris's

144

competency when it came to spell locks. "So what's our next move?"

"I thought you and Luc were investigating that warehouse this morning?"

"We are. I meant after that." I hesitated. "Where is he?"

"He went to a hotel to shower and change. He'll be back by the time Mia gets here."

"I thought he was staying at the King's Tower?"

"There's no point now that the throne has been taken."

The toast popped up. I grabbed the butter out of the fridge and slathered it on. "Given Mia's still minding the store, I take it you have plans?"

Mo nodded and began dishing up the bacon. "I'll continue following Tris. The Leaf is new, so he won't immediately recognize it."

"Except he's been here twice now and might have seen it parked over the road."

She shrugged. "A risk, but a small one, I think. He was never really that observant."

"Maybe once that was true, but he's playing a very different game now."

"I've lived long enough that the likes of Tristan Chen will never catch me unawares. And you'd better put more toast on—Mia's just arrived."

The door downstairs opened even as she spoke, and Mia's bright voice said, "Hello, anyone awake?"

"Upstairs," I said, "and he's not here."

"Damn." She bounced up the stairs with far too much energy for this hour of the morning. "But at least I get a bacon butty in compensation."

I laughed and motioned her toward the table. "Have you got the tracker or does Ginny?"

She pulled it out of her handbag and placed it on the

table. "We talked to the barman once Tris and the brunette had left. They used the internal stairs, suggesting they'd gone up to his room."

Or hers, possibly. "Did the barman know her?"

"He said she wasn't one of his regular patrons, but I did get a description." She pulled out her phone and handed it over. "Oh, and before you say anything, I placed a slight restriction on him. He won't be able to tell Tris we were asking after him."

"Good." I glanced down at her phone, but it was a pretty generic description except for the small sword tattoo on her left shoulder. I glanced at Mo. "If we send this to Barney, do you think he'd very discreetly ask around about her?"

"Yes—he's been itching to get more involved in the investigation. I'll send it to him now."

I handed her the phone. "What about the first woman Tris met?"

Mia grimaced. "From where we were sitting, she looked drunk—he had to help her into the car."

"Where did he pick her up?"

"The Bolton Guesthouse. They went straight to the factory from there. I took a photo as they were coming down the stairs, but it's somewhat blurry thanks to how far back we were parked."

Mo found the image and showed me. It was both grainy *and* somewhat out of focus, but she had shortish blonde hair and wore jeans, a red-and-green striped sweater, and orange runners. Color coordination was obviously not her thing. "And you didn't see her leave the factory?"

"No, but Tris did leave via the pub, so it's possible she was still there." She paused. "I'm gathering you think they're something more than simple pickups?"

"The first one surely was."

"Yes, but there's every indication the second one wasn't."

"I know." And it was telling that I couldn't muster any real annoyance or anger. I had no real doubt that they'd fucked like rabbits, if only because there'd been something very frenetic in Tris's lovemaking the other night. It was almost if he was making up for lost time ... or simply didn't have enough of it left.

I finished buttering the extra bits of toast, then pulled out a chair and sat opposite Mia. Once I'd slapped some bacon in between my toast, I glanced at Mo. "Did Luc mention casting a locator spell to ensure Max really is in Paris?"

She nodded. "It's already been cast, but I won't activate it until he rings. It requires less personal energy if I can pin it to a phone call."

"Wouldn't it be easier to simply do a tracking spell using something personal?" Mia asked. "You've a whole room filled with his stuff upstairs."

"Tracking spells can be combated with other magic," Mo said. "Pinning a locator to something electronic doesn't have that problem, because few know it is possible."

"I certainly didn't," Mia said.

Mo patted her arm. "You're young, that's why. Knowledge gathers over time."

"I'm pretty sure my parents don't know it, either." Her eyes crinkled with amusement. "They sure as hell would have used it when I was a teenager. It would have been far easier than hair-based locator spells."

"Only fractionally," Mo said. "And it's a one-shot spell, whereas DNA-based spells can be used over a longer period of time."

"I don't suppose you could teach me it, could you?"

"Certainly, but why?"

Mia's grin flashed. "For the next time I suspect a partner is cheating on me, but don't want to go to all the time and effort of breaking into his house and stealing some hair."

"As I've noted before, the young men in this town need to be bitch slapped for their lack of good sense." Mo's gaze hit mine. "I believe Max is about to return your call."

"Why would—" I cut the rest off as my phone rang. With a mix of amusement and resignation, I pulled it out of my pocket and looked at the screen.

"No," Mia said. "It can't be ... can it?"

"It is."

She shot Mo a bemused look. "How do you fucking do that?"

"I am a woman of many talents."

"Many you shouldn't have."

"As I've said many a time to Gwen, it's thinking like that that keeps everyone in their set little boxes." She pulled another old iPhone out of her pocket and then activated it.

As her magic surged around us, as sharp as dozens of gnats, I hit the answer button. "It's about fucking time, brother."

"Hey, if you wanted a quicker answer, stop telling me it's an emergency every damn time you ring. It gets to a point where disbelief sets in."

"And if you stop ignoring me and your damn problems, then maybe I wouldn't have to keep saying it's urgent."

He sighed. "I take it the Blackbird has been bothering you?"

"Yes. Have you taken his damn call yet?"

"No, because I was busy."

"Doing what?" I glanced at Mo; she held up a finger. Another minute before she locked onto the signal.

"Enjoying my damn holiday," Max said.

"Then you're still in Paris?"

"Of course I am." He paused. "Why?"

"Because Lucas swears he saw someone fitting your description in Ordsell."

"What the hell would I be doing in Ordsell?"

"Eating at McDonald's, apparently."

His pause was just a little too long for my liking ... or was I simply looking for reasons to distrust my own damn brother?

"I love McDonald's, we both know that, but I'm not about to fly all the way to Ordsell just to grab a burger," he growled. "Especially when there are plenty of McDonald's here in Paris."

"Got him." Mo turned the phone around. On it was a small map of the 1st arrondissement area, with a small star next to the Castille, Paris—one of his favorite hotels.

Relief—tainted with a large portion of guilt—surged. He still wasn't lying to me.

"Then call Lucas once we've finished talking, or I'm going to fly over there and pin you down until you do."

He laughed. "You would, too."

"Yes, because it's no damn fun being shadowed by the man, let me tell you. A third wheel is not needed on dates."

"You mean you've actually had one? Color me surprised."

"Thanks for the confidence boost, bro."

He laughed. "I hear Tris is back in town—why don't you hook up with him again?"

"Been there, done that, not going back for seconds."

"Why?"

I hesitated. "He's changed."

"Not that much. I saw him in London a few weeks ago, and he seemed like the same Tris to me."

"Why were you meeting Tris?"

"Because he wanted to talk about some old book he was being commissioned to find."

Annoyance stirred to life. It seemed I wasn't the only one Tris was using. "Why would he come to you looking for a book? He knows you don't read that much."

Max laughed again. "No, but I do have access to the Okoro London library, and he was told it might have been kept there."

"Who told him that? And what book was he after?"

"He didn't say who his employer was, and I didn't ask." He must have shifted the phone from one ear to another, because the background voices sharpened. Just for an instant, one sounded familiar, but it was gone before I could place it. "But it was the family bible."

My stomach began to churn. What were the chances of two different parties searching for two different family bibles? They had to be connected. Had to be. "Did he say why?"

"Nope. He just said he'd been commissioned to grab it and wanted my help."

"And you said?"

"I said I'd photocopy the relevant pages if he told me what they were looking for. He said no, and so did I."

"And is the bible actually there?"

"I don't know—I didn't bother checking."

"Could you?"

He sighed. It was a rather put-upon sound. "I suppose I could ring and have someone check."

"That would be great. Have you been in contact with Tris since then?"

"I've had no reason to." He paused. "What's all this about, Gwen?"

"I think Tris's search for the bible might be linked to the break-in at the museum and the attack on Jackie."

"Is she okay now?"

"Bruised but alive. She's staying at a friend's place for a while."

He grunted. "Do you want me to contact Tris and question him a bit more?"

"He'd probably think it suspicious, and that's the last thing we need."

"I've a somewhat justified reputation for being a playboy who not only changes his mind as quickly as the weather, but is always chasing the next big deal." His voice was dry. "He won't be suspicious."

I hesitated. "Okay, but be careful. It's possible you've got a target on your back."

He snorted. "I'm not the one who's been attacked several times. How about you start listening to your own advice?"

"I will. Just make sure you talk to the damn Blackbirds."

"All right, all right, I will." The irritation was back in his voice. "Is that it?"

"For now, yes."

"Good. I'll let you know what Tris says once I talk to him."

"Thanks—and enjoy the rest of your holiday."

"If you'd stop ringing, I just might."

He hung up. I pocketed my phone and glanced at Mo. "You heard all that?"

She nodded "I might put in a call to Lance Okoro this

morning. I think we need to place that bible into safe keeping."

Lance wasn't one of Ginny's relations—he was the patriarch of the London Okoro line. "Why do you think Tris—or whoever is employing him—is after it? From what I saw of Jackie's research, the Okoros aren't recently linked to the Witch King's line."

"That may not matter. There are only seven witch lines, remember, and there's been a lot of intermingling over the years. It's possible the true heir could come from any bloodline."

"And yet Luc said there're only thirteen direct heirs and seven indirect."

"That they know of."

"It *is* their job to know."

She shrugged. "There's one point everyone seems to have forgotten—if it was just a matter of claiming the crown and drawing the sword, someone would have done so by now."

"Aside from the fact the real crown is lost, *is* there more to it than that?"

"Most likely." She motioned to the food that remained on the table. "Eat up, before it all gets cold."

We did so. As the last drop of tea was all but squeezed out of the pot, Mo cocked her head sideways and said, "Luc is almost here—you might want to put on more toast."

"Seriously," Mia said. "How?"

Mo's grin flashed. "I have ears, and he rides a motorcycle."

"Meaning he'll be in leathers? Fabulous."

I rolled my eyes and then rose to make more toast. Luc came up the stairs a few minutes later, looking suitably dark and dangerous in black leather. Mia's eyes briefly widened, then she shot me a grin.

"I totally agree with Ginny's assessment." She rose and offered him her hand. "Mia Lancaster, at your service."

"Lucas Durant—a pleasure to meet you." He accepted her hand briefly but his gaze was on mine. "Your brother finally rang me."

"That's because I threatened to fly over and beat him up if he didn't. Did you get the answers you needed?"

"Yes. Believing them is another matter entirely."

"Why are you so certain he's lying?" Mo leaned back in her chair and studied him critically. "There must be a reason, Lucas."

He hesitated. "In truth, there isn't. All we have is circumstantial evidence and a gut feeling."

"The gut being yours?" I asked.

"Yes." He glanced my way again. "I cannot ignore instinct any more than you can."

"As long as instinct is not based on dislike, we should be good," Mo commented. "Though I'd be interested in knowing why you've such a fierce aversion to someone you've never actually met."

Luc shrugged, a casual movement at odds with the tension radiating from him. "When you spend time in London, you hear the stories. Perhaps I'm not being fair, but I can only react to what I'm told by people I trust."

"What sort of stories?" I put his toast on a plate and handed it over.

Once again I felt the impact of his gaze. His fury was deep and dangerous, and it was definitely based on something more than rumors.

He shrugged again. "Nothing significant."

Mo snorted. "You still can't lie for shit, but we all know Max is no angel, so we'll let it pass for now."

Luc didn't comment. He simply placed the remaining bacon onto his toast and ate it.

I pushed to my feet. "I'll head upstairs and get changed —do I need to bring my helmet?"

"No; mine are Bluetooth paired. Makes it easier."

"Take Nex and Vita," Mo said. "Just in case."

I nodded and bounded up the stairs. After climbing into my gear—which consisted of leather boots and jacket, teamed with Kevlar-reinforced jeans—I grabbed the daggers, shoved them into the backpack, and headed back down. Luc was once again nowhere to be seen.

"He's waiting for you outside."

Mo handed me a small glass vial filled with a clear liquid. I frowned at it. "Holy water?"

"Of sorts. It'll turn to mist once you smash the vial, and forms a protective vapor barrier that darkness won't imme-diately get through. It'll give you an escape route."

I swung the pack around and tucked the vial into a padded inner pocket. "I'm not liking the fact you feel I'll need one."

"It's precautionary, nothing more. After what the dark elf said and the attack on Jackie, I think it better we don't take any risks."

"Agreed, as long you also heed that advice."

She smiled. "I haven't survived this long to fall at the final fence. Trust me on that."

"Another odd statement you won't explain." I kissed her cheek. "Once we finish at the factory, I'll give you a call to find out where Tris is."

She nodded. "You might as well search his room when you're in there getting his hair."

"I intended to."

And a part of me—a very small part of me—hoped like hell that we wouldn't find anything incriminating, that he was involved only as far as attempting to grab the Okoro family's bible, even if that very obviously wasn't the case anymore.

I clattered down the stairs. Mia's grin flashed. "The hot man has a hot bike."

"I expected nothing less. I'll update you on the journey later."

"I'll be waiting with bated breath."

I snorted and headed out. Luc's motorcycle wasn't, as I'd half expected, something fierce, black, and sporty, but rather all gleaming red-and-silver comfort. It was an Indian Roadmaster Elite, a top-of-the-line, full of every gadget imaginable, touring motorcycle—something I knew only because Tris has spent many a teenage year drooling over the damn things.

"I didn't expect you to be a man who prefers comfort over excitement."

He shrugged and handed me the helmet. "I'm often traveling long distances, so it makes sense. Ready?"

I climbed on. Once we were both settled, he moved off, cautiously at first but then gathering more speed once he realized I was indeed an experienced passenger. And the bike, it had to be said, was glorious.

I was almost disappointed when we reached Bolton and began to wind our way through the streets. Once we neared the address, Luc found street parking and then stopped. "The factory should be just around the corner."

I nodded and, once I'd climbed off, handed him the helmet. He stored both and then glanced casually around. Old brick warehouses lined either side of the street, but only the plastics factory down the road and the small pub further up looked to be in use. There were very few people about and few cars on the street.

Luc held out a gloved hand. I eyed it somewhat suspiciously. "What?"

"I won't bite."

That's a shame. "And?"

"I'm going to manipulate the light so we disappear. It's easier to do so if we're in contact."

"Huh." I gripped his hand. With both of us wearing gloves, it should have felt impersonal, even with hormones aroused by the closeness of our ride.

It didn't.

He tugged me toward the corner of the street. Energy stirred around us and the air sparkled, gently at first and then with increased ferocity. Glimmers of gold flared across his body, down his arm, and then up mine; it felt as if thousands of gnats were gently biting. It wasn't painful, but it *was* uncomfortable. It continued to spread until both of us were covered and then, rather weirdly, he stepped away so that there was a good six inches or so of space between us.

He was still very visible, and so was I.

I frowned. "Isn't the sparkle a dead giveaway?"

"No, because its only visible from the inside. It's a means of ensuring whoever I'm sheltering doesn't move beyond it."

"Clever."

"And necessary, especially when you're dealing with someone incapable of seeing magic."

I raised an eyebrow. "I didn't think Blackbirds bothered with ordinary folk?"

"We don't, but not all witch-born are capable of magic. There are some outliers—some family lines where the link to witch ancestors is so tenuous that they do not possess the ability."

"A statement that suggests one of the heirs might be from such a line, and yet I wouldn't have thought he'd be capable of even drawing the sword."

"He was, yes, but there's a line of thought that the ability to perform magic is *not* a prerequisite for claiming the sword, simply because the sword itself is a means of drawing the power of all four elements together."

"Yes, but surely he'd have to have some understanding of magic, otherwise he wouldn't be able to control it."

"That is also true, and why many discount the theory."

I studied the street ahead for a second. "You said 'was.' I take it he's now dead?"

"He was one of the three killed." Luc grimaced. "We got him to a safe house but unfortunately, he broke protocol and contacted his friends. They were followed."

"He wasn't under protection?"

"Not directly. There are only ever twelve Blackbirds active at a time, so our resources are limited."

"You can't put more on?"

"No."

"Why?"

A smile touched his lips. "Because that is the way it has always been, and that is all the table fits."

"Bigger tables can be built, you know."

My voice was dry, and his smile grew. It did good things to his already divine features. "But none could never replace this. It's original, from the time well before the last Witch King, when the sword was first drawn."

"*That* is seriously old. Like, before medieval type old."

"Indeed."

"What about my cousins, then? Jackie was investigating

a possibility that the Okoro line could be traced back to Luis Valeriun."

"That is the rumor, but one that's never been confirmed."

"Why not? The bible might be missing, but surely there'd be other records—I mean, weren't all births recorded in parish registers back in the day?"

"*If* the parents were churchgoers. Many witches at the time weren't."

"Well, that's inconvenient."

He raised an eyebrow at me. "Do you go to church?"

"No, but times have changed. The church was considered the heart of any village back then, wasn't it?"

"Yes, but that still doesn't alter the fact that many witches were not comfortable or indeed welcome in many places of worship." He shrugged. "Anyway, we have distant heirs on a watch list, but not under full protection due to the fact that, like your brother, the bloodline connection is severely diluted."

He stopped at the corner, forcing me to do the same. The side street wasn't very long—the brick wall of the factory to our left ran down to the gates of a timber yard. The warehouse was over the road, sitting between the pub and the yard. It was a single-story brick building that had a two-tone paint job—candy pink on the bottom and around the trims, and gray everywhere else. The roof sheeting was dark with dirt and moss, and the windows had been boarded up. There was a thick padlock on the double wooden doors that sat in the middle of the structure.

"It doesn't look as if there's an easy way in."

"No." He tugged me across the road and down to the end of the pub, where he rose on his toes and looked over the fence. "There's a couple of windows on the side, but they're boarded up. Wait here while I check things out."

Before I could protest, he released my hand and disappeared over the fence. The surrounding shimmer winked out of existence, no doubt meaning I was visible again.

I walked back up the street and peered into the pub's windows. No one appeared to be inside, which wasn't surprising given the early hour. I stepped back and studied the first-floor windows. The curtains were closed but music played softly somewhere up there, suggesting someone was home—maybe even Tris's first date.

I walked down to the far end of the old warehouse. A sheet of metal divided the back of the building from the timber yard's wall, but the bottom edge of it had been bent up to provide a crawl space. I looked around again, then quickly went down onto all fours. Getting through the gap was a tight fit, but after a bit of shoving and swearing, I was in. The strip of ground beyond was littered with old booze bottles and take-out containers, suggesting either teenagers or the homeless had been responsible for the fence break.

I climbed to my feet, dusted the muck off my jeans, and then walked forward. There were no windows on this side of the building, but there was a door down the far end—and the lock had already been smashed.

I peered around the long edge of the building and saw Luc approaching. "Found a way in."

He raised an eyebrow. "Good teamwork generally means one partner following the orders and actions of the other, more-experienced partner."

"We're hardly a team, and I got bored." I gripped the handle and carefully opened the door. The room beyond was dark, and the air filled with damp moldiness ... and something else. Something that hinted at ash and anger.

"On second thought—" I stepped back and waved him on. "The senior partner may now precede me."

He reached back and drew his sword—a process that seemed extraordinarily easy considering how many experts declared it impossible—and then stepped through the doorway. Just for a heartbeat, the darkness seemed to consume him. Then light flared—light that was a dark and dangerous red. Hecate burned.

"Does that mean what I think it means?" I asked softly.

"Yes. There were demons or dark elves here."

"'Were' is certainly far better than 'are.'" I drew my daggers and followed him in. Light dribbled down both blades, but it was a somewhat muted reaction that confirmed evil was currently absent. "I was really hoping Tris wasn't neck-deep in all this shit."

"I doubt he is the brains behind said shit, if that's any comfort."

"It's really not."

Under Hecate's glow, the factory looked long and eerie. Cobwebs hung in strings from metal roof rafters, and bits of old machinery and what looked to be hoists lay scattered all around. There was no indication that anyone used this place on a regular basis—the rubbish that lined the strip of land behind us was absent here, which was rather odd if homeless people had been responsible for the mess. The factory would have provided them with protection against the elements, and given the lock had been broken and there was no evidence of magic being employed within the factory to deter—

I stopped abruptly, my nose twitching as the air stirred with a brand-new scent. One that vaguely smelled of decay and rot. "Is that—?"

"Death," Luc finished for me. "Yes."

"It smells rotten."

I crossed mental fingers even as I said that. I really hoped it was both rotten *and* old. That it was dead vermin or some other poor animal rather than a woman in a red-and-green striped sweater. Common sense said it couldn't be, that her body wouldn't have decayed that swiftly, and yet instinct was stirring again.

Instinct, I thought savagely, needed to shut the hell up unless it could provide a damn basis for its guesswork.

Luc glanced over his shoulder, his jade eyes burning with the same deep fire as Hecate. "Would you prefer to wait here?"

"I think you can guess the answer to *that* question."

"And impolite it is, too." His smile briefly flashed. "The scent comes from the far corner."

My gaze jumped past him; the corner held a broken jumble of machine parts and railings. Maybe the death we could smell lay beyond it, tucked in the corner ... I swallowed heavily, torn between needing to see and not. Between needing confirmation that the worst of my fears about Tris were true, and hoping like hell that I was wrong, that Luc was wrong, and Tris was doing nothing more than searching for a damn book.

Even if the mounting evidence suggested otherwise.

The closer we got to the jumble, the stronger the smell became. My stomach churned, but I forced my feet on. It wasn't like I'd never come across death before—I'd seen it in both demon and animal guise many a time. But this ... this was human. Every inch of me was certain of that, even if I couldn't yet see the body.

In Hecate's bloody light, the stone floor near the mess of metal glistened black; the dark pool stretched from the broken edge of a machine to the dirt-splattered rear wall. Oil, not blood, I thought, even as my pulse rate jumped.

"There're stairs behind the mess." Luc's voice was even, at odds with the tension that radiated from him. "I think it's safe to say the stench is about to get a whole lot worse."

"Oh, joy."

He glanced at me. "Be ready—the scent of darkness is stronger down there, too."

"Double joy."

A smile ghosted his lips but didn't quite reach his eyes. "Most normal women would be running right now—you know that, don't you?"

"I have Mo as a grandmother. I think it's safe to say I've never been normal."

"I can see that." He paused. "I like it."

My eyebrows rose even as warmth pulsed through me. "Is this your version of 'we might get dead, so I might have an admission' thing?"

"Could be. Let's go."

He moved forward without a backward glance. I followed close, Nex and Vita at the ready, their glow increasing as we cautiously moved into the basement's bowels. Our steps echoed on the metal steps and, just for a second, something stirred in the ink beyond Hecate's light. I faltered, my pulse tripping into a higher gear and fear sitting like a thick lump of ice in my stomach. There was something here. Something beyond the smell of death. Something that spoke of evil.

The deeper we moved into the basement, the more certain I became that there was far worse here than the mere scent of death and decay—although *it* was now so ripe and raw it was almost liquid. I tried breathing through my mouth but it didn't help. The putridity clawed at the back of my throat, clung to my clothes, and clogged my pores.

As we neared the bottom steps, a faint, almost sickly glow appeared—spell strings. They not only lined either side of the stairs but also washed across the bottom step and then ran across the floor, walls and ceiling, entirely encasing the basement area.

Were they keeping something in? Or something out?

I narrowed my gaze; the exterior strings were some sort of containment barrier and it was aimed inward, suggesting that part of the spell was designed to prevent something escaping. If it was the smell, then it was beginning to fail. I had no idea what the greater portion of the spell was designed to do. It was, however, far more complicated than the spell the dark elf had unleashed at the King's Tower.

"Luc—"

"I see it." He paused on the second bottom step and raised Hecate. "Radiate."

She immediately did so. Her light exploded, casting bloody fingers through the darkness, peeling it back and revealing the basement's secret.

It was filled with bones and bodies.

Hundreds and hundreds of them.

EIGHT

*O*h Tris, what have you done? What the hell have you gotten involved in?

The words tore through me but remained locked inside. I'd been expecting death, but this ... this was a slaughter yard. I shuddered, swallowing heavily, staring in disbelief and utter horror at the broken remnants of humanity that were literally everywhere—hanging from ceiling struts, pinned to the walls, piled into white mounds on the floor. There were clothes, shoes, and other unrecognizable pieces of material, some of which still clung to small bits of their wearers. I clapped a hand across my mouth and nose, though I wasn't sure whether it was meant to provide a physical barrier against the bile rising up my throat or a vain attempt to keep out the smell and horror.

The containment portion of the dark spell, I thought grimly, had to be the only reason this place hadn't already been discovered. The pub next door should have been overwhelmed by the stench, even with all the factory's windows boarded ... The thought died as I spotted the one thing I didn't want to see.

A red-and-green striped sweater.

"Oh fuck, *no*."

The words were whispered and yet they echoed through the shadows as loudly as any shout. I stared at that sweater, sorrow and anger surging in equal amounts. The man I'd grown up with, the man I still loved as a friend, was a murderer. One who was undeniably working with the demons and the dark elves. There could be no dismissing it now. Not that doubt had ever really existed anywhere beyond my own fragile hopes that he couldn't—wouldn't— go to depths such as this.

Damn it, Tris, *why?*

"What?" Luc said.

I briefly closed my eyes, fighting the useless sting of tears, and then silently pointed.

"Oh." He hesitated. "I'm so sorry."

My gaze shot to his. "Why are *you* sorry?"

"You've lost a friendship you clearly valued, and under the vilest of circumstances. That's never an easy situation to accept."

There was such a depth of understanding in his eyes that I once again found myself blinking rapidly.

"No." My gaze went back to the remnants of the woman's body. "We need to find out who she was."

"Yes, although I doubt there'll be any form of identification left on her. Or, indeed, any of them."

"She certainly wasn't carrying a purse or anything when Tris picked her up last night." I hesitated. "She looks torn apart. They all do."

He nodded. Though his expression gave little away, there was an almost haunted look in his eyes. "I've seen this in one other place. I was hoping never to see it again. It's a hecatomb."

"And that is?"

He didn't immediately answer, but a muscle in his jaw ticked, and turmoil radiated from him. Fighting the memories, I guessed. I lightly touched his arm, felt his muscles jump in response. "I'm sorry, you don't have to answer. I can guess."

He briefly placed his hand over mine and squeezed. Though the contact was not direct, thanks to the gloves we both wore, awareness surged. But it wasn't sexual in nature; it was something far deeper and totally unexpected. Because, just for that moment, I was in his memories. I saw Hecate flaming and heard her scream. Felt his desperate determination against the hordes that were coming from all angles, tearing and biting and destroying. Saw a woman in a red dress at his feet, her blood flowing from deep wounds in her chest and her head, staining the cobblestones with her life ...

"Thank you, but I'm fine. The question is a natural one; you just caught me a little off guard."

His words broke the reel of images and I blinked, disorientated, as if somehow that connection had bled me of strength.

He noticed it, and though I doubted he guessed the true reason for it, there was a flash of sympathy—and perhaps even protectiveness—in his eyes. He lightly touched my arm, pressing heat into my skin. "I may be fine, but are you?"

I took a deep, somewhat shuddering breath. "Yes. Go on, please."

His gaze swept me briefly, concern evident. But he didn't voice his obvious doubts. "Traditionally, a hecatomb was a public arena where the Greeks sacrificed one hundred oxen to their gods. It was also used later for arenas in which human sacrifices were performed."

"The Greeks had nothing to do with this."

"No." The smile that ghosted his lips held little warmth. "In this instance, a hecatomb is a place of exchange. A life given for a service or information received."

"Between demon and human? Or is this depth of carnage a dark elf thing?"

"They are capable of it, although they generally only eat human flesh on special occasions."

"Oh, that's comforting." My gaze swept the basement, and horror surged yet again. "That does suggest this atrocity is demon based."

"If our suspicions are true—if the demons and the dark elves are working as one for their greater good—then that assumption is likely false. The sheer numbers involved here would also suggest the exchanges have been happening for far longer than we ever expected."

"Doesn't this just get better and better." I pointed Nex at the faintly glowing threads hovering close to the bottom step. "Do we tempt that? Or do we just walk away?"

"The latter. Neither of us have the skills to contain this. I'll call it in once we're out in the fresh air."

I turned around and quickly retreated, although I didn't sheath my daggers until I'd reached the litter-covered rear yard. And just for a moment, everything hit, and I bent over, my body shaking as I fought back tears and sucked in air.

Luc didn't say anything. He just wrapped his big, warm arms around me and held me close. It was a closeness that wasn't only physical but also, rather oddly, emotional. As if, in that one brief moment, we were one.

It was *that* connection that told me he wasn't as immune to me as I'd feared.

Once the shakes had eased, I sniffed and pulled back. "Sorry. I guess the shock of it all just hit."

"Unsurprising." He tucked a stray strand of hair behind my ears, his touch tender. "I've seen men and women with years' of fighting experience fall apart far quicker after such a discovery. You did well to hold it together for as long as you did."

A smile touched my lips. "I'm thinking you lie, but I nevertheless appreciate it."

He nodded and eyed the gap in the fence I'd crawled through. "We'll go back over the other fence. There's no way I'm going to fit through that; I'm rather surprised you did."

"At any other time, I'd take umbrage at such a statement, but it seems petty in the face of what lies below us."

"It was not meant as an insult."

"Then it's the strangest compliment I've ever heard." I hesitated, eyeing the door into the factory. "Should we do something to block that and prevent others from entering?"

"I'll disguise it. You go check the coast is clear so that we can get out of here without raising suspicions."

I nodded, and as I walked away, his power surged. Though I wondered how he intended to conceal it, I wasn't curious enough to go back and see. The quicker we got away from this place, the better.

I clambered up the fence to check no one was near or watching, then jumped down on the other side and pulled my phone out to call Mo.

"Where's Tris?" I asked the moment she answered.

"Buggered if I know." Her tone was annoyed.

"You've lost him?" I couldn't help the surprise in my voice.

"Yes, because he went to the damn station and caught a train."

"Why didn't you follow it?"

"Because I wasn't sure which damn one he was on." She blew out an aggrieved breath. "What was at the factory?"

"According to Luc, what is known as a hecatomb."

"Well, fuck."

"Yeah. It was horrible. The first woman Tris picked up last night was there."

"Meaning he must have collected something in return for her sacrifice."

"And that something is probably being taken to London or wherever else he's headed."

"Unless he gave it to the brunette he met in the pub last night."

"Possibly." I glanced around at the sound of approaching steps. "You're clear, Luc."

He immediately climbed over, and a whole lot more elegantly than me. "Mo?"

I nodded and flicked over to speakerphone. He caught my elbow and escorted me across the road.

"Where are you headed now?" Mo asked.

"If Tris is currently on a train, it gives us the perfect opportunity to search his room. You?"

"Barney got a hit on the brunette. We're going over to have a chat with her."

"She's a local?"

"No. Visitor from London, staying at The Grand."

Which is how Barney found her so quickly—his daughter was the manager there. "Do we know anything about her?"

"Not at this stage." She paused. "Barney just arrived. Talk later."

She hung up. I shoved my phone back into my pocket. "Do you mind returning to Ainslyn straight away?"

"No, because it's better to search Tris's hotel room while there's no danger of discovery. If we don't find anything, we'll come back and see if the guesthouse's manager knows anything about the woman Tris brought here."

I nodded and climbed onto the bike. "I take it you've called your people about the factory?"

"Yes, but we haven't the power to deal with the erasure of a hecatomb. The job will fall to others."

"What others?"

"Asking questions really is your natural state, isn't it?"

"And answering them really should become yours."

He chuckled softly. "I'm talking about the Preternatural Division of the National Crime Agency, who have some of the strongest witches on their books as advisors. We've worked with them for many a year now."

I blinked. "I had no idea such a unit even existed."

"Few do—and that's just the way they like it. Ready?"

"Yes." I lightly gripped his jacket, taking comfort in his closeness, in the warm press of my thighs against his. After the horror we'd just left, I was grateful to have someone to lean on, however briefly. However much he was still a stranger.

We cruised back to Ainslyn. Once we'd parked and the helmets and gloves had been stored, Luc said. "What's his room number?"

"Two-ten."

"Once we're invisible, we'll grab a master key, then make our way up there."

He held out his hand. I twined my fingers through his, and once again the contact was fierce—electric. And this time, he definitely felt it. Awareness and desire burned—all too briefly—in his eyes.

But he didn't say anything. He didn't even acknowledge it. As we strode toward The Cherry Tree, the air once again shimmered, but faster this time, thanks no doubt to the fact we were in a public place. Just before the glitter entirely concealed us, a woman came out of the nearby sweet shop, and her mouth dropped open. Then we were gone and she blinked, looking around in some confusion.

Once in the hotel, Luc walked to the desk and, after sending the desk calendar crashing to the floor, waited for the lone receptionist to come out from behind the counter, then quickly leaned over, opened a drawer, and pulled a keycard out. We headed for the stairs.

I glanced around to make sure no one was close. "How do you know that key will open the door?"

"A lot of smaller hotels keep a master key close by for guests who lock themselves out."

"Yeah, but there's no guarantee that's it."

He shrugged. "If it's not, I'll go back down and find it."

"Meaning you've done this before."

"Many a time."

We reached the second floor, but he didn't release my hand. He swiped the keycard through the lock and, when the door opened, flashed a warm smile. "See? Good things happen to those who believe."

I snorted softly. "I think luck had more to do with it than belief."

"Could be." He ushered me inside, then closed the door and put the chain on. "Do you want to go through his bags? I'll check the cupboards and drawers."

I nodded and walked across the room to the carryall sitting on the foldout stand. I didn't look at the bed. I didn't want to remember the fun we'd had, even if that was where the doubts had first seeded.

I undid the bag's top zip and carefully pulled clothes out. There wasn't a whole lot—just a couple pairs of jeans, a few shirts, socks, and underpants—suggesting that despite him saying he didn't know how long the job would take, he hadn't intended staying too long. Delivering that woman to such a vile death obviously hadn't initially been a part of his task here—not given he'd only done so after receiving orders from the man he'd met at McDonald's. But that made it even more important we find and stop that man—and before he could give any more damn orders.

Luc began opening and closing drawers. "Anything?"

"Not really." I stacked the clothes back and then checked the bag's side pockets. There were a few coins and some used train tickets. "He's been to both Carlisle and Bath via train, though."

"Interesting. There's a witch library in Bath."

"And Carlisle?"

"Was the location of an heir until we got him out last week. What's the date on the ticket?"

I quickly looked. "Seventeenth."

"Meaning he might have been scouting the area. We got the heir out on the eighteenth."

"Was it a direct heir?"

"From Rodella's second marriage, yes."

I shoved the tickets back into the side pocket, but as I was about to zip it up, I spotted a torn bit of white tucked in the far corner. I carefully pulled it out. On it was a partial phone number. I finished checking the rest of the pockets but didn't find anything else.

I walked over to where Luc was sweeping a hand across the wardrobe's top shelf. "Here, found this."

He accepted the bit of paper and then grimaced. "Half a phone number is not of much use."

"Where's that belief you were speaking of earlier?" I asked. "It might not be useful now, but could come into its own later on."

"Perhaps." His somewhat amused expression suggested he doubted it. "There's nothing here. Do you want to check the bathroom?"

I nodded and continued on. The bathroom contained little more than his toiletries. I unscrewed the cologne's lid and tentatively took a sniff. It was aromatic and woody, and very definitely *not* the cardamom, bergamot, and lavender-based scent I'd now smelled a number of times. Which did at least provide a sliver of relief. Tris might have killed that woman, but he wasn't yet closely involved with the attacks on me.

For now, anyway.

After plucking hair from his comb and wrapping it carefully in a tissue, I walked out. "Nothing there, either."

He held out his hand. "Then it's time to go."

"Back to the guesthouse?"

He nodded and, as the shimmer crawled over the two of us again, said, "But I've a feeling we'll not find much there, either."

I frowned as we clattered down the stairs. "She would have had to check in."

"I doubt she did so under her own name."

"Given we don't actually know her name, that's not going to make much difference. On the plus side, we do have a photo."

Which was blurry, but still gave us a starting point. Once he'd returned the keycard, we headed out to his motorcycle and journeyed to the guesthouse. The manager

173

was less than helpful and had absolutely no reaction when I showed him the somewhat blurry photo. Either he was a damn good actor, or he really hadn't seen her.

"What are you thinking?" I asked, once we were outside.

"That's it's probably the night manager we should be talking to. I also think it's about time we had lunch. I'm starving."

So was I, and not just for food. I squished that thought back into its box and said, "There were a few nice pubs on the ride up here."

He nodded and pressed a hand against my spine, lightly guiding me back to the Indian. "We'll stop at one of them and plot our next move over food."

"You're buying?"

He glanced at me, eyebrow raised. "Last I heard, the De Montforts weren't poor. I, on the other hand, am just a struggling foot soldier."

I smiled. "No one who owns a manor house in Somerset is poor, but never let it be said that *this* De Montfort is a miser. But you can buy the next meal."

"Deal." He handed me a helmet. Once we were on our way, he added, his warm tones so clear over the Bluetooth, "Would it be worth talking to Tristan's parents?"

"No. You probably know more about his activities in London and who his friends are there than they ever would. I doubt they even know he's back in Ainslyn."

"Has he talked to you about his activities in London?"

I half smiled. "Is that your way of asking if we had a long-distance relationship?"

"No." He hesitated. "Did you?"

"No. We were simply friends who sometimes had sex when he came back home—and you know well enough how

174

often that's been lately if you've been keeping an eye on him." I paused as he took a sharp left. "Have you searched his London premises?"

"No, but after this, we certainly will. We've also put an arrest order on him."

I frowned. "If you arrest him, we may never uncover the man he's reporting to."

"Trust me, the Preternatural Division have the means to make even the most reluctant witness talk."

"Which suggests they skim the edge of the law."

"They don't skim—they crash right through. Anyone working with the dark realm is considered to have waived any right to the laws of this land and is treated accordingly."

"Which is no doubt why the division remains secret."

"So secret, few in parliament even know about it."

"Then how does it get funded?"

He shrugged. "Their funding would be part of the NCA's overall budget, but I can't tell you how the division is listed."

"What about the Blackbirds? Are you government funded?"

His amusement was a warm wave that briefly washed over me, though how that was even possible I had no idea. "No. We are entirely self-funded—always have been, even though we've always been responsible for the protection of the Aquitaine line and have over the years received compensation in the form of land and holdings from the various kings."

"If it isn't for the money or even the glory, why are the Blackbirds so devoted to the crown? Especially these days?"

"Because it was a duty entrusted to us by Vivienne, a Celtic water goddess who also gave the Aquitaine line the sword."

"And just what did your ancestors do to receive such an onerous and never-ending task?"

"They were on the wrong side of a war—one that cost thousands of lives. The duty to protect light against all darkness was their penance."

"Odd that it was given by a water goddess."

"It's said that the waterways ran with so much blood and gore that it stained the banks and *her* for years." He pulled into the parking area of a small, stone-built pub and stopped. "Will this do?"

I took of my helmet. "As long as they'll serve me a pot of tea, I really don't care."

"A woman with simple tastes, huh?"

My gaze found his. "That depends entirely on what we're talking about."

The rather sexy gleam—one that was part amusement, part awareness—made another brief appearance in his eyes. "Food. We're talking about food."

"Shame."

"Perhaps. But it is far safer."

I raised my eyebrows. "The attraction exists, however much you pretend otherwise. And we're both consenting adults."

He opened the door and ushered me inside. "Yes, but there are ethics to be considered."

"What ethics?"

I scanned the surprisingly busy dining room and saw a table for two down the far end. Luc must have seen it too, because he pressed a hand to my spine and lightly guided me that way. There was nothing light about the effect his touch had on me, however.

This *wasn't* normal. It couldn't be. And I had a sudden feeling that Mo would know exactly what was going on.

Once we were both seated, a waitress bustled over, handing us a menu and then taking our drinks order. As she hurried away, he said, "The ethics of being involved with the sister of a suspect, especially when she's already been the target of what we call a 'sleep and steal' effort."

I frowned. "Tris couldn't have stolen anything from me magically, because I'm immune to it."

"Really?" Surprised edged Luc's voice. "Since when?"

"Since birth." I studied the beautiful planes of his face for a moment. "I'm surprised you didn't know, given you appear to have done your research when it comes to my family."

"Yes, but that was never mentioned anywhere."

"Then you didn't look hard enough—it's listed on my license to carry."

He shrugged. "Perhaps it was there and I simply missed it. It *was* your brother we were more concerned about." He paused. "Has Max this same immunity?"

"Of course not—he has the elemental ability to control storms, which means it's impossible to also be immune."

"Not necessarily. There are some who believe that Uhtric himself had a similar immunity—at least until he drew the sword."

"The thing I've never got is why he even drew the sword in the first place? He wasn't the firstborn son."

"No, but he was nevertheless the one the sword chose."

Before I could reply, the waitress reappeared with our drinks—tea for me, and a black-as-ink coffee for him—then said, "Ready to order yet?"

I glanced hurriedly down the menu and ordered the bangers and mash. Luc settled on the steak-and-kidney pie with a side order of chips. The waitress nodded, collected the menus, and hurried away again.

"I hope you're prepared to share those chips," I said with a smile.

"That's the reason I ordered a large bowl. You look like the sort of woman who'd steal a poor man's last chip."

"I'm not that mean—I'd definitely split it." My smile faded. "How could the sword help choose a king? It's only ever drawn when darkness rises."

"It may not be drawn, but it *is* gripped. The sword reacts by emitting a pulse of blue light when a true heir touches it."

My heart began to beat a little faster. "That's what happened up on the knob."

He nodded. "Unfortunately, whoever was up there used strong concealing magic. I wasn't aware they were there until I saw that pulse—and by the time I got across to the island, they were gone and you were in trouble."

"I never did thank you for that, so, thank you."

"You're more than welcome. Besides, I could hardly question you about your brother if you were dead."

"Then why did you disappear so abruptly?"

"I had to follow the distortion of light the concealing magic left behind before it totally disappeared." He grimaced. "I got as far as that parking area. He'd obviously been picked up by someone, because your car was the only other one in the area both before and after."

"So why didn't you come back? Or hang around?"

He shrugged. "Other business to attend to."

I poured some tea and then added milk and sugar. "There *is* one major problem with your statement that the sword only reacts to heirs."

He raised his eyebrows. "And that is?"

"It reacted to me."

He sucked in a deep breath. "That is—"

"Don't say impossible, because it clearly isn't."

"I was going to say unexpected." He frowned. "But perhaps it really shouldn't be. You're a twin, and your brother is an heir, however distant. Perhaps it simply reacted to the bloodline's presence rather than the actuality of gender."

"Has there ever been an attempt by a woman to draw the sword before?"

"Oh yes. There's been many a royal maiden desperate to claim the Witch King's Crown. There've been wars fought over it, in fact, and some who *did* succeed, however briefly. But the sword was never drawn by any of them."

"Maybe because they were never given the chance, thanks to the fact the dark realm wasn't threatening."

"And maybe it was because only males can draw the sword."

"As Mo would point out, those sorts of grand statements were invariably written by men more concerned about promoting the greatness of their gender than the actual truth."

He grinned. "*That* is a truth I cannot deny."

"Then it makes you a rare man."

"Possibly. Acknowledging such statements does not change the facts, however." He paused as the waitress delivered our meals, placed the chips in the center of the table, and bid us to enjoy. I immediately stole a chip, which drew a smile.

"If it *is* a recognition of blood kinship," he continued, "then it becomes even more urgent that your brother stops avoiding us. He may yet be in danger."

"I'll ring him and tell him, if you want." Although I could imagine his response, and it wouldn't be polite.

Luc hesitated, and then shook his head. "I'll consult with others in my order first, and we'll go from there."

"A statement that suggests your lot operates on a consensus of opinion rather than having a set hierarchy."

"We do. That is why the table is round—everyone there has equal standing and an equal say."

"What happens if a vote is split down the middle?"

"A very long and tedious debate occurs until a suitable middle ground is found." He waved the fork at my lunch. "Eat, before it gets cold."

"Yes, sir." I grabbed another chip and saluted him lightly with it.

He rolled his eyes and started eating. The sausages were divine, especially with the onion gravy. I grabbed a dinner roll to mop up the last remnants from my plate and then sighed in satisfaction. "That was lovely."

"There're chips left, you know."

"Sadly, I've only enough room left for another cup of tea."

The waitress chose that moment to appear and immediately said, "Coming right up." She glanced at Luc—who shook his head—then she collected my plate and disappeared again.

"So what's the plan for this afternoon?" I asked.

He hesitated. "I have to touch base with Gabe—"

"Is he the Blackbird who helped you get rid of the demon's body?"

"Yes."

"Why was he in Ainslyn, when you said it was your patch?"

"Why do you think? I can only ever be in one place at a time, and I did warn I'd be your shadow—"

"Only until my brother turned up." And there was a

tiny fraction of me that suddenly hoped Max was his usual obstinate self and decided to stay longer than a week.

"Given recent events and your brother's reputation for being uncooperative, I dare say my duty will remain exactly where it is for the foreseeable future. Speaking of which—" He got out his phone. "What's your phone number?"

A smile teased my lips. "I don't give that out to any old Tom, Dick, or Lucas, you know."

"It is for professional purposes only."

"Well, that makes it doubly easy to refuse."

He didn't look amused. "If something does happen to you, I can use it to trace you."

"Mo can find me far easier and faster than a damn app."

"Perhaps, but it is nevertheless a sensible thing to do."

"Well, if we're going to be sensible, you'd better give me yours then, too."

Amusement finally touched his eyes. "Only if you promise not to abuse it."

"I promise not to abuse it unless totally and absolutely necessary. Or until all this is over and the ethics are no longer a problem."

"Fine," he said. "In the meantime, I'll have to be strong enough for both of us."

"Oh, please don't."

He didn't laugh, as I'd half expected. Instead, his expression was briefly consumed by shadows and sorrow. "Things can go badly wrong when distractions happen, Gwen. I'll not be caught like that again."

The woman in the red dress, I thought, but resisted the urge to ask who she was. I'd basically stolen that memory from him, and until he willingly shared it, I had no right to mention it.

After we'd exchanged numbers, I poured the last bit of

tea into my cup, but my phone rang before I could drink it. The ringtone told me it was Mo. I hit the answer button and said, "What's up?"

"Fucking everything." Her voice was filled with a wild mix of fury and sorrow. "I just got a distraught call from Ada."

My pulse leapt several gears. I knew what was coming. Knew, and feared it.

"Are her brothers ...?"

I didn't finish the sentence. I didn't need to.

"Yes," Mo bit out. "Gareth's been murdered, and Henry is missing."

NINE

"**N**o." The denial was torn from me.

"Yes." Mo's voice was grim. Unrelenting. *Angry.*

I closed my eyes, battling the need to scream even as tears threatened.

Gareth dead and Henry missing. It just didn't compute. It didn't make sense. They weren't direct heirs—why would someone want them dead?

I swallowed heavily, trying to maintain composure. Trying to *think.* The thought that came was one that made my gut churn even harder.

"Both Gareth and Henry were on Jackie's list. Max and a person named Jules were the next two."

"I know. I've sent Max a message to ring one of us urgently."

"Let's hope he actually takes notice of it." I took a deep, quivering breath. "I take it you're going to help with the investigation?"

"Ada's asked me to, yes. I'd like you and Luc to meet me at Gareth's."

"I'm not sure what I can—"

"I'll need Luc's help if I'm to get entry into the crime scene, and I'm certainly not about to leave you in Ainslyn alone. Not after this."

They don't want to kill me, I wanted to say, but that wasn't really the point. Not anymore. Not if they wanted to get to Max *through* me.

"I still don't get why they're going after the indirect heirs," I said. "It doesn't make any sense."

Luc abruptly straightened. "Someone's been attacked?"

I glanced at him and nodded. He immediately motioned to the waitress and asked for the bill.

"I can't answer that question." Mo's voice very much suggested doing so had hit the top of her to-do list. "I'm leaving within the hour; ring me when you get there."

"Hang on," I said, and quickly filled Luc in.

"It'll take us a good four hours to get up there." He glanced at his watch. "We won't arrive until after nightfall now."

"That'll do," Mo said, obviously overhearing.

"I'll call when we arrive." I hesitated. "Did Ada say anything else? Give any clue as to how ..."

"She couldn't—wouldn't—talk about what she saw."

Meaning what she'd seen was pretty brutal.

"She called the police," Mo continued, "but it now appears the NCA has taken over the investigation."

That was no surprise, given what Luc had said about them. "Take it easy when you're flying, Mo. Don't kill yourself trying to get to London as quickly as possible."

"I'm too ornery to be taken down by something as simple as a heart attack, my girl. Besides, there's too much left yet in this world that I have to do."

The waitress came back with the check. Luc added a

generous tip to his payment, then rose and pulled on his leather jacket.

"Talk soon, then."

I hung up and stood.

"You okay?" Luc asked softly. He grabbed the jacket out of my hands and held it for me to put on.

"I don't know." I hesitated, and then shook my head. "I honestly don't know."

I'd just lost one, if not two, family members, and yet I was numb inside. Maybe it was shock. Or maybe it was disbelief. Maybe the reality wouldn't really hit until I walked into their house.

Luc didn't reply. He simply caught my hand and led me outside. Once we were on the road again, he said, "Let me know if you need to stop. Otherwise, we'll ride straight through. The sooner we get answers, the better."

With that, I could only agree. From that point on, there was little conversation to be had. We stopped once for a bathroom break, but otherwise pushed the speed limits where and when we could. Dusk had faded from the sky by the time we reached South Kensington, where Gareth and Henry co-owned a five-bedroom, four-story terrace house.

Luc wove through the traffic quickly and easily, and pretty soon we were in Thurlough Square. There were cops everywhere. He parked the bike and then helped me off. After the long day of almost constant travel, my muscles were a bit stiff, despite the Indian being built for comfort.

I eyed the official vehicles uneasily. "How are we going to get in?"

"I'll make a call." He hesitated. "Do you need to contact Mo?"

I nodded. "She wants you to make arrangements for her to get in."

"I'll see what I can do."

I crossed my arms and waited, my gaze scanning the building's beautiful old façade as Luc organized our entry.

"We're in luck." He shoved his phone back into his pocket. "Jason's in charge of the investigation."

"And he is?"

"An old friend." He caught my elbow and guided me across the road—and didn't immediately let go once we were on the other side. I rather suspected he didn't want to —that he enjoyed the contact as much as I did.

Which was just another of those little insights that at any other time—with any other man—could have been wishful thinking. It wasn't.

"Did Mo get clearance?"

"Yes."

"Thanks." I pulled out my phone and sent her a quick text.

"No need to thank me." Luc's amusement was evident. "I rather suspect Jason is looking forward to finally meeting her."

I glanced up curiously. "Why?"

"Because there are few enough true mages left in the world today."

I frowned. "She's many things, but a mage isn't one of them."

He raised an eyebrow. "Isn't a mage defined as someone proficient in all forms of magic?"

"Yes, but that doesn't apply to Gran."

"How many De Montforts do you know that can perform the sort of magic she does?"

"None, but it's not like I have a whole heap of kin to go by." And I had even less now. I blinked back tears. "Besides, she's only ever done minor magics."

But even as I said that, I remembered the energy she'd unleashed in the vaults and had to wonder. There was so damn much she hadn't told me, so many questions that still lay unanswered. It would actually make a great deal more sense if she *were* a mage.

"In this day and age," Luc was saying, "the ability to perform multiple magics—however minor that ability might be—qualifies her as a mage. And that's *without* taking into account her great knowledge of all magics."

I wrinkled my nose, though I wasn't really sure why I resisted the idea. Maybe it just made my *lack* of knowledge and power all that more ... galling.

"If you doubt," he continued, obviously noting my expression, "why don't you simply ask her?"

"Because it'll be just another of those damn questions she won't answer."

Down at the other end of the road, a silver-haired man came out of Gareth's house, then ducked under the police tapes and strode toward us. He looked to be in his late forties, with a craggy brown face and a slim build.

"Lucas," he greeted, holding his hand. "It's been too long."

Luc gripped the other man's hand and pulled him into a fierce hug. "It has. I wish it was under better circumstances, though."

"Yeah, it's pretty grim inside." Jason's gaze switched to mine. His eyes were the same vivid shade as Luc's, suggesting there was at least some Durant heritage in his bloodline even if he didn't immediately feel like a witch. "And who's your pretty partner?"

"Gwen De Montfort," I said before Luc could.

"Ah." All trace of amusement fled. "Sorry for your loss."

I nodded. "Has there been any sign of Henry?"

"Not as yet, no, although there's also no immediate indication he was home when the murder happened."

"Have you requested a locator?" Luc asked.

Jason nodded. "She didn't have much luck, though. Either he's magically concealed or ..."

"He's already dead," I finished when he hesitated.

"Yes. I'm not sure it would be wise for you—"

"Are you—or anyone else on your team—able to track witches by their tells?"

He frowned. "No, but a witch wasn't behind this murder."

"Are you sure of that?" Luc asked. "Because we've now got concrete evidence of at least two witches working with the dark realm."

Jason swore. Vehemently. "Why did I not know this?"

"It was only confirmed today, and I did contact your office to put out a warrant."

"Tristan Chen," Jason said instantly. "I'd heard it had been issued, but I've been too busy here to follow updates."

"So he hasn't been found as yet?" Luc asked.

"No. He's not at his apartment—hasn't been for over a week, according to neighbors. We've got it under surveillance." Jason's gaze came back to mine. "Are you absolutely sure you want to go inside?"

"We've just come from a hecatomb," Luc said softly. "If she got through that, she can get through anything."

"Another one of *those* is the last thing we need." Jason's voice was grim. "Old or new?"

"Old. Older than even the last one we found."

"Well, fuck." Jason shook his head and then turned on his heel and led the way back. "Don't things just keep getting better?"

"Yeah." Luc held up the police tape and ushered me through. "Any luck with the break-in at the museum?"

"Nothing new, but we're still following leads."

Luc grunted but didn't comment as a police officer came out of the house and handed us shoe protectors, hairnets, and gloves. My stomach immediately started churning; part of me really didn't want to see what I was about to see, but I had to. Gareth might be dead, but Henry was still out there somewhere. I needed to find him. Needed to save him. I didn't want to lose two relatives in one day.

I followed the two men into the rather opulent hallway and up a couple of steps to the raised ground floor's reception and kitchen area. There were cops—uniformed and not —searching every inch of the room, but we didn't stop, moving up two more flights to the top floor and what looked to be the master bedroom.

I'd barely entered when a gasp escaped and I stopped, unable to force my feet any further. There was literally no part of the bedroom that had not been visited by bloody destruction. Just like the people in that basement, Gareth had been torn apart. Blood, gore, intestines, and limbs were tossed all over the place. The scent of death and blood rode the air, accompanied by a pain so deep it seemed to invade my bones and make them ache.

I took a deep, somewhat shuddery breath and fought back my horror. I needed to maintain control, to not cry or make a scene. To think and see clearly, so that Gareth's death might be avenged and Henry found.

"Are you okay?" Luc asked softly.

I nodded and rubbed my arms. He didn't look convinced but after a moment, he followed Jason into the huge suite and began questioning him. I remained exactly where I was. Any closer might be tempting an already unsteady stomach.

I briefly closed my eyes and took another deep breath, gathering the courage to look beyond the gore, to look for any possible reason for this madness. Surely it couldn't have happened because of his tenuous link to Luis Valeriun—surely there had to be a more logical reason, especially given there were direct heirs still alive and well.

The bedroom, I noted, was as big as the top two floors of our building combined. There were three huge sash windows through which the interior lights poured, highlighting the street below. All three were closed and locked. Full-size bookcases had been set into the walls either side of the bed and held more photographs and knickknacks than books; nothing immediately appeared to be missing. There was a long, built-in wardrobe to my left and, to my right, an en suite.

My gaze returned to the gore, and it suddenly struck me as over the top. No death by demon was ever pleasant but this ... this was a frenzy. It was out-of-control madness—the sort of thing usually found in a random late-night encounter. It was not something you'd expect to find in what amounted to a contract killing. There were surely easier ways to kill someone without bringing the full glare of the police world down on you. Hell, if you had the right witch contacts, you could buy a spell to do the deed from a distance. By the time anyone wised up, any hope of tracking the spell would have dissipated. So why send in a demon to unleash bloody mayhem? Why advertise your connection to the dark realm like that?

Had it gotten to the point where the witch figured his secret was out and there was no point hiding it anymore? Or was there something more practical behind the use of the demon? Had it simply been a means of quickly curtailing Gareth's response to someone breaking past the spells protecting this place? After all, no witch—however strong—could retaliate while being torn apart ...

I closed my eyes and swallowed heavily. I couldn't stay in this room. I had to get out, to get away from the scents of death and agony, even if the retreat was only as far as the en suite.

"Jason, is it okay if I look in the bathroom?"

He glanced up. "Yes, but if you find anything, notify me immediately."

I nodded and went in. The bloody destruction in the other room was thankfully absent in the en suite. It was huge—the shower alone was bigger than our entire bathroom at home, and the bath could have substituted for a kid's swimming pool. I stopped in the middle of the vast space and looked around. White marble adorned the floor, the wet areas, and the long vanity unit, while the walls were gold-patterned white wallpaper. Gold tapware and twin rain showerheads completed the feeling of opulence. My gaze went to the sash window. The spell surrounding it—just like the ones that protected our place—had been designed to keep darkness *out* rather than in, but the fact it remained active had hope surging. Spells never lasted beyond the death of their creator, which not only meant that its source was Henry rather than Gareth but also that he was still— The thought stalled as I caught the faintest flicker of energy clinging to the window's catch.

It was a goddamn *tell*. One that suggested the witch—and maybe even the demon—had both entered and exited through this window.

And while the fragment probably wouldn't lead me to the witch who'd magically unlocked this window and unleashed untold horror onto Gareth, it would at least give me some sense of him if our paths crossed again.

I very carefully approached the window, trying not to cause any sort of draft that would fragment the tiny tell any further. Once close, I covered my nose and mouth with one hand to prevent any chance of my breath disturbing the tell and then leaned in.

The ethereal piece of DNA held no familiarity, and there was a tiny bit of me that was relieved. I'd half expected Tris to be behind this atrocity as well, but this tell wasn't his.

There was, however, a trace of Okoro in its patterning. I carefully rolled off a glove, then reached out with one finger and gently touched the fragment's center. Its energy wrapped around my fingertip, briefly allowing me to tap into its secrets. There was definitely Okoro in its molecular setup, but it was entwined around something that was far darker. Something that spoke of ash and death.

It was also unclear whether the tell came from a man or a woman, which wasn't something I'd come across before.

Before I could gather anything else, the tell faded, leaving me with far more questions than I had answers.

"Mo's just arrived" came Luc's comment from the doorway. "Did you find anything?"

"Yeah, a tell."

"Big enough to track?"

"No, unfortunately. But it was from whoever broke in here."

"Not Tristan, I'm gathering?"

"No."

"For your sake, I'm glad."

"So am I." It might not make any sense, given he'd already proven himself willing and able to escort an innocent woman to her death, but I just didn't want to believe he'd betray me—betray our lifelong friendship—so easily. The man I'd grown up with *was* still there, even if he was now tainted by darkness. I really wanted to believe that, when push came to shove, he'd walk away from causing any actual harm to me or Max or Mo.

Which might be nothing more than a fool's hope, but still ...

Luc stopped beside me, his big, warm presence doing little to chase away the chill that seemed to have settled into my bones. "Is there anything odd about the witch who did this?"

I hesitated. "He or she is an Okoro, but there's an odd edge of darkness woven through their magical DNA."

"You weren't able to define gender?"

"Oddly, no."

He grunted. "Is it possible the darkness you sensed came simply from working with a demon?"

"This wasn't something that had simply rubbed off. It was ingrained."

He frowned. "Are you suggesting the murderer is part demon? Or even dark elf? Because you know that's impossible, right?"

"I once would have said Ainslyn having an open gateway into Darkside was impossible, and look how wrong that proved to be."

"Yes, but demons would rather eat humans than fuck them."

"The images on that gateway suggest otherwise."

"Only because they use it as a form of torture, and the human is generally consumed in the process."

"What about dark elves then? They're not only humanoid in form, but possess all the right anatomical bits."

"Yes, but there's never been any mention of such a cross happening—not in all history."

"That you know of."

"Blackbirds have spent eons protecting the crown from darkness in all its forms. If such a cross were possible, we'd surely know."

I wanted to believe that. I certainly didn't want to believe such an abomination could exist, let alone thrive, in this day and age. But I also couldn't ignore what instinct and training were telling me.

I crossed my arms and lightly rubbed them. From the room behind me came Mo's familiar voice.

"Why on earth would she—or he—be involved in destroying possible heirs?" I asked. "There's nothing she could gain by doing so. It's not like she can claim the sword herself, even if she is a direct descendant of the Witch King."

"A king always needs a queen," he commented. "The prestige and power that comes with such a title might be incentive enough."

He carefully unlatched the window and then slid it open. The night air swirled in, thick and cold with the scent of rain, but it was the snap of several magical strings that had my heart leaping—and not in a good way.

Henry's magic might still be protecting this place but the fact it had broken rather than bent around the window being opened said he was swiftly running out of strength.

"Mo?" I yelled. "You need to get in here."

She appeared in the doorway. "What's wrong?"

I stepped to one side and waved a hand toward the window. "It's Henry's magic protecting this room, not Gareth's—and his magic is now fracturing."

She narrowed her eyes, expression intent. "He's not

close ... but we need to get to him, and fast."

"Can you track him?" Jason asked.

"Via his tell, yes. We'll ring when we find him."

"There's no way you're going without us," Jason said. "This is our investigation—"

"And my damn family," Mo cut in. "So unless you can fly, you're out of luck on this one."

With that, she shifted shape and flew out the window. I swung my backpack around, pulled out my daggers, and quickly lashed them together. Then I shoved the pack at Luc and followed Mo out the window, flying hard to catch up with her.

The trail of Henry's fading magic led us over Lord's Cricket Ground and a large cemetery, but by the time we reached a long body of water, the delicate threads were so fragmented they were now drifting apart; we wouldn't be able to track them for much longer.

Without warning, Mo dove. I tucked my wings in close and followed, but the trailing daggers hampered the speed of my descent. She banked and swept through treetops before shifting shape near the ground and landing. I did the same, and then lunged forward to grab her as her damn moonboot snagged in a tree root.

She patted my hand absently. "Thanks. He's here somewhere—"

A scream rent the air, the sound one of fury more than pain. Henry, somewhere in the trees to our right.

Mo swore. "The demons have followed him here—go, Gwen. I'll sweep in from behind."

Demons. Plural. *Fuck.*

I drew Nex and Vita, threw the sheaths on the ground, and bolted across the small clearing, jumping a log and then crashing through the bushes beyond it. The demons would no doubt hear me, but that was exactly what I intended. It was far better they attacked me than finish the job on Henry. I darted around several trees and leapt thick tree roots, following the scent of ash now simply because the remaining wisps of Henry's tell were being swept away by the breeze.

The ground rose steeply and the brush got thicker. I raced on, the fierce light from the blades both lighting my way and letting me know just how close I was to darkness.

Another scream rent the air, but this time a fierce stab of pure energy followed it.

Henry, using the De Montfort ability to take life rather than heal it.

I crested the hilltop. Saw, in a swift glance, Henry on the ground but backed up to the standing stone in the center of the clearing. Saw the ashes of two demons fluttering to the ground at his feet and three more break through the cover of the trees to our left and fly toward him.

I screamed in fury and ran at them. Though their speed barely altered, two immediately twisted around and came at me while the third continued toward Henry.

I raised the daggers, clapped the blades together, and swept the twin forks of lightning in a bright arc, ashing the first two demons before sweeping the light across the clearing to destroy the third.

Movement, behind me.

I twisted around, caught a glimpse of scaly brown hurtling through the air. Dropped and rolled, coming in underneath the demon and slashing up high with both blades. Their tips cut through scaly flesh as easily as they might butter, and blood and guts sheeted down. I swore, wiped the stinking muck from my face and eyes, and then scrambled to my feet as yet more screams rent the air.

Three more demons were charging toward Henry.

I ran, with every ounce of speed I could muster, toward them.

Mo got there first.

She shifted shape, hit the ground in a crouch, and slammed her hand *into* the soil. Power surged and the earth rose up in a wave, catching the demons in its swell and then sweeping them away—sweeping them down. Smothering them within the earth.

She remained crouched, her gaze scanning the area and the ground trembling under her touch.

No more demons appeared. After a moment, she relaxed and climbed a little unsteadily to her feet. I grabbed her elbow again, holding on until she nodded an okay.

"How many more were there out in the woods?" I asked.

"Only two, but they were browns and easily destroyed."

Especially for someone who had such power at her fingertips ... "I don't suppose you'd care to explain what you just did?"

She frowned. "You know what I just did—used magic to destroy demons."

"That was Chen elemental magic, not ours. Luc's right, isn't he? You *are* a mage."

She grimaced. "Some might call me that, but it's not a title I use or want. It comes with too many connotations."

I raised my eyebrows. "What sort of connotations?"

She waved the question away. "Now is not the time to be discussing this. Let's go save Henry."

Exasperation surged, but she was right—Henry had to come before the need for answers. I spun and followed her across to the standing stone.

Henry's eyes were now closed, and his face an odd

waxy color. Blood matted his dark hair and covered the front of his dress shirt, and his breathing was fast and uneven. His hands were on his stomach; through his spread and bloody fingers I could see not only a torn red cummerbund but also the intestines he was attempting to hold in. How he'd escaped the house, let alone mustered enough energy to smoke two demons, spoke volumes of his determination to survive.

Now we just had to keep him that way.

Mo knelt in front of him and clucked her tongue. "You're a right mess, aren't you, laddie?"

Life stirred behind closed eyelids. "Mo?"

The question was barely audible, but it nevertheless had relief surging. If he was conscious enough to speak, then Mo had a good chance of saving him.

"Yes, it's me. Give me the rundown, laddie, and I'll fix what I can."

As Henry obeyed and Mo began the long task of healing the worst of his wounds, I grabbed my phone and used Google Maps to find out exactly where we were, then rang Luc.

"Is Henry alive?" he immediately said.

"Yes." I gave him our location. "Mo's healing what she can, but he's still going to need medical attention. And given the number of demons that were chasing him, he's also going to need one hell of a protection detail."

"I can arrange that. Hang on." He put me on hold for several seconds. "Right, there's a specialized recovery team on the way. Man in charge is Bishop Lancaster. He'll get Henry to a private medical facility and arrange twenty-four-hour protection."

"And you?"

"I'll meet you in Ainslyn tomorrow."

Meaning he was heading first to the private facility so he could question Henry. "Don't forget to bring back my pack. There's stuff in there I need."

"It's in the storage compartment already."

"Thanks. See you in the morning."

I hung up, shoved my phone away, then stripped off my jacket and used the inside of it to wipe off the worst of the blood and gore. Which still left the stink, but there wasn't much I could do about that, given I didn't have a change of clothes and wasn't about to run around near naked.

After another ten minutes or so, Mo's magic faded and she sat back on her heels with a sigh. Henry's guts were no longer threatening to spill past his fingers, and his breathing had eased dramatically. He still had deep puncture wounds across his chest, a bloody left arm, and a thick cut that stretched from his left temple to the back of his head, but his skin color was healthier. At the very least, he no longer looked like death warmed up.

"That's the best I can do." The tremor in Mo's voice indicated just how far she'd pushed her strength. "Now, dear boy, you'd better tell us exactly what happened."

Henry didn't immediately respond, but tears edged past the corners of his eyes and trickled down his cheeks.

"Gareth—"

"We know." Mo shifted position, resting her back against the standing stone and then gently twining her fingers through his. "We were there."

"You warned us. We should have—"

"Regrets won't change anything, laddie. You need to tell us what happened, starting with how the demon got in."

He took a deep, shuddering breath. "Someone unlocked my protective spell, and so damn proficiently I didn't even sense the breach."

"Where were you?"

"Downstairs waiting for an Uber. By the time I got upstairs—" He stopped, a sob escaping. "Why would anyone do that? To Gareth, of all people?"

"Answers are the one thing we're short on at the moment," Mo said. "But trust me, that will change."

"Good." He swiped at the tears with a bloody left hand. "If you do catch the bitch who held the demon's leash, I want—"

"You saw her?" I cut in.

He looked up. His blue eyes were so bloodshot there was very little white left—a result of having been pushed to his utter limits, both magically and physically.

"I'm not entirely sure whether it was a him or a her; could have been either, in truth. I'm just saying 'her' for expediency."

"Can you describe her then?"

He hesitated. "Her facial features were Okoro, but her skin had a grayish tint, her long hair was white, and her ears had an odd point to them."

So I hadn't been imagining it. We *were* dealing with some sort of crossbreed.

"How did you escape?" Mo asked.

"They'd left the en suite window open. I was out the damn thing and thought I was safe when the demon lunged at me." He grimaced. "That's how I ended up gutted."

And why there was no blood inside the bathroom or on the window frame. It didn't explain why the window was shut when we'd found it, however.

"It's a miracle you even could fly in that state, laddie."

"It wasn't a miracle—it was simply luck. The demon's claws somehow went under the cummerbund rather than slicing right through it. As you can see, it did eventually fray open, but it kept things intact long enough for me to shift shape and fly away."

"Do you know how they found you here?" I asked.

"Tracking spell," Mo said. "I destroyed its remnants before I did the healing thing."

"I have no idea when it was attached," Henry commented. "I didn't feel anything hit when I was flying away."

"That is not surprising, given the situation."

"No." Another tear tracked down his cheek. "What happens now?"

I squatted down in front of him so he didn't have to keep looking up. The slash across his head might not be pouring blood, but he had to have one hell of a headache. "You're going into protective custody."

He frowned. "I'm thinking the police won't be able to stop this bitch if she uncovers my location."

"The police won't, but the Preternatural Division—who are a part of the NCA—will."

"Never heard of them."

"They have some of the strongest witches on their books," Mo said. "You'll be safe with them."

"What about Ada?" he suddenly asked. "Is she okay? Is she in any danger?"

"We don't believe so, but I've already spoken to her," Mo said. "She's quietly disappearing for a few days, just to be on the safe side."

"But if she stays with friends or family, she risks being tracked down."

"Which is why we've booked her a little place up north under an alias. She'll keep to herself and not contact anyone. I've a friend who'll keep an eye on her and act as an intermediary for any phone calls that need to be made."

His expression was a mix of pain and resignation. "I know it's better if I don't see or talk to her but she's the only sibling I've got left—"

"And we need to keep it that way," Mo said firmly. "You need to remain out of contact. It's very possible that if they found her, they'd use her as bait to force you out of hiding."

"But why?" The edge in his voice spoke of both anger and confusion. "Why would anyone want me? Why did they want Gareth? Christ, he was practically a saint compared—"

He cut the rest of that sentence off, but it was pretty obvious where he'd been heading—*compared to Max*. And he was right. But that didn't mean my brother was any safer from death—in fact, Gareth's death now doubled the danger to Max. Whether or not Jackie was right in thinking my mother's branch of the Okoro line ran with the blood of Luis Valeriun, the gray-skinned bitch was going after them ... what few of them there were left, anyway.

Henry sucked in a somewhat shaky breath, then blew it out slowly. "Just keep her safe, Mo. Promise me."

"I'll do my best, Henry. That's all I can promise."

"I guess that'll have to do."

He closed his eyes and rested his head back against the stone. Mo glanced at me. "How soon is help getting here?"

I glanced at my watch. "Probably another ten minutes."

"You want to head up to the road and wait for them? I'll keep guard here."

"You don't think there'll be more attacks, do you?"

"Hard to say—especially given the overkill of sending nine demons after one man."

"Then perhaps—"

"Gwen, I'm fine. It'll take more than the magic I've expended here to fully erase my energy stores."

She still looked rather drawn, but I knew better than to say anything. I handed her my daggers, then took to the wing, heading first to the clearing where we'd initially landed to collect the knife sheaths before flying over to the road. Two black vans rolled up about eight minutes later. I somewhat warily stepped back into the trees as they came to a halt a few yards away. The man who jumped out of the first van was a short, somewhat rotund figure with thick ginger hair and merry blue eyes. He wasn't a witch but there was odd energy about him that suggested he wasn't without power, either. What that power was, I couldn't say.

He strode toward me and held out his hand. My skin prickled at the contact, and though the sensation wasn't unpleasant, I had a vague feeling it was connected to the energy I couldn't place. "I'm guessing you're Gwen De Montfort. I'm Bishop Lancaster. We're here to pick up your cousin."

"Excellent," I said. "But I'd like to see some form of identification before I take you anywhere near him."

He chuckled softly. "Lucas said you'd probably say that."

He reached into his pocket and pulled out his wallet. His credentials looked legit, even though I'd never actually viewed a Preternatural Division badge before.

"Why the black vans? And where's the ambulance?"

"The second van is fully equipped," he said. "No matter what state he's in, we can cope."

Relief swept me. Mo might have healed the worst of his wounds, but it was good to know that if he did take a bad turn, they could keep him alive. "He's located in the forest—we'll have to walk there."

He nodded and motioned to the second van. Three men got out and approached with a stretcher and a full medical kit. All three flashed their IDs, which made me think Luc had been quite clear about reassuring me they were the real deal.

I led the way back to Henry. Mo's gaze scanned the four men and then she nodded, as if in satisfaction. "Thank you for your prompt arrival, gentlemen."

Bishop held out his hand and introduced himself. Mo's energy output flickered when she clasped his hand, though whether it was in response to that strange tingling I'd felt or something else, I wasn't sure. She ran through Henry's injuries and then told them what she'd healed.

Bishop's gaze widened. "It's a wonder he survived all that."

"He's a De Montfort. We're built tough."

"Obviously." Bishop motioned his medics to proceed. "I'm afraid that until you're given clearance, we can't divulge the location of our hospital unit. But Lucas will be sent updates, and we'll get you in there as soon as possible."

"At this point in time," Mo said. "It's probably safer for all involved if we remain away. Updates will be fine."

Bishop nodded, then turned and followed his men from the clearing. I glanced at Mo. "What was his power?"

"He's a reader."

"Meaning a telepath?"

She shook her head. "Telepaths read direct thoughts. Readers get the measure of a person via skin-to-skin contact."

Suggesting that's what he'd been doing when we'd clasped hands. "Then why does his energy feel oddly dangerous?"

"Because most readers can also project their own energy into another person. It can have catastrophic results."

"Remind me never to get on his bad side, then." I studied her for a minute. "There was a quaint-looking tavern not far from here—why don't we go grab something to eat and drink before we fly home?"

She arched an eyebrow. "Are you cossetting me?"

"Possibly. But it's been one hell of a day and I think we both need to replenish before we do anything else."

She patted my arm. "A sensible reply, but you forgot one major problem."

I frowned. "What's that?"

"You stink worse than a demon's armpit."

I closed my eyes and swore. She chuckled softly. "Home it is."

"Just take it slow—"

"I'm fine, Gwen."

"Yeah, but I'll be carrying the damn daggers and it's been one hell of a long day."

"Neither of us believe *that* to be anything more than a lie to protect my ego, but we'll run with it. Go."

Once I'd sheathed my daggers and loosely tied them, I shifted shape and swept skyward. It took far too many hours to get home, and by the time we did, I was exhausted. Despite her protests that she was fine, I helped Mo upstairs, ran her a bath, and then made her a hot toddy before taking care of my needs.

With my leathers in the old boiler and the stench of demon washed from my skin, I picked up my phone and tried to ring my brother. As per usual, the call went to voice-mail, so I left a message stating I had urgent news about Gareth and Henry and that he needed to ring me as soon as he could.

With that done, I made myself a whiskey-laced hot chocolate and returned to Mo's room. It was very much a reflection of the woman herself—a riot of bohemian-inspired color and textiles. The large, rather ornate bath took pride of place underneath the window, while the toilet and basin sat behind a half wall in the corner. I plonked down on her bed and sipped my drink. I'd overdone the whiskey and it burned all the way down but had little effect on the ice that had settled in my stomach.

"Did you and Barney manage to talk to the brunette Tris met with at the hotel?"

"No—her room was cleaned out by the time we got there."

"When did she check out?"

"She didn't—she skipped out without paying the bill."

"The hotel would have taken an impression of her credit card, though, so were you able to at least get her name?"

"Jane Smith."

"If that's her real name, I'll give up whiskey."

Mo chuckled. "There's no danger in that—the payment was rejected. Apparently, the card had been canceled."

"Did they get an address or phone number when she checked in?"

"Yes; the phone rings out and the address is a false one —a young family lives there and have never seen or heard of the woman."

"And you believe that?"

"Yes. There was no lie in her words or fear in her eyes."

While that was good, it nevertheless left us with another dead end. "I wonder how she knew you were coming to see her? Do you think someone tipped her off?"

"Possibly." Mo shrugged. "Barney talked to his daughter over the phone, so it's possible someone overheard and passed it on."

Possible, but unlikely, her tone implied. "What about Lance Okoro? Did you contact him about the family bible? It might be the only way we're going to get to the truth of Gareth's murder."

She nodded. "He sent a courier across to get it immediately, but the bible wasn't where it was supposed to be."

"Meaning we're too late."

"Possibly." She grimaced and raised her foot, using her toes to flick on the hot water tap. "Although he's of the opinion it's merely been misplaced, given there's been no indication of a breach."

"There wouldn't be if Tris was responsible."

"He only returned to London today—or yesterday, as it now is. I doubt, however, the Okoro bible is the reason behind this particular attack."

"Then what the hell is?"

"It might just be a precautionary measure, especially given they're also looking for the Valeriun bible."

"But why are they even searching for them? Why are they killing indirect heirs when direct descents of the Aquitaine kings remain alive?"

"*That* is a jolly good question." She held out her now empty mug. "Another wouldn't go astray."

I put my drink on the nearby bedside table and then grabbed her cup and headed out. "What did you think of Henry's description of the woman who attacked him?"

I raised my voice slightly, even though Mo's hearing was probably better than mine.

"I'm thinking your thoughts are probably more interesting."

I doubted that. I poured hot water into her glass, then added the whiskey and honey and quickly stirred. Once the honey was fully dissolved, I picked the glass up and returned to the bedroom. "The fragment of tell snagged on the window catch suggested she was either part demon or dark elf. Luc said crossbreeds couldn't exist, but Henry's description suggests otherwise."

She accepted the toddy with a nod of thanks. "There's a long history of dark elves stealing human women to refresh their own bloodlines. And while it's normally rare to find crossbreeds—or halflings as they're more commonly known —outside the darkness in which they're born, they do exist. They're also hermaphrodites and able to function as either male or female as they desire."

Which also fit in with what Henry had said. "I'm not finding the term 'normally' comforting. Not in this situation."

"And you shouldn't. I rather suspect we're going to find quite a few more of them before this is all over."

"Fabulous." *Not.* "How on earth could any human woman live long enough in Darkside to give birth?"

"Elves are not only capable of great magic but are also great influencers. And weak minds are easily swayed."

"Yes, but we're talking Darkside here. You know, the place many call hell?"

"Only fools and religious folk believe it to be so. As I've said, it is simply a dark reflection of this world."

"Filled with twisted, bloodthirsty, crazy beings."

Mo's chuckle drifted softly on the warm air. "In case you've not seen the news of late, there're more than enough of those types existing right here in the light."

A fact I really couldn't dispute. "Okay, so presuming said women gave birth and their halflings somehow survived into adulthood, why aren't they subject to the same restrictions that the dark elves have here?"

"There are theories suggesting that while human blood

does steal magic from dark souls just as it does witch, it also offers halflings protection against the light."

"Whose theories might they be? Yours?"

She chuckled again. "No. There was reportedly one who existed in Layton's court. It's even said her wickedness is the reason he combined the two thrones and ended true witch rule in England."

I raised my eyebrows. "How could a halfling get past a court full of witches? The darkness in her tell would have given the game away in an instant."

"Unless she inherited the elf ability to influence."

"Even the greatest influencer wouldn't be able to fool an entire court, surely? Besides, this particular halfling was capable of magic."

"Not necessarily—the tracker on Henry was a simple one and held no hint of darkness in its strings. I think it likely she purchased rather than made it."

I scrubbed a hand through my still damp hair. "Then how in the hell do we catch this bitch?"

"By tracking down whomever she's dealing with."

"Because that's going to be *so* much easier."

My voice was dry, and Mo smiled. "We start with the one real lead we actually have—Tristan Chen. You did get some of his hair when you went to his hotel earlier, didn't you?"

I nodded. "It's in the backpack Luc still has."

"Good." Her voice was crisp. Decisive. "Then once he arrives in the morning, we'll find your treacherous ex and make the bastard talk."

The sharp ringing of the phone dragged me from a deep

sleep. I groaned softly and groped around on the bedside table for several seconds before I found and answered it.

"Good morning, dearest sister—how are you this fine morning?"

I forced open an eye. It was met by darkness. "It's not morning here yet, fuckwit, and you well know it. What the hell are you doing up at this hour?"

He chuckled. Evilly. "I haven't gone to bed yet. What's this about Gareth and Henry? What saintly thing have they done now?"

Gotten themselves dead ... or close to. I rubbed a hand across my eyes. "You sitting down?"

"No, but I very soon intend to be lying in the arms of a gorgeous man, so be a dear and get to the point."

I took a deep breath, gathering courage, and then told him what had happened.

He was silent for a long time, and then softly said, "Fuck."

"Yeah."

"How's Henry?"

"He's alive. More than that, I can't say. The Preternatural boys whisked him to one of their secret hospitals."

"Under full witch guard, no doubt."

"Yes. But the attack makes no sense, Max. None of this is making any sense."

"It does if the De Montfort link to kings is stronger than everyone thinks."

"If that were true, there'd be some evidence of it somewhere. Besides, everyone is searching for the Okoro and Valeriun family bibles, not the De Montfort."

"That's because the De Montfort bible was destroyed decades ago."

"You knew about that?"

"I asked Mo about it a few years ago," he said. "What's she planning to do now?"

"Go after the bitch behind it all, obviously."

"But how? Even *she* can't track someone without some form of their DNA." He paused. "The halfling didn't leave behind a tell or anything else trackable, did she?"

"There was a tell fragment, but it disintegrated before Mo got there. If there was anything else, I dare say the Preternatural boys will let us know." Or rather, Luc would.

He grunted. "Then how the hell is she planning to find the halfling?"

"Via the one person who seems to be the connecting force—Tris."

There was a long note of silence. "Tris is looking for the bibles, true, but that doesn't mean he's involved any deeper."

"Except he is." I quickly told him about the hecatomb and the woman Tris had driven there. "He's responsible for at least one murder, Max. Given the number of bones in that place, it's very possible he's responsible for a whole lot more."

"*Fuck.*" It was a short, sharp explosion of anger. "I can't believe he was—" He cut the rest off and took a deep breath. "You're right—there's no other option now. He has to be caught and questioned. You're doing so today?"

"Yes. As soon as Lucas arrives."

"Good." He paused. "Given what's happened to our saintly cousins, what're Mo's thoughts on the likelihood of darkness drifting my way?"

"Given the list we retrieved from Jackie's—"

"What list?" he cut in sharply.

"She was doing some sort of Okoro family tree. You,

Gareth, and Henry were all on it, along with some guy named Jules."

"Jules Okoro? Never heard of him."

"He wasn't directly related to Mom's family."

He grunted. "Are any other family members on it?"

"No, thank god. It's bad enough that you are."

"Well, at least there's one more person between me and death."

He sounded far too cheerful for my liking. "Hey, Gareth and Henry didn't take any of this too seriously either, and look what happened to them."

He sighed. "I promise to be careful and keep a low profile. "

"If that's even possible for you."

He chuckled softly. "You'd be surprised."

I would indeed. "Seriously, watch your back, Max. And make sure you send me a text every morning and evening, just so I know you're okay."

"That will get tedious very quickly."

"Better tedious than dead, bro."

"You do realize that by the time you *don't* get a text from me, I could be dead and there's nothing you could do about it?"

His tone was dry, and I couldn't help smiling. "So you're volunteering to text every hour?"

He snorted. "Morning and night it is. Just be sure to take your own advice, sis. I can't protect you on this one, and the Blackbirds' priorities will always lie with the heirs rather than the sister of an heir."

"I'm aware of that."

"Good. Chat later."

"Enjoy your gorgeous man."

"Oh, I intend to."

At least one of us was, I thought, and shoved the phone back onto the bedside table. Sleep, however, proved elusive and, hearing someone moving around downstairs, I threw the covers off and shivered my way into trackpants, a thick woolly sweater, and my zombie slippers.

It wasn't, as I'd expected, Mo, but rather Luc. He wore old leather boots, jeans that hugged him in all the right places, and a woolen sweater that was the same glorious shade as his eyes. Max's last comment rose to taunt me, and I couldn't help feeling a little envious of him right now.

Luc's gaze scanned me briefly, leaving in its wake a trail of prickly heat that did not help my mood.

"Good morning," he said, his tone warm and soft.

"It's definitely morning, but calling it good could be a stretch." I grabbed the kettle and filled it. "You've obviously still got the key."

"I do." He put a dob of butter into the frying pan and let it sizzle. "Thought it would be easier than constantly knocking and then being forced to hold a conversation out on the pavement."

"It's definitely easier, but nowhere near as amusing. How's Henry?"

He poured the mix into the pan—he was making omelets, I realized. The fact he could cook only added to his appeal—especially when combined with the whole unshaven thing he had going at the moment. It was pretty damn sexy.

"Henry's stitched up, drugged up, and still alive as of an hour ago."

"I gather you and Jason questioned him last night?"

"Yes, although I doubt we got anything more than you or Mo did."

"Probably not." I paused. "Did he tell you about the woman?"

Luc flipped the omelet, added ham and cheese, and then glanced at me. "It appears you were right."

"And it's the one time I really wished I wasn't." I leaned against the counter and crossed my arms. "Did Jason or his team pull anything out of Gareth's bedroom that could help us track her?"

"The only DNA found was either Gareth's or the demon's. The woman must have been fully covered up and prepared."

"I know she got in through the window, but from everything Mo's said about halflings, they're human in shape and can't fly like many demons. So, how did she escape? She can't have jumped out of the window—aside from the fact it was closed when we found it, it's a three-story drop to the ground."

"We have no idea who closed the window, but we do know she went up, not down—we found a tie-off point. We're not exactly sure what happened to her after that."

"Huh." I glanced around as Mo's door opened and she stepped out. She looked a whole lot stronger this morning, despite the shadows under her eyes. "Would you like a tea?"

"That," she said, her severe tone at odds with the amusement lurking in her expression, "is a very stupid question for someone I've raised since practically a babe."

I grinned. "Not really. Not considering just how often you change things up."

"Tea is the one constant in my life, as you're well aware." She sat down at the table. "And one of those omelets would make a fine accompaniment, young man."

Luc smiled, slid the omelet onto a plate, and then handed it to her. "It's ham and cheese."

"Perfect." She accepted the cutlery I gave her with a nod. "Did you bring our backpack?"

"It's sitting over on the coffee table."

"Good." She popped some omelet in her mouth, and something close to bliss crossed her expression. "Gwen, if you don't marry this man, I damn well will. This omelet is close to perfection."

Luc chuckled. "A compliment from the woman who issues so few immediately has me wondering what she wants."

Her offended expression was at odds with the devious twinkle in her eyes. "It's a sad state of affairs when a simple compliment raises suspicions."

"In this case, I think it could be justified."

"Possibly." She waved her knife somewhat grandly. "But we'll get to that after I finish this divine omelet."

I pulled three mugs out of the cupboard and began making our tea and his coffee. "Finding Tris's location via a spell will be easy enough, but how are we going to restrain him? He'll be suspicious the minute he sees me. No matter what you think of him, Mo, he's not dumb, and he knows how rarely I leave Ainslyn."

"He might well be suspicious, but I doubt he'll react immediately. And if he does—" She shrugged. "His magic can't actually hurt you."

"Yes, but let's not forget, he *is* physically stronger than me."

"While that may be true, there's more to fighting than mere strength," Luc said. "I've seen you fight. I'm not sure I'd back *me* against you if it came down to it."

I snorted softly. "A lovely compliment, but one that is total bullshit."

"Not necessarily." He handed me the next omelet, his

expression serious. "You're fast, your fighting style is unconventional, and you don't react as most would expect."

"The 'most' in that statement being men," Mo observed with some amusement. "Simply because most men are *always* underestimating women. Tris will be no different, my dear."

I transferred the drinks across to the table and then sat down to eat my omelet. It was, as Mo had already observed, quite divine. "That still doesn't address the point of how we're going to capture him. The minute he sees Luc, he'll react."

Luc frowned. "Why? We've not yet—" He paused. "He saw me entering the shop the night of the storm?"

I nodded. "I said you were Mo's guest, but I'm pretty sure he suspected the truth."

"It shouldn't make that much difference," Mo said. "Once you've distracted him, our Blackbird can take him down the old-fashioned way."

I raised my eyebrows. "The old-fashioned way being?"

"Blow darts, of course."

I laughed but cut it short when I realized she wasn't joking. "Seriously? In this day and age?"

"In this day and age"—Luc plated the last omelet then joined us at the table—"a dart gun is a simple and easy method of taking someone down without raising any major suspicions."

"Except darts in real life don't work like they do in the movies. It can take up to ten minutes for the drug to take effect."

"Which is where you'll come in," Mo said. "Tris has never been one to refuse a free feed—take him to a nearby café or something."

I didn't think it would be that easy but, given the only

real certainty in this whole situation was our ability to find him, I guessed we had no option but to play it by ear.

I finished the omelet, then, as Mo began preparations to make the tracker, went upstairs to do my teeth and pull on warmer clothes. Once I'd found my spare bike jacket, I dug out my stone knife from the back of the drawer and strapped on its wrist sheath. Then I grabbed my wallet and phone and headed downstairs.

Mo had woven Tris's hair into a ball of gently pulsing golden strings. "He's in Nottingham."

"What the hell is there?" I asked. "Aside from a fictional sheriff, that is."

"The High Sheriff of Nottinghamshire *is* an actual position that still exists, although it's mostly ceremonial these days," Mo commented. "And I think if Tris is sniffing around the place, there's either an heir living there or perhaps one of the bibles they were looking for."

Luc's expression was grim. "It's the former."

Anger surged through me; at Tris for stepping so thoroughly into darkness, and at me for not sensing something was so desperately wrong sooner. Maybe if I had, I could have changed ... nothing. Absolutely nothing. Tris had never been one to be swayed from a course of action once he'd set his heart on it. "Is the heir already under guard? Or is he another indirect heir?"

"He's indirect; I'll contact Jason and ask him to send people over."

I returned my gaze to the pulsing sphere sitting in front of Mo. "I take it Luc will be using that?"

"I've already tuned it to his energy. It hasn't got a very long range though, so you might have to cruise around for a while before it activates. Oh, and Betty lives there now, so feel free to use her as an excuse if Tris initially questions your presence. I'll word her up."

I nodded and glanced at Luc. "We'd better go. If he gets wind of the protection detail, he might just leave the area."

Mo followed us across to the top of the stairs. "Once you've secured him, give me a call. I'll fly in and get the truth out of the little bastard."

"Will do."

We headed out. Once Luc had sent his text, I said, "I'm surprised you weren't annoyed by Mo's insistence she be the one to question Tris."

"I expected it." He tossed me a helmet. "Besides, she's probably forgotten more about interrogation than I've ever been taught."

Undoubtedly, given at one point very early on in her life—well before Max and I had ever come onto the scene—she'd worked for the High Witch Council, which had once been the equivalent of the Privy Council and responsible for advising the king and his executive on matters of the state. These days they were little more than an oversight council who settled disputes between witch houses. Of course, said disputes—while rare—were often brutal, bloody, and complicated, and only the most powerful spells could cut through all the crap and magic to ferret out the truth. Mo had been one of five witches tasked with ferreting.

It took us nearly two and a half hours to reach Nottingham, thanks to road works on the A50, but the finder spell came to life as we entered the city and guided Luc through a myriad of streets. Eventually he stopped not far from what looked to be an old market square.

"According to this," he said, "Tristan's coming from the right, walking toward that Costa Coffee place."

I studied the red-and-black building for a moment. "How are you going to dart him without raising suspicions? It's rather open here."

Not to mention busy.

"I'll loop around him and dart from behind. No one will see me or the gun."

"But won't Tris, at the very least, sense you manipulating light?"

"Did you, up on the island? Or in the King's Tower?"

"Well, no, but—"

"It'll be fine, Gwen. Stop worrying."

"I can't help what is part of my nature." I stripped off my jacket; I couldn't risk Tris recognizing it. I might not have worn it too often unless we'd gone riding, but he knew well enough I didn't own my own bike and would wonder who I'd come here with. "How are we going to play this once the drug takes effect?"

"If I've the dose right, he should simply fall asleep."

"Someone suddenly falling asleep in the middle of conversation *will* attract attention." My voice was dry. "And what happens if, once he feels drowsy, he decides to leave?"

"Then I'll follow." He briefly grabbed my hand, his fingers so warm against mine. "This will work. Trust me."

I did trust him. I just didn't trust the fact that things would go the way we wished them to.

But I squeezed his fingers in appreciation and then headed across the road, weaving through the morning crowd until I got to the corner. After briefly scanning the entire area, I turned right. A few seconds later, the crowd briefly parted, and I spotted Tris. He wore a hoodie, dark jeans, and old boots, all of which were caked with grime, and he walked with his head down and his hands shoved deep into his pockets. He looked ... different. Defeated, somehow.

Or maybe that was imagination at work again.

I took another of those deep breaths that did little to calm the inner butterflies and then strode toward him. When I was close enough, I said, adding a touch of disbelief in my voice, "Tris? Is that you?"

His head shot up, and an odd mix of consternation and pleasure raced across his expression. What lingered after, however, was a decided frostiness.

"Gwen? What the hell are you doing here?"

"I was just about to ask you the same question."

I stopped an arm's distance from him—close enough to see the utter tiredness in his dirt-smudged face. Close enough to see his clothes were damp, and to smell the mix of sweat and earth on him. The latter had me wondering who he'd been with—and what they'd been up to—given Tris didn't have the Chen ability to move or control earth.

"Had a night job."

"It's not exactly night now, my friend."

He grimaced, but his gaze remained on mine and was filled with suspicion. "Which is why I'm now heading back to the Plaza and bed. What about you?"

"Mo wanted to visit a friend," I said. "I'm playing chauffeur for the day."

He scanned the immediate area with narrowed eyes. "She's obviously not near here."

"No—she's at Betty's." My smile felt forced; I hoped he didn't notice. "The last thing I wanted was to listen to them gasbagging about the past, so I left them to it. I haven't been to Nottingham before, so it's a good chance to look around."

"Betty's living here now?"

"Well, if she wasn't, we'd hardly be here, would we?" I waved a hand toward Costa's. "Would you like to join me for cake, or do you have to be somewhere? Like a shower?"

He didn't react to the—perhaps a little forced—amusement in my question. "It's quite a coincidence, isn't it?"

"What is?" I hoped like hell he couldn't hear the rapid pounding of my heart. It seemed abnormally loud to me. "Me asking you for cake?"

"More the fact that you're here in Nottingham the same time as I am, and walking past the same Costa."

"Meaning what? That I deliberately sought you out?" I snorted. "Seriously, Tris, I'm not *that* desperate to sleep with you again."

"We both know that Mo is more than capable of getting anywhere she desires under her own steam, so why would she ask you to drive her?"

"She's ninety-five, Tris, and she recently broke her goddamn leg." I threw up my hands and stepped back. "But fine, don't fucking believe me. I'll just go get myself some cake, and you can take your foul-smelling clothes and your goddamn suspicions back to your hotel room alone."

I spun and strode toward the door, my heart racing and all mental fingers crossed that I hadn't taken things a step too far.

For too many seconds, I thought I had.

But as I reached for the door, he grabbed my arm and stopped me. "I'm sorry. It's been a shit night. If you can stand the grime and the smell, coffee and cake would be great."

I raised my eyebrows. The last thing I actually needed was to go inside before Luc had darted him. "Are you sure? Because, seriously, if you're going to be all grumpy and taciturn, I'd rather eat alone. I'm not in the mood for your nonsense right now."

"I'm sorry. Really, I am. A decent cup of coffee with an old friend will definitely be an improvement over—" He cut

221

the rest of the sentence off and slapped at his back. "Fuck, something just bit me."

Thank *god* for that. I forced a note of amusement into my voice. "What?"

"I don't fucking know. Probably one of the goddamn beetles that were crawling all over the place." He turned around. "Can you see anything on my back?"

"Something other than the six-inch tarantula crawling down your spine, you mean?"

"I'm being serious here."

"And you think I'm not?"

"Gwen, please. It's burning."

Which suggested he might be having a reaction to whatever drug Luc had used on the dart. If he was, then it was likely he'd leave sooner rather than later. "Stop fidgeting and let me check."

He immediately did so. I pressed my fingers across his shoulders, and then down his spine, covertly removing and pocketing the small dart in the process. "There's really nothing here, Tris."

"Are you sure it's not a damn beetle?" He half turned. "Because it felt—"

The rest of his words cut off and moisture sprayed across my face. I frowned and wiped at it, and saw, in a moment of utter horror, that it was blood. My gaze jerked back to Tris; I saw the hole in his head, and the blood, and bits of bone and god knows what else oozing from it.

He'd been shot—and killed—between one word and another.

TEN

He didn't collapse. Not immediately. He simply stood there, his expression ... odd.

Then, without sound, he crumpled to the ground at my feet.

For several seconds, I didn't move. Couldn't move.

I just stared at the man who'd been both friend and lover as his blood dripped from my chin.

A scream rent the air.

Not mine, though part of me certainly wanted to.

Another joined it, and the crowd surrounding us swelled. As a man pushed past me with a curt "I'm a doctor," I somehow reined in my horror and disbelief and stepped back through the immediate press of people. I couldn't save Tris, but I could certainly catch his murderer ... if I was fast enough.

I scanned the buildings on the other side of the road. The shot must have come from up high, because if anyone had produced a handgun in a crowded street, there would have been reactions. And if the shooter *had* been a passerby, they surely would have done a body shot rather than head—

it might not have killed him instantly, but it would have been safer.

I couldn't see anything untoward on either the rooftops or in the windows of the building opposite, but would I, if this was a professional hit?

A hand clamped my wrist, and I reacted instinctively, reaching across to grab my assailant's pinkie and use it as a lever, twisting his whole hand up and around. The soft curse that followed had me quickly releasing.

Luc.

"Oh, sorry."

"My fault." Though his voice was flat, anger practically vibrated from every pore. Not at me, but rather the situation, I suspected. "I should have learned the first time. This way."

I followed him out of the still-gathering crowd. "Did you see where the shot came from?"

"No, but the trajectory suggests the other side of the square. Can you scout?"

"Yes, but wouldn't they be gone by now?"

"Probably, but we still have to try. If you see anything suspicious, wait for me. Don't go in alone."

I nodded and, after a quick look around to see if anyone was paying attention, shifted shape and flew skywards. Pigeons scattered as my shadow raced across them, filling the sky with a cloud of gray. They briefly obscured my vision but ultimately saved my life; the bird in front of me exploded into a bloody mass of bone and feathers.

I swerved sharply and arrowed toward the bus shelters lining the side road. I'd barely reached the first one when its glass exploded; as the glittering shards cut through the air, people screamed and ran. I rose, keeping close to the underside of the building's awning, hoping that, despite my light plumage, it would be more difficult for the shooter to spot me. The back of another bus shelter disintegrated, and just for an instant, I spotted something glinting in a dormer on the top floor of the department store across the road. The shooter, either shifting position or leaving.

A third shelter was shot out. Any minute now, a bullet might do to me what it did to that pigeon ... I forced the fear down and concentrated on getting out of his range as quickly as possible.

I reached the end of the building and climbed skyward, fear so thick in my throat I could barely breathe. No shots chased after me.

Either I was now out of sight or he'd left.

I swept over the department store's roof, saw the dormer window, open and empty, and arrowed in fast—only to slam beak first into a net that had been stretched across the back of the dormer. I crashed to the floor, the shock reverberating through my body forcing a change into human form. For too many seconds, I simply lay there, the netting wrapped tightly around my body, making it difficult to move, to breathe, even as I waited for a bullet to tear through my skull as easily as it had Tris's.

The kill never came.

Even as relief stirred, fear rose. The mere fact that a net had been strung across this window meant he'd been prepared to counter a shifter ... but how could he have even known I'd be here?

How, how, how?

The sharp sound of retreating footsteps dragged my attention back.

The shooter ... he couldn't be allowed to escape.

I sucked in a deep breath, then flicked my knife down into my hand and quickly cut the net from my limbs. Once free, I reached for the shifting magic again and then paused. Flight might be faster, but as a blackbird I couldn't open doors, and surely the first thing the shooter would do was head into the store and get lost in the crowd.

I thrust upright and ran through the dusty, box-filled room. After punching through a set of swinging exit doors, I paused, head cocked as I listened for the footsteps. They were coming from the nearby set of stairs, heading down just as I'd guessed.

I raced after him, taking the steps two and three at a time, my speed reckless. Two flights down, the sound of footsteps was lost under the babble of noise now coming from the store, but on the next landing, an exit door swung lightly. I went through hard and crashed into two men standing on the other side. We tumbled to the ground in a tangle of arms and legs and I swore, fighting to get free. They yelled at me, grabbed at me, trying to stop me from escaping. Guards, I realized, as I elbowed one in the gut and punched the other in the balls. As twin "oomphs" of pain echoed, I scrambled to my feet and quickly looked around. I couldn't see anyone suspicious—couldn't see anyone carrying anything that vaguely resembled a concealed gun.

I grabbed the guard still clutching his vitals and unceremoniously hauled him upright. "Did someone else come through this door a few seconds before me?"

"No," he wheezed, "and you'd best—"

I pushed him back with enough force to unbalance him again and returned to the stairwell, pounding down the stairs to the next level. Another quick scan didn't reveal anyone who tweaked my instincts.

I continued on, repeating the check on each subsequent floor. By the time I crashed through the last set of doors, the guards were on my tail and I'd basically given up any hope of finding the assassin.

I spotted Luc striding through the main doors and walked toward him, my hands raised. "Yes, I disobeyed orders, and yes, I've lost him. Sorry."

"I'm not surprised by either event." He plucked a piece of string from my arm, his expression concerned. "Netting?"

"It was strung across the window."

"Meaning he'd been prepared for the presence of a shifter. Interesting."

"I'd say it was more alarming."

"Yes, if only because it suggests we have a leak somewhere along the pipeline."

"If there *is* one, it has to be your side. There's only three of us, and we don't leak."

A smile flirted with his lips despite the seriousness that remained in his eyes, but it fell quickly away as his gaze moved past me. It was only then I became aware of the commotion. I half turned; the two guards I'd knocked down raced toward us. Others were coming in from the left and the right.

Luc calmly reached into his jacket pocket, pulled out his wallet, and produced a badge. "Sorry for the commotion caused, gentlemen—Officer De Montfort was chasing a suspect in a shooting. He was located on your top floor."

The guard's anger turned to horror. "We knew something had happened given all the police and ambulances, but we had no idea—"

"I wouldn't expect you to," Luc intervened smoothly. "Is that floor in everyday use?"

The most senior-looking of the guards shook his head. "It's storage only—"

"Good. I want guards placed on all exits to and from

that level, to ensure no one goes up there until my colleague —" He paused and glanced around as his name was called. "Ah, here he is now. Gwen, do you want to go clean up while I update Dan?"

Dan, I noted, was one of the Preternatural Division men who'd been at Gareth's. After grabbing directions from one of the guards, I departed for the bathroom, where I discovered that not only was my face smeared with blood and tiny fragments of feathers and bone but also my hair. I bent over the sink and did my best to rinse both. Thankfully, the hand dryers were the old-fashioned type, which meant I could at least duck my head under one and use my fingers to help dry my hair. Which made it frizzy, but that was far better than having bits of pigeon and Tris—

I savagely cut off the rest of that thought and headed out.

Luc leaned against a nearby wall, his arms crossed. "At least you no longer look like something the cat hacked up."

"I'm not entirely sure that's a compliment."

"Best I can do on short notice. Here—" He dug into his jacket pocket and pulled out a pink hairband. "You might want to use this to restrain the mane."

I accepted it with a smile and quickly used it to restore some order. "And what would you be doing with pink hairbands in your pockets?"

"I've a younger sister who believes a brother's pockets are designed to carry all the small necessities. I've discovered quite a number of tampons and lipsticks in various pockets over the years." He caught my elbow and guided me toward the nearby exit. "Dan will look after the situation here. We've got other leads to chase."

"Did he give you that badge you're carrying?"

"No—Jason did last night. It's a temporary badge given

to the specialists they call in for a set job. Saves constantly having to clear their presence with the regular force."

"Which leads on to my next question—how on earth did Dan arrive here so fast?"

"He's one of the extra guards who was called in to protect the heir living here."

The wind swirled around us as we left the building. I shivered, even though I wasn't really cold. Luc shifted his grip from my elbow to my fingers; while the warmth of his touch didn't really do much to battle the inner chill, it was nevertheless comforting—as it was no doubt meant to be.

The street in which Tris had died was now cordoned off, and there was a multitude of police cars and ambulances surrounding the Costa building.

I swallowed the bile and grief that rose and tried to concentrate on the job at hand rather than the specter of death. "I take it there're still people guarding the heir? Because this might just be an over-the-top diversion."

"That thought had occurred to us, and yes, he's still well protected. Did you see the shooter at all?"

"No. I just heard his departing footsteps."

"Heavy or light?"

I hesitated. "What difference does that make?"

"Light could mean a woman, heavier a man."

"Unless, of course, we're dealing with a thin, tall man. Or maybe even someone who could be either."

"Also possible. How did you know where he was located?"

"I spotted his rifle."

"Suggesting this hit was *not* a professional one."

"Whoever did this was a damn good marksman—"

"Yes, but a professional could have made the shot through the open window from the back of the room. He or she certainly wouldn't have let any part of the rifle hang out the goddamn window."

I frowned. "Professional or not, how could they have known Tris would be walking down that street?"

"Perhaps by the same means we did—a tracking spell."

"So how did they know we were intending to question him? We only really decided this morning, and that wouldn't have given them enough time to set this all up, surely."

"It might have something to do with the hecatomb being sealed and cleansed—the dark spawn would have felt its loss and perhaps suspected Tristan had been compromised." He paused, waiting for a car to move past before tugging me on. "I don't suppose he mentioned where he was staying when you were talking?"

"At some hotel with plaza in its name. Why?"

"Because it's possible that once the killer has stashed his gun, he'll head across to the hotel to clean out Tristan's belongings and wipe down the room. I think we need to arrive first."

I pulled my hand free and did a quick Google search. "The closest possibility is only a block away."

"Then we'll start with that."

It didn't take long to get there. Luc once again showed his badge and explained the situation. Luck, for once, was on our side. Tris had booked a room yesterday evening.

The manager escorted us up to the room, but remained outside as we went in. The room was basic but comfortable, with a double bed on the left, and a desk, flat-screen TV, and a wardrobe to the right. There was a good six feet of space between the two, which was rather unusual in a three-star hotel. Tris's bag—the same one he'd been using in Ainslyn—sat on the desk rather than a foldout luggage stand propped against the wall.

"You check that," Luc said. "I'll check the drawers and bathroom."

I nodded and walked over. A look inside revealed only one complete change of clothes, which suggested he hadn't really planned to be here more than a night. I dumped them all onto the desk and ran my fingers around the base of the bag. Nothing unusual met my touch. I checked his jeans pockets and shook out the shoes, with the same result. I shoved them back in and checked the side pockets.

"Nothing here," I said as Luc came out of the bathroom.

"And yet again nothing but basic toiletry items in there." He motioned to the bedside table on the other side of the bed, close to the window. "You want to check that?"

I did so. On the top of the table, beside the phone was a notepad and pen. Though there was nothing written on the paper, something had obviously been written on the previous page and then torn off. I picked the notepad up and held it closer to the window.

"It looks like he jotted something down, but I can't make out what it is."

"Let me look."

I tossed the notepad across and then opened the drawer under the bedside table. Something rattled in response. I frowned and opened it wider. The item rolling around was a ring—a blue-stone ring. One that reeked of darkness and power, and which bore uncanny similarities to the ring I'd found in the ashes of a demon.

I shouldn't have been angry or even surprised—not after everything I'd already learned about Tris. And yet I was.

I grabbed the pen, shoved it through the ring, and brought it out into the light. "Look what I just found."

Luc sucked in a breath. "An oath ring."

"Yeah, and it's almost exactly the same as the one the demon that attacked Jackie had been wearing."

Luc moved around the bed but made no move to touch the ring. "It's not the control ring but rather one of its subsidiaries."

I frowned. "How can you tell?"

"The lack of script on the surface of the ring."

"Why would Tris have it then?"

"Because he'd bound himself to whomever holds the control ring."

"But why would he even contemplate that? He might not have had Chen powers, but he was by no means lacking when it came to magic."

And yet even as I said that, I remembered his desire to be far more than he was. Remembered how his father's disdain for what he *could* do had always colored his actions and decisions. It wouldn't have taken much to convince Tris to swear an oath if the ultimate end prize had been great enough.

"A throne—or rather, helping a king regain it—would surely provide more power and wealth than even Tristan could have imagined."

"I don't know about that—he was capable of imagining quite a bit." I paused for a moment, uneasily watching the light flicker across the ring's almost oily-looking surface. "There's one thing I don't get in any of this—"

"Only one?" Luc said, echoing an earlier comment with an amused glint in his eyes.

I nudged him lightly with my shoulder. "Even if the heir gains the crown and draws the sword, what good will it do him? He can't claim rule over the UK—Layton's spells are still in effect and they utterly protect the current royals."

"All spells can be broken—you've noted that yourself."

"Yes, but we're talking about a spell that has survived for hundreds and hundreds of years—the fact it still stands is testament to its strength and Layton's skill in crafting it." I hesitated. "Or has it not been tested before now?"

"Oh, it's been tested, but never by the Witch King's heir bearing the sword of all power. And if he opens Hell's Gill ..."

The last thing I wanted right now was to worry about *that* possibility. "Surely Layton would have also woven countermeasures into his spells to protect his heirs against the use of the sword."

"Perhaps, but by all accounts, Layton wasn't always on good terms with common sense or sanity."

"So Mo said." I motioned toward the ring. "Is there any way we can use this to track down the master?"

"I don't personally know, but I daresay someone at headquarters might."

He tugged a small silver-lined bag out of his pocket and opened it up. Once I'd tilted the pen and let the ring slide inside, he sealed the bag and tucked it away.

"Did you manage to see what had been written on that notepad?"

He shook his head. "But it'll be easy enough to figure out—all we'll need is a pencil."

I raised my eyebrows. "Does that old trick actually work?"

"You obviously don't watch many mystery movies—the technique *always* works."

I smiled. "I think it's pretty well established that movies don't often deal with reality."

"True, but in this case, it *is* fact based, as long as Tristan placed enough pressure on the pen for the writing to be indented on the page underneath—which it obviously has."

He motioned me to follow him, and we headed out. Once he'd told the manager to lock the room until forensics arrived, he borrowed a pencil and lightly shaded the indented area.

What appeared was an address.

"That wouldn't happen to be where the heir is stashed, would it?" I asked.

"No, thankfully." He pulled out his phone and tapped the address into it. "It's over Radcliffe-on-Trent way, a stone's throw from the river."

I frowned "That's some distance from here, isn't it?"

"Seven miles or so. Why?"

"Is that via car? Because Tris was walking when he was murdered, so it's possible he was dropped off somewhere near Costa."

And *that* would explain how the killer had not only known exactly where he'd be but also what time he'd likely get there.

"That's presuming this address is actually where he was last night."

"I think it was."

"Why?"

"Because my gut is saying it was."

"Then in the gut we must trust." He pulled out his phone and then motioned me forward. "I'll get Jason to order a check on security and traffic cams. We might get lucky and spot who he was with."

We returned to his motorcycle and quickly drove across to Radcliffe-on-Trent. The house located at the address was a small pebbledash bungalow and was the last house in a dead-end street. The river lay behind it, and a tree-covered cliff ran the full length of the street on the right—though this house was the only one of the three that had it as part of its boundary.

Luc stopped in the parking space in front of the bungalow and killed the engine. There was little evidence of life in any of the three houses, and the only car in the street was parked up the other end, close to a line of green bins.

The bungalow was small but neat-looking. Lace curtains covered the only front window, and a small green garden shed sat between the house and the cliff. To the left, a hedge-lined concrete path led to the other side of the house and, I presumed, the front door.

I got off the bike and handed him the helmet. "How are we going to tackle this?"

"You go knock on the front door. I'll scout around the yard."

I nodded and followed the path around to the front door. There was no doorbell, so I knocked. The sound echoed but drew no response. I tried again, and then looked around as Luc appeared down the far end.

"Anything?"

He shook his head. "But the lawn is neat and the garden beds are well tended, so someone obviously lives here."

"No one's answering the door."

"Is it deadlocked?"

"No. It's a simple latch bolt from the look of it."

"Good." He stopped beside me and pulled a credit card from his wallet. "Keep watch while I open her up."

I stepped back, but only kept half an eye on the street, watching as he forced the card in the gap between the door and the jamb. He grabbed the door handle and, after several seconds of twisting and pushing the card around, turned the handle, opened the door, and motioned me in.

"And just where did you learn that trick?"

"Jason taught me—it's fair to say he skirted the edges of criminality when he was younger."

We'd entered straight into a combined kitchen-living area. The carpet on the floor was worn, as was the rocker-recliner that faced the small TV on the wall opposite. A two-person sofa sat under the lace-lined window, with an old-fashioned radiator to the right of it. The kitchen was small but neat, and there were a bowl and two cups sitting upside down on a draining board. The air had a slightly musty smell, suggesting the house had been closed up for a while.

"How'd he get from being a thief to being a chief investigator with the Preternatural team?"

"Luck," Luc replied. "Let's see what's down the hall."

As it turned out, there wasn't a whole lot beyond two bedrooms and a bathroom. The place was pin neat, and there was nothing to suggest anything untoward had happened to whoever was living here.

I followed him back into the living area. "Why the hell would Tris have written this address down? There's nothing here to find."

"Maybe because he found and removed whatever it is they were looking for."

I motioned toward the furnishings and the various knickknacks scattered about. "This place obviously belongs to an old couple—what on earth could they possibly have that would interest a killer heir and his allies?"

"That's something we may now never know."

I looked around for a second and then frowned. "Tris

made a comment that wherever he was last night was crawling with beetles. I haven't spotted one here yet."

"Maybe they went somewhere else after they raided this place."

"Except there was no indication anyone else had forced that door." Not that they needed to when Tris was a magical locksmith. "What about the shed? Anything in there?"

"Nothing more than a mower and a few garden tools."

"Then why the hell were they *here*?" The inner frustration was very evident in my voice. "Are you sure there's nothing outside?"

"Nothing in the garden, but maybe there's something closer to the river."

"Or maybe the cliff—the trees are certainly thick enough to be hiding all manner of things."

"Possibly." He motioned me out. "Let's go explore."

We made our way around to the back of the house and pushed through the shrubs providing a boundary between the yard and the long grass slope leading down to the river. There was no indication of digging, nothing to suggest that whatever Tris had been sent here for lay between where we stood and the river itself. Nor were there any moorings or short piers along the riverbank, either here or further along to the left.

The tree-lined cliff dominated the skyline to our right. Cars following the road up top were briefly visible through the gaps in the trees, but there was little else to be seen. Frustration stirred as I studied the slope again ... and spotted a very faint path—the sort of path that could have been left by someone walking through the long grass a few hours ago. Anyone could have been responsible for the trail, of course, but my heart nevertheless leapt. A vague hope was better than no hope.

Luc had obviously spotted it, because he immediately followed it. The grass soon gave way to trees and scree.

"There appears to be a very old path cutting across the base of the cliff."

"I guess that's better than heading down into the water."

He glanced over his shoulder, his eyes bright in the muted light. "Blackbirds don't swim?"

"They can. They just have no desire to." Especially when the day wasn't exactly warm.

The path was little more than a goat track that meandered haphazardly through the trees. Though cars continued to rumble along the road high above us, there was little in the way of birdsong and no sign of squirrels or even hares. Which was odd, given gray squirrels, at the very least, were something of a pest in areas like this.

"Hear that?" Luc said, after a few more minutes.

"Define 'that.'"

"Running water."

I paused and listened. After a second or two, I heard the soft splashing. "If that's a waterfall, it's a pretty puny one."

"There's no waterfall in this area that I'm aware of, so it's more likely runoff from all the rain we've had of late. But Tris's clothes were wet, and it wasn't raining here last night."

"Then it's worth investigating." And it wasn't like we'd found anything else.

He continued on; the ground grew rockier and more uneven, with much of the scree looking fresh. There'd obviously been some kind of landslip here recently.

We came out of the trees into a clearing filled with rubble and dirt. Several thin streams of water meandered down the slope toward the river; to our right, sitting in the middle of the semicircular landslip, was a jagged rupture that led into deeper darkness. The waterfall we'd heard splashed over the cave's top lip and then joined the rest trickling toward the river.

"Well, that certainly presents one possible reason for Tris clothes being wet," Luc said.

I eyed the gash uneasily. "You don't think we're going to find another hecatomb in there, do you? Because I really think my stomach has had its fill of bloody deaths today."

"It's generally not the sort of place they set those things up—but I can't give you any guarantee." He glanced at me. "You can wait here, if you want."

"You already know the answer to that," I replied mildly, "so why even suggest it?"

"Because it *is* the gentlemanly thing to do."

"Maybe that's why I'm not used to it—there're no gentlemen in my life."

"That's a very sad state of affairs."

"On that, we agree. But you could help fix the problem if you'd put your ethics aside."

"If a gentleman loses his ethics, he has nothing."

"Nothing except exceptional sex with a very hot blonde."

Just for a moment, something flared between us—something that was so raw and powerful, my breath caught in my throat and my pulse rate leapt.

It disappeared as quickly as it had risen, but left chaos in its wake. At least it did in me; it was hard to say what effect it might have had on Luc. He was the poster boy for utter control.

"Perhaps, once this is all over, the hot blonde and I can discuss that possibility."

"Which is the surest way to take all the passion out of

the situation, Luc." I motioned to the jagged entrance. "I don't suppose you have a flashlight on you?"

"No, but I don't need one." He raised a hand and wiggled his fingers. "Come along. I won't let you trip over anything."

I twined my fingers through his and let him tug me forward. The water dribbling over the lip of the cave was icy and the rocks around it slick and slippery. We squeezed through the gash and moved forward cautiously. Other than a distant drip-drip, there was little sound in this place, and while the air smelled damp, it was free of the more "earthy" scent I'd smelled on Tris. If he *had* been underground digging shit up, it hadn't been anywhere near this tunnel or cave or whatever the hell it was.

"Wait here," Luc said abruptly, and released my hand.

I crossed my arms as he moved away. After a few seconds, there was a soft click and light flared, so bright it made me blink.

"I'm thinking it's not a good sign that they've left flash-lights here."

"Flashlights *and* hard hats." He tossed me one.

I shoved it on and studied the rough-hewn but narrow shaft that stretched ahead for a good fifty feet. The ground fell away at that point, and the space beyond was obviously large, given the light hit neither the ceiling nor a far wall. "How could a place like this have remained undetected for so long?"

He shrugged. "There used to be a lot of mines in Nottingham—maybe this was one of them."

"Mines don't usually create caverns though, do they?"

"No, but there have been instances where tunnels have intersected such spaces. Shall we continue?"

He walked on without waiting for a reply. The bright

light failed to reveal anything more than fallen rocks and dripping water. The cave ahead wasn't giving its secrets away easily.

The floor began to angle down sharply, and the stone became slick with moisture and slime. My foot slipped out from underneath me, and I threw out my arms for balance, one hand catching the jagged edge of a rock. I gripped on tight and stopped the slide, my heart going a million miles an hour.

Luc didn't say anything; he simply held out his hand again. I accepted it. Now was not the time for any sort of pride-based foolishness; one broken leg in the family was more than enough.

We reached the end of the slope and came out into the cave proper. It was huge—so vast the thick, glittering stalactites scattered across the roof high above looked more like barely developed pins than the centuries-old limestone structures they undoubtedly were. A stony forest of stalagmites dominated much of the floor, but there was a section to our right that was little more than a pile of stony rubble.

I motioned toward it. "Is it possible that whatever caused the landslide also caused that?"

"Maybe. Whether it's the source of the smell on Tris is another matter, as it doesn't look fresh."

No, it didn't. We nevertheless picked our way across to investigate. Luc's suspicions were right; not only was the fall relatively old—as evidenced by the fungi growing on the top layer of stones—there was absolutely no indication that anyone had dug into it recently.

Luc swept the light around again; across the far side of the cavern, half hidden by a fat, ten-foot-high stalagmite, was a second tunnel. Thick slabs of wood lined its sides and supported the ceiling, which meant the tunnel wasn't witch made. No Chen worth their salt would ever do work so shoddy that it had to be shored up by timber at a later point.

We walked over. Luc swung the light across the timbers; they were black with age but appeared solid enough. Looks could be deceiving, however, as I'd very recently learned.

I once again pushed the bitter sadness away and studied the tunnel. It was narrow, with rough-hewn walls that dripped with moisture. The dank, earthy smell that had been so evident on Tris very faintly touched the air. Something moved right on the edge of the light; after a moment, I realized what it was. Beetles. There were a number of the damn things crawling up the wall and over the rotting timber.

"Whatever Tris was doing, it's down there somewhere," I said. "He was complaining about beetles before he was shot."

"Then on we go."

We entered cautiously. The ground was as rough as the walls and wet underfoot, which meant our pace was by necessity slow. What was more dangerous, however, were the creaks and groans coming from both the timber supports and walls around us. It felt like this whole tunnel was in danger of an immediate collapse, although surely if that were even a remote possibility, Tris and whomever he was working with would have done something to stabilize it.

Unless, of course, they'd gotten what they needed last night, and this whole place was now nothing more than one big trap ...

I shivered and shoved my imagination back into its box. Tris's demeanor certainly hadn't been that of a man who'd successfully found what he'd been looking for. Besides, they couldn't have known we'd find the address on that notepad and investigate; couldn't be certain that we'd walk further than the bungalow and find the landslip and tunnel entrance. If there *was* a trap here, then it hadn't been set for us but rather anyone who'd stumbled onto this place.

As thoughts went, it didn't actually do a lot to ease my growing fear.

The deeper we moved underground, the louder the creaking grew and the stronger the smell of fresh, damp earth became. Then, up ahead in the distance, something twinkled.

"What's that?" Though the question was soft, it echoed loudly in the pressing silence of this place.

"I don't know." He shifted the light upward. "I'm more worried about them at the moment."

The "them" in question were the tunnel's timber supports. The two immediately ahead had partially broken at their midpoint and now formed a shallow V that was barely holding the earth above in check.

"We've only two choices," I said. "And you already know which one I'll be voting for."

"Never let it be said that the De Montfort women have no gumption."

"I don't think anyone who has ever met Mo would dare say anything along those lines."

"Not if they have any sense, anyway."

He pressed forward, ducking under the broken beams and being ultra careful not to touch the side supports—a somewhat difficult task for someone as broad shouldered and as tall as he. I followed cautiously, watching each step. The last thing we needed right now was me slipping again.

We came out into another cavern, although this one was small and enclosed. There were three more tunnels leading off it—one of them looked like a natural crevice, but the other two were manmade and shored up by rotten-looking timbers. The twinkling was coming from the second—and most dilapidated—one.

We walked over. The twinkle turned out to be a ring—a silver ring that held a deep red stone surrounded by diamonds. Its setting was old-fashioned and masculine in style rather than feminine, and it looked relatively new rather than something that was centuries old.

"How on earth did something like this get here?" I sat on my haunches and held a hand just above the ring. My skin tingled in response. "It's emitting the faintest caress of magic, but I'm not seeing any strings to suggest it's active."

"Neither am I," Luc said, "but there's definitely something embedded in the stone—and it's got the faintest whiff of foulness to it."

"A dark spell?"

"Possibly." He shifted slightly and studied the shaft's opening. "I'm not seeing any sort of trip wire, be it magical or physical."

"Which doesn't mean there isn't something hiding further in." I studied the tunnel for a second. "I guess I could fly in and check it out—if this is a trap, they've likely set it for a human rather than a bird."

"Not necessarily. Not given the netting across that window."

"True, but it's nevertheless worth the risk. Besides, I'm immune to magic, remember."

He hesitated and then nodded. "But be damned careful. At the first sign of trouble, retreat."

"I will."

I briefly touched his arm, drawing strength from the contact, and then stepped back. Once I'd shifted shape, I grabbed the flashlight with my claws and flew in. The tunnel was long and narrow enough that the tips of my wings brushed the sides. The timber supports deeper in were in even worse shape than the ones near the entrance, and several had given way, causing a semi collapse. How Tris or indeed anyone else had gotten in here without bringing half the mountain down on top of them, I had no idea. The tunnel curved slightly to the right and then opened up into what looked and felt like a small antechamber, albeit one made of earth. In the center of the chamber was a freshly dug hole. Several shovels leaned against the wall to the right of this, and Coke cans and plastic wrappers littered the floor. I hovered for a few second longer, looking for any indication of magic, then shifted shape and dropped to the ground.

"You there, Luc?" I called softly.

"Of course I'm here—where else would I be?"

I smiled at the tetchiness in his tone. "I've reached the end of the tunnel—they've been digging a hole in the middle of what looks to be a natural chamber."

"Any spells or traps?"

"No."

"Then I'm coming—"

"Don't. The tunnel is in a really bad state, and there were a couple of collapsed sections. I doubt you'll get through them."

"Tristan and whoever was with him obviously did—"

"Yeah, and maybe them coming out last night is the reason the tunnel is in such a state—Tris did look as if he'd been caught in a slide."

Luc grunted. It was not a happy sound. "Is there any clue as to what they were looking for?"

"Not immediately." I propped the flashlight on the nearby pile of rock and earth and then knelt next to it. The hole was quite large—nearly five feet wide and at least three deep. "Given the amount of rock that has been excavated, though, they've obviously been at it for a few days."

"They used shovels?"

"Yes, which is odd. Chens aren't exactly hard to find or hire, and it would have saved a lot of time and effort."

It would have galled Tris no end that he—a Chen—was unable to do the one thing his family was renowned for. And it certainly wouldn't have helped his mood any to be physically digging when his baby brother could have done it with just a flick of his hand.

"Maybe," Luc commented, "they didn't want anyone else to see what they were digging up."

I leaned in and brushed a hand across the dirt and rock fragments lying on the bottom. Energy stung my fingertips, its caress sharp but brief. I jerked them back, my heart racing a million miles an hour. No magical strings followed. No spell rose. I hesitated, then leaned in a second time; once again, energy bit at me. This time, I resisted the urge to pull away and instead studied it. It wasn't a spell; it was, in fact, pure energy, and its caress reminded me somewhat of the pulse that had come from the sword when I'd gripped it.

"Luc, there's something here."

"It would be helpful if you elaborated on that statement just a little bit more."

Despite the tension running through me, a smile tugged at my lips. He really *didn't* like being kept at a distance. "It's energy, and it rather feels like the pulse that erupted from the king's sword."

"Can you see what's causing it?"

"No." I pushed to my feet and walked over to the shovels. "It can't be too far from the surface though."

"If it was close to the surface, why would they have left before digging it out?"

I jumped into the hole and shoved the shovel into the ground. It barely dented the surface. I could only hope the item was indeed close to the surface; otherwise, I was going to be here all damn day.

"Maybe they weren't aware how near they were."

"Or, given this thing is emitting the same sort of energy as the sword, they simply didn't have the capacity to feel the pulse."

"Technically, *I* shouldn't be feeling it."

"Yeah, but you're also Moscelyne's granddaughter. I rather suspect you have the same capacity to do things you shouldn't be able to."

"If Mo's to be believed, you've got that the wrong way around."

"She thinks you're capable of far more than what you currently are?"

"Apparently."

"Then you should believe her."

"You haven't grown up with her. She makes lots of grand statements that aren't always backed by reality."

I tossed what was little more than a scraping of soil onto the rock pile and then tried again, this time stepping on the shoulder of the shovel and pressing my full weight onto it. It only went a few millimeters deeper. I swore, took off my jacket, and kept digging. By the time I spotted a thin stick of gold, sweat dripped from my hair and I'd stripped off to my bra.

I dropped to my knees, flicked my knife down into my hand, and carefully picked the bits of soil and rock away from that glimmer of gold. My knife did a far better job than the shovel did and the more it revealed, the more my heart raced.

It was a crown—a very old crown—and one whose

247

image I'd seen only very recently, in an ancient book of fables. The band was thickly threaded gold through which a thin string of blue stone had been woven. A thick, leaf-shaped piece of gold sat in the front of the band, and in the center of this sat an oval-shaped, blue-gray stone. Zigzagged bands of gold surrounded this centerpiece, oddly reminding me of lightning frozen midstrike—albeit the wrong color.

I carefully pressed my fingers under either edge of the crown and eased it free from the soil; power pulsed across my fingers, and jagged light flashed across the surface of the stone.

I gulped and tried to contain my excitement.

"You're not going to believe this, Luc, but I think I just found the Witch King's Crown."

"The stolen one?"

"No. The original."

His sharp intake of breath echoed. "Why makes you think that?"

"As I said, it has the same pulse of power as the sword."

"Why the hell would something like that be here, of all places?"

"You tell me. Your lot was supposedly guarding the thing, not us."

I put the crown to one side and brushed my fingers across the base of the hole. This time there was no response —which didn't mean there wasn't anything else here to find, just that there was nothing else holding the power of the crown.

I pushed to my feet and pulled on my jacket. Then I wrapped my sweater around the crown and tied it around my waist. Though I wasn't entirely sure why, instinct was saying to keep it close but out of sight. After everything that had happened over the last few days, I wasn't about to gainsay it.

I put the shovel back then checked everything was almost as I'd found it. "Coming out."

And kept my fingers crossed as I said it; I'd never shifted carrying a gold artifact before and had no idea if it would react the same way to the change as silver—that is, be immune to it.

The shifting wave swept over my body and, thankfully, encased the wrapped crown as easily as it did the backpack. In blackbird form, I grabbed the flashlight and then carefully made my way through the tunnel, moving back into human form when I neared the entrance. My foot slipped as I landed. I stumbled and would have fallen had Luc not jumped forward and caught me.

"Thanks," I said but didn't immediately pull free. His body was warm and hard against mine, and his arms held me so very tenderly. He felt too damn good ... and too damn right.

"A more suspicious man would think you did that deliberately." The roughness in his voice spoke of desire. "But I've learned you're very straightforward when it comes to stating what you want."

"For the little good it's done me so far."

I forced myself to pull free and then stopped, an odd feeling of dread suddenly clutching at my innards. The ring at our feet now pulsed, sending a bloodred light spinning across the darkness.

"I'm thinking that's not a good sign." All trace of desire had fled Luc's voice. "Let's get out of here."

He caught my hand and we raced across the cavern, the flashlight's beam dancing erratically across the walls, catching the tiny flecks of dirt falling from the roof.

The pulses of red grew sharper, brighter, and were now accompanied by a surge of energy. Dark energy. Angry energy. We'd obviously tripped whatever spell lay deep in the heart of that ring, and though I wondered how, I really had no time to do anything more than concentrate on keeping up with Luc.

We swept into the next tunnel. The shower of earth was more noticeable here, and all too swiftly became a constant rain that poured all around us. A tremor ran through the earth, and a deep rumbling began, a sound that chased us through the tunnel, growing ever louder as it drew closer and closer. As a thick cloud of dust overtook us, all but cutting out the flashlight's beam, I realized what it was.

The tunnel was collapsing.

"Gwen, fly—get the fuck out of here."

"We both get out of here or we both get buried. There is no other option."

"The crown is far more important—"

"Not to me, it's not, so shut up and run, Blackbird."

He swore but obeyed. We pounded through the dark and disintegrating tunnel, pummeled by dirt and rocks and chunks of wood as the tunnel's support beams gave way under the force of the pulsing energy. As the rumbling grew louder and stronger, the ground rose like a wave under our feet and threatened to sweep us away. Slabs of stone and wood fell all around us, hitting with enough force to bruise. We crashed through growing slopes of debris, fighting to get free of the tunnel and the danger it represented.

Finally, from up ahead, came a distant flicker of light. Sunlight, somehow filtering through the jagged entry point.

We were so damn close ...

With a gigantic whoomp, the tunnel collapsed. Somehow, in the midst of it, Luc spun, grabbed my waist, and threw me forward. I flew through the air, the shifter magic sweeping my body as the survival instinct kicked in. The light grew closer, nearer; escape was close, so damn close.

Then a weight hit my back and I was tumbling, falling, through the air. I hit the ground hard and fell into darkness.

ELEVEN

Waking was a painful experience. For too many minutes, I fought it, not wanting to deal with reality, not wanting to know just how bad my situation had become.

But consciousness would not be denied.

Without opening my eyes, I began a check. My fingers and toes all moved, so that was at least something. It felt like a hundred horrible little men were gleefully banging drums inside my head, and the warmth trickling down my cheek suggested I'd either split my forehead or my scalp open. There was a secondary ache in my left thigh, and something hard and circular biting into my spine.

The crown ... and it was still very much intact by the feel of things.

I forced my eyes open and saw the stalactites high above. I'd made it as far as the first cavern ... but had Luc?

There was no sound, no indication of movement, from the tunnel that now lay behind me. Dust still rolled out of the entrance, which meant I hadn't been unconscious for all that long. The ground had stopped quivering, and the dark energy no longer pulsed.

I tried to move but there was a weight on my lower body pinning me down. I lifted my head—which only set off the bastards with the drums—and saw that half an old beam and a good chunk of earth lay across my stomach and legs. I pushed upright as far as the muck would allow and then, using my knife, began to shovel the loose soil away from the beam. Luck had obviously been with me—it was one of the older, semi-rotten timbers and held none of the weight of the more intact ones. Had one of them hit me, I might not now be moving at all.

Once the beam was as exposed as I could make it, I shoved my knife back into its hilt and then reached for the jagged end of the beam. With a grunt of effort, I lifted the thing, then shoved it sideways and released it. One jagged side edge caught my right leg as it thumped back down, tearing through jeans and skin alike. Pain rolled up my body, another heated ache in what seemed to be a growing mountain of them. I took several deep, quivering breaths and then pulled my feet from under the loose soil.

I was free. Bloody, but free.

But the task—and the danger—was far from over yet.

I rolled onto my hands and knees, remaining there for several seconds as fresh aches erupted across my body and the idiot drummers intensified their efforts.

Then, slowly but steadily, I climbed to my feet. I didn't fall back down in a dead faint, which I considered a win. After a deep, steadying breath, I looked around for the flashlight and spotted it a few yards away. Nothing happened when I pressed the button, but after a few shakes, the light came back on, even if a little half-heartedly. It was good enough.

The cut on my leg was quite deep and bleeding profusely. Though I wanted, with every inch of my being, to do nothing more than find Luc, I needed to tend to my wounds first. Me bleeding to death wouldn't help either of us.

I swung my backpack off and pulled out the medical kit. After pouring a vial of the sanctified water over the worst of the wounds, I sprayed Mo's antiseptic sealer onto them and then wrapped bandages around the wound on my thigh and the deep cut on my head—more to help keep the sealer intact than anything else.

I carefully picked my way through the rubble and paused at the tunnel's entrance. It was partially blocked by a pile of earth, stone, and wood, but the pale light revealed pockets of emptiness beyond it. Despite what it had felt like, not all of the tunnel had collapsed. Some timber still stood. Hopefully, that meant Luc might yet be alive ...

I mentally crossed all things, then very carefully climbed up the rubble pile and squeezed through the gap at the top. After half sliding, half stepping down the other side, I paused again at the bottom and swept the light around. There was another partial blockage twenty or so feet away.

"Luc?" I said softly. "You there?"

No answer came. I thrust fear away and carefully walked on. Dirt rained from the ceiling, and the multitude of creaks and groans suggested the tunnel remained unstable. It didn't matter; until I knew what had happened to Luc, I wasn't going anywhere.

I reached the second blockage. This time, the left-side support had given way, but it had jammed hard against the roof beam that rested on the debris pile to the right, and the combination had basically stopped a full collapse. There was a triangular gap between the two beams, so I shone the light through and caught sight of a booted foot.

A *moving* booted foot.

He was alive. My heart leapt, even though I had no idea yet of the state he was in or how injured he might be. He could move, and that, right now, was a good start.

"Luc?" I said. "You need to answer me. I need to know what the situation is like in there before I can do anything to help."

Silence stretched for several seconds, and then, his voice raw and somewhat croaky, he said, "I'm alive. Bleeding and bruised, but alive."

"If you were dead and still talking, I'd be hightailing it out of here. Zombies aren't my thing."

"Well, that puts *Shaun of the Dead* out of the running for a possible date night in." His foot disappeared and, a few grunts later, his dirt-grimed, bruised, and bloody face appeared. "Is there a way out of this hell hole, or is the exit blocked?"

"If you can make it through this gap, we should be right."

He eyed the two beams dubiously. "We might need something to prop the edge of that top beam up—if any of the supporting dirt moves, the whole thing will cave in."

I hesitated. "There's a beam near the exit that might be the right size. Wait here."

I rose and made my way back down the tunnel. After sliding back down the rubble, I took off my jacket, looped one sleeve around the end of the broken beam and tied it off, and then began the difficult task of hauling it back up the slope. By the time I got it into the tunnel, sweat poured down my cheeks and my head was pounding so bad my vision was going in and out of focus.

If I didn't have concussion, I'd be damned surprised.

I dragged the beam down the tunnel. By the time I got back, I seriously felt like throwing up.

"You're not looking too great," Luc said, concern evident in his expression and voice.

"That's because I don't feel all that great." I propped the flashlight against the wall and then shoved the beam into the gap. "But let's get you out of here before we worry about anything else."

It took a bit of effort and a whole lot of swearing on my part, but we eventually got the beam upright and in place.

"That should do the trick," he said. "But keep well clear, just in case this doesn't work and the whole thing comes down."

I nodded and retreated, but kept the light centered on the gap. He might be able to see in the dark, but in a case like this it was always better to be safer than sorry. He turned on his side and, using one arm and the force of his legs for momentum, inched his way through the gap. Dirt continued to rain down, but our makeshift brace held.

Once out, he rolled into a sitting position. There was a deep gash across his forehead and another down his left arm, but unless there were internal injuries, he'd come out of the collapse better than I had.

He accepted my offered hand and rose but didn't immediately release me. Instead, he tugged me close and brushed his lips ever so sweetly across mine. It felt like he was branding me.

Felt like heaven.

"If we weren't still in such a precarious situation," he murmured, his breath so warm against my mouth and his jade eyes glowing with heat, "I'd kiss you more thoroughly."

"What about the whole ethics thing?"

"They'll survive a kiss."

A smile tugged at my lips. "I might not."

"You're made of sterner stuff than that." He released me. In the flashlight's fading glow, the strength of his desire was very evident. But that was no real surprise; it was well enough documented that a heightened sex drive was often the result of a near-death experience. I just had to hope that it lasted past us getting out of here and remained strong enough to perhaps delete those ethics of his. Otherwise, I could foresee a number of sleepless nights in my future.

We carefully made our way back through the tunnel and down the rubble pile. Once we were well clear, I grabbed the pack and pulled out the first aid kit.

"Here, you might want to use this on that arm—" I stopped, my gaze snapping toward the jagged tunnel entrance. Though the faint sound wasn't repeated, unease prickled up my spine. "Was that a voice coming from outside? Or am I just overly jumpy right now?"

"It might just be a nearby resident out for his daily stroll, but I doubt we can take that risk—"

"Not given how thoroughly we sprang their trap."

"Yeah. I'll go investigate. You move over to that large stalagmite and turn off the flashlight."

Once I had, the shadows stole him from sight. I crossed my arms and shifted my weight from one foot to the other but couldn't find a position that didn't make various bits ache. He reappeared a few minutes later—something I heard rather than saw, as the shadows remained around him.

"We have a serious problem."

"How many problems are we talking about?"

"Five, one of whom is a Chen."

To clear the fallen earth, obviously. "They got here

rather fast, didn't they? I mean, we haven't been in here that long—"

"We've been here for several hours, at least. If the spell on the ring came online when you flew into the tunnel, they'd have had plenty of time to get here."

"Great." I flexed my fingers in a vague effort to ease the tension pulsing through me. It didn't help. It never did. "Can't you just spin the daylight around us? Or are they already too close to the tunnel?"

"They're close, but under normal circumstances, it wouldn't matter because we could hide in the shadows and wait for them to move deeper into the cliff side. But they've brought several bloodhounds with them. Light manipulation doesn't alter or contain scent."

"Then we fight it out—it's five against two, after all. The odds aren't hugely in their favor."

Though I couldn't see his smile in the ink, I felt the warmth of it deep inside. "Never let it be said that the De Montforts aren't up for a challenge. The only problem here is the fact they've also got guns."

"Ah."

"Yeah. I think our best option is to split up—"

"No."

"Gwen, under no circumstances are these bastards to get the crown. In fact, it's better if they don't even realize we have it."

"Yes, but—"

"I can draw them away—I can move faster and quicker if I'm not shielding you. Once I've pulled them from the entrance, you can fly out and get the crown to safety."

I hesitated and then nodded. I hated the thought of him being bait, but he was warrior trained and would be far better off without having me to worry about.

"What if they've got your bike under watch? And what if only a couple of them chase you?"

"Oh, I guarantee they'll *all* chase me."

There was a savage edge in his tone, and it sent a chill tripping down my spine. It was an odd reminder that no matter how much Mo or I trusted him, we really didn't know that much about him.

"Where will we meet?"

"Fly home if you can, then call me. I'll join you there when I'm able."

I touched his arm to make sure of where he was and then rose up on my toes and dropped a kiss on his cheek. "Be careful."

He lightly cupped my face and brushed a thumb over my lips. "Oh, I have a kiss yet to claim, and no one and nothing is going to stop me."

With that, he turned and walked away. There was nothing I could do then but wait.

I didn't have to do so for long; a scream rent the air, then men were shouting and dogs baying, the sounds swiftly moving away from the tunnel's entrance.

I remained where I was, listening intently, trying to uncover whether they'd all fled or if one or two had remained behind. But there was no sound other than the increasingly distant cry of the dogs.

I'd have to find out the hard way ...

I took a deep breath and then shifted shape. I kept close to the jagged roofline, my gaze on the shadows ahead, looking for movement or any indication that men were out there, waiting to trap a fleeing blackbird ...

Sunlight pierced the gloom and cool, fresh air played across my wingtips. Closer and closer I drew ... and then I was out, in the open, pumping my wings hard, reaching for the treetops and beyond.

No shout followed me. No magic or gunshot pierced the air in an attempt to bring me down.

Luc had, as promised, drawn them all away.

All but the man whose severed head now lay several feet away from his body.

I hoped Luc wouldn't face legal consequences for that, but I couldn't imagine the law would be too impressed with someone running around beheading people, whether or not said people deserved it. He was working with the Preternatural boys, though, so maybe they'd simply come in and clean up the mess. It surely wouldn't be the first time they'd encountered a situation like this ... not when they seemingly worked with the Blackbirds on a semiregular basis.

I circled above the trees for a few seconds, uncertain where to go. As much as I ached to go home, instinct said that wasn't the wisest option right now. Whether or not the dark forces realized we'd stolen the crown from under their noses, they were certainly aware that I was working with Luc, and our building would be the first place they checked. But if not home, where?

Though I didn't really know, my first action had to be getting well away from the immediate area. I swooped around and headed in the opposite direction to Luc. After flying for about twenty minutes, I spotted an old barn sitting in the middle of an empty field and circled down. It was half-filled with hay, which meant it would give me somewhere comfortable to sit and block the worst of the wind while I called Mo.

She answered on the second ring. "What the fuck is going on? I'm getting all sorts of bad vibes from the cosmos."

I gave her a quick rundown on everything that had

happened in Nottingham, and then added, "But I've saved the best bit for last."

"I hate to imagine what *that* is," she muttered.

"I found the crown. The real crown—Uhtric's crown."

She sucked in a breath. "Are you sure?"

"As I can be. It emits the same sort of energy that the sword does. But I have to ask—how the fuck did it get in an abandoned cave in the middle of nowhere Nottingham?"

"An even better question would be, how the fuck did the other side know about it when we damn well didn't?"

"They've obviously got better information sources than we have."

"And *that* is a worry." She paused. "You can't bring the crown here. It's not safe."

"That's why I'm ringing rather than flying home. We need a plan."

"Indeed." She paused again. "How bad are those wounds of yours?"

"Every bit of me hurts. And if I haven't got concussion, I'll be very surprised."

Mo grunted. "Do you remember that bookstore café we stopped at outside Buxton a few years ago?"

"Vaguely."

"You think you can meet me there?"

"I'm in no fit state to be seen in public, Mo."

"No, but the parking area is large and surrounded by trees. You can perch there until I arrive to collect you."

"And then?"

"And then, once your wounds are fixed and we've rested for the night, we'll head on over to Windermere Lake."

I frowned. "Why? What the hell is over there?"

"A lady who should be able to help us if she feels so inclined. Depends what mood she's in, really."

"Well, that certainly cleared everything up."

Mo laughed. "You'll get your answers soon enough. Fly on over to Buxton, and I'll meet you there in around an hour and a half."

"Bring a thermos of tea. And food. Lots of food." I hesitated. "Shall I tell Luc where we're headed?"

"No. I'd rather no one knows where the crown is—it's safer that way."

"I thought you trusted the Blackbirds?"

"I do, but given what happened to Tris, there's obviously a leak somewhere." She paused. "I wouldn't tell your brother about the crown."

"Max hasn't always played on the right side of the law, but he wouldn't betray us like that."

"Perhaps not, but he can't give away what he doesn't know. And if Darkside suspect we have the crown then they have an additional reason to go after him."

"Surely they'd come after you or me first?"

"Not if they want him dead anyway."

True. "Luc suggested Tris's murder happened simply because the hecatomb was uncovered and sanctified not long after he was there."

"Which may well be the case. We can't, however, discount the possibility of a traitor in our midst. See you soon—and don't damn well sleep. Not if you do have concussion."

"I'll keep in bird form. That way if I do start drifting off, I'll fall from my perch and wake myself up."

Mo snorted. "Did I not tell you to practice the art of sleeping in form when younger?"

"Yes, you did, and yes, I did." I just never got the hang of it, because I could never really see the damn point.

I hung up but didn't immediately move. Instead, I

raided the backpack for the emergency chocolate bar kept there. It didn't really fill the hunger hole, but at least the sugar influx would temporarily prop up the strength reserves.

By the time I reached Buxton, the weather was closing in again. I circled the area a few times before I spotted a couple of familiar landmarks and found the bookstore. The trees were bare, providing no shelter against the increasing ferocity of the wind, so I swooped in under the awning and perched on the top of the doorframe. There wasn't a whole lot of room, meaning I had to concentrate or fall off.

Mo arrived what seemed an eternity later. The gates into the parking area were locked, so she simply stopped in front of them and then leaned across and opened the passenger door. I swooped over, shifted shape, and climbed into her car. And immediately turned up the heating. My fingers and toes were like ice.

"Well, you weren't exaggerating when you said you were in a bit of a state."

"And now I'm half-frozen to boot."

"So I can see." She reached into the back seat to grab the thermos, then poured me a drink and handed it to me. I was shaking so hard, tea splashed over the rim of the metal cup and splattered my jeans. I barely even felt it. Mo made a clucking sound and steadied the cup. "There's no need to be wasting perfectly fine tea like that, my girl."

I smiled at the severity in her tone, as she no doubt intended. "I'll be perfectly fine in an hour or two."

"You'll be scalded inside a minute at this rate."

She retrieved the cup, placed it on the console between us, and then held out her hands. "Take them."

The second my fingers caught hers, her power rose, a

fierce force that flooded my system with heat, erasing the chill that had settled deep into my bones in seconds flat.

Feeling returned to my toes and the shaking eased dramatically. "Thanks."

She nodded and returned the cup to me. "I'll fix the rest of the aches once we're settled for the night. Is the crown in the backpack?"

"No, it's wrapped in the sweater and pressing into my spine." I undid the knot and then tugged the sweater away from my waist. The crown sparkled in the dull light of the evening but the stone remained mute and the power didn't pulse.

Mo sucked in a breath, and something close to awe crossed her expression. "It is indeed Uhtric's crown."

"It looks nothing like the replacement they made."

"No, because the replacement was fashioned after the crowns worn by human kings, not witch." She motioned to it. "Wrap it back in your sweater and tuck it in the backpack. If the dark ones realize we've beaten them to their prize, they'll soon have an army out searching for it."

"If that's the case, why aren't we heading to Windermere straight away?"

She smiled and touched my shoulder. "Because, dear child, you are far more precious to me than an old king's crown."

"Yes, but—"

"We'll be fine. There's no spell set onto the crown, so they can't track it, and even Darkside can't flood the entirety of England searching for us." She reached into the back seat again and then handed me a stack of plastic-wrapped sandwiches. "Eat and drink, and let me worry about everything else."

After wrapping the crown up again and tucking it safely

into the backpack, I sipped my tea and made inroads into the pile of sandwiches. Though we didn't drive for all that long, it was dark by the time Mo pulled onto a graveled drive. After a few seconds, the headlights picked out a little, whitewashed thatched cottage. Mo stopped under the cover of some trees and we both got out. The air was cold and silent. Nothing stirred; even the rumble of traffic from the nearby highway was inaudible.

Mo grabbed a duffel bag from the back of the car, then walked over to the red-painted door, lifted the mat, and grabbed the key.

"Well, that's a totally secure place to hide a key, isn't it?"

Her smile flashed. "We're in the country, darling girl. Folks tend to be more honest than not."

She stepped into the cottage and turned on the lights. I followed her in and looked around. The place was small but cozy, consisting of little more than a combined kitchen-living area, a bedroom to the right, and a bathroom to the left. A small fireplace dominated the rear wall.

"How'd you get onto this place?" I dumped the back-pack on a nearby chair—there were only two—and walked across to the fire. It had been already set with kindling, and there were matches sitting on the mantelpiece.

"It belonged to a former lover."

I struck the match, shoved it under the paper, and then glanced at her. "Then let's hope the dark ones don't know much about you or your lovers—"

"He's long dead, and his granddaughter only ever uses the place in summer. No one will think to look here."

She pulled several vials out of the duffel bag, dumped them in the bathroom, and then said, "Right, let's get you patched up, and then you can soak the remaining aches away."

I sat on the chair and let her work her magic. Once she'd healed the worst of my wounds, I filled the bath and shook in her various salts and oils. After I'd soaked in it long enough for the water to be on the cool side, I made us both another cup of tea and then headed to bed.

A too-loud ringing woke me who knew how many hours later.

"Grab that, will you?" Mo rolled over, taking half the bedcovers with her.

I groped for the phone, then realized there was no table on my side of the bed and the phone was charging in the other room.

I swore, climbed out of bed, and padded, shivering in my T-shirt, into the other room.

I swore again when I saw the time.

I hit the answer button and said, "It's four in the goddamn morning, Luc—why the fuck are you ringing at this hour?"

"You were supposed to call me. You didn't. I was worried."

It was a statement that mollified some of the annoyance. "Could you not have worried a little bit longer? I mean, seriously, four a.m.? Who gets up at that hour?"

"The man who has been up most of the night looking for you."

"So why didn't you ring earlier?"

"I did. I kept getting a 'this number is not available' message."

"Oh. Yeah. Sorry, the phone was flat." I cleared my throat. "You obviously got away from the bad guys okay."

"Yes. Where are you? I checked the bookstore, but you're not there."

"No, but we're safe. Are you going to get into trouble for beheading that guy?"

"No. Where's the crown?"

"Still with me."

I could practically feel the exasperation rolling down the line. "And where might that be?"

"I'm actually not sure—it was dark when Mo picked me up, so I have no idea where we landed, other than it's a little cottage out in the middle of nowhere."

He grunted. It was not a happy sound. "Well, when she wakes, find out where you are and let me know. We need to discuss what we're going to do with the crown."

"We're going to hide it."

"Yes, but we need—"

"No, I mean Mo and I are going to hide it."

He was silent for a long moment. "She doesn't trust us?"

"She believes we have a leak, and it doesn't matter if it's within your lot, the Preternatural team, or someone close to us. If only she and I know where it's hidden, it limits leakage possibilities."

"And makes you both targets."

"Only if they realize we found the crown." I paused. "You didn't tell Jason, did you? Or your people?"

"No."

Relief spun through me. "Then don't. I'll contact you as soon as the crown is hidden."

He made an aggravated sound. "Fine. I'll head up to headquarters and see what we can do about tracking down the controlling oath ring."

"Just be careful. They'll guess we have it and may use it to entrap."

"I'm well aware of that, Gwen."

"Okay then." I hesitated. "Talk to you later."

"You will." He still sounded rather annoyed, and I couldn't say I blamed him. But his sensibilities were a whole lot less important than protecting the crown. Generations of De Montfort women had dedicated their lives to protecting the damn sword; we could do no less for the crown now that we had it. Especially when only the crowned king could draw the sword.

"That Luc?" Mo said from the other room.

"Yeah. He's not happy."

"Well, that's to be expected. We have the crown and they, the defenders of said crown, do not."

"You sound overly happy about it."

"They had it once. They obviously lost it, given where it ended up. Now it's our turn." She appeared in the doorway. "Do you want to make the thermos up? We might as well get going, seeing we're both up. If we can get to the lakes by dawn, it'll make things easier."

"Who exactly are we entrusting the crown to?"

"The woman from whom the sword came."

I frowned. "Didn't the Lady of the Lake give the sword to the Aquitaines?"

"Yes."

"We're giving the crown to the Lady of the Lake?"

She frowned at me. "Did I not just say that?"

"Yes, but I had no idea she actually still existed."

"Well, of course she exists. Just because humans no longer believe in the old gods doesn't make them any less real."

"I guess—"

She patted my arm. "Vivienne has been quiet for many a century, I'll grant you that. But that doesn't make her any less real or any less powerful. Make that tea while I go freshen up."

We were on the road ten minutes later. The predawn darkness was still and calm, and the storm that had threatened yesterday evening had blown past without a huge amount of rain, meaning the roads weren't dangerously slick. The little Leaf ate away the miles with surprising speed, and Mo's old rock playlist kept us both awake.

Dawn was just beginning to stain the clouds with various shades of pink by the time we arrived in Windermere. Mo wound her way through the empty streets, then turned onto a secondary road that basically followed the shoreline.

"Well, this place has certainly built up since I was last here," she commented.

"When was that?"

She shrugged. "Well before you were born."

"Were you here for a holiday or was it business?"

She glanced at me, amusement evident. "Both."

"Did it involve the Lady Vivienne?"

"No. One does not bother a water goddess unless absolutely necessary. Here we are."

The "here" was the parking area of what a sign said was the Windermere Jetty and Museum. "Here? We're going to call on a goddess from a *jetty*?"

"Not the jetty itself, but the shoreline just up from it. It's close enough to the center of the lake and gives us the best call coverage. Now stop your fussing, grab the backpack, and follow me."

We climbed out of the car. The morning was crisp, and fog clung to the dark water, hiding the end of the jetty and all but the masts of the sailing boats moored nearby. Mo walked over a bridge that spanned a concrete water channel, then through the treed park beyond, heading for the shore of a U-shaped inlet.

Stones crunched under our feet, but the fog drifting across the water's surface dulled the sound. Despite the fact there were multiple houses not that far away, it very much felt as if we were alone is this place.

Mo bent and pressed her fingers into the water lapping at the shore. As tiny waves rose around her hand, she said, "Lady of the Lake, I beseech thee, heed my call."

Her voice was soft and yet filled with a power that echoed across the fog-caressed lake. Nothing stirred. Nothing happened.

"Lady of the Lake," Mo repeated. "Your presence and your help are requested. Please, heed my call."

Still no response. My gaze swept the fog-shrouded lake; there was nothing out there but those barely visible boat masts. "Perhaps—"

Mo held up a finger, silencing me. I bit my lip and waited. After another minute, the fog stirred, sluggishly at first and then gaining traction and power as it rolled toward us. As the wave of white rolled over us and the world disappeared from sight, a voice that was both otherworldly and powerful said, "What is it you wish of me, Moscelyne?"

"Darkness has risen and the true king has not."

"This is not something I can change."

"No, but we have found the crown of the king; it needs to be held safe until the time of rising arrives."

"That time is not now."

"No," Mo repeated. "The sword remains unclaimed."

"That will not be the case for very long."

Mo's uncertainty spun through a wall of white, sending little whirls skittering away. "The sword cannot be claimed without a coronation."

"Your knowledge is not as complete as you think,

270

Moscelyne, if that is what you truly believe. Bring forth the crown."

"Gwen?"

I stepped up to the edge of the water. "It's here."

"Throw it to me."

I glanced down at Mo, though I could barely see more than the ring of gold around her eyes. A ring that glowed as fiercely as the crown itself.

"Do it," she said softly.

I pulled the crown free from the pack and, with all my might, tossed it across the water. Blue light pulsed from the gem at its heart, clearing a path through the mist in front of it. A hand rose from the water—a hand that was as pale as ice, with nails that were as red as blood—to catch it. It was held aloft for several seconds and then pulled back into the water.

"I will keep it safe until the time of the king has truly risen."

"Thank you, Lady of the Lake."

The mist stirred, and a sense of amusement swirled around us. "I am not used to such formality, Moscelyne. Not from you."

"It has been a long time, Vivienne. Formality is a prerequisite until advised otherwise."

"Then consider yourself so advised. Until we next meet."

The fog rolled back, and waves retreated from Mo's fingers. She washed the mud from them and then rose. "Well, that was interesting."

"Indeed. I had no damn idea you were on first-name terms with an ancient goddess."

"There are few enough of us left these days who do

have the capacity to call on the ancient gods. It's natural she would know the names of those who do."

"A perfectly reasonable answer, and one I do not for a second believe."

Mo clucked her tongue. "It is a sad state of affairs when your granddaughter mistrusts your explanations."

"That's because your explanations rarely actually explain anything." I crossed my arms and studied her for a second. "How many other mages are there?"

She grimaced. "Technically, only two others remain. Gwendydd resides in Europe, and Mryddin has yet to leave the cave in which he was trapped quite some time ago."

"If he was trapped in a cave, why did no one rescue him?"

"Because he didn't deserve to be rescued. He fell in love with the wrong woman, despite frequent warnings. It's his penance." She shrugged. "Of course, it's also possible the old fool simply considers the entrapment an extended holiday—a nice break from the troubles of kings."

"There haven't been any kings to worry about for eons. Not witch kings, at any rate."

"Ah, but trapped in his cave, how would he know that?"

I blinked. "That suggests he was alive during Uhtric's time, but that's impossible, surely?"

She shrugged again. "Mages tend to live a very long time. And before you ask, he's the oldest of us. I'm the youngest."

I stared at her, and then swallowed heavily. "Does that mean you'll outlive me? Or even any children I might have?"

"Outlive you? Possibly not, given my blood runs in your veins."

"So just how old are you?"

Amusement twitched her lips. "Old enough."

"Gran!"

She sighed. "It'll do your head in if I actually answer that particular question."

"It'll do my head in if you don't."

"Well, then, given the results will be the same either way, I might as well not."

"Seriously? Just answer this one question for me. Please."

"Fine. I am not your grandmother. I'm not your mother's grandmother. I'm older even than that."

I sucked in a breath. "No—"

Her eyes twinkled. "What is the point of me answering if you're not going to believe me?"

"But that's—"

"Impossible, yes, I know. But here we are."

"But ..." I swallowed. "How?"

She shrugged. "It is said mages come from a union of gods and witches. Or, in Mryddin's case, an incubus and a human. It gifted offspring with long lives and great power."

"So you're basically immortal?"

She smiled. "No. I can be killed just the same as any witch or human. I just age at a fraction of the speed of either."

"Which means—given I've aged rather normally—that you *will* outlive me."

She patted my arm comfortingly. "The whole ageless thing doesn't kick in immediately. It happened to me only after I had my three children."

I stared at her. "Three? Why have you never mentioned them?"

Something shone in her eyes—something that was sadness and pain, even if it disappeared all too quickly.

"Because none inherited the god gene. I have buried children, grandchildren, and great-grandchildren, just as I buried your mother."

And would bury me, if that was necessary. She didn't say that, but it was nevertheless in the brief wash of sorrow emanating from her.

I gripped her arm. "I'm sorry, Mo. I didn't mean to stir old hurts."

"I know." She patted my hand comfortingly. "There is one bright spot for you, at least, if you have inherited the gene."

"And what might that be?"

"Gwendydd's bloodline runs through the Blackbirds; it is possible that Luc is a bearer."

"Luc is committed to his work," I said, voice dry. "It won't matter one way or another whether that's true or not."

She motioned me forward. "I've seen the way he looks at you—"

"That look is lust, Mo, and his ethics aren't going to allow anything too exciting to happen."

"Then you'll just have to spin your wiles a bit harder."

"Mo, you've seen me spin my wiles many a time in the past. You know just how successful that's been over the years."

"Sadly, yes. But I *am* hoping my genes will eventually kick in." She pressed the remote, and the car's lights flashed in response. "Let's go."

"Where? Home?"

"Yes. Barney's nephew was able to enlarge and enhance the image you took of the writing on the back of the throne. Barney said he'd bring it over this morning."

"It'll take us a few hours to get back there."

"Barney's idea of morning is closer to midday than dawn."

I grinned. "I do often wonder how he manages to keep his job."

"Easy. He sets his own hours."

I laughed and climbed into her car. We made our way back to the M6, and though the traffic was fairly light, it still took us over three hours to get home, thanks to a couple of lavatory pit stops.

Once Mo had parked, I grabbed my pack and the now-empty thermos and then climbed out. The street was surprisingly busy considering it was winter, but maybe they were bargain hunters here for the winter sales. I waited for several cars to move past, then crossed the road. But as I got my keys out and went to open the door, I stopped, the hairs on the back of my neck rising.

Something was inside.

Something that felt a whole lot like a demon.

TWELVE

I backed away from the door and then glanced at Mo as she joined me on the pavement. "There's a demon inside."

She studied the building, her gaze narrowed. "Feels like there's at least one up on the first floor, but that shouldn't be possible given the time of day."

I looked up at the front windows. The blinds in the living area had been drawn—not something we normally did. "Could they be half-breeds?"

"Maybe." She glanced at me, her expression grim. "If they are, we have a bigger problem than I'd thought."

I frowned. "Why would halflings be a worse problem than full demons?"

"Because it suggests they've enough to be wasting them on a suicide mission such as this."

"Or they simply have no respect for either of us." I glanced up at the windows again. "What are we going to do?"

"Did you lock Max's window?"

"Yes, but that doesn't mean it's not open again. They

276

seem to have an uncanny knack for getting around your protection spells."

"Yes, and it makes me wonder why. But let's worry about our intruders first. I'll head in through the window if it's open—"

"And if it isn't?"

"I'll open it."

"Any sort of magic will warn them—"

"Which means they'll either fight or run, and the two of us can cope with either." She paused. "Do you have your daggers with you?"

"Only the stone one."

"Then that'll have to do. It might be wise in the future to start carrying Nex and Vita whenever you're out on any sort of investigation—until all this shit is sorted out, it's better to be safe than sorry."

"The only way we're going to sort shit out is by finding and stopping the murderous heir. How long do you want?"

"I'll shift shape behind our cars so it's less noticeable. Give me a minute after that."

She waited until a car had rumbled past and then hobbled across the road. Once she'd taken blackbird form, she flew up the building and disappeared. I flicked my knife down into my hand, waited the allotted minute, then shoved the key into the lock and opened the door.

The small bell chimed merrily into the silence and I silently cursed the thing. On the floor above, all movement ceased, but the air now crackled with energy. It wasn't a spell; it was more a gathering of power—a whip ready to strike.

I studied the bookstore, but there was no movement and no evidence of anything being tampered with down here.

Whatever they were doing or were after, it involved the upper floors.

A loud crash had my gaze snapping toward the stairs. It was glass shattering. Mo had obviously forgone spelling and just broken through the window.

I raced across the room. Saw a shadow move at the top of the stairs and heard a slight whistle as energy cracked toward me. I dropped instinctively and the dark whip that would have taken off my head sheered instead through the top rail and split the balustrade underneath it.

As sparks and splinters flew, I pushed upright and lunged up the stairs. The dark-skinned man standing at the top was *huge*—a great hulking figure whose head and trunk were partially wrapped in shadows but whose arms and legs were the size of trees. My stone knife looked wholly inadequate, and I wasn't entirely sure *I* was up to combating the monster, either.

The air whistled another warning. I had nowhere to go, so I simply raised the blade to counter the invisible force of energy. The two met in a shower of sparks, but the knife not only held, it sliced straight into the whip. I twisted the blade around and cut down hard. As the knife's edge severed the thin stream of energy, I shifted shape and flew straight at the gigantic figure. He raised the severed whip to strike again, but I shot through his legs and quickly shifted back to human form. As he lumbered around, I shoved him hard toward the stairs. He bellowed and windmilled one arm, trying to balance even as he struck at me. The severed end of the dark whip caught the edge of the backpack and the smell of burning canvas filled the air. Fire leapt down my side as the ragged edge skimmed my flesh, but I ignored it and slashed with my knife. The blade caught several reaching fingers and severed them. As they plopped to the floor and his blood spurted across my body, I twisted around and kicked, with as much force as I could muster, at his knee. There was a loud pop and then his leg buckled underneath him. Another shove had him tumbling down the stairs, but I didn't wait to see if the fall killed him. I followed him down and made damn sure of it.

Only then did I take a deep, somewhat shaky breath.

Only then did I become aware of the fighting still happening upstairs.

I swore and raced back up. Saw, in one quick glance, Mo with Einar in hand, trading knife blows with a tall, thin woman. I raised my knife, screamed hard, and charged.

It was enough to momentarily distract the woman; rather surprisingly, Mo didn't finish her off. She simply knocked the woman out and let her fall in a heap onto the floor.

"You okay?" I stopped beside Mo and studied the unconscious woman. She was pale-skinned, with long black hair and human features. Only the slight point to her ears hinted at her darker ancestry.

"Yeah, but the bitch is immune to magic so I had to do things the hard way. Go grab the silver rope out of the bottom of my wardrobe, will you?"

I nodded and sheathed my knife as I walked across the room. The rope was made up of three slender silver chains woven around thin, high-tensile wire, which gave it strength while prohibiting any possibility of spell casting or shifting shape when bound by it. I'd never seen Mo use it before now, but that didn't really mean anything, given she was centuries old ... I shook my head, still unable to comprehend that fact, and walked back. Mo had dragged the woman onto one of the wooden chairs and bound her hands with some old cable ties.

She accepted the rope with a grunt of thanks. "Go grab your daggers and take care of that pile of shit at the base of our stairs. I'll bind this bitch and then go grab the blessed water."

I ran up to the next floor and discovered chaos. My room had been turned upside down—drawers were open, and my clothes and shoes scattered everywhere. Even the damn mattress had been torn from the base and slashed open. What the hell had they been searching for?

It surely couldn't be the crown. Luc had taken out the men who'd come to the cave, and they wouldn't have had the time to get any more people back there. Even if they *had*, it'd still take hours to remove all that debris. So why— The thought stalled as I remembered the stuff I'd taken from Jackie's. That had to be it—we had nothing else here that could interest Darkside. And given both halflings had still been here when we'd arrived, there was a good chance they hadn't found the family tree or the book I'd shoved it in —but I'd nevertheless better check when I got back down there.

I poured some holy water over the area that had been lashed by the whip, then changed into fresh clothes and searched through the mess to find Nex and Vita. By the time I'd ashed the man mountain and returned to the living area, Mo had stripped off the woman's leather armor and bound her with the silver rope.

I skirted them and went to the coffee table. The book remained; the papers I'd tucked inside had gone.

I swore softly. Mo glanced around sharply. "What?"

"The family tree I found at Jackie's is gone. I don't suppose you found it on her, did you?"

"No."

"So either the man mountain had it, or there was a third person here."

"Given someone got them through our spells, I'd vote the second option. It does make me wonder how the hell they knew we had them." She paused. "Did you tell Tris?"

"No, but it's possible he spotted them the night he snuck up here—we did sit on the sofa and share a drink."

"I can't see how he could have picked out one old book with notes from all the others sitting there."

Neither could I. Especially when he wouldn't have been able to see what little of the notes had been visible from where he'd been sitting. "I did tell Max about the list, but I didn't mention where it was hidden—and I still won't believe he'd betray us."

"He was willing to work with Tris to get the relevant information from the Okoro family bible, remember, so maybe Tris's controller contacted him direct. Max rarely sees the bigger picture—he's all about the immediate deal and what it can do for him." She shrugged. "But let's sort out one problem at a time."

She unscrewed the bottle of blessed water and poured it over the woman's head. Her response was instant—her scream was a high, piercing, and inhuman sound that sent chills skittering down my spine.

"That," Mo said, casually placing the empty bottle on the table before reaching for another. "Was only quarter strength. You can expect increasing increments if you do not answer my questions."

The woman hissed and opened her eyes. They were a weird red-brown, and filled with hate and fury. "You'll get nothing from me, witch."

"Oh, I think I will. You're human enough to want life

over death, halfling." She poured the second bottle over the woman's head.

Another scream, and deeper anger. The woman's pale skin gained a slightly pink sheen.

"We're both aware that even full-strength blessed water won't actually kill you." Mo's voice remained conversational. "But it will erase the imprint of ash and darkness from your skin, and make it impossible for you to ever return to the nest."

"There will be no return. We both know this also."

Mo raised an eyebrow. "Not necessarily. If you answer my questions, I will release you."

My gaze shot to Mo, but she didn't acknowledge it. Her attention was wholly on the halfling.

The woman's laugh was sharp and disbelieving. "I am not so foolish as to trust the word of a witch."

"It is the truth, halfling."

"Those who live in light know not the meaning of that word."

"Those of us who are mages are bound by certain rules. If I swear that you will, indeed, leave this place alive, then I'm bound by the rules of my order and my gods to do so."

Something flickered in the woman's red-brown eyes. Uncertainty, and perhaps even hope. "And do you so swear?"

"Yes."

The uncertainty remained, but the woman nevertheless took a deep breath. "I am nothing but a menik. I do as I'm told, nothing more."

"Even foot soldiers such as yourself have those who they report to. I want a name."

"It will do you no good."

"Then you should have no fear of telling me, should

you?"

The woman contemplated Mo for several seconds. "Is this all you want?"

"That, and where she resides. I also want the name of the person who let you into this place."

"And I can leave after I tell you this? You do not lie?"

"You can go."

Cunning flickered through her eyes. She was going to give us information, all right, but it wasn't likely to be the truth.

"My control is Orika. She resides in Nottingham."

That raised my eyebrows. I doubted it was a coincidence that she mentioned the town where Tris was shot; I also doubted this Orika was actually her boss or even the shooter. It was more than likely to be the name of another halfling like her.

"Address?"

The woman gave it to us. "I do not know the name of the person who let us in. But he was a witch."

"What type of witch?"

The woman shrugged. "You all emit the same stench. It is hard to tell."

"So he used a key to get in here?" I asked.

"Key and then magic," she replied. "I know not what kind."

"Can you describe him?" Mo said.

"It would do no good. He was using a shield that altered his appearance."

The man Tris had met at McDonald's had been using a similar shield, and I doubted it was a coincidence. Perhaps as well as receiving his orders from the stranger, Tris had given him a copy of our key. Just because I'd gotten one off him didn't mean it was the only one he'd had.

But how could he have woven exceptions into the magic protecting this place? Only a very strong witch who was familiar with Mo's magic could have done something like that without leaving some sort of tell behind.

Mo released the rope and then cut the cable ties. "You may leave the same way you entered, halfling."

The woman's gaze darted between the two of us then she rose and fled—not out through Max's broken window, but rather down the stairs and out the front door.

I quickly sent Luc the information we'd gleaned from the menik, then scurried after Mo as she snapped a quick "Come along" at me and strode toward the stairs.

"Where are we going?"

"Following her, of course." Mo looked over her shoulder. "You didn't actually think I was releasing a dark spawn, did you?"

"I figured you had some sort of plan, but she's stripped down to her underclothes and immune to magic—where the hell did you hide the tracker?"

"I didn't. I called Ginny for help. She does this sort of thing for a living. Might as well make use of her."

"Did you tell her it could be dangerous?"

"Indeed. That only made her doubly eager to help. She should be waiting for us out the front."

Ginny's racy-red Audi sat across the road in our parking area. She climbed out of the driver side as we ran across and handed me the keys. "Be gentle with her, or I will get cross."

I grinned. To say Ginny loved her car was something of an understatement. "I promise not to mash the gears more than once or twice."

She patted the car's hood lightly. "It's okay, baby, we'll get through this together."

"Ladies, we need to move." Mo pushed the passenger

seat forward and climbed into the back. It was a tight fit for someone of her height.

"We won't lose her—I got a good feel for her when she left the building. And can I just say, I've never seen anyone whose radiating energy is such a weird, murky gray."

I shoved the seat belt on and started the car. The soft rumble of the engine filled the air, and anticipation shot through me. I might thoroughly love my Mini, but it was a rare treat to be driving the Audi.

"That's because she's a halfling," I said. "Which way?"

"She's moving east but still on foot at this point." Ginny glanced at me. "What the hell is a halfling?"

"You know all those bedtime stories your mom used to tell you about demons coming to steal you from your bed?"

Ginny shuddered. "I used to have damn nightmares. Not entirely sure what Mom's point was, other than to have me too afraid to get out of bed during the night."

"That," Mo said, amusement evident, "was entirely the point."

"Well, it worked. Left here. She's at the end." Ginny paused. "Look's like she just picked up transport."

"Which car? There're three up ahead."

"Green one. And she can't be a demon—she's out in the middle of the day."

"She's a half-demon," Mo said. "Born of a stolen human and dark elf father."

Ginny swung around, her expression one of horror as she stared at Mo for several seconds. "Seriously?"

"I'm afraid so."

"Well, fuck, I'll be locking my windows from here on in."

"They don't come after witches," Mo said. "Not strong, opinionated ones, anyway."

"That does not comfort me in the least."

We were soon out of the old town and motoring toward Clifton. I glanced at Mo through the rearview mirror. "Where do you think she's going?"

"Back to base."

I frowned. "How is that going to help us? Other than revealing another dark gate?"

"She won't be heading to a dark gate. Not when she still reeks of holy water." She shrugged. "She's a menik—"

"Which is?" Ginny cut in.

"A foot soldier. They have little free will and are trained to return to their temporary base and report if a mission goes sour. Given the number of halflings that have been in play, we've obviously got a clutch of them somewhere near Ainslyn."

"Wouldn't them all hanging out together be dangerous? They're not exactly human identical." And the man mountain I'd killed would certainly have been hard to miss.

"They'll be somewhere out of general sight, probably in an abandoned house surrounded by trees and with few neighbors." She paused. "I would also think that there are 'human identical' halflings living unnoticed within various communities."

"Not witch communities," I said. "Their stink would give the game away."

"Not necessarily. The one who almost brought down Uhtric's reign certainly didn't smell like a demon."

"Do you think the woman Tris met is a halfling?" Ginny asked.

"I'd say it's highly likely," Mo said. "I'd truly love to know what he received in exchange for that woman in the hecatomb."

"A whole damn lot has happened since we last talked,

hasn't it?" Ginny said, exasperation in her voice. "What the hell is a hecatomb?"

I explained, and her face went white. "I didn't know such things even existed."

"They used to be everywhere before Uhtric locked Hell's Gill down," Mo said. "Unfortunately, it could happen again if the wrong person claims the sword."

"Next right," Ginny said. "And wasn't the sword created to combat darkness?"

"Yes and no. It was designed to combine and draw on the power of all four elements, thereby creating a weapon Darkside had no answer to."

"So that's why they're running around killing people— they're trying to prevent anyone raising the sword against them?"

"I think what's happening is far darker than that. I think we've got an heir who's been seduced by Darkside running around killing rival heirs so that he might claim the power for himself and his dark masters."

Ginny sucked in a breath. "Surely no one would be that foolish. Not in this day and age."

"Power has always been a dangerous lure for the weak willed," Mo said.

I glanced at Mo through the rearview mirror. "Do you think this woman will lead us to the one Tris met?"

"Maybe, though she's further up the chain of command and unlikely to be stationed at the menik's base."

"What about the name she gave us? Do you think that has any value?"

"It's likely to be someone involved on a peripheral level. She wouldn't be foolish enough to attempt a total lie—she'd be wary of me sensing it."

"Just as well I passed the info on to Luc, then. At least he can get someone to check the address straight away."

We drove out of the old town toward Clifton Springs. Ginny directed me through a number of smaller streets and we eventually found ourselves in a tree-lined lane.

"She's stopped at that chapel down the far end, by the look of it," Ginny said.

I pulled over to the side of the road. "Isn't a chapel a rather odd place for half-blood demons to be hiding out?"

"It would have been deconsecrated when it was decommissioned," Mo said. "So whatever protections the religious blessing gave it no longer apply."

"Whatever blessings?" Ginny said. "I thought it was an undisputed fact that no demon could step across holy ground?"

"It depends entirely on the strength of the demon and the piety of the priest. Update Luc while I go scout. If we are dealing with a clutch, we'll need Blackbird help."

"Luc said he was going back to headquarters; if he did, then he's in London and hours away."

"There are twelve Blackbirds in all, remember. I'm sure there'll be one or two close enough to render assistance."

I crossed mental fingers that *that* was the case. "Be careful out there."

Her smile flashed. "It'll take a demon far wilier than a mere menik to get the better of me."

As Ginny got out of the car, then popped the seat forward for Mo to exit, I dragged my phone out of my pocket.

Luc answered second ring. "What's happening?"

"The halfling has led us back to what we think is a clutch."

He sucked in a breath and then swore, softly but vehemently. "Where are you?"

"Outside Clifton Springs." I quickly gave him the address. "Are you able to get someone here to help deal with this?"

"Yes, but it could take them some time to get there."

"I'm pretty sure Mo has no intention of tackling this alone, but the sooner you get either your people or even the Preternatural squad here, the better it'll be."

"I'll organize it now and see you soon."

Meaning, no doubt, he was now on his way here. I studied the old chapel down the far end of the street. Unease stirred, though I wasn't entirely sure why. "I'm heading down to help Mo. Do you want to reverse back into that dirt lane we passed and wait there?"

Ginny nodded. "Yell if you need help or a quick getaway."

"Will do."

Once she'd reversed into the lane, I shifted shape, grabbed Nex and Vita, and then flew over the trees toward the old chapel. It was a small redbrick building, with plain glass arched windows rather than stained, and a slate roof covered in moss. The grounds around it were well tended, which to me suggested someone came here regularly to look after them. I couldn't imagine halflings bothering with such a mundane chore.

With a flick of her wings, Mo appeared. I followed her into the tree-lined field to the right of the chapel and shifted shape to land.

She didn't look happy. "I can't get close enough to see what we're dealing with. There's a tight weave of magic around the entire building."

"Can you disconnect it?"

"Possibly, but it'll take some time and I may need help."
She held out her hand. "Lend me your phone, and I'll call
Barney."

"I don't mean to be rude, but how can he help us? His
gift is personal magic—"

"And what do you think dark elf magic is? It's not
elemental—they don't source it from the world around
them, as most witch houses do. It comes from their inner
darkness."

"Yes, but dark magic is still very different—"

"But still ultimately involves spell strings, which means
he should be able to at least guide me. Keep an eye on that
chapel while I—"

A huge whoomp drowned out the rest of her sentence.
As bits of brick, glass, and slate went flying skyward, a huge
wave of heat and magic rolled toward us, setting the trees
lining the field alight and blackening the grass.

"Gwen, fly—now!"

I immediately shifted shape, swooped around to grab
my daggers, and then leapt skyward. The shimmering wave
of invisible flames and magic rolled over the spot where
we'd been standing, crisping the blackened grass and
scorching the ground.

But it didn't roll on across the rest of the field. It leapt
up, chasing us into the sky.

I flew hard, desperately trying to get clear. Heat shimmered across my tail feathers and the stench of burning
filled the air. I squawked and shot up vertically in an
attempt to shake the deadly fingers. Faster, higher, I went,
my heart pounding so hard it felt like it was about to tear out
of my chest.

Finally, the fingers fell away and the wave collapsed.
We were free. Relief hit so hard that for several minutes my

entire body shook. It took every ounce of concentration just to keep flying.

Mo squawked, an imperative sound that basically meant "follow me." I swung around and we flew back to the little chapel. The roof had been partially blown off, no glass remained in any of the windows, and a fire raged deep in its wooden heart.

A heart that held no whole bodies, only bits.

Mo swooped down, shifting shape as she neared what remained of the entry doors. As I landed beside her, she raised a fist; energy shot from her clenched fingers, punching up to skies that were thick with clouds. It hit, and the clouds began to stir, gently at first and then with increasing speed as the wind whipped up and chased them toward us. Lightning flashed and thunder rumbled; a heart-beat later it began to rain. Not lightly, not gently, but so damn hard it was little more than a wall of water. The flames in the church were doused in an instant.

Mo unclenched her fist and her energy beam immediately dissipated. The wind fell silent and the clouds lightened and moved on at a gentler pace.

"Wow." I reached out to steady Mo as she sucked in a deep breath. "You okay?"

"Yeah." Her smile flashed, though her cheeks were on the hollow side again. "Haven't called to the skies like that in a while, and I forgot about the cost of doing so."

The roaring of a car engine had me half spinning. Ginny. She slid the Audi to a halt and scrambled out. "Are you both okay? What the fuck happened?"

"The bad guys were erasing evidence," Mo said. "Gwen, why don't you go into the chapel and see if there's anything useful left. I'll park on that little bench under the tree and recuperate for a few minutes."

I helped her across then strapped on my daggers and returned to the chapel. Ginny followed me over.

"You might want to stay outside." My voice was grim. "It isn't going to be pleasant in there."

"It can't be worse than some of the things I've seen as a cop."

"I wouldn't bet on that."

"I'll guess we'll soon find out." She motioned me forward.

I didn't bother arguing any further. Truth was, I was happy to have company even if it wouldn't make the gore any easier to cope with.

I stepped through the remains of the doorway and stopped inside the porch. Despite the cleansing downpour, the stink of ash and death was strong. Light streamed through the gaps in the roof, highlighting the utter destruction caused by both the heat wave and Mo's storm. There were large chunks of what had once been halflings scattered in-between jagged bits of furniture and the colorful remnants of clothes. From what I could see, there'd been at least five other meniks here. That they'd been killed so swiftly spoke of their master's determination to keep us in the dark. About *what* was now the question we needed to answer.

That, and how they'd even known we'd found the nest.

There couldn't have been more than ten minutes between our arrival and the chapel's destruction. Even if we'd been immediately spotted by the meniks, it would have taken time for them to report back and a decision to be made. Unless, of course, there'd been some sort of automatic self-destruct button installed within the magic protecting the place. Maybe Mo's effort to get close was what had triggered the explosion. The dark elves were notoriously efficient when it came to destroying things, if what the old literature said about them could be believed.

"You were right," Ginny said, her expression one of horror. "This *is* worse than anything I've seen before."

"Yeah."

I stepped into the main building. The chapel was a simple cross shape, with the apse and chancel down the far end. Two small wings sat on either side of the nave halfway down, and that's obviously where the ignition point of the fiery explosion had been. The walls were charred, and the one body I could see there was little more than half a skull and, rather weirdly, finger fragments.

Ginny motioned toward them. "They might be intact enough to get a print from. I know these things were part demon, but they were living in this world, and the one we followed probably had a license. At the very least, we might be able to use her information to help track down others like her."

I glanced at her, amusement tugging at my lips. "We?"

She raised an eyebrow. "You don't seriously think I'm going to step away now, do you? Not after seeing this and knowing there are goddamn half-demons roaming about the world."

"Ginny, I'm not sure that's a good—"

"Um, don't finish that." She waved a finger up and down her body. "Grown-up person here. I'll decide what is and isn't a good idea."

I raised a hand. "Fair enough."

Her gaze narrowed. "I don't trust you when you use that tone."

And she was probably wise not to, given I had no intention of placing her in the line of danger if I could at all help it. "Let's discuss this later."

"I'll make damn sure that we do." She looked around. "What exactly are we looking for?"

"I don't know."

"That's helpful."

The smile tugged at my lips again. "They blew this place up to stop us finding something—"

"Something other than a slew of half-demons, you mean?"

I nodded. "We already knew about them, so they either did this to stop us interrogating them, or there was something else here."

She grunted. "Well, if there's anything left to find, then it's going to be found up in the apse area. That's the one place that hasn't suffered much damage.

My gaze returned to the apse. Though all the windows had blown out, the area seemed relatively intact compared to the rest of the chapel. It looked as if the meniks—or whoever controlled them—were using it as an office area, because there were several blackened desks and upturned chairs in the chancel area, and a larger, relatively untouched desk where the altar would have been.

"Let's check it out."

We carefully made our way down the center aisle. I did my best to ignore the stench of burned flesh, and tried to avoid the multiple body remnants and bloody pools of water. But it was damned hard.

We checked the chancel desks on the way through; while the heat had warped some of the drawers, the ones that did open were empty. There wasn't even the usual assortment of dead pens and paper clips that often collected in desks.

We moved on. A gentle breeze stirred through the broken windows and paper fragments drifted out from behind the larger desk. Ginny reached down and, using a tissue, carefully picked up one of the bigger pieces. "It's something of a miracle that any paper survived the blast."

"Yeah." I moved around the desk and checked the drawers. They were as empty as the ones in the chancel, so the papers had obviously been sitting on top.

"There's writing on it," Ginny said. "But I have no idea what language it is."

I picked a couple of pieces and my gut clenched. The writing on the scraps very much resembled the writing I'd seen on the dark gate Luc and I had found. "I think it's elvish."

"No surprise, I guess, if we're dealing with half-breeds."

"No."

We collected the remaining useable fragments and put them all on the table. Jigsaws weren't my thing, but Ginny was pretty good at them. I left her to it and moved back to the side wing that had sustained the most damage. Though light streamed in through the roof not very far away, this area lay in semidarkness. Whether this was a result of there being no windows, or something more arcane, I couldn't immediately say. But it was definitely where the ignition point had been. Aside from the fact that there was very little left of the menik who'd been standing here, string fragments still floated in the air and a hole had been blasted through the wall at the far end. Though I didn't understand the intent behind most of the strings, newer layers had been interwoven through the old, and suggested the protections here had very recently been adjusted.

The soft sound of a footstep had me reaching for Nex and spinning around. Mo stepped into the nave and, after a quick look around, strode toward me.

I released the half-drawn knife. "I thought you were

resting?"

"Curiosity got the better of me."

"You know what curiosity did to the cat."

"And the rest of that proverb is 'but satisfaction bought her back'. Which, of course, is appropriate given it refers to a cat's nine lives. Bit of a mess, isn't it?"

"Understatement of the year."

"Not really. It could have been a whole lot worse if we hadn't stepped in."

"If *you* hadn't stepped in," I corrected dryly. "And by the way, I intend to sit you down once this is all over and question the hell out of you about your life and these powers you've concealed all these years."

"Powers?" Ginny said, her gaze still on the bits of paper in front of her. "What powers?"

"That's a question that can be saved for later." She stopped beside me. "And I haven't concealed them, Gwen. There was simply no need to use the majority of them before now. What have you found?"

I waved a hand toward the strings. "Are there enough remnants to track the spell back to its creator?"

Mo pursed her lips and narrowed her eyes. "Worth a try. Step back."

I did so. She raised a hand; light leapt across her finger-tips, a golden glow that had the shadows shifting uneasily. As the pulse of her energy grew stronger, Mo formed the light into a half-sphere, and then stepped deeper into the nave. The strings immediately drifted away from either the movement or the light itself. Mo stopped and raised the glowing half-sphere, softly blowing on it. As it rolled from her fingers and spun lightly on the spot, Mo stepped to one side and cast a rope spell. The invisible line of power ran around the outside of the dark strings and looped back to

Mo. As she drew it back in, the strings were caught and bunched up. Once she had a thick knot, she ran the half-sphere through the mass, and then capped it to form a complete sphere. It rather resembled a mass of twisting black vipers caught in a cage of gold.

She studied it critically for a few seconds and then nodded, satisfaction evident in her expression. "The cage will keep them viable for a few hours longer. What's Ginny studying so intently up there?"

"It's some sort of list, by the look of it." Ginny stepped to one side. "Gwen suspects it's elvish."

Mo stopped beside her and studied the scraps. "Gwen would be right. Unfortunately, it's not a language I know."

Ginny smiled. "I think it's fair to say there're very few who do—other than the elvish or their halflings."

From beyond the walls came the wail of approaching sirens. Either someone had called the cops or the Preternatural boys were now screaming toward us.

"If we can find the bitch Tris met with, or even the meniks' controller, it's possible they could translate for us." I waved a hand at the scraps. "Do you think they erased the nest as a precautionary measure, or do you think this list is what they were trying to destroy?"

"Possibly both, though how they knew we were following their menik is worrying. It's not like we told anyone."

"Could they have placed some sort of listening spell or device in your home?" Ginny asked.

Something within me went cold, and I swore. Loudly.

Mo raised an eyebrow. "You've had a thought?"

"Yeah." I scrubbed a hand across my eyes. "I doubt we're dealing with a listening spell, because you would have sensed any tampering with the magic that surrounds—"

"Not necessarily," she cut in. "Not if it was done by a witch of this world who was familiar with my magic—and that's already been proven the case a number of times."

"Breaking magic is one thing," I said. "Weaving a spell through it without you knowing is entirely another."

"Which does not mean it's impossible." She made a "continue" motion with her hand.

"If it's not a spell, it leaves us with the bug option, and Tris. I think the night he snuck in he'd actually been in the shop for a while, because it was the sound of him moving around that woke me. I presumed he'd been looking for something, but what if he wasn't? What if he'd been placing something? Something like a bug."

"They're easy enough to get these days," Ginny said, "and they're quite sophisticated."

"And we were talking about following the menik as we were coming down the stairs this morning." The wail of sirens was now so loud I had to raise my voice to be heard. "If the devices are being monitored full-time—and they'd logically have to be—then they would have had time to organize the destruction here."

"What sort of range do the things have?" Mo asked.

"Depends on their size, and what sort of receiver they're using." Ginny shrugged. "Some can have a very long range, but generally it's somewhere between a hundred and fifty to five hundred meters."

"A range that gives them plenty of places to hide," I said.

Ginny shook her head. "With the density of buildings within old Ainslyn, they'd probably want to be close."

Mo pursed her lips. "You know, Saskia next door closed her shop for a few weeks to visit her Parisian relatives. It would be a perfect hideout for anyone intent on keeping an eye on our comings and goings."

The sharp sound of the siren abruptly cut off, leaving a briefly eerie silence. Then doors slammed and footsteps came running toward the building.

"Then the first thing we'd better do when we get home is check the place out."

"I can borrow a scanner from work," Ginny said. "It will be pointless clearing out your listeners if you don't also clear out their devices."

"That would be awesome—thanks." I glanced around as a familiar figure stepped into the room. "Jason? What are you doing here? I thought you were in London?"

"No, I left to ask Henry a few more questions."

"How is he?" Mo asked.

"Pretty good, considering. What happened here?"

As Mo filled him in, I tugged the phone out of my pocket and took several quick snaps of the various bits and pieces of paper.

"Righto," Jason said. "We'll take it from here. But the next time you unleash a menik, call us in on the hunt. We might have prevented all this if we'd been here."

"I very much doubt that, dear boy, but I will attempt to let you know in the future." Her tone suggested he shouldn't rely on her actually doing it. "In the meantime, does the name Jules Okoro mean anything to you?"

"No." He frowned. "Should it?"

"It was one of the names on a list we found—the same list that had both Gareth and Henry on it."

"A hit list?"

"For a killer heir."

"Which means Henry could still be in danger. I'll alert the team at the hospital. What about the sister?"

"She's safe."

"Good."

Mo motioned to the papers on the desk. "You might want to get the Blackbirds to have a look at this list. They used to have scholars familiar with elvish text, though I'm not sure if that's still the case."

"Elvish?" Jason stepped forward and looked at the papers. "Interesting. And is that a tracker sphere you're holding?"

Surprise ran through Mo's expression—not something that happened too often. "You know what it is?"

Jason smiled. "You don't get to be in charge of preternatural investigations without being familiar with all forms of magic, old or new. I will admit, however, I've only ever read about spheres like that. There're not many around today who can create them."

"Up until recently, there hasn't been a need for them."

"Good point. I take it you're about to track whoever unleashed the destruction here?"

"Yes. We'll let you know if we find anything."

"That won't be necessary, because I'm assigning one of my men to accompany you."

Awareness and heat prickled through me. I turned as Luc stepped into the chapel. Just for an instant, his gaze met mine and that indefinable force once again surged between us. It was far deeper than just awareness and desire now; it was almost elemental in feel, and spoke of a connection that stepped beyond the physical, beyond the emotional. It whispered of destiny and age, and of a bond not just days in the making, but years. Decades.

Centuries.

And it shook me to the core.

He felt it. That was evident in the slight widening of his

eyes. But that was all the acknowledgment he allowed. His expression otherwise remained the same and the quick tattoo of his steps didn't hesitate for even a second.

The damn man had the control of stone.

"No need," he said. "I'll go with them."

"The two of us won't fit on the back of your bike," Mo said. "And you definitely won't fit in the back of Ginny's Audi."

"Much to my eternal chagrin," she muttered.

"Take my car," Jason said. "I'll arrange for your bike to be transported back to headquarters."

"Thanks."

Jason tossed him the car keys. "Keep us updated. These ladies seem to have trouble understanding the concept."

"It's an age thing," Mo said. "I'm too old to remember, and these ladies are too young to care."

Jason rolled his eyes and motioned us to move on. Luc spun around and led the way out. As I fell in step beside him, the connection stirred to life yet again and my pulse skipped. I did my best to ignore it and said, "Is there a Jules Okoro on your list of possible heirs?"

Luc shook his head. "Why?"

"Because he was on that family tree Jackie was working on. Given he was listed after Gareth and Henry but before Max, it's possible he's not only an heir, but the next one to be hit."

"Do you remember any of the names above Gareth?" he asked.

"I only scanned it for a few seconds." I wrinkled my nose, trying to recall. "I think it was someone called Remy or Randy or something like that, but he can't be the one behind these murders."

"Why not?" came Mo's question.

"Because it appeared they were listed in age—Max is younger than either Gareth or Henry, and he was at the very bottom. Why would this Remy or Randy want to murder those younger than him?"

"Because there have been instances where the sword has deemed the firstborn son unworthy," Mo said.

"Uhtric was one case in point, as I mentioned earlier," Luc added. "He was third in line, but the sword reacted to him over either of his older brothers and he subsequently became king."

"Given how tenuous the Okoro link is, let alone the De Montfort," Ginny said, "why are they coming after either line? Why not hit the direct descendants first?"

"There's obviously a link we've all missed somewhere," Luc said. "If we could track down your family's bible, we might have a better idea of what's going on."

"I did ask Dad about it," Ginny said. "He vaguely remembers seeing it in a cousin's house, but that was years ago and the cousin has since moved to Australia. He's trying to find him."

Mo grunted. "Well, that would certainly explain why no one can find the thing, but not how Darkside appear to know more about the Okoro and De Montfort lines than we do."

"Are you sure the De Montfort bible was destroyed in that fire decades ago?" I asked. "Did you actually find any remnants to suggest it had been there and destroyed?"

Mo pursed her lips. "The entire house burned to the ground but, yes, we did find some charred remnants amongst the ashes. I suppose it *is* possible those bits were strategically placed."

"If they were, it would certainly explain a few things." Though in all honesty, how could they actually know more about recent generations than Mo, given how long she'd lived? If there *was* a direct link, it must have originated from a time *before* she'd been born.

"What it doesn't explain is why this Jules Okoro is on that list between Gareth, Henry, and Max," Luc said. "If there's a direct line of succession through the De Montforts, why would he be between them? Have you asked Jackie about it?"

"Yes," Mo said. "She found a brief mention of him, but hasn't as yet been able to find a record of his birth or even his death. I've asked her to keep investigating."

"Perhaps that's why they're searching for the Okoro bible," Ginny said. "Maybe they want to know whether he is a threat or not."

"If Darkside believed he was a threat, they'd kill him regardless," Mo said. "And that means we need to find him before they do. Ginny, can you go back home and see if either of your parents knows who he might be? And then would you mind heading over to Browne's cafe and keeping an eye on Saskia's store?"

She nodded. "If someone leaves, I'll follow and report back."

"Just be wary," I said. "If they in any way suspect we're on to them, you may be led into a trap."

A smile touched her lips. "I *am* a cop, remember. I do know how to follow suspects."

Mo touched her arm. "These suspects have a tendency to murder first and ask questions later, so carry your blade *and* your gun."

"I will."

She jumped into the Audi and drove away. We followed Luc to an unmarked black sedan and climbed in—me in the back and Mo in the front.

Luc started the engine. "Where to?"

Mo raised the glimmering, string-filled sphere and studied it for a few seconds. "Head into Clifton Springs, and I'll direct from there."

As Luc turned the car around and accelerated down the road, I said, "Did you send someone out to investigate the information I sent about the menik's controller?"

His gaze briefly met mine in the rearview mirror. Though there was nothing more than calm remoteness in those jade depths, desire nevertheless flickered through me.

The damn link between us was definitely getting stronger, and it wasn't helping the state of my errant hormones *at all.*

"Dan detoured over and checked it out. The woman who'd been using the room unexpectedly checked out an hour earlier."

"Any evidence that she was our shooter?"

"Dan viewed the security tapes, and she was carrying a long ski bag that could easily have concealed a rifle. He's put out an APB on her."

"I hope you mentioned that she could be dangerous."

"They've been told to keep their distance and notify the NCA immediately."

"What about the oath ring we found in the hotel room? Did you have any luck trying to trace it?"

"I sent it to London. As far as I'm aware, they're still working on it." His amusement spun around me, a warm yet insubstantial caress that had goose bumps tripping down my spine. "You really do like your questions, don't you?"

"It's a family trait, dear boy, and one you'd better get used to," Mo said before I could reply. "It'll make your life together easier. Take the next left."

He did so, then glanced at her, eyebrow raised. "I'm a

Blackbird; that's all I ever wanted to be, and all I ever will be. Long term is not something I'm interested in."

I couldn't help wondering if he was trying to convince himself or me with statements like that. "You let me go and you'll end up regretting it, Blackbird."

"No," he said softly, his gaze on mine again. "I won't."

Mo leaned across and patted his knee. "While I do appreciate the practical and stoic nature of the Blackbirds, what is happening between you two is something way beyond your control and determination."

"Attraction—no matter how fierce—will never rule my actions, and my heart will never again be on the table."

It was a statement that stung, if only because—for one brief moment in that cavern—I'd truly believed his heart *had* been on the table. There'd certainly been more than just a fierce attraction; it had been deeper than that. Stronger than that.

So who was kidding themselves? Him? Or me?

"I'm not talking about attraction," Mo said. "And not even the most hardened heart can fight destiny."

"I don't believe in destiny."

"Ah, well then." Mo shook her head. "Your fall, when it does happen, will not be pretty."

Luc didn't reply, and silence fell for a while. After a few more directions from Mo, we entered a street that was filled with redbrick bungalows all made in the same mold. There was a large paddock area down the far end and—beyond a somewhat scraggly hedge—the tops of shipping containers were visible.

"Stop here," Mo said. "It's the last house in this row."

Luc pulled over. I leaned forward and rested my arms on the front seats. The house in question had double-width windows at the front and two dormer windows in the roofline. The front garden had been concreted over and there was a white van sitting to the right of a longish brick planter that divided the yard from the footpath.

Mo unclipped her seat belt. "I'll go scout—"

"It's better if I do," Luc said. "Especially after what happened at the chapel. They're likely to be watching for any over-inquisitive birds."

Mo hesitated, and then nodded. Luc climbed out of the car and disappeared from sight.

"You obviously have a good idea what this goddamn connection between me and Luc is," I said. "So how about you explain it? Because I have to tell you, it's frightening the hell out of me."

She frowned. "Why on earth would you be frightened of it?"

"Because it's not natural to be connected on such a deep level with someone you barely even know. And it's certainly not natural to touch that person's arm and suddenly be immersed in their thoughts, sharing a memory that caused them great pain."

Mo sucked in a breath. "That usually doesn't occur until after consummation of the relationship."

"Then I hate to think what's going to happen if and when we ever get around to sex." I paused and looked through the front window. Though I couldn't see him, the odd awareness told me he was now moving down the side of the house. "What exactly is it?"

"It's what was once known as *anima nexum*—a Latin term that means soul connection."

I raised my eyebrows. "Soul mates? You're saying we're *soul* mates?"

"Not exactly." She grimaced. "It can certainly refer to two people who are connected at a soul level, but it can also refer to souls doomed to battle each other through time eternal, or souls who are destined to re-meet until whatever went wrong in their initial relationship has been rectified."

"So are we the first or the third? Because we're obviously not the second."

"I suspect, given what you just said, that it's the third option."

"Why? I would have thought my ability to touch him and see his pain was something a soul mate could do."

"No. The soul mate connection is simply a recognition of fate. It's of the moment—of *this* life rather than the past. It can be fierce and instant, to be sure, but it certainly does not imbue either party with any sort of psychic ability."

"And the third option does?"

"If the souls have been meeting for centuries then, yes, because the bond deepens with each rebirth, becoming something that is heart, mind, *and* soul."

"Forcing lovers to relive their doomed relationship certainly seems like something the old gods would do," I muttered. "Does it happen often in the De Montfort line?"

She hesitated. "I've seen it before, yes."

"I'm sensing there should be more to that answer."

"The more is nothing but a cautionary tale used to scare adulterous young women."

"Why young women? Why not young men?"

She smiled. "Because the history of this world is written by men determined to cast women in the worst light."

"So what was the tale, and where did you hear it?"

"It was one my grandmother told me and she was, like you, rather enraged that it was Gwenhwyfar rather than her lover who paid the ultimate price for falling in love."

"And Gwenhwyfar was?"

"The chosen wife of the first witch king. As was often

the case in those days, it was an arranged marriage—one that held political and military benefits. The king sent the Blackbirds to escort Gwenhwyfar and her family to the ceremony. It's said that along the way, Gwenhwyfar and a Blackbird fell in love."

"And what about the fabled Blackbird ethics?"

"It applied to kings, not their queens—or future queens. As I said earlier, affairs often happened."

"I gather the king found out?"

"By my grandmother's account, Gwenhwyfar was not one to hide her emotions in secrecy and lies. She told the king she would not marry him."

"And?"

"The Blackbird was banished and Gwenhwyfar beaten. She was then forced—by both her father and the king—to honor the arranged marriage."

"She didn't run? She didn't get rescued by her Blackbird?"

"No."

"What a bastard, abandoning her like that."

Amusement touched Mo's lips. "As I've said, their duty is to their king, not their heart. He was honor-bound to leave as ordered."

"Technically, honor should have stopped him ever getting involved with her." I shook my head. "So, what happened to her? Did she live a long and unhappy life? Or did she reconcile with her king?"

"Neither. She bore him one son to save her family's honor, and then she killed herself."

"How the hell is *that* a cautionary tale against adultery? Seems to me it's more a warning to keep your big mouth shut."

Mo chuckled. "I always thought that, too."

"What about the Blackbird? What happened to him after he was banished?"

"He went to the Lady of the Lake and begged her to help him regain his love."

I blinked. "How on earth could she have helped him? I mean, she's a goddess and all, and probably could, but I wouldn't have thought she'd interfere in mere matters of the heart."

"Vivienne did help, but not in the way he might have wished. She's a romantic and was somewhat incensed that he simply walked away rather than fighting for the woman he loved."

"She sounds like my kind of goddess. What did she do to him?"

"She decreed that he would have a long and lonely life to regret his actions, and that his soul and Gwenhwyfar's would then meet time and again down through the ages. If he did not repeat his mistake—if he held true to his heart rather than his duty and allegiance to the king—his wish would be granted."

"Is there a happy ending to this story? Because other-wise I'm not liking the sound of it."

"That I can't say. It is but a tale, after all."

I gave her a long, somewhat disbelieving look. "You rarely waste time telling me tales like that unless there's a point behind them."

"The point, my girl, is pretty obvious."

"I'm not Gwenhwyfar, Mo."

"Perhaps not, but it certainly *is* evident that you and Luc have formed a connection generations in the making. It would explain your instant attraction to the man and your ability to sense his presence, his emotions, and at least some of his memories."

"Well, all I can say to *that* is, we must have done something pretty damn shitty way back in our past—especially given that in *this* life, he's determined not to get involved long term."

"Perhaps, like Gwenhwyfar's lover, he is paying a penance for abandoning his heart for duty."

Something cold went through me as the image of the woman in red rose, and I shivered. "I think he might have fallen for someone he was protecting. I think she died and he blames himself."

"Ah." She wrapped a hand around mine and squeezed lightly. "If that *is* the case, then this lifetime is not likely to end happily for him."

"Meaning I should just stop hankering after the man and get on with finding someone else."

She smiled. "I doubt the hankering will stop, and it may well be that you could have a very happy sex-based relationship with him. But I would not expect much more than that."

"I had sex-based with Tris. I want more, Mo."

She squeezed my hand again. "We all do. And you will perhaps find that. You have in the past."

Before I could question *that* particular statement, Luc opened the driver door and leaned into the car.

"There's a minor boundary alarm around the windows and the doors, and at least two people inside, as far as I can ascertain. There're two doors—one on the side and one at the rear—as well as the open dormer window."

"Gwen, you take the latter," Mo said. "I'll hit the front and Luc can take the back."

He nodded and disappeared once again. Once Mo and I had climbed out of the car, we shifted shape and flew across to the bungalow. I waited until Mo had retaken human form and then swooped around and arrowed in through the open dormer window. I landed in a half-crouch and quickly looked around. It was a bedroom, but not one that had been used recently. There were no spells protecting it, either, which was odd. I rose, strapped on Vita and Nex, and then padded toward the door. As I reached for the handle there was a crash followed by a quick curse from the back of the house. A heartbeat later Mo's magic surged. I flung the door open and ran out, only to cannon into a half-shadowed figure racing toward the nearby stairs. We went down in a tangle of arms and legs, his weight landing across my body, pinning me. I bucked, trying to shift him, trying to get the arm twisted underneath me free. He snarled—a guttural, almost inhuman sound—and lashed out with a clawed fist. I jerked away; the blow aimed at my face smashed into the side of my head instead and left my ear ringing.

I raised my free leg and kneed him hard in the side, then flicked the stone knife down into my hand and thrust it deep into his body. He bellowed, another fierce sound that was more feline than human.

I stabbed him again, and then bucked, this time hard enough to dislodge him. I rolled sideways and climbed upright, but he somehow twisted around and kicked my legs out from underneath me. As my arse hit the carpet, he lunged at me, a catlike move that was frighteningly fast. I scrambled backward but hit a wall, swore, and threw myself sideways, twisting around and rolling underneath his leap. Claws lashed at me, slicing down into skin, drawing blood. A scream tore up my throat, but I gave it no voice. As the stranger bounced off the wall and came at me again, I dropped my stone knife and drew the other two. He hit me just as the blades crossed; lightning surged, encompassing the two of us, but ashing only one.

For several minutes, I didn't move. I just sucked in air and tried to get my zooming heart rate back down to survivable levels.

"Gwen? You okay?" Mo asked from somewhere near the base of the stairs.

"Yeah." I sheathed my daggers and rolled onto my hands and knees. The idiots with the drums had obviously decided to do an encore performance inside my head; the result had me blinking back tears. "There was a fucking halfling up here. I had to ash him, I'm afraid."

"Just as well we got the other three, then. You coming down?"

"After I investigate his room."

"Be careful."

"Always."

I pushed upright. Pain rippled down my left side and I hissed, clapping a hand to my ribs and feeling the wetness there. I spun and went into the nearby bathroom. The side of my sweater and the T-shirt underneath were both shredded; his claws had sliced me open from the top of my ribs down to my waist. While the cuts there were relatively shallow, the same couldn't be said for the upper portion of the wound. Thankfully, he hadn't punctured a lung or broken my ribs because, while the cuts hurt like blazes, I had no trouble breathing. I dribbled water down the three slashes to clean them and then grabbed a dressing to help stem the bleeding. It would have to do until Mo had a chance to heal the wound properly. I wrapped a bandage under my breast to help hold the dressing in place, then pulled my clothes back on and drew Nex. I picked up and sheathed my stone knife on the way through to the other bedroom.

Where I discovered a body.

A half-eaten, *human* body.

THIRTEEN

Bile rose and I swallowed heavily. This death was nowhere near as bad as the ones I'd seen in the hecatomb, but only because it was a whole lot fresher. He simply hadn't had the time to completely flesh-strip her.

Blood still ran from the multiple wounds over her torso, and her right leg had been skinned, leaving muscle and fat exposed. Her left leg was missing—torn from her body from up near her hip.

It made me wish I'd taken the time to make the bastard suffer a whole lot more, rather than simply ashing him.

As I stepped into the room, something crunched under my foot. I looked down to see several small bones. They looked like the remnants of toes ...

My stomach stirred anew, and I clapped my free hand to my mouth in an effort to stop the bile.

"Help," a voice said. "Please, help."

My gaze darted around, but there was no one else in the room. No one but me and the victim ... and surely that soft plea couldn't have come from her. Surely not ...

Her fingers twitched. Dear god, she was still *alive* ...

"Mo, Luc, you need to get up here—*now!*"

I darted forward and dropped onto my knees beside her. Blood soaked into my jeans and stung my skin; demon, she was part demon.

Fuck.

"Help," she repeated, her voice a fading whisper. "I can't—"

Despite the rise of wariness, I leaned a little closer. "Can't what?"

"Reach you."

Even as she replied, she lunged at me, her taloned fingers swiping at my throat. I lurched back instinctively and slashed up with Nex. The blade sliced through her hand with ease and her severed claws plopped onto my body even as her blood spurted across my face. The stumps of her fingers scoured across my neck, leaving a wet and stinging trail.

Movement, behind me. Not another demon; Luc.

"Drop completely to the floor," he said.

I obeyed, my head smacking against the carpet hard enough to see stars. The air howled, then silver flashed over my head and thumped into the halfling's body, knocking her down, pinning her to the floor. She screamed and writhed but couldn't escape. Hecate was silver; she couldn't touch it, let alone draw it from her flesh.

I took a deep breath and closed my eyes against the ridiculous sting of tears. A heartbeat later, Luc was on the floor beside me, his hands gentle as he cupped my face. Fear vibrated through his fingertips; fear and a caring so deep it made my soul sing.

This connection had definitely spanned lifetimes—and it suddenly made me angry that he was only prepared to explore it on a physical level and, even then, only temporarily.

"Gwen? Talk to me."

I took a deep, quivering breath and then opened my eyes. "You took your fucking time getting up here, Blackbird."

He frowned, obviously catching the edge in my voice but not understanding it. "How bad is that wound on your side?"

"Bad enough."

"Then go down and see Mo. I'll question this bitch."

"Sorry, but there's no way in hell I'm about to miss *that*. Help me up."

I held out a hand and, after a moment, he took it and carefully pulled me upright. A hiss of pain escaped and warmth trickled faster down my side. Obviously, the padding wasn't doing a whole lot right now to stem the tide.

Luc frowned. "I think—"

"The sooner you question her, the sooner I can go downstairs and get healed."

"May the gods save me from stubborn women," he muttered, but turned and walked over to the halfling.

He stood above her for a second, examining her, then bent and tore a section of her shirt away from her shoulder, revealing a small sword tattoo.

This was the woman Tris had met.

Obviously, she'd become a liability to her dark masters and, subsequently, lunch.

Luc gripped Hecate's pommel and turned her blade fractionally. Light flickered down her edges, then split and flowed across the halfling's body, enmeshing her. Her back arched and she screamed, a high-pitched sound of agony, but she made no move to attack. She couldn't. Hecate's fiery threads had her arms pinned.

"Tell me your name." Luc's voice was cold. Emotionless.

The woman spat. Luc swayed away from the globule and then turned Hecate's blade a fraction more. The light lines pulsed and tightened; the woman's eyes widened, and fear rather than hatred stirred across her features.

"Your blood pours from your body even as we speak, half-breed. We both know you will be dead soon enough. We also both know that if the silver remains in your flesh, your soul will not find its way back to the great cauldron."

"I care not."

"Good. I'll leave the sword exactly where it is, then. In the meantime, you *will* answer. You have no choice."

He turned the blade another notch. As the fiery threads tightened even further, her mouth opened, closed, and then opened again.

"Orika," she snapped. "I am Orika."

So I'd been wrong earlier. The other halfling *had* given up her controller—though given how quickly Orika had left Nottingham, she'd obviously been warned of that fact straight away.

"And what is your connection to Tristan Chen?"

The halfling fought the urge to reply but in the end, she said, "I am his contact."

"And his lover?" I couldn't help but ask.

Her gaze flicked to mine and she snorted. "I could find a better lover in the pit of despair."

A statement that had me briefly wondering just what half-demons considered essential attributes in a lover ... and whether their lovemaking to each other resembled the scenes I'd seen depicted on the dark gate. I shivered and shoved the rather disturbing images from my mind.

Luc cast me a warning look. I raised an eyebrow, silently challenging it. He of all people should know I wouldn't be silenced. He had, after all, commented on it often enough.

His attention returned to the halfling. "Who do you report to?"

The woman hissed but couldn't deny Hecate's magic. "Winter. That is all I know."

"Description?"

"She was one of the gray ones. Had long white hair, blue eyes, neutral features."

Which sounded a little like the woman—or man, given Henry hadn't been entirely sure of gender—who'd attacked Gareth.

"And the name of the witch working with this Winter?"

Her teeth flashed, though I wasn't entirely sure if it was a smile or a snarl. "Name is bound by magic. Not even your witch sword can force it."

"Did this witch order the kill on Tristan Chen?"

"Yes."

"And on me?" I asked.

Her gaze flickered to mine. The fierceness was leaving her eyes—death was only a few heartbeats away.

"No."

"Then why am I being targeted?"

"Price."

I frowned. "What sort of price?"

She didn't answer. *Couldn't* answer. She was dead.

"Well, fuck," I muttered. "Why do they always die just as it's getting interesting?"

"It's the gods' way of making us work harder for our

answers. Now, will you please go downstairs and get that wound tended to?"

"What are you doing to do?"

"Search the room—and I'd rather not have your blood dripping everywhere contaminating whatever evidence might be here."

"It's not *that* bad."

"It *is* that bad. Go. Please."

"Fine. But only because you asked so nicely."

He didn't look amused. I sighed and left, my footsteps echoing as I trundled down the uncarpeted stairs. Mo appeared in the doorway of the room to the right.

"In here." Her gaze raked me and she frowned. "Seriously, my dear, you really need to stop injuring yourself. We've too much yet to do for you to be on the sidelines."

"Hey, it's not like I'm deliberately getting hurt." I followed her into the small living room. There were two men and a woman stretched out on the floor, all of them bound with magic. None looked happy. "Have you got anything out of them?"

"They're meniks, I'm afraid, so they really haven't that much to tell." She motioned me into the kitchen. "But they share the same controller as the menik we caught in the bookstore."

"And *she* was being consumed by a catlike halfling upstairs. Both are now dead." I pulled out a chair and sat down.

"I take it Luc managed to question her before she died?" She helped remove my sweater and T-shirt, and then began unwinding the bloody bandage.

"She gave us a name—Winter—and a description that sounds like the woman who attacked Gareth and Henry."

The dressing fell away and she tsked. "Nasty, but at

least it's not as bad as the bleeding makes it—" She stopped, alarm in her expression. "What the hell did you do to your right side?"

I twisted around to look but the movement sent pain burning down my left side and had me hissing. "I don't know—why? What's there?"

"It looks as though something melted your flesh. Your whole side is a mess—it's a wonder you're not rolling around in agony."

"I don't know how that—" I stopped, remembering the halfling with tree trunks for limbs. "The fellow on the stairs had some sort of energy whip—it hit my backpack and skimmed my side."

"Well, it's going to leave scars, I'm afraid. You're just lucky that it hasn't gotten infected."

"I did pour some holy water over it, but it didn't look or feel that bad at the time."

"The holy water has obviously taken care of any infection, but it hasn't removed all the heat from the wound." She knelt in front of me and placed her hands on either side of my body, just to the side of my breasts. As her power rose and her fingers warmed against my skin, she asked, "Did Orika say anything else?"

I repeated everything she'd said and then added, "I also asked why they were trying to kill me. She said it was the price. Any idea what she meant?"

"The dark ones tend to exact a blood price for their help." The heated force of her healing energy swirled through my body and my skin rippled and twitched in response. "Perhaps you were Tris's price. You were, after all, probably the only person he cared about almost as much as himself."

I wrinkled my nose. "If that's true, why was he wearing

319

an oath ring? Why would he swear allegiance to either Darkside or another witch and yet pay a blood price?"

"Normally he wouldn't, but these are not normal times." She paused. "It's also possible they're trying to get to Max through you."

"Killing me isn't going to get them Max."

"The dark elf destroying the throne didn't mention killing you, did he?"

I frowned. "Well, no—"

"Then it's possible." Her magic reached a crescendo and the burning ache in my side and head disappeared. She sat back with a sigh and opened her eyes. "As I feared, I couldn't repair the melting, but I did at least erase the embedded molecules that were causing all the damage. But next time you get hit by a dark whip, tell me immediately."

"I will." I pulled my sweater on but didn't bother with the T-shirt. It was too damn wet with blood. "Is it possible that Tris swore an oath to Jules Okoro? Because no matter what you might think of him or how deeply he might have fallen into darkness recently, I really can't imagine him swearing fealty to a demon."

"Actually, neither can I." Mo squeezed my arm and then rose. "Perhaps our next move should be to search Tris's apartment."

"We already have; there's nothing there." Luc came into the kitchen. His gaze scanned me and came up concerned. "You're still looking pale."

"I'm fine. Stop fussing."

He raised an eyebrow, expression unconvinced, but all he said was, "There's nothing helpful upstairs. I've called Jason—he wants me to stick around until he can get someone here."

The connection between us stirred, whispering his

secrets to me. *He'd* been the one to suggest it, not the other way around. He'd wanted to place some space between us again in the vague hope it would somehow halt the gathering momentum of that connection.

Well, if he wanted distance, he could have it.

Mo nodded. "We'll fly back home, then. We've some bugs to get rid of."

"Bugs?"

She patted his arm. "We'll fill you in later. I want to get my girl home before her stubbornness collapses under the weight of exhaustion."

"Not going to happen." I crossed my arms and frowned at her. "And since when have you ever cossetted?"

"Every now and again, the long-absent mothering gene does kick in. Come along."

She turned and walked out. I studied her retreating back for a moment and then stepped close to Luc, rose on my toes, and kissed his cheek. He half raised a hand, as if to draw me close, and then hesitated.

"I will not break," he murmured, letting one finger drift down my cheek and rest lightly on my lips. "I cannot."

"Because of the woman in red. The one who died even as you tried to save her."

He blinked and stepped back. His eyes were a cold and stormy green. "How do you know about her?"

"That connection you're ignoring? It showed me. It's why Mo said this is bigger than either of us."

"Gwen, we need to get moving," Mo said from somewhere out in the backyard.

"I have no control over what you choose to believe, Gwen, but I am a—"

"Blackbird and married to the job, et cetera," I cut in. "Yeah, heard all that. You might want to look up the legend of the first witch king's wife. It might provide some useful information."

"A legend cannot and will not alter *my* life."

I smiled, though it held very little humor. "A legend is already changing our lives, Luc."

He waved a hand. "Yes, but we're not talking about the king's sword, are we?"

"No." I touched his arm, felt the muscles underneath my fingers jump. Awareness surged, along with heat and desire—both his and mine—but I pushed it aside. "And relax. I don't have to be hit over the head multiple times before I get the point. You're safe from my wicked wiles from now on, Luc."

With that, I turned and walked out. His gaze burned a hole into my spine, but I didn't look back. I'd been open and honest about my attraction to the damn man; the next move —if there ever was one—had to be his.

Mo was standing near the back fence. "I gather from your expression the man is still in the denial stages of your relationship."

"I'm beginning to think it'll never get beyond that point."

She patted my shoulder. "All good things come to those who wait."

"A saying developed by gods who delight in seeing humanity suffer, I'm sure. Why are we leaving? Don't give that crap about cossetting, because I'm not believing it."

"This is why you're my favorite grandchild—you have such a skeptical nature."

"Technically, I'm not your grandchild. And you didn't answer my question."

"Ginny is watching Saskia's store from Browne's café,

remember. I think we should go join her, as I suspect things might get interesting once night falls."

I raised my eyebrows but simply motioned for her to proceed. She shifted shape and leapt skyward on brown wings that glimmered with gold. I followed close behind, a far paler shadow.

Sunset was just starting to stain the clouds by the time we got home. We waited until several women had walked past and then landed in our parking area.

"You might want to go shower and change, as you're in no fit state to be seen in public," Mo said. "I'll talk to Ginny and see if there's been any activity."

I nodded and walked over to our store, but paused just inside the door to scan the shadows. There was no immediate indication that the spells or the store had been broken into while we'd been out, but that didn't really mean anything, given how easily these people seemed to be getting past Mo's protections.

I locked the door and moved across to the stairs, one hand on my knife and the other running along the underneath bit of the handrail. Three quarters of the way up, I found a small metal device. The first of many bugs, no doubt.

I left it where it was and continued on to the bathroom. Mo and Ginny hadn't appeared by the time I'd showered and redressed, so I strapped on all three of my daggers and then pulled on a long coat to cover them. After grabbing my keys, I walked past Saskia's place, then crossed over to the restaurant. There was a pot of tea and a sticky bun waiting for me.

I slid into the booth next to Ginny and said, "So, any movement?"

"The curtains twitched every time a motorcycle went past, but that's about it."

"They're watching for Luc." I picked up the teapot and poured the tea into the delicate china cup. "I found a bug under the stair handrail. It was probably close enough to pick up anything we were saying in the kitchen and living area."

"Which is how they were able to remain one step ahead of us," Mo said. "Quite annoying."

"Understatement," I said, amused. "I also sensed a vague glimmer of darkness as I walked past Saskia's shop. There's one, if not two of them inside."

"Two would be more logical if they don't want to be obvious about their presence there," Ginny said. "They could work in shifts without the risk of being seen coming and going."

"Which means we may have to mount an attack rather than sit here and wait for them to come out." I bit into the bun and groaned in pleasure.

"Good?" Ginny said.

"Better than sex."

Amusement danced across her expression. "That rather sadly says a lot about your sex life."

"Which is nonexistent now and looking even bleaker for the future."

"What? That gorgeous man isn't willing to play? Is there something wrong with him?"

"Yeah, he has ethics."

"Ladies," Mo said, voice dry. "Can we concentrate on the problem at hand?"

"Sorry," Ginny said, though she didn't in the least look it. "I've requested the bug finder and should get it tomorrow."

"Excellent," Mo said. "Though I rather suspect that after the events of today, they'll be pulling their forces back tonight."

"Aside from Tris, they've only lost meniks and one controller," I said. "In the scheme of things, I wouldn't call it a huge blow."

"True enough, but they have no idea how much information we might have gotten from Orika or the others," Mo said.

"Retreat isn't something I thought demons would do," Ginny said.

"If we were just dealing with Darkside, then an immediate, full-on assault would be likely. But we're not. We're dealing with a witch who has so far predicted all our moves."

"Thanks in part to the bugs," Ginny said.

"It's more than that. They appear to have an unfortunate familiarity with my magic."

"Then what's the plan? We can't sit here all night." If only because Browne's wasn't open past six in the winter months.

"Actually," Ginny said. "We can. I told Mary there was an undercover op happening and that we might need to use her premises as cover. She's more than happy for us to do so, and we can use the rear lane exit to come and go so those over the road won't suspect anything."

"Excellent," Mo said. "Gwen, contact Luc and tell him what we're doing."

I dragged my phone out and sent a text. I really didn't feel in the mood to talk to the man right now. "What if whoever's inside uses the rear window or door to come and go?"

Mo pursed her lips. "I'll put an alarm at the far end of

the lane—it'll be far enough away that they won't sense me doing it, and yet close enough that we can react if they set it off."

I nodded. "Do you want me to take first shift while you grab some sleep?"

She gave me a long look. "I may be old, my dear, but I suspect I have a whole lot more energy and strength than you right now. You go recuperate. I'll call if anything eventuates."

I narrowed my gaze. "Promise?"

"The battle that looms is yours, not mine, Gwen. I am merely the tactical advisor."

I raised my eyebrows. "Since when did all this become a full-blown battle?"

"It hasn't—and hopefully won't." She shrugged. "Ginny, it might be best—"

"Don't be thinking of sending me home," she said. "Because I ain't shifting. In fact, it might be good to call in Mia; she'll be able to sense anyone breaking through your spell, and I'll be able to trace the bastards."

Mo hesitated, and then nodded. "Okay, we'll work in four-hour shifts—I'll start, you and Mia can do the middle, and Gwen can take the tail end. And Ginny, you'd better move your car—they might notice it's been sitting in the same spot for a while."

"I'll see you in four hours, then." She rose and left.

I picked up my tea and sipped it. "You agreed to letting Ginny and Mia help us way too fast. Why?"

"Because I've an inkling nothing will go down until predawn. It's always been their preferred option."

"It may be the demons' preferred option, but we are—as you've already noted—also dealing with a wily witch."

She smiled. "Yes, but even wily witches know better

than to tackle an older and cannier witch when she's awake and aware. They won't do anything until two or three at least, when they're sure we're asleep."

"And that's why you gave Ginny and Mia the nine-to-one shift."

She nodded. "They can be safely tucked away in their own beds before the shit goes down."

Knowing both of them as well as I did, I rather suspected that neither Ginny nor Mia would leave quietly once their shift was over. "What if the opposing witch guesses this is what you'll do and the shit goes down during their shift?"

"Mia has quite a formidable arsenal of spells under her belt and Ginny is no easy target. They'll be fine—but I'll run a little additional protection around the inside perimeter here, just to be sure."

"Good idea." I finished my tea and rose. "You'll wake me for the last watch session?"

"I will."

I leaned over and kissed her cheek. "I'll set my alarm, just in case you sleep in."

Her eyes sparkled. "Anyone would think you distrust me."

I grinned. "Anyone who knows you would think said distrust was justified."

She harrumphed. "Go, horrible child. But make sure you sleep with all three daggers close to hand, just in case I'm wrong and the shit hits earlier than expected."

I grabbed the last bit of bun and headed home. My room was still a mess, but I couldn't be bothered restoring order, let alone dragging the mattress back onto the base, so I left it on the floor. I couldn't find my PJs so I changed into a pair of track pants and a T-shirt. Once I strapped my knives back on, I found my pillow and the duvet, and then crawled underneath the feathery warmth. I was asleep within minutes.

My laziness saved my life.

A large whoomp provided the first inkling of trouble. I jerked upright, daggers somehow in hand, and looked around wildly. Saw darkness ... and dust.

Why was there dust?

There was another whoomp, and the whole room shuddered. Then, with little warning, the roof collapsed. Plaster, wood, and slate fell like rain into the center of my bedroom, spraying the rest of the room with deadly shards of debris. Chunks of roof thumped around me—onto me—cutting through the thin material of my T-shirt and leaving bloody trails. The dust was so thick it was impossible to see, let alone breathe, and panic surged. If I didn't get out now, I wouldn't.

I kicked the duvet free of my legs and scrambled toward the door. Saw a shadow move and the gleam of black metal. Demon sword. I swore and rolled to one side, coming up in a half-crouch and smashing Nex and Vita together. Lightning flashed, a searing heat that melted both the blade and the demon who held it.

More shadows, followed by the thick scent of demon. I swore again and directed the lightning through the door, arcing it around in an effort to kill the ones I could see and the ones I couldn't.

But there were far more of the latter—and they were still pouring in through Max's bedroom.

I cursed again and spun away from the door. If I could reach the windows ... but a mountain of unstable debris now lay between them and me, and the dusty, deadly rain showed no sign of abating. The collapse might have happened over my bed, but it was now racing toward the front of the building.

I could wait it out—wait until the collapse had eased and then smash through a window and escape ...

The thought had barely crossed my mind when the floor began to tremble. Then, with a loud crack, the broken mess that covered my bed dropped away.

It wasn't just the roof that was collapsing. It was this goddamn floor as well.

I sucked in a breath, then faced the door and once again slapped the knife blades together. As the killing light flickered out, I ran into the hall. Heard a slight whistle and dropped hard onto my knees; a fiery whip cracked over my head and smashed into the wall behind me, sending plaster and wood flying. I swore for a third time and lashed out with Nex; a shudder ran through the blade as it connected with flesh but the lightning continued to burn from both blades even though they were now separated.

Demons died.

But not enough. Nowhere near enough.

A scream rent the air—a high-pitched inhuman scream. Not the demons. Hecate.

Relief surged, but Luc and his bloodthirsty sword were on the stairs and there was a never-ending tide of darkness between us.

Energy snapped through the air. I slashed up with Nex again and caught the whip's tip. White light flared against red and sparks flew, brief stars that lit the shadows, revealing the mass of demons all but crushing each other in their efforts to get through Max's door. I rolled Nex around the whip's electric thong; lightning flickered down its length, hit the handle, and then leapt at the massive demon holding it. As his body exploded into dust, I spun around and slashed at the demon arrowing toward me, slicing through the top of his head and sending blood, bone, and brain matter flying.

The trembling in the floor was now so bad that the nearby walls were shaking. I had to get out before the whole place collapsed.

I thrust up and crossed the blades once more. The lightning flickered and became strong again, even as a pulse of pain began deep in my brain. It was almost as if the daggers were now drawing on my energy ...

With another loud crack, the floor underneath me gave way. I screamed and threw myself forward, thrusting the daggers into more solid-looking floor and momentarily halting my slide just as my legs dropped into emptiness. Demons lunged at me, tearing my arms, forcing me to free Nex and slash wildly upward; lightning flickered back and forth, forming an odd sort of netting that stopped the majority of the blows coming at me. Some still got through, and pain rose like a red mist ...

With a scream of utter fury, Luc leapt into the fray, Hecate a blur as he killed the demons between us with cold and ruthless precision.

The warrior was in full flight, and it was a glorious thing to behold.

As the demons momentarily fell back from his onslaught, he leaned down, grabbed my hand, and pulled me out of the hole.

"Go," he said. "I'll be right behind you."

"Where's Mo?"

"She's trying to keep the ground stable—the bastards hit the building with earth magic, top and bottom."

A huge chunk of plaster came down just in front of me, forcing me to leap over it. I stumbled forward several steps before I caught my balance, then saw a flash of movement to my right. I slashed Nex sideways, but Luc was there before me. He buried Hecate in the demon's flesh and then spun, his jade eyes burning bright in the dusty darkness.

"Go, now."

I stumbled down the stairs and raced toward the door. I could hear the fighting behind me—Hecate's fury all but lost to the screams of the demons. Dust fell all around me, and the front windows were cracked. Mo knelt in the street beyond, both hands on the cobblestones and her power pulsing out in waves. Ginny and Mia were standing either side of her, protecting her against the demons that ringed them. I raced through the door, screamed in fury, and once again called on the power within Nex and Vita. Deadly forks of light streaked out, whipping around the demons, destroying them between one heartbeat and another. The ache in my head got stronger and that mist of red momentarily blurred my vision again. I ignored it and ran for Saskia's place.

"Wait—" Ginny said.

"Protect Mo," I shouted.

Footsteps behind me. Luc, not Ginny or Mia.

"I'll go around the back," he said. "Can you open the front door?"

"No—I'll go through the window."

"Give me a minute then."

As he disappeared around the corner, Mia shouted, "Step back from the door, Gwen."

I obeyed, and a heartbeat later, she punched the door open with a spell. "Thanks, Mia!"

I ran through, then paused near the counter to scan the room. The floor plan here was basically the same as ours—although Saskia sold pretty fabrics rather than books—and the floor immediately above held stock rather than accommodation. There were no demons in this lower section that I could see or smell, although the latter was nigh on impossible anyway thanks to the thick scent of death and defecation drifting down the stairs.

The back door crashed open, and from above came a scramble of movement. I swore and raced for the stairs. Another door slammed open and then wood screeched. It was a sound I was very familiar with.

"Luc, they're jumping out the back window."

The thump of his footsteps immediately turned and retreated. I took the stairs two at a time, but at the very last moment caught sight of a thin line of silver stretched across the top step. I leapt high above it and landed in an awkward half-crouch on the landing. Saw a flicker of flame and then heard a whoosh ... *fire*. The bastards had set fire to the place.

I raced toward the extinguisher on the wall opposite but caught movement out of the side of my eye. I slid to a halt and sucked in my gut. As the demon's blade sliced through my sweater but not my flesh, I stabbed Nex sideways. The blade blazed brightly in the darkness, and even as the point buried deep into the demon's chest, the lightning ashed his body.

I grabbed the extinguisher, ripped out the lock pin, and sprayed it across the flames that were just beginning to take hold of the papers and material piled in the center of the room.

The rest of the place resembled a goddamn pigsty, and the stench was horrendous. There were take-out containers, drink bottles, and piles of toilet paper and shit everywhere. Saskia did have a toilet, but maybe the meniks had been warned against using it in case we heard it flushing— The thought cut off as air stirred past my cheek.

I switched grip on the extinguisher and swung it around hard. The tank smashed into the face of the demon sneaking up on me and knocked him back. I dropped the extinguisher, leapt forward, and stabbed Nex into his dark heart. Then I leapt over his body and ran for the rear room. There were no more half-demons—they'd obviously fled out the open window. I walked over and peered out. The body of a man who'd been cleaved in two lay directly below, and the sound of fighting echoed from the far end of the lane.

I resisted the urge to go help Luc—he was far more capable than me when it came to fighting demons—and locked the window. The last thing I needed were more demons sneaking up on me.

Outside, the stairs creaked, and I suddenly remembered the wire. "Careful," I shouted. "There's a tripwire on the landing."

"Spotted it" came Mia's comment.

As I stepped out of the room, a broom came down on the wire and snapped it. For a heartbeat, nothing happened; then, with a crack, the landing's floor gave way and crashed down onto the shelving below.

"See, I told you it was nothing exotic," Mo said.

"The trap may not be, but the goddamn stench wafting down definitely is."

"Nose plugs would definitely be an asset up here." I walked over to the edge of the hole and peered around the corner. There were only the two of them on the stairs. "Where's Ginny?"

"She's making sure no one enters the bookstore," Mo said. "I called Jun and asked him to come over and check the integrity of the walls and what remains of the roof and ceilings."

Jun was Tristan's father. "Does he know his son is dead?"

"He didn't say anything, so I doubt—" She stopped, her gaze narrowing. "So it begins."

"What begins?" I said, exasperation evident. "Or shouldn't I ask?"

She smiled, though it held an odd sort of sadness. "You've been using Nex and Vita, haven't you?"

"Yes, of course, but—"

"And this time, the power didn't fade."

"Well no, but—"

"Which means the immersion begins."

She held out her hand. I gripped it and guided her across the remains of the joists. The tremble in her fingers alarmed me, but I didn't say anything. Now was not the time to cosset.

"What immersion?"

"The ancient power within the blades is finally forming a deeper connection with you." She squeezed my fingers, and I released her.

"And why would that happen when I'm a witch without power?"

"It is a recognition of strength and will more than power."

"So why would it happen now rather than earlier?" I gripped Mia's hand and guided her across the joists. "It's not like I haven't fought demons before."

"No, but you've never used the blades with such frequency before, which means they haven't had the chance to truly assess you before now."

"That almost sounds like they have a life and will of their own," I said. "There's not a screaming banshee of a witch locked inside them, is there?"

She snorted and strode across to the pile of paper the demons had tried to destroy. "No. But they *are* born of magic, rather than the forge, and that does come with complications."

I followed her across and squatted on the other side of the small paper pile. "What kind of complications?"

She waved a hand. "Your eyes, for starters."

I frowned. "What's wrong with my damn eyes?"

"They're seriously bloodshot," Mia said. "It almost looks as if they've been bleeding."

The red mist, I thought uneasily. "How bad can the bleeding get?"

"Bad enough, but that's a discussion we can have later. Let's uncover what these bastards were trying to destroy first."

Frustration stirred, though it wasn't exactly an unexpected reply. I picked up a sheet of paper and scanned it. "It looks like they were recording absolutely everything. This even notes what we had for breakfast."

"I don't know a whole lot about demons or their habits," Mia said. "But surely to god even they'd have the sense to only make a note of the things being said."

Mo grimaced as she shuffled through the layers. "It would depend on the wording of their orders."

Awareness prickled across my skin; a second later, Luc stepped into the room. I didn't acknowledge him ... and it was way harder to do than it should have been, given my annoyance with the man.

"I killed two of the demons attempting escape, but the third took flight." His gaze was on me as he spoke, but I picked up another piece of paper and studiously examined it. He added, "It was the red monster in charge of the mob that attacked us up on the knob."

That had my head snapping around. "Why would he be here? I'd have thought it too risky for a demon of his stature to be appearing in the middle of a major town."

"Unless the stakes were great," Mo said. "They do seem to want you dead pretty badly."

"Then why does the red one keep flying away? Why didn't he attack me up at the knob, after Luc had left? Neither Nex nor Vita had that much fire left in them—I would have been an easy target."

"Except he couldn't have been sure that I wasn't still around," Luc commented.

"Fair enough, but he must have sensed me coming through the front door here alone—why flee out the back? Especially after going through the effort of bringing a building down on top of me." I paused. "Just how did they manage that? I had no sense of magic in the seconds between that first whoomp and the second."

"They used earth magic," Mo said. "But it was a form I've not seen before—one that disrupted the internal integrity of stone and wood and made it fluid."

"That doesn't sound like a positive development," Mia said.

"I doubt the red demon was behind the destruction," Luc commented. "I think it more likely to be the person who was astride his back."

"Which would explain why he fled," Mo said. "He was protecting the asset."

Luc nodded. "Reds are middle hierarchy though—he wouldn't have left unless he was ordered to do so."

"Can full demons work magic?" Mia asked.

Mo shook her head. "Only the dark elves, and even then, they use personal magic rather than elemental."

"Is it possible," I said slowly, "that this asset is a full

witch? One stolen as an infant and raised in this world by the halflings?"

Mo stared at me for a moment, horror crossing her expression. "Oh my god, *yes*. I didn't even think—"

"You're hardly alone in that," Luc cut in.

"Yes, but I *knew* it was possible, because it's happened before."

I frowned. "When? Because once again it's not been mentioned in any of the history books I've ever read."

"Well, no, because there weren't many who realized what had happened. Most thought the collapse of the castle's eastern wall was due to the heavy rain and the river flooding."

Luc frowned. "Didn't that happen just before Uhtric was born?"

Mo nodded and scrubbed a hand across her eyes. "They pushed *that* child too far, too soon—we found him dead in the ruins of the wall. It would seem they might have learned some restraint."

"'We?'" Mia asked, eyebrows rising.

Mo waved a hand. "Figure of speech."

Like hell it was—though it did mean she was far older than what she'd already admitted. "Why wouldn't they just wait until their fosterlings reach adulthood and therefore full capacity as a witch?"

"That I can't say. Perhaps it has something to do with the differences I felt in the magic." She flicked a piece of paper around. "Do you recognize the address here? It's not one I've heard mentioned."

Luc plucked it from her fingers and then swore. "It's the address for the hospital where Henry's being kept."

I glanced at Mo and, as one, we scrambled to our feet.

"We need to get over there," she said. "*Now*."

"The hospital is fully protected both magically and physically," Luc said. "They won't get to him, I guarantee that."

"*Our* building was fully protected," Mo bit back. "And look at the state it's in now. Ring Jason and warn him. Tell him to get their Chen consultants over there immediately, and mention we're on the way."

"I will, but—"

"We haven't the time to stand here and argue, Luc. Gwen, let's go. *Now.*"

She ran into the smaller room, thrust open the window, and flew out. I tore off a strip of fabric to wrap Vita and Nex in, then changed and flew after her, the blades held secure in my claws and pulsing with an odd sort of heat.

A heat that weirdly spoke of both anticipation *and* strength.

I had no idea what it meant, and no time to dwell on it.

We flew hard and fast through the darkness, but it still took us far too long to reach the hospital.

By the time we got there, it was under attack and in flames.

FOURTEEN

The entire left wing of the small, T-shaped hospital burned. The ground around the other wing was surrounded by demons, but the main mass wasn't attacking. They were simply standing there, their howls filling the night with their anticipation and desire for blood. Two secondary forces had gathered near the exit points, one of them currently trying to batter down one set of the doors with a ram, the others hacking at the second set with axes and swords.

Magic lit the air, the strings a mix of dark and light, ebbing and flowing as each spell momentarily gained dominance over the other. It meant the Preternatural's main witch force here were Lancasters rather than elemental witches—though there was at least one Valeriun within the building, if the deadly shards of ice pelting over the force with the ram was anything to go by.

Mo flew over the hospital and headed for the three black vehicles situated in the parking lot. She shifted shape and then strode toward them. Once I'd also reclaimed

human form, I swept my daggers up from the ground, and
ran after her.

"Situation?" she snapped as Jason appeared from the
back of a van.

"Henry's wing is under heavy attack, but we're
currently holding them."

"How many people have you got inside?"

"A dozen soldiers, three Lancasters, and a Valeriun," he
said. "Spells are preventing any breakthrough via the doors
and the roof; they should be able to hold them off until the
army arrives to deal with the bulk of the demons."

"How far away are they?"

He glanced at his watch. "Ten, maybe fifteen minutes."

Mo grunted. It was not a happy sound. "Have there
been any reports of a red demon?"

"Yes—why?"

"Because that bastard is carrying a child who's capable
of bringing down a building. How many Chen witches have
you got on site?"

"Only one—"

"Tell him to meet me at the far end of Henry's wing in
five minutes."

"That's too dangerous, and I can't spare—"

"I don't want or need your men's protection. What
room is Henry in? Have you got a floor plan?"

"Yes, in the van."

"Gwen, go in and protect Henry. If I can't stop the
collapse, I'll work on a means of getting you out. Signal
when you get to the exit."

She flew off without waiting for an answer. Jason swore
and immediately ordered his witch to meet her. Then, with
a curt "follow me," he moved back to the van and jumped

inside. He ordered the floor plan up on the screen and then said, "Look, my men are holding them. Once the army gets here—"

The rest of the sentence was lost to a massive whoomp. It was starting ...

"What's the quickest and easiest way for a blackbird to get into that wing?"

"There isn't one."

"What about the windows?"

"Barred with silver-coated iron."

"Standard sizing?"

He frowned. "Yes."

I motioned to the floor plan. "Where's Henry's room?"

He pointed to an inside room at the midpoint of the wing. "He's in the isolation rooms here."

"And these rooms here and here?" I pointed to the rooms on the outside walls. "What are they?"

"Wards here," he said, pointing, "And storeroom and offices behind."

"Great. Contact your men, ask them to shoot out the window in room one-eighteen, and warn them that I'm coming in."

"I still don't see—"

"That whoomp you heard? That's the first warning that Darkside's witchling has been unleashed. The building will begin to collapse with the second one."

The words were barely out of my mouth when it happened. I swore, jumped out of the van, and leapt into the sky. As I flew hard for the far side of Henry's wing, the roof above the first exit began to shimmer and melt. A shout went up from the demons holding the ram, but they didn't run. Instead, they increased their efforts to batter down the doors. This time, the magic holding them together buckled. Either the strength of the spells or the witches were fading, or the witchling could not only disrupt the integrity of wood and stone, but also magic.

I swooped around, spotted a broken window, and arrowed in. The bars skimmed my back and stomach, and the daggers clanked as they hit the metal. I shifted shape and landed amongst the glittering glass shards. Became aware of the two men in the room and the guns aimed my way.

"I'm Gwen De Montfort," I said. "Where's Henry?"

"Inside. This way." The bigger of the two men spun and led the way out of the room. Dust filled the air and spiderweb cracks were now appearing in the ceiling above.

We were rapidly running out of time.

A third whoomp echoed, and the walls began to vibrate. The soldier in front of me looked around, his expression uneasy. "Sounds like they're attacking the walls."

"They are. How many people have you got down near the eastern exit?"

"Five."

"Order them back here immediately. The roof there was on the point of collapse as I came in."

He immediately got onto coms, and from the quick response, he was obviously the commander. I strode into the room; there were three more soldiers here, as well as Henry, who wore both a flak jacket and helmet.

"Gwen?" he said, "What the fuck—?"

"There's no time to explain. We need to get out of this building—now."

"We have orders to remain," one of the three soldiers said.

"If you follow orders, you'll be dead inside of five minutes. Henry, move."

He hesitated, his expression uncertain. I swore, but before I could do or say anything else, the walls began to shake and the falling dust became chunks of plaster.

"This entire building is about to come down on our heads. Move, before I goddamn force you."

I drew my daggers and pointed Vita toward the dusty corridor beyond the door. Lightning flickered from her tip and spun around the room, a thin sliver of dangerous white light that surrounded the four men. I had no idea how or why it had happened, but it looked pretty fucking awesome.

Henry stared at me for a heartbeat, his expression a mix of surprise and awe, and then walked out the door. Two soldiers followed. The third motioned me ahead of him.

"Where now?" Henry said, then jumped sideways as a huge chunk of plaster crashed down next to him.

I glanced around at the sound of footsteps. Men and women appeared through the dusty gloom—four soldiers and a witch. The latter was pale, her eyes bloodshot, and her chest heaving.

"They've broken through the doors," she said. "I laid a few traps, but it won't hold them."

"Retreat to the other exit," I said. "I'll delay them."

"We can't get out there," the commander said. "There's a secondary force of demons."

"That will change," I said. "Go. Trust me."

"Mo's there, isn't she?" Henry said. I nodded, and relief stirred through his expression. "Then we're safe. Do as she says."

The commander didn't look convinced but he nevertheless motioned his men to obey. He stayed right beside me and hefted his weapon. "We buy them time."

"That's the plan."

I faced the dark corridor resolutely, Nex and Vita alight in my hands and tension thrumming through my body. Dust and plaster continued to fall around us, but the main roof collapse was happening further down the hall—it was a distant but slowly approaching rumble.

I wished the same could be said of the demons.

Their screams rent the air, a cacophony of noise that made my ears ache and my pulse race. I gripped the daggers tighter, and the lightning responded, flickering out in ever lengthening whips. They lit the darkness and reflected brightly in the eyes of the approaching horde.

The commander raised his weapon and calmly fired. I crossed Nex and Vita and sprayed the lightning across dusty darkness, disintegrating the first line of demons and searing the legs of several behind them.

As each one fell, two or three more took their place. They didn't seem to care—not about the lightning or the gun or the quivering walls.

A huge crack appeared in the ceiling halfway between them and us. A heartbeat later, it came down, burying several demons and sending a thick wave of tile, wood, and plaster rolling toward us.

"Run," the commander said.

I obeyed. While the cascade wouldn't stop the demons, it at least gave us some cover. We pounded through the unsteady hall, showered by dust and plaster, chased by that wave of debris and the howls of the hunting demons.

We skidded around a corner. Up ahead, clustered to the right of the exit doors, were the rest of the soldiers and Henry. Strings of magic flickered and pulsed across the door, but their force was fading as the witches weakened.

I sucked in a deep breath, then raised the daggers and

crossed the blades. Light shot out, twin forks that blasted through the glass doors and seared the demons beyond.

It was best I could do, signal wise.

Howls echoed through the darkness, coming from ahead and behind. As the walls around us began to shake and the ceiling started coming down in chunks, the commander bit out an order for his men to surround and protect Henry, then began firing. The bullets tore through flesh and bone, but the tide wasn't stopped. As the two witches began spinning their magic into a barrier between the demons and us, a sword stabbed through the nearby window, skimming my side and drawing blood. I swore and lashed upward with Nex, cleaving the sword in two even as lightning wrapped around the demon beyond and disintegrated him. As I directed more spears of light through the smashed glass doors, the ground beyond began to rumble and then rise, slowly at first and then with increasing speed, arching up each side of the door until it had formed a solid dome. An exit tunnel—Mo was creating an exit tunnel.

I smashed the rest of the glass away and then spun around. Saw the thick mass of flesh almost on top of us.

"Commander, we have an exit—move."

"Team one, go," he said, shouting to be heard above the blasting of guns, the screams of the demons, and the roar of the oncoming collapse. "Team two, rear protection."

Six soldiers immediately retreated, Henry safe in their midst. As they ducked through the broken doors, the ceiling above us cracked and the walls began spitting missiles of rock and plaster as the full collapse began.

"Commander, get your men out of there." I crossed the daggers and blasted lightning at the wall of demons in front of them. Red mist momentarily blurred my vision, and moisture dribbled over my lashes. I swiped it away and swept the lightning back and forth, keeping the demons at bay even as the ceiling and walls began to collapse around them.

"Gwen, come *on*," Henry shouted.

I sent a final surge of light toward the horde, then turned and ran, chased by chunks of roof and walls. As the doors began to buckle under the weight of the roof collapsing above it, the ground started to rumble once more. A thick slab of earth rose to enclose us totally and then the tunnel began to extend—lengthen—away from the building.

"Benson, Reggy, to the front," the commander barked. "Everyone else, on guard. We may be surrounded by earth but there's still a ton of those bastards outside and the tunnel may not protect us against their weapons."

A statement that proved all too true as a spear stabbed through the earth and sliced into the leg of the nearest soldier. Weapons fired in response, the noise deafening in the confined space. The commander picked his man up and motioned everyone to move on.

More spears shot through the sides of the tunnel, and all too quickly it became a deadly forest that claimed the life of one soldier and left the rest of us bloody. We might just have stepped from the frying pan into the fire ...

From the top of the pod came heavy thumping, and then earth began to shower down. They were attempting to break through ... I swore and raised Vita and Nex, but the lightning hit the dome and crawled along it, as if searching for an exit point.

Claws broke through the earth and the lightning leapt forward, spinning up into the gap. If the demon screamed as his body was ashed, I didn't hear it, thanks to the explosion of gunfire and the sudden howling of the wind.

The cavalry—in the form of the army and air witches—had obviously arrived.

The earth pod continued to move forward, shuffling us away from the sound of fighting. Then the wall of earth at the front of the pod began to disintegrate; the commander snapped an order and the soldiers—bloody and limping—formed a barrier in front of Henry, their weapons at the ready. The night air, thick with the scent of smoke and death, rushed in, but no demons followed.

A woman stood in front of us. Wind streamed through her dark hair, and her eyes were lit with stars.

"This way," she said, and then punched sideways. A vortex of air shot from her fist; the clawed feet of a demon made a brief appearance as he was flung up and away.

She turned and ran toward a thick clump of trees. The soldiers kept in tight formation around Henry, with the commander and me at the rear. The sounds of battle were now fading, the gunshots fewer. The wind still howled, however, though its force was not aimed our way.

Perhaps the demons were in retreat ...

The thought had barely crossed my mind when my foot sank ankle-deep into the soil. I frowned and glanced down, using the light dripping from Nex and Vita to see what was happening. Water was bubbling up from the ground, forming little streams that ran away quickly through the longish green grass. Maybe there was a natural spring nearby ... The next step went deeper. Up ahead, the soldiers were now struggling knee deep through mud.

Then I caught the faintest of magic. Dark magic. *Earth* magic.

The demon's witchling was still active.

"Get out of here," I shouted. "It's a trap."

The soldiers didn't hesitate. As one, they moved

forward, the two on either side of Henry shouldering their weapons and gripping his arms to move him along at a faster clip.

I lunged after them, but with every step, I sank deeper and deeper into the ground. Then a huge wave of power rolled over me, setting my skin afire with the sheer depth of depravity so evident within it. It sent me sprawling forward, and I hit the wet ground hard, sinking underneath the soil; water and muck flooded my mouth. Panic surged even as someone grabbed the back of my shirt and pulled me upright.

A scream rent the air. I twisted free from the commander's grip, saw Henry and the two men holding him upright drop straight down into the ground.

"No!" I threw myself forward, somehow latching on to his hand a heartbeat before it disappeared. His fingers wrapped around mine, his desperation a force that pulsed through his grip. I rose onto my knees and pulled back with every ounce of strength I had, trying to free him. The commander dropped beside me and thrust his hands into the soil. With a fierce growl, he slowly rose; the head and then shoulders of one of the soldiers came out of the ground.

Henry wasn't budging. I simply didn't have the strength.

"Help—I need some help here."

Soldiers appeared, some plunging arms into the ground, others reaching down and taking a firm grip further down the arm I held. Yet more appeared to help save the other trapped man. He came free, coughing and spluttering but alive.

There was still hope for Henry ...

I screamed in fury and pulled back with all my might,

trying to break the suction-like hold the ground had on Henry. Energy pulsed around us as the forces of light and dark magic fought for control over the ground that was drowning Henry.

We had to get him up. He couldn't die. Not like this ...

He moved. Only a fraction, but it was a start.

"On three," the soldier closest to me said, and then counted down.

As one, we all pulled. Slowly, ever so slowly, more of his arm came free.

Mo's magic joined the fray, but it was little more than a pale whisper of her usual force. The dark pulsed again; it gripped Henry and ripped back down, deeper into the earth, pulling the three of us down with it. My face hit the soil and liquid earth rushed into my nose and mouth. But I refused to release Henry's hand and, with a surge of strength from god knows where, pushed back up, clear of the ground, somehow halting Henry's slide deeper into the earth.

But the strength in his fingers was gone; there was no life in them, no pulse. If we didn't get him out soon, then he was truly dead.

There was only one way to save him. I had to find and kill the witchling.

"Here," I said to the soldier kneeling next to me. "Grab his hand."

He immediately did so. I thrust up, loosely wrapped the daggers together, and then sprang skyward. Smoke was thick in the air, distorting the view, but I could see that the demons who remained were on the run, their asses chased by winds that occasionally caught their heels and flung them high.

The red demon and his witchling wouldn't be where his

forces were running. He'd be somewhere safe—somewhere apart from the conflict and yet still able to see it.

I circled around and spotted the tor on the nearby summit. There. They were there.

I arrowed toward it, the daggers trailing behind me, hampering my speed. For one insane second, I considered dropping them, but they were the only real advantage I had over the demon. I just had to hope the few seconds of delay they were causing wasn't the difference between life and death.

As I drew closer to the summit, I saw them.

But they also saw me.

Something small and wiry scrambled onto the red demon's back. A heartbeat later, he was in the air, his wings pumping hard enough to stir a vortex of dust and debris. It didn't stop me from seeing him—I was higher than him.

But I wasn't faster.

As he began to pull away, I did the one thing Mo had told me never to do—I changed shape in midair and, as I plunged downward, unwrapped the daggers and clapped the blades together. Lightning shot across the distance between us and clipped the red demon's tail. He bellowed in fury and swooped upwards, the wiry figure clinging like a limpet to his back. I followed his movements and forced every ounce of remaining energy into the blades, demanding—wanting—death.

Nex responded.

As moisture filled my eyes and pain exploded through my brain, a thick bolt of lightning shot across the night sky and hit the demon dead center. It cindered the wiry figure and burned a hole right through the red demon's chest.

He dropped.

So did I.

As the ground loomed at alarming speed, I reached for the shifting magic. It answered far too slowly, and the ground approached far too fast ... I banked my wings, desperately trying to slow down, and hit the ground in a crunching tumble. The pain in my head exploded through the rest of my body, and I knew no more.

FIFTEEN

Waking was a painful process. The mad drummers were back in my head and working hard, and my eyes were sore and gritty.

But my fingers and toes all moved and I wasn't wrapped in bandages, which meant enough time had passed to give Mo a chance to recover from her efforts at the hospital and then heal me.

I shifted slightly, felt silk sheets run across naked skin, and suddenly wondered where the hell I was.

I opened my eyes. The first person I saw was Mo. She was asleep on an old brown chesterfield, her feet propped on the end of the bed, her skin pale but holding none of the gauntness that came with expending too much energy.

The other person was a presence I felt rather than immediately saw. Just for an instant, our connection surged to life. His relief, his caring, and his desire ran through me, a fierce wave that made my heart sing and body ache.

Then it was gone, ripped away by a will of steel.

I took a deep breath that did little to calm the tide of anger, and then said, "Where are we?"

"At a friend's country estate, not that far from Ainslyn." His voice was calm but remote. "It's safer to stay here until we can figure out our next move."

I wanted to jump up, grab him by the shirt, and shake some goddamn sense into him. But there was little point. He was holding strong, and arcing up against it would only harden his resolve.

"And Henry? Where's he?"

His long pause said it all. I closed my eyes against the tears. Damn it, we'd come so close, fought so hard, and it had all been for naught.

Fingers twined around mine. Mo, not Luc.

"They did get him out," she said softly. "But his mouth and nose were blocked by earth and by the time they cleared it—"

I studied her for a moment, seeing the grief. Seeing the guilt. "How's Ada coping?"

"As well as can be expected." She squeezed my fingers. "Her grandmother has come down from Scotland to be with her."

"And the funerals? When are they?"

"Tomorrow. We can't be there, Gwen."

"But—"

"You would only put Ada and everyone else in danger," Luc said, a gentle note of compassion in his voice. "They may have succeeded in killing Henry, but they missed you. I have no doubt they will try again."

I took another of those deep breaths that really didn't do a whole lot. "Have you contacted Max? Is he still safe?"

"He's still in Paris, but lying low, as promised. I've convinced him to move out of the Castille. He's now in a small apartment under an assumed name."

I grinned. "I bet he's unhappy about *that*. I mean, there's no room service to cater to his every whim."

"He did mention that. Several times."

I could imagine. "That leaves us with the unknown Jules—are we any closer to knowing who he is?"

Mo shook her head. "I contacted Jackie again and asked if she'd found anything else on him. She said there was an Okoro line that had a direct link back to Aquitaines, and she believed it was possible his claim to the sword was stronger than Max's."

"Meaning she did find a royal connection in the De Montfort line?"

"Not as yet—she still believes it's more a combination of bloodlines that brought Gareth, Henry, and your brother into the firing line."

I frowned. "I get Gareth and Henry being targets—their mom was a Valeriun, and they've a strong history with the Aquitaines. But the Okoros—or at least, Mom's branch of it —don't."

"That we know of," Luc said. "But remember, both family bibles are missing—"

"I think it would be fairly safe to say that, given recent events, the bibles are not missing but rather in the hands of our enemy," Mo said. "Which means we must now proceed on the presumption that the unknown Remy or Randy is the one behind these murders."

I gripped the silken sheet, keeping it close to my chest as I sat up. "Do you think that now both Gareth and Henry are dead, our would-be king will make another attempt to draw the sword?"

"More than likely," Mo said. "It would be the only way of testing whether he'd succeeded in erasing the competition."

"And that's what I don't get," I said. "You both said earlier that the sword makes a judgment on worthiness—wouldn't erasing all other heirs result in unworthiness?"

"In peaceful times, undoubtedly," Mo said. "But we've now taken several gigantic steps closer to a war."

"A war they can't win without the sword to open Hell's Gill," I pointed out. "So why don't we just hide the sword? It may take a couple of strong Chen witches to break the knob away from the stone circle, but surely—"

"That's been tried in the past," Mo said. "The De Montfort blessing hasn't always held out for the full year, and gold will always draw the greedy."

I grunted. "Then we need to place a round-the-clock watch—"

"We haven't exactly been sitting around idly while you've been unconscious," Luc said. "No one will get onto the island, let alone draw the sword."

I hoped he was right, but there was a niggling doubt deep within. Everything that could go wrong had, up until this point, so why would things suddenly start changing? I opened my mouth to say as much, but Mo squeezed my hand, drawing my gaze, and then shook her head.

Luc's phone rang. He pulled it out of his pocket and glanced at the screen. "Sorry, I have to take this."

I watched him leave, and then returned my gaze to Mo's. "How long was I out?"

"Three days."

I stared at her. "Really? Why? How badly was I broken after my nosedive into the ground? Or was it more a case of you needed to recover first?"

"I did have to recuperate, but that is neither here nor there simply because there were no broken bones to fix."

"That's impossible. I hit at speed—"

355

"Yes, and Luc witnessed it." Her smile was one of absolute delight. "Trust me, that boy is yours. You just have to give him time to get used to the fact."

"I don't think there's enough time in the entire world for that to happen," I muttered. "So how in the hell did I escape without breaking anything?"

"I would imagine you have Vita to thank for that."

"What in the hell has a knife got to do with it?"

"She is life, remember, and they have obviously accepted your heritage and your claim."

"Well, great, but I still don't see how that—"

"It's very possible you did break multiple bones when you crashed, because as Luc raced toward you, he said you disappeared under a strange golden glow. Life is golden. Death is harsh white."

I blinked. "But how can that possibly be when I don't have the De Montfort healing ability?"

"As I have said, your problem has always been your negativity—"

"It's not negativity, it's fact."

"And yet the daggers recognized you. They would not have done so if you were completely void of magic."

"Then it has to be buried damn deep," I muttered, "because I kept coming up as null whenever I was tested."

"Null simply means no visible force was detected. It doesn't mean you are without power."

I snorted. "That's splitting hairs, and we both know it." I waved a hand. "So why was I unconscious for three days if Vita healed me?"

"She healed you of the physical damage done by the crash, but she could not heal the damage caused by using her and Nex."

I stared at her for a moment, unease stirring through me. "But it was just a headache—"

"One that caused blood vessels in your eyes to burst and your body to go into a type of hibernation." She hesitated. "In your case, it was only three days. In the past, there have been cases of hibernation lasting weeks. Even years."

I scrubbed a hand through my hair. "I take it the more I use the daggers, the greater the toll on my body?"

"Yes. There will come a point where even I cannot save you."

"That'll teach me to watch what I wish for," I said. "What are we going to do about the sword?"

"There is nothing we can do, beyond watch and wait."

"So you do think our murderer will go up there to test his claim."

"Yes. And I also think the Blackbirds will not stop him."

I frowned. "Luc seemed pretty certain they had all options covered."

"All except the sky."

"Okoros can't fly."

"De Montforts can, and we could be dealing with an unknown offshoot line, remember."

"Then what are we going to do? We can't camp on King's Island—we'd be too easy to spot."

"As humans, yes. As blackbirds, no we won't."

"As plans go, it isn't one of my favorites."

She grinned. "It'll be fun."

"Your idea of fun and mine are two very different things."

"That's the trouble with young things these days—you're all too soft." She squeezed my fingers and then released them. "I'll go organize some food for you. Once you've eaten and showered, we'll head off."

"What, today?"

"I can't think of a better day to start. Besides, the new moon rises tonight."

And for witches, that meant a time of new beginnings—a time when goals were renewed, desires were set, and new intentions made. It would be the perfect time for a would-be king to draw the sword.

I took a deep breath and then nodded. I might not fancy spending the night in feathered form up some tree, but if it stopped a would-be king claiming his prize and also brought him to justice, then I'd do that and a whole lot more.

I had a brother to protect and cousins to avenge.

Once I'd eaten and taken a very hot—very long—shower, we headed out. Luc had argued against our actions but, in the face of Mo's determination, had in the end reluctantly agreed. Not that he had the power to stop either of us, and we all knew it.

Night had set in by the time we reached King's Island. We flew along the length of the island, heading toward the knob. The stars twinkled brightly and the energy of the moon pulsed even though she wasn't visible.

Trees gave way to rocky, barren ground and then the stone circle came into view. I followed Mo down to the ground and stepped into the stone monoliths, my gaze on the knob and the stony sheath that held the sword.

It took me a few minutes to realize what I was seeing.

Or rather, what I *wasn't* seeing.

The sword was gone.

The new witch king had claimed it.

All hell was about to break loose.

ABOUT THE AUTHOR

Keri Arthur, author of the New York Times bestselling Riley Jenson Guardian series, has now written more than forty-eight novels. She's won a Romance Writers of Australia RBY Award for Speculative Fiction, and two Australian Romance Writers Awards for Scifi, Fantasy or Futuristic Romance. She was also given a Romantic Times Career Achievement Award for urban fantasy. Keri's something of a wanna-be photographer, so when she's not at her computer writing the next book, she can be found somewhere in the Australian countryside taking random photos.

for more information:
www.keriarthur.com
kez@keriarthur.com

Fireborn (July 2014)

Wicked Embers (July 2015)

Flameout (July 2016)

Ashes Reborn (Sept 2017)

Dark Angels series

Darkness Unbound (Sept 27th 2011)

Darkness Rising (Oct 26th 2011)

Darkness Devours (July 5th 2012)

Darkness Hunts (Nov 6th 2012)

Darkness Unmasked (June 4 2013)

Darkness Splintered (Nov 2013)

Darkness Falls (Dec 2014)

Riley Jenson Guardian Series

Full Moon Rising (Dec 2006)

Kissing Sin (Jan 2007)

Tempting Evil (Feb 2007)

Dangerous Games (March 2007)

Embraced by Darkness (July 2007)

The Darkest Kiss (April 2008)

Deadly Desire (March 2009)

Bound to Shadows (Oct 2009)

Moon Sworn (May 2010)

Myth and Magic series

Destiny Kills (Oct 2008)

Mercy Burns (March 2011)

Nikki & Micheal series

Dancing with the Devil (March 2001 / Aug 2013)

Hearts in Darkness Dec (2001/ Sept 2013)

Chasing the Shadows Nov (2002/Oct 2013)

Kiss the Night Goodbye (March 2004/Nov 2013)

Damask Circle series

Circle of Fire (Aug 2010 / Feb 2014)

Circle of Death (July 2002/March 2014)

Circle of Desire (July 2003/April 2014)

Ripple Creek series

Beneath a Rising Moon (June 2003/July 2012)

Beneath a Darkening Moon (Dec 2004/Oct 2012)

Spook Squad series

Memory Zero (June 2004/26 Aug 2014)

Generation 18 (Sept 2004/30 Sept 2014)

Penumbra (Nov 2005/29 Oct 2014)

Stand Alone Novels

Who Needs Enemies (E-book only, Sept 1 2013)

Novella

Lifemate Connections (March 2007)

<u>**Anthology Short Stories**</u>

The Mammoth Book of Vampire Romance (2008)

Wolfbane and Mistletoe--2008

Hotter than Hell--2008

CPSIA information can be obtained
at www.ICGtesting.com
Printed in the USA
LVHW111826120322
713212LV00001B/45